POISONED SOUL

A BLACK FATES NOVEL

Christine Roi

This is a work of fiction. Names, characters, places, and incidents either are the product of the author's imagination or are used fictitiously. Any resemblance to actual persons, living or dead, events, or locales is entirely coincidental.

Copyright © 2024 - Christine Roi

All rights reserved. No part of this book may be reproduced or used in any manner without written permission of the copyright owner except for the use of quotations in a book review. For more information, email *authorchristineroi@gmail.com*.

Book design by Alison Cnockaert
Cover by Natalia Junqueira

ISBN 979-8-218-49864-1 (paperback)
ISBN 979-8-218-49865-8 (eBook)

www.christineroi.com

For all of the eldest daughters.

And for Lily, the sniffer of flowers and my protector.

TRIGGER WARNINGS

This story contains graphic content that might be troubling to some readers, including, but not limited to, depictions of and references to:

Intimate Partner Violence

Child Abuse

Forced asphyxiation

Severed appendages

Murder/Assassinations

Dismembered bodies

Torture

Discussion of Sexual Assault

Trauma

Your mental health is important to me. Please be mindful of these triggers before reading this book. Seek assistance if needed.

AUTHOR'S NOTE

This is the third book in what I'm referring to as the Caccia Trilogy in the Black Fates series. The official reading order of these books is as follows:

Nemesis

Sworn in Blood

Poisoned Soul

These books are works of fiction. They were written in the spirit of entertainment. Though I do take the issues presented within the plot of this book very seriously, this story is presented here without an agenda.

Please enjoy.

A DARK AND STORMY NIGHT - MANY YEARS AGO

A clap of thunder woke me from a dreamless sleep. I always slept well here. Even far away from the family in the converted attic, I felt protected. My eyes opened, attempting to take in the darkness of my room. Surrounded by soft pink bedding and the scent of lavender, it would have been easy to fall asleep again. To let the warmth take me.

Our parents had gone out for the evening to celebrate their anniversary and left us in the care of our grandparents, as they often did whenever they had dinner to attend. After curling up to watch Pride and Prejudice with my grandmother, I had gone to bed. My sister had locked herself away in her bedroom well before that, but not before helping herself to the tea and biscotti that had been laid out in the kitchen.

Light flashed through the sheer curtains. With a blink, I sat up to find a figure sitting at the end of my bed. My grandfather. I rolled over and turned on the small bedside light on my nightstand. It was my nightstand. My light. My room. Even at his house, he'd always had rooms for us.

Soft light filtered out from the opaque globe lamp. Scooting up to sit, I leaned against my pillow and headboard. Pattering rain filled the silence. Silence thickened with every unspoken word on my grandfather's face. I swallowed. Before I could speak, ask why he looked that way, color leached from his face and aged a decade in a single night, thunder clapped again.

He flinched.

"Nonno," I whispered. "What's happening?"

Then I heard it—my sister's heaving sobs. My grandmother's pleading.

"Please, Kaia Mia. Take a breath. Bambina, please."

His head turned, looking toward the open door, toward my weeping sister and his wife. Oily dread coated my gut. With his attention returned to me, I waited. A wail sounded from below and my grandfather shook his head, wiping a hand down his face before looking at me again.

"They're gone, Mia Principessa."

It was my turn to shake my head.

"I don't understand."

A flash of lightning was quickly followed by thunder that seemed to rattle the house. The biscotti in my stomach turned leaden.

"Your mother," he said, eyes filled with anguish. His eyes were tired as they searched my face for the right thing to say. The right way to break my heart. "Your mother and father... there was an accident."

1

Lilith

I always assumed I would go first.

It's not a natural thought, me being the younger of the two Caccia sisters, but my line of work made it more probable. Sneaking into houses, offices, and hotel rooms to help people meet their maker. Fighting strangers for my life. Stephen Bryant nearly killed me. Benjamin Camden got closer still. That idea didn't haunt me. When your business is death, it's easy to think about without feeling. It's a part of life. We arrive. We depart. Everything in between is merely a footnote.

But Kaia. My older sister. I'd taken a blood oath to protect the family with my life. Protect her. And I'm still standing because she took a bullet for me. I could still feel her dying in my arms. This was never supposed to be the way our story ended.

Standing on a cliff's edge, I stared down into the waters below. The tympanic boom of the waves filled the air like the mist they created. Icy wind numbed every extremity. Couldn't feel my face. Couldn't hear anything. Nothing but the roaring inside my head. It's an empty chamber with a howling wind pushing through the cavernous space. A raging tempest in a cathedral of stone.

"People are starting to arrive," Nico said with an even tone. The kind you use when speaking to an untamed animal.

Nico put his arm around my shoulders and guided me away from the cliffs. West stood, watching me from the garden. Like the rest of us, he was clad in white. It was easier to look at him. The man who'd taken on all of my burdens. Easier to let myself think about how he'd stood by my side these last few weeks as I shattered. Easier. Because as I entered the garden, I was met with a sight I could barely stomach.

Rows of small white chairs circled her open casket. Fluffy white hydrangeas were pierced with lilies and larkspur, surrounding the polished wooden box. West didn't move from my nephew's side, but continued to watch as I approached the gleaming casket.

My sister's Armani suit was unwrinkled. I picked a piece of lint off of her shoulder and smoothed her hair around her face. Even in death, Kaia was flawless. Her high cheekbones and jawline had always been sharper than mine. Smooth olive skin that had once glowed with her youth was now more grey than gold like someone had turned off the light in her. Not one blemish. Except for one. I couldn't stop thinking about it. The wound beneath the layers of fine fabric. The one that took her from me.

It seemed a cruel irony for it to be such a beautiful day when my sister's eyes had closed forever. The cold winter day was only slightly warmed by the sun hanging high in a cloudless sky. It wouldn't be long before the service started.

It's a beautiful place for a funeral. It reminded me of her. The garden was the picture of tranquility contrasted by the raging sea. White everything. She loved white. She spent her life dressed in black. Worked always in various black tones. But at home, with me and Daniel, she wore shades of white.

I smoothed my dress as I stepped away from her and surveyed the gathered mourners. Many from our family. Many from businesses we owned. As the boss of the Caccia family, a feared power in Los Angeles, people valued her. Respected her. Everyone respected my request to wear white. I couldn't stand the idea of black. Not today. My sister deserved better than the darkness that swallowed her life.

West took my hand as I sat down beside him, between him and Daniel. Lupo's arm was draped around the small boy's shoulders. I was glad to see it. Glad that Daniel had a grandfather. Someone steadfast. Someone stronger than I could be for him right now. The way my grandfather had been strong for me. For us.

Kaia's will had been clear. No funeral. She wanted to slip away. Be forgotten. But funerals aren't for the deceased. They're for the people you leave behind. The ones who have to suffer the agonizing moments remembering you've gone when they think of something they want to tell you or feel the urge to make contact, only to be rebuffed by your permanent absence.

This wasn't for her. It was for Daniel. For her story, to end with a taste of the heavenly hereafter I knew I would never see.

"IT WAS A beautiful service," a kind female voice said as a hand rested on my shoulder.

I hadn't been aware of her presence until she touched me. Only distantly registered the words she had spoken as I searched the room for Daniel. If he was anything like me, he was hiding from the crowd. As a child at my parent's funeral, I couldn't understand my discomfort with the mourning masses. But now I could. Making other people feel better about your grief is more draining than some will ever know. Especially when the person you're grieving is your mother.

Lanna's kind, dark eyes were soft as they met mine. "You look very nice. This dress is..."

I looked down at myself. The fitted white dress had sheer bell sleeves that were embroidered with small flowers. My finger traced over a small bloom on my wrist. I'd been finding comfort in the garden that was only a few yards away. In the silence of flowers.

"Thanks," I muttered. "I'm glad you're here."

"Can I?" Lanna held her arms out, inviting me in for a hug.

I shook my head.

"Alright then. When you're ready, it's here for you. So am I."

I nodded and looked around the dining room, unable to meet her eye. The space was filled with people. People I'd known for years as Kaia's little sister. People I was getting to know better as the new Caccia family boss. They stood around, talking in hushed voices with small plates of food in their hands. Taking bites of the feast I'd had brought in for this affair that I was starting to deeply regret. This affair meant strangers in her house. My house now, I guessed, even though I wasn't sure it would ever feel that way.

It was why I was hiding out. Ducking every conversation I could. Tomorrow. Tomorrow. Tomorrow I could bring myself to put on a brave face. To be the leader of this family. But their kind words. Their pitying faces. I couldn't take much more of that.

West walked out of the kitchen, toward his sister and me. We'd hardly spoken two words to each other today. Like he knew the lack of conversation was more comforting to me than any words. He held two tumblers of what looked like whiskey, extending one to me as he joined us.

As I took the glass, my eyes snagged on an arrangement of flowers I'd not seen before. Large lilies and hydrangeas burst from a sterling silver tapered vase. Far too ostentatious for a funeral. Whoever had sent them wanted me to know they had paid a lot of money. I stormed over to the kitchen counter, snapping the card out of the blooms to examine it.

"Who sent that?" West said, peering over my shoulder.

My gut twisted as I read the black monogrammed initials on the card. Initials that were burned into my brain.

Don't make a scene, I told myself. *He's just taunting you. It's not important.*

Tucking it into my bra, I turned to face West.

"Where's Daniel?"

He slipped his free hand to my back, a warm weight that steadied the building discomfort in me.

"In his room."

MY HEELS SANK into the carpet as I ascended the stairs into the finished attic. The one my grandfather had turned into a playroom for me. Huddled in the corner beside his open bedroom door, Daniel sat in a sack lounger with a book.

Everything about this felt familiar. A grieving child retreating into a book. An adult who had no idea what to say. Only this time I was the adult and no one was here to tell me everything was going to be alright.

"Hey buddy," I hesitated, unsure of my welcome. I remembered what it was like to lose my mother. The loneliness in it. No food sated me. Sleep didn't bring me rest. And every comforting word grated on my ears, even then.

"Hi," Daniel said, not looking up from the book he was reading. I glanced at the cover and sat down on the floor beside him, tucking my legs under myself.

"I remember this one," I said as I nudged the cover with my finger. "This was the first chapter book I ever read."

He made a small humming noise of acknowledgment and kept reading my worn-out paperback. I made a mental note to find him more books. We sat there for a while. I quietly read over his shoulder about the pig and its unlikely new friend. When he finished the chapter, I spoke again.

"You know, when my mother died, I stayed up here for weeks. Didn't eat. Barely talked to anyone. I just sat right here, where you are, and read one book after another."

Daniel's eyes shifted to me, but he kept the book propped up in his lap. A small finger was placed where he must have stopped reading at the beginning of the new paragraph.

"That's when Nonno planted the garden for me. He knew I liked plants. But it was to get me outside, probably."

I looked around the little playroom, searching for anything else to say. What had once been my haven, a place of respite for a girl, became Daniel's when he was born. Everything in the playroom now said that a little boy lived there. Spaceships dangled from the ceiling and blocks were stacked in the corner. Dinosaurs and superheroes littered the floor.

Daniel went back to his book when I didn't continue speaking. A comfortable silence settled between us. I stretched out my legs and took off my shoes, continuing to read over his shoulder. The light in the room began to wane. Gravel crunched beneath tires as mourners left the house.

Stairs creaked beneath the weight of West's footsteps as he came into view with a small plate of food. He'd kicked off his shoes. His sock-covered feet approached us carefully.

"Did you eat?" West asked the boy beside me, though his eyes were on me. Daniel shook his head. West lowered the plate to him. Grilled cheese. I hadn't heard him make it, but it certainly wasn't on the menu for the service. Thick crusty bread, golden with butter. The sandwich was cut diagonally and placed so neatly on the plate.

Daniel tucked a baseball card into the book to mark his place and set it down beside him. He took the plate and thanked West, but didn't eat. I gave the boy's shoulder a little squeeze.

"Looks tasty," I offered.

West sat down beside me, leaning back against the wall. I shifted and tucked myself into his side, keeping one hand on Daniel. He looked at me and then to West.

Every single thing West had done since my sister died was to take care of us. Moved my sister's things into the warehouse she'd been keeping. Sold her car. He even retrieved the rest of my things from my old apartment and brought them to the house. Said that if this was my house now it should feel like home.

I had been too lost in my pain to do anything except thank him. But it was a silly thing. My degrees. My blankets and throw pillows. Half-burned candles. None of it felt like home. This place wasn't it, anyway. Not really. For me, home would never be things. It was people. It was my sister. I would never be home again.

2

WEST

Daniel was limp with sleep as I carried him the short distance to his bed. He'd taken a few bites of the sandwich I made for him, which I considered a victory. Even if it was a small one. Lilith stood in the doorway, watching me tuck him into his small bed with a look in her eyes that I was noticing more and more.

Half sadness. Half love. Maybe there can't be sadness like that without love. Before I could reach her to give any comfort, she walked away. And it wasn't just a physical distance I felt between us.

Lili was standing in our room with her dress half unzipped, staring out the window at the moonlit sky. Night black hair swooped in curls and waves down her exposed back. The pointed high heels she'd been wearing were abandoned beside the bed. I wasn't sure if it was the loss of those inches or her grief that made her look so small now.

"Is he still asleep?" Lili asked, not looking at me. Her voice was flat. Tired.

"Passed out cold," I answered, striding toward the window. Unable to resist touching her, I let my hand brush through her hair to the zipper. "Do you need help with this?"

Lili nodded absently. I stepped closer and dragged the zipper down slowly, savoring her nearness. The garment loosened and fell to the ground around her feet. She turned away from me and approached the bed, removing her bra and throwing it atop the discarded dress, content to sleep in her underwear. With a slow but deliberate movement, she was under the covers.

I picked up the clothes to take them to the hamper. The Lilith Caccia I knew hated clothes on the floor. She cleaned when she was stressed. That woman was a stranger to this one.

"Don't," she said. Pulling up the covers, she continued. "Come on."

Obeying her command, my clothes joined hers on the floor. Moving to the side that had become mine, I slid into the bed beside her and pulled her body against me. The feel of her skin against mine still sent a jolt through me, but I ignored it.

Positioning one arm beneath her head, I let the other drape over her waist. Her breath fanned across my skin, and I could almost feel the moment her despair pulled her under into a deep sleep.

I had everything I ever wanted at the tips of my fingers, but now it felt like she was just fucking gone. A ghost in the sheets beside me.

―

"COME IN."

I'd only been in this office a few times. When I interviewed for the job working the door. The woman sitting at the desk was more terrifying than my first commander. She didn't look up from her laptop as I peeked through the door, instead lifting a hand to wave me in.

Suddenly feeling I had been called into my fleet admiral's office, I approached the desk and let my hands come to rest at my back. An old habit, but not the worst one I could have.

"Have a seat."

Clicks and taps sounded from the keyboard as she continued to work. I waited. She was the one who called me in here. The club wouldn't open for another hour. I had time. Still, I checked my watch. Maybe just to fill the time.

Kaia turned her attention to me. Brown eyes. Sharp, intelligent in a calcu-

lating way. So unlike the wild hazel-gold color of her sister's. Sharp eyebrows, sharp cheekbones, and make-up that highlighted her beauty. Kaia Caccia was gorgeous. But her appearance was calculated. As was her suit, her expression, and probably everything else about this room. So completely unlike her little sister.

"You served in the military, correct?"

I nodded. I'd half-expected for her to call me "commander." Kaia looked down at her laptop, scanning her screen for something.

"A Navy SEAL. Retired," she read aloud.

Medically discharged. But I wasn't about to correct her. An alert sounded from her computer. She continued to look at it, probably reading whatever had just popped up. I tapped the arms of the chair I sat in and waited. A minute went by. Then another.

"How well would you say you know my sister?"

I blinked.

"I, uh. I don't know. We train together. She's a good fighter. We met at the gym. She referred me here."

Was I in some kind of trouble? I reviewed everything I'd done here. Maybe she caught me reading during a lull. I never got the impression that it was a problem before.

"Right. And you see each other every day."

Not a question. I waited for her to continue.

"Mr. Hale, I don't have time to beat around the bush. Do you care about her?"

I swallowed, trying to think of an answer that she wouldn't repeat to her sister. *Lilith Caccia was my best friend. That's all.* I repeated that to myself. As I opened my mouth to speak, a thoughtful expression crossed Kaia's face. She nodded.

"I thought so. I need something from you."

With a roll of my shoulders, I cleared my throat.

"Alright," I answered. "What can I do?"

Kaia shut her laptop and tapped a perfectly manicured nail on her desk. A knock at the door followed the sound.

"Boss?" Nico Ricci said as he entered.

"Just a minute," she responded, holding up a finger while looking at me. "I need you to follow her."

Follow her? Kaia stood from her desk, looking down at me expectantly. Our meeting was over, I guess. She bent over and picked up a black leather purse from inside a desk drawer. Shrugging it over her shoulder, she rested a hand on the strap.

"Follow her. Keep an eye on her for me. I don't care if you have to leave during a shift. It's covered. I'll pay you. Let's call it hazard pay. Lilith is your only responsibility. Protect her."

"PLEASE."

Lilith stiffened in my arms with a sharp inhale. Small whimpers came from her. And that same word over and over. Muffled. Whispered like a prayer. Fuck.

"Lili," I whispered, trying for gentle even though she'd just scared the hell out of me. "You're dreaming. Wake up."

We couldn't have been asleep for very long. Lanna had left before I joined Lilith and Daniel. Lupo stayed over and now slept in the guest room across the hall. He'd said since he was family now that he wasn't going anywhere. The burden of the day had sent all of us to bed early. I looked at the clock on the bedside table as Lili whimpered again. Just after midnight.

"Wake up, Trouble. Come on."

Gorgeous eyes blinked, struggling to focus on me as I jostled her awake. Lili's face crumpled. With a sniff, she buried it in my neck. Her tears soaked my skin as she let out wet, hot breaths. I stroked her back and sighed.

"I'm sorry," she whispered.

"There's nothing to be sorry for."

She hadn't cried. Not at the funeral or in the time before. I sure as shit wasn't going to stop her now, even if it was a nightmare that did it. If the brave face she was showing to the world was cracking with me, I was thankful for it. With long strokes down her back, I waited.

"I'm right here, Lili."

With a deep breath, she retreated from my neck and looked at me. Even in the dark, I could see her. Like my eyes couldn't stand not to take her in. I stopped stroking her back to sweep damp black strands of hair away from her cheeks. As I did, I saw the frown. The gleam of tears in her eyes. How do you protect someone from this?

I couldn't stop myself as I pressed a kiss to her mouth. It was salty, still wet. She sighed as she sucked on my lower lip. I groaned. Every cell in my body leapt at the chance to get closer. Fuck, I couldn't help it. Couldn't help but pull her against me. Or the way my body responded to her nearness, ready to be inside her again after these last few weeks. It had been that long since we'd slept like this. Skin to skin. All I'd wanted for years was to hold her like this. We'd gotten so close to something great. Something life altering.

She pulled away and looked at me. Something crossed her eyes. As she settled against me again, I stared into the dark and pictured that look over and over again. Gold ringed irises. And a door slamming shut behind them.

"HOW'S SHE DOING?" Clayton asked as he lifted a beer to his lips.

"The same."

"Shit."

"It hasn't even been a month. Lanna says Lili just needs time." The sentiment felt empty even as it came out of my mouth. "Have you talked to Casey? She didn't show up at the funeral."

Clayton's stubble-shadowed jaw ticked in a way I'd not seen since our first tour together. Hardly anything bothered him, but he and Casey had struck up a friendship since we pulled her out of that hellhole in Joshua Tree. It didn't make sense. She was peace and he was chaos. But somehow they found things to talk about. What was eating at him now? I had no idea.

"She's been staying with her dad and working at the bar. I drop by sometimes. Feels weird to call. Either Ronan or Killian is always around, and I prefer my head attached to my body."

I chuckled as I lined up my shot and pulled the trigger. The shot echoed in the cement room. Clayton let out a low, appreciative whistle.

"Bullseye. Big surprise. Anyway, we're talking about you, Blackjack."

"Don't call me that."

What was I supposed to say? Things with Lilith felt like they were at a standstill. When I woke up this morning, she was gone. She went to the office, her sister's office hidden away at Muse, every day.

Lupo was in the kitchen with Daniel when I had come down, making the boy a breakfast he didn't seem to have any interest in eating.

"She's at the club," the old man confirmed as he flipped bacon in a pan. "I caught her on the way out. Surprised you didn't hear the car leave. That Camaro is loud as hell."

I reloaded my weapon and looked down at my phone. Still no response to the text message I'd sent her hours ago.

> Going to Clayton's for a while. Let's have dinner tonight. Just you and me.

It was a desperate attempt, but damn. I just wanted to be alone with her. Get her to talk to me.

"She's got a lot on her plate now, man," Clayton said, watching me check my phone again. "You keep checking that phone, but if you had a bunch of businesses dropped in your lap, would you be sending text messages to your boyfriend?"

I grunted and put the phone down.

"Let me ask you something else."

Clayton put his hand on my rifle, forcing me to set it down.

"You love her?"

It was a stupid question. A stupid fucking question. Love was not the right word. It was too small. Too insignificant compared to what I felt. She was all I thought about. Day in and day out for six years since the moment I laid eyes on her. Looking at her made my chest ache. The night she told me she loved me too may have been the happiest I'd ever been in my damned life. Even though it was a month ago, it felt like a distant memory. I nodded.

"You know what she is. You know what her family is and what they expect of her. That's a lot for anybody to shoulder already. Damn near impossible. So don't add to it. If you love her, what are you going to do to help her?"

3

Lilith

Kaia's blood dried on my hands. My arms. My legs. I was covered in what remained of her. It made my skin itch as it flaked away. Bit by bit. Kaia disconnected from me.

In the back of the van, there was just me. Me and Kaia. I looked at her eyes, brown and warm like our mother's, forever closed. The rosy color of her cheeks. The subtle glow to her skin. All of it was fading away. Death had come to sip at her beauty instead of taking it all at once, tasting her like wine.

My sister had always been there to guide me. Talk sense into me. She was the anchor that I needed when I was drifting away. Staring at her motionless body, I felt myself floating into dangerous waters.

A black pit of rage and pain expanded inside me with every breath. Every thud of my still-beating heart. Every time my mind tried to digest what happened, it rubbed up against this fresh hole inside of me.

Crummy white cotton soaked in red. Had the spot grown? The wound had been so quick to take her; I hadn't examined it. A shot to her chest. So close to her heart. I wouldn't let myself imagine the damage, my education haunting me with the bitter truth.

Someone turned on the radio. Plucking guitar strings from a sad song my sister used to love filled my ears. The mournful singer's voice came through the *speakers. I found myself simultaneously hoping someone would speak to me and terrified that they would.*

WHEN YOU'RE BARELY sleeping, each day blends into the next seamlessly. Before I knew it, a week had passed since my sister's funeral.

In the mirror, there was a woman I didn't even recognize. But it was important for the men to see me as an authority figure. Someone with self-respect, or at least someone good at pretending to have some. Even if I'm just a poor man's version of my sister, it's what they'd expect.

She showed up every day to this place with perfect makeup, usually a bold lip. Flawless suit or dress. Imperious expression. A queen who was ready to greet her subjects. Plan battles. Run her kingdom.

I found the small gold tube of lipstick in her desk drawer. YSL. Twisting the bottom, I watched the center twirl up. Red like... Fuck, never mind. Putting on the red lipstick felt like a lie. Stage makeup for the character I was playing. I'd always been more of a natural tones makeup kind of girl.

Inside I felt like there's a power line that's come loose. Whipping in every direction. Snapping at passersby. A danger to everyone. Even myself.

A soft knock tapped on the door.

"Boss?"

"You don't have to call me that," I protested as I walked out of the bathroom.

"Yes, I do. They're here."

Imposter syndrome isn't a thing for assassins. Setting out to kill someone always produced a result. But I wasn't just an assassin anymore. Now I was the boss of the Caccia family. Something I was never supposed to be.

Emerging from the bathroom, I ran my hands over myself. I hurried toward the desk and picked up the ledgers, taking them to the safe. The keypad beeped as I typed in the combination. A polished walnut file box sat amongst other precious goods. I tugged it forward to set the ledgers inside but was distracted by a black card falling on the floor.

No larger than a business card. I looked at both sides. A phone number and a nondescript email on one side. Nothing on the other. My eyebrows pulled in confusion. Another knock sounded from the door. Quickly stuffing the card into my pocket, I closed up the safe.

Nico pulled his gun from his holster, checked to make sure it was loaded for what was likely the tenth time, and sheathed it again. I glanced toward the safe. Closed. Web of confusing information safely tucked away. The door opened and my guest stepped in. I straightened my jacket, standing behind my sister's desk. My desk. Here the fuck we go.

"For an Italian, you've got good taste in whiskey."

Ronan took a pull from the crystal tumbler and eyed it in the light. The late afternoon sun filtered in through the blinds, causing the tawny liquid to look almost amber. I sipped from my glass and set it on the desk.

"It's Japanese."

It still felt foreign to me. Sitting behind this desk in a suit. Like I was pretending to be my sister. Playing a role. Holding her place for her. Waiting for her to show up and take control of this meeting. The door stood out in stark contrast against the rest of the room. Vibrating with potential energy. Like at any moment, it would swing open and she'd be here. Instead, Nico stood behind me, where I had once stood behind her.

Dark eyebrows shot up as Ronan examined the glass, giving the tumbler an approving nod as he took another sip.

"I didn't ask you here to drink up my whiskey, Arawn."

Ronan rolled his dark brown eyes and drained the whiskey in his glass before speaking again. The lean bodyguard he'd brought with him took the empty crystal tumbler and set it on the bar.

"We haven't been in business together long, Caccia. But you can't think I'm a stupid fucker. Get on with it then."

"You and I had an agreement," I said, finishing the whiskey from my glass.

"Aye. Destroy the people who kidnapped and assaulted my daughter. Same ones who murdered your sister."

The whiskey went sour in my mouth. My left hand flexed as I tried to maintain a cool exterior. Nico shifted behind me. He'd seen it. The reaction I'd tried to hide. I looked down at my desk, my sister's desk, and took a breath.

"Yes."

"What do you purpose? Because I have a few ideas about the punishment, but I'm not quite sure where to begin."

The chair squeaked as I leaned back in it and squeezed my eyes shut for a moment. This damned chair. Brand new. Ozzie's blood never came out of the one that belonged to my sister. This chair was the only new thing in this whole office. Nothing else had been added. Everything in this room had been hand-selected by Kaia to create her perfect aesthetic. She'd had it redecorated as soon as she could following our grandfather's death. I couldn't bring myself to change a damned thing. My sister had even picked the whiskey.

"You and I have been in this business for long enough to know how things work. If we cut off the head, another will grow back in its place. This Duke Harrison Augustus-Stanley. He's just the head. We need to destroy the infrastructure or there's no point in doing any of it."

Ronan nodded. He thoughtfully rubbed at the salt and pepper stubble on his jaw.

"Hyphenated name. Sounds like a cunt."

"We can't do anything until we know what we're dealing with. During my time with Benjamin Camden, I learned they traffic women and ship them off to different port cities all over the world using shipping containers. Thanks to Augustus-Stanley's fucking villain monologue, we learned they're also trafficking children."

The smoking skull on Ronan's hand seemed to yawn as his hand flexed and relaxed. My eyes flicked to his bodyguard as I sensed him tense beside the door. Nico's feet shuffled behind me. None of them had been ready to hear that.

"I've got someone who can start looking into that for me."

I raised an eyebrow at Ronan.

"I believe you know Mr. Clayton Wrigley. Quite versatile for a mercenary. We'll see what he's able to unearth for us."

WINTER DARKENED THE sky at this relatively early evening hour. The white Georgian house glowed like a lantern behind the cypress trees that hid it from the world as lights from inside the house illuminated the first-floor windows. The Camaro rumbled, announcing my arrival as I pulled the car in on the gravel driveway next to West's Bronco.

The day had been difficult. Various updates from men in my employ filtered in as I sat and planned with Ronan. I walked toward the house in a fog, but it began to lift as I heard Daniel laugh from inside. A few excited barks soon followed.

But the warmth that had bloomed in my chest was quickly extinguished as I noticed a package sitting outside the front door, placed in the center of the doormat. A long, gleaming black box with a matching black ribbon. I took off my blazer and draped it over the box, stuffing the concealed item under my arm before entering the house.

The door creaked as I let myself in. Garlic and something savory perfumed the air. Something sizzled as I heard the oven door open and close.

"Shit," Lupo grunted.

"Bad," a small voice replied. "That's a bad word."

"Sorry," the old man muttered.

"Hi Zia," Daniel said, twisting in the stool at the island to look at me, no doubt hearing my heels on the tile floor behind him.

West looked up from the bottle of wine he was opening. He lifted the bottle and gave me an inquisitive look. I nodded. Yes, I wanted a glass of wine. I wanted the entire bottle.

"Hey, buddy," I replied, hefting the box under my arm, hoping it remained hidden. "I'm going to go upstairs and change. I'll be right back."

Stepping out of my heels to leave them at the bottom of the stairs, I quickly climbed toward the bedroom. The black box poked me in the ribs like its presence alone wasn't irritating enough. The bedroom door lock clicked as I shut it behind me. Unsheathing the box from my jacket, I tossed the garment on the bed and set the box atop the dresser.

The black ribbon fell away, cascading to the floor as I pulled it off of the long box. I could smell what was inside before I opened it. A slight squeak of the glossy box and a quick intake of breath were the only sounds as I looked inside to see what awaited me.

A perfectly cut long long-stemmed black star calla lily. And a card. A card with the same black monogrammed initials. Only this time it came with a message scrawled across the back in fine handwriting. Probably written with a fucking fountain pen.

> *I'm quite fond of hunting foxes. You're certainly more lovely and intelligent prey. Perhaps you'll be more difficult to snare than your sister. But this is not going to be the only pretty Lily I put inside a box.*

No signature. But I didn't need one. The initials were enough.
H.A.S.
Blood coating my hands. A rasping rattle of air. White stained red. Arid desert wind. Dust stinging my face. Kaia's eyes fixed on the sky.
H.A.S.
It was him. The man responsible for my sister's death. The man I hadn't stopped thinking about since her last breath rattled in my ears.
The Duke.

4

WEST

Steaming meat, cheese, and noodles had my mouth watering. I heaped a portion onto a plate for myself. Then one for Lili. Lupo did the same for himself and Daniel, then handed the boy a glass of milk to carry to the table.

I tried to ignore the irritation I felt at not hearing from Lilith all day. She'd seen my text message. I knew that much. Instead of having dinner with me, we were here. I could accept that. Seeing how tired she looked when she walked in the front door made the fight die in me. Clayton's words replayed in my mind.

"You know what her family is and what they expect of her. That's a lot for anybody to shoulder already. Damn near impossible."

I didn't want to add to her problems. I waited for her for six years. I could wait a little more. But I couldn't help but feel like she was putting distance between us. Lili almost bumped into Daniel as she stepped off the stairs. Wariness filled her expression as she saw the plate I'd made for her.

"Don't even start," Lupo grunted, passing her on his way to the dining room. "I worked all afternoon on this thing. You're gonna eat."

An annoyed sigh through her nose, but I didn't miss the way her full lips quirked with the barest hint of a smile. The sight damn near knocked me over. My girl was still in there.

"I'm going to need a refill," she sighed as she retrieved her glass from the counter and lifted it to her mouth for a couple of gulps.

There was a glimpse of olive skin as a bare shoulder peeked out from the flannel shirt she was wearing. Seeing her in one of my shirts still felt satisfying. Just as it had in my cabin or the weeks after, wrapping her up in my clothes was a new intimacy I savored. Knowing she'd chosen that, along with a pair of sweats, to give her comfort was a relief. Though I had no idea how to help her, I could comfort her. Even if it was just in this small way.

"Come on," I nodded toward the dining room as she moved to take her plate. "I've got it."

The walnut table was elegant in its simplicity. Over the weeks in this house, I'd gotten to know Kaia better simply by being around her things. She preferred function over form but never sacrificed style. A beige linen tablecloth covered it. Matching napkins sat atop it. Lupo had even lit the white tapered candles in their tiny marble holders.

"Italian sausage mixed in with the beef is the key to a good lasagna," Lupo was telling Daniel as I set Lilith's plate down in front of her. Sitting cross-legged in her chair, she leaned backward with her glass curled toward her chest as she watched them talk.

"It is?" Daniel pulled his fork up from his plate, creating a long string of mozzarella that he sucked into his mouth.

"Yeah," Lupo laughed. "Then you've got to use fresh ricotta and fresh pasta."

"Fresh from a box," Lili muttered into her glass as she took another gulp.

"Watch it," Lupo warned.

Lili put her free hand up with her wineglass in the other in mock defeat. She hadn't put herself at the head of the table. That seat remained empty for the woman who wasn't there.

This was still new to her. Lilith was the head of a family. Not only in name, but in her ability to take everything on. To protect those she loved, yes. But also to be there for them. It showed in the way she listened to Daniel go on about the book he was reading, even though her eyes were heavy with exhaustion. It also showed as she took the boy upstairs to get ready for bed, telling him she'd read a chapter with him.

Soap and tomato sauce frothed in the sink as I scrubbed baked cheese off of the casserole dish. The jingle of Remus's collar announced his arrival. Lupo wasn't far behind his old dog, approaching from the dining room with the last of the dishes.

"She cleared her plate," I said, glad to see that she'd done that much. Even if it had been accompanied by two glasses of wine.

"I need to talk to you," Lupo grunted as he opened the dishwasher to put away the dirty plates.

"About?" I asked, not taking my eyes off of the dish in my hand. The damn thing had so much cheese on it. I sighed and set it down to soak. Turning the water off, I looked over at him.

"She's alone now."

I angled my head, confused.

"She's not alone. We're here."

"No. Not like that. I mean, she's alone in the family. The last Caccia."

"What about Daniel?"

"Daniel is her nephew. If she died right now, the seat would go to the underboss. If there's no underboss, it would go to her child. Right now, she has neither. And she has no one to protect her."

The proclamation made the noodles and cheese go leaden in my stomach. I gripped the counter, trying to force down the rage. Lilith would never be vulnerable, and she wouldn't be in any danger. Not while I was around.

I dried my hands on the kitchen towel and tossed it onto the counter, leaning against it as I waited for Lupo to make his point. Crossing my arms to hide my balled fists, I tried to keep my voice down as I spoke.

"Why in the hell didn't you bring this up with her. Why me?"

A look of pity crossed his weathered face.

"She needs to get married."

I felt my eyebrows shoot up my forehead as my fists squeezed. It hadn't even been much more than a month since Lili and I got together. Sure, we'd been friends for six years and she knew me better than anyone, but I couldn't pressure her to marry me. With everything going on, rushing Lili to the altar for this was... I shook the thought from my head. Getting married now would be insane.

"Kaia didn't need a husband," I argued.

Remus looked up at Lupo as though agreeing with me. His thick grey head tilted, awaiting his owner's answer. I always liked that mutt.

"Lilith was her underboss. Also, Kaia had an heir the same day she became boss. She had a legacy. Lili doesn't have that and you know it."

The day their grandfather died. I'd forgotten that detail. It wasn't long after that I'd met Lili. I blew out a breath and looked toward the stairs, hoping she didn't overhear this conversation. She didn't need this. Not now.

"I'm not going to pressure her to marry me. She's going through enough right now."

Our conversation halted as I heard footsteps coming down the stairs. We both watched Lili appear, muttering something about going to check on her plants as she stuffed her feet into her boots and walked out the front door.

Lupo's attention returned to me. His mouth quirked to one side like he was trying to decide how to explain what he'd already told me. That pitying look returned to his face as he said something I wasn't ready to hear.

"Lili needs strength. Not just physical strength. Political strength. A support system. She needs to marry someone from within the family. Or someone from another family. A stronger family," he said, looking down at his shoes before he dared to finish. "Not a bouncer."

5

Lilith

When I was a little girl, my grandfather was at war with the Bratva. No matter what he did, Ilia Kramnik, their boss, seemed to always be a step ahead of him. If my grandfather tipped off the police for a drug bust at their warehouse, the place was clean when the cops got there. If he paid off an informant, the man was found dead a few days later.

Matteo Caccia was not bested by many, but Ilia Kramnik almost broke him. It was during this time that he became obsessed with his Camaro. I suppose my Camaro, now. If he was found working on the car for long stretches, it was likely because of a problem with the Bratva he couldn't solve.

"Something about getting my hands dirty settles me, Mia Principessa."

The grind of the pestle against the mortar was enough to send my mind into a dormant state. Stone on petals. Stone on berries. Grinding, grinding, grinding. Busywork in my little apothecary. It was the only place I could stand to be alone. Working with my hands had a way of settling me, too. Even though that flower was all I could think about. My hand drove the pestle down again and again, thinking about the card, the card, the card.

A glance down into the bowl had confirmed I'd created a fine enough dust to add to the boiler for distillation. I dumped the powder into the receptacle and removed my gloves with a quick tug. Then I dropped the gloves on my work table.

Lupo had told me that since I became the boss of the family, I was no longer the Wolf. No longer responsible for protecting the family because I was the one in need of protection now. As if caring about my family was a job I could quit.

My mind drifted back to that night in my sister's office. When I got on my knees, drank her blood, and swore to protect her with my life. I could still taste it. The mixture of wine and blood. My sister. I made a vow. I made a vow to her and I failed.

Well, it would be a frosty fucking day in hell when I stopped getting my hands dirty. I looked down at them, as though I could see every drop of blood I'd shed in the name of protecting my family. They needed my protection now. From him. The Duke. But I wasn't stupid enough to disappear into the night to eliminate this enemy.

Not alone, anyway.

My hand drifted to the spot between my breasts as my eyes landed on the gleaming black box and the Duke's message inside of it. It wasn't just a threat. It was a challenge. That piece of human garbage was challenging me. I may not technically be the Wolf any longer. But I would always bear the mark. It would always be inside me. The howling beast. The protector.

The box thudded into the small metal trash can, along with the card and flower inside. Hefting it into my arms, I left my small laboratory and plodded down the small stairway to the driveway.

Metal clanked on stone as I set it down in the gravel. Sulfur and smoke stung my nostrils as I struck a match and tossed it into the can. As the small pyre raged, I remembered the last fire I lit. That one containing the bones of a man who'd killed my friend. Isabelle. Strangled to death by a man who decided she was disposable. This one contained a promise. A promise to hunt me and kill me.

I couldn't help the smirk as I thought about the irony. The Duke may have learned to hunt, but I was born to it. Violence wasn't my first language, but being immersed in it since childhood made me fluent. Hunting was in my blood. Hell, it was my fucking last name.

"STOP IT! STOP it! Stop it!"

My screams rattled my brain. Tears cut cool trails down my burning cheeks as I begged him again to stop. But he didn't. And my mother hit the side table as she fell to the floor. Blood trickled from the open wound in her head. With a finger beneath her nose, I knew she was still breathing as I knelt beside her.

Kaia had gone to our grandparents' house, at my grandfather's request. He'd suggested I come along, but my father had refused. Said that I wasn't needed there, so why should he go to the trouble of bringing me when I could just come home from school? My mother had made the mistake of arguing with him.

Hands clamped and pinched the skin around my shoulders as my father lifted me from the floor. First to stand. Then to face him. His grip tightened as he looked me in the eye with golden irises that matched my own. Irises I'd grown to hate.

"Don't yell at me, you little shit," he fumed, every word coming out of his mouth through clenched teeth. They were accompanied by small drops of spit I fought to ignore as they dusted my cheeks.

"You could have killed her," I whimpered, barely audible even to my ears. His hands squeezed my shoulders, hard enough that I knew I'd need to wear sleeves the next day. My father's face neared mine as I squeezed my eyes shut, afraid of what would come next.

"I should have killed her. I should have killed all of you. You are a waste of life, Lilith. You are nothing to me but a walking, talking reminder of my regret."

The grip on my shoulders loosened. He'd let me go. Let me go and walked away. I knelt beside my mother, whose head wound was still bleeding as she remained unconscious. My hand clasped hers as I looked down at her, unsure of what to do. Then I felt the barrel press to the back of my skull, at the top of my spine.

"You were supposed to be a boy."

Warm wetness pooled around my knees, soaking into the carpet I knelt on as I wished for my sister. The safety on the gun clicked, reverberating into my skin.

"Jesus Christ," my father spat, setting the safety. "Clean this up. You're making a fucking mess."

My wet pants clung to me as I ran out of the room and up the stairs, into the bathroom Kaia and I shared. The pink shag rug cushioned my knees as I fell before the toilet and vomited until I was sure I'd broken a rib.

THE CLUB WAS still quiet at this early morning hour. I'd come alone to work on the family accounts. That damned box was already haunting me, so sleep wasn't a fucking option. Work would have to do. After all, if I couldn't trust the men I was meeting here now, it would defeat the purpose of the meeting itself, wouldn't it?

Kaia had been an accounting major in college, which meant that she had a much better head for numbers than I ever did. Don't get me wrong. Banging away at formulas always quieted my mind. Hard figures were easier to figure out. Applied formulas with chemistry always made perfect sense to me, but when she would start discussing finances and interest rates, I got bored.

"What the fuck, Kai?" I muttered to myself as I calculated again, eyes stinging from the meager light of the desk lamp. Or maybe it was the lack of sleep.

The only thing my sister and I had in common was our code system. She used a similar code key to track the accounts in her spreadsheets as I did for my recipes and formulas. Another shared skill taught to us by our grandfather.

I had her code key set out beside my sister's laptop as I went through her accounting records to sort things out. It was what I'd been coming here to do. The family attorney had reviewed my sister's will with me. Except for some savings in Daniel's name, everything was mine. But what did "everything" add up to?

Blinking, squeezing my eyes shut, I shook my head to clarify my thoughts. All of the investments and LLCs. Interest on loans coming in from people who owed us thousands. What I was looking at couldn't be right. It just couldn't.

"Hey boss," Nico muttered as he entered.

It didn't stop the word from repeating in my mind. The word flashed like billboards in Times Square as I sipped my coffee. It repeated like a song stuck in my head as I locked the laptop back in the safe. Denial wouldn't change it. Denial wouldn't stop my life from being changed forever upon seeing that damn number. Again and again and again.

Billion.

The cup of coffee on my desk had to be cold at this point. It hadn't tempted me enough to drink, even when I was running on no sleep. Nico yawned. At almost six in the morning, anyone would be tired. My other guest perked up, turning in his chair to look at the entering man. They exchanged glances and turned their attention to me as Nico took the other guest chair before the desk.

"Nico, I'm sure you remember Damon Roma."

Damon extended a tattooed hand toward Nico in greeting. Looking over the soon-to-be former underground fighter, Nico raised an eyebrow at me in curiosity after giving him an appreciative nod.

"I had Damon come straight here after his last fight, so I apologize for the early meeting. But there's something I need to ask of both of you."

"Anything, boss," Nico grunted, adjusting himself in his seat.

"Yeah, whatever you need," Damon agreed.

I stood from my desk and picked up the bottle of wine I'd brought in from my sister's selection at the house. After poisoning the bottle and glass in the desk for Ozzie, I'd had to get rid of everything. Two crystal tumblers from the bar would have to do for this.

"Are both of you familiar with what the Wolf does in this family?"

Nico nodded, knowing that his father was the first person to serve as the Wolf. His brother was the next. I was the last. I was the only one who had failed.

Failure.

I shut the thought out. Damon shook his head in answer to my question. I went on.

"Well, Damon, the Wolf is like a knight. A knight who swears himself to the kingdom. To his queen. By doing so, you promise to put my life and the life of my family before yours. You've proven yourself to be a great fighter. Would you stand by my side, Damon? Would you fight for me?"

A faint smile tugged at Nico's lips. I didn't ask him because I knew what his answer would be. To swear the vow. I'd needed men I could trust. Men who I was sure hadn't been corrupted by Ozzie's influence.

Those were the men I needed these two to hunt.

I couldn't face the enemy at my front if I didn't know who had their knives pointed at my back. The silence stretched out in the room as Nico and I awaited Damon's answer.

"Yes, boss."

I nodded. Uncorking the bottle, I poured a small serving of wine into each tumbler. Unsheathed the hunting knife from my belt. It may have become part of my routine to wear a suit as the boss of the family, but I wasn't going to stop carrying it. I sliced into my palm and squeezed several drops of blood into each glass. Damon's eyes flared as Nico grinned.

A lone wolf is a dangerous and unnatural thing. I thought about all of the nights I hunted alone, waiting for my prey in the dark reaches of their homes or following them down alleyways. Alone.

I'd started training with West so that I could fight off anyone who tried to defend themselves against me. But now it was my turn to defend myself. And I needed people I could trust to guard my back.

"Kneel," I said, watching the blood run down my hand into the second glass. "Both of you."

Nico looked up at me with pure joy. He'd wanted this. Wanted to be more than a bodyguard. I was grateful for that desire. It meant I didn't have to explain what would happen next. He knew. And Damon would learn by his example. I painted an attempt at a peaceful smile on my face and stepped toward him with the first tumbler.

"Say the words."

6

West

The coffee pot gurgled and bubbled. It was Lili's old pot from her old apartment. It looked odd sitting next to the high-end espresso thing that belonged to Kaia. Out of place. A sudden sputter shook me from my dazed state. I slept like shit last night. Lili tossed and turned. I heard her muttering in her sleep. But she didn't wake. As I filled my cup from the pot, Lupo's words came flooding back.

"She's alone now."

Cream swirled into the black liquid.

"She has no one to protect her."

Sugar dropped in behind it.

"She needs to get married."

My palms pushed into my eyes with force, trying to rub away the thoughts from the outside. The thought still made my stomach turn. Lupo left no room for argument. Even if I had the opportunity, I didn't know what to say. How could I argue? I wanted to. Wanted to break the dishes in front of me. Scream at him. Rage about it.

The front door swung open and the foyer filled with the sound of heels hitting the marble floor. Shining black leather points peeked out from the wide hem of her pants. Grey herringbone, like the rest of her suit. A black sheer blouse peeked out from under a vest.

"Good morning," Lili sighed.

"Early day?" I asked.

She'd been gone when I woke up. Seeing her in her mafia boss getup confirmed what I'd already guessed. Something at the club. Something she didn't want to tell me.

Lili picked at the tie holding up her hair and pulled it free, the inky dark strands falling as she shook it loose. She nodded and shrugged off her jacket.

"Did you eat?" I asked, already knowing the answer as I grabbed a mug to pour another cup of coffee for her. Only, there was no answer. I looked up from the cup to find the room empty.

A creak from the stairs informed me of her location. We were alone in the house. Lupo had taken Daniel with him to another appointment, but not before reminding me that I should excuse myself from this situation.

"You know I can't do that," I'd reminded him.

"I know how you feel about her. I do. But she was never supposed to be this. If I'd known this would happen, I wouldn't have let you get near her."

An entire army couldn't have stopped me from getting near Lilith Caccia. With everything going on, I wasn't going to throw marriage into the shitstorm she was dealing with, but that didn't mean I was going to step aside and let someone else take her hand.

She reemerged on the stairway, trotting down in her black leggings with a flannel thrown over her sports bra.

"Do you want to work out?" She asked with an elastic in her teeth, braiding her hair.

"You didn't answer my question?"

"You're not answering mine," she argued.

I sighed through my nose and unclenched my jaw. Instead of speaking, I raised my eyebrows at her. Lili rolled her eyes.

"No, I haven't eaten today yet."

"Then you know we're not working out."

Lili tied off her braid and placed her hands on her hips, the flannel pushed back. Clayton had told me I should be helping her. That I shouldn't be adding to her problems. I didn't understand everything that she had to deal with now. But I could at least get her to eat some fucking breakfast.

Her lips twisted to one side. I watched her consider her options. Go to the gym without food and without me. Or eat something. She huffed and walked to the cabinets behind me, picking out a bowl and then a spoon from the drawer in front of her. They clanged angrily on the countertop as she stormed into the pantry.

I turned and watched her, sipping my coffee as she poured chocolate frosted puffs into the bowl. A splash of milk. She leaned against the counter and angrily spooned it into her mouth. Milk dribbled down her chin as she ate.

Mission accomplished.

"YOU KNOW WHAT to do."

I took my time getting ready to go to the gym. Let her stew. Let her wait. Let her digest that damn bowl of cereal. But most of all, let her be angry. Angry was better than nothing. The hours of nothing she'd spent in bed. Sleep. Wake. Nothing. Sleep. Wake. Nothing. I couldn't go back there. I wouldn't let her go back there. Even if it meant making her hate me.

We'd been coming here every day. After the days she spent in bed, it was the first normal thing I'd been able to get her to do. I'd thought if I could get her to connect with her body, that the distant look in her eyes would diminish. And it did. But that distance was replaced with storms.

"Again," I coached, holding up the punching mitts to take her blows.

Sharp exhales accompanied Lilith's hits. Her first strikes were hard, firm enough to rattle my bones. I adjusted my stance, ready for more.

"Again," I said.

Brutal efficiency made her attacks look elegant. Like a dance.

"Again."

Lupo's words played through my mind again.

"She has no one to protect her."

After all those years of training with her, he should know this woman better than that. She was bruised and battered when I met her, standing in this ring with him. Maybe losing Kaia had affected the old man more than I knew. But he was letting fear cloud his judgment.

"Let's switch to kicks and then we can come back to this," I offered, hoping to give her fists a break.

She wiped her forehead with her elbow and nodded. Sweat trailed down her neck, disappearing into the faded black bra. I turned away, swapping the punching mitts for Muay Thai kick pads.

"Alright," she said, walking in a small circle. "Are you ready for me to kick the shit out of you?"

It took over six years for us to get here. There were a lot of times during that period I'd told myself she wasn't ready or I was going to ruin things between us. But she had to know on some level how I felt about her, even then. Lili's a smart girl. All that time could have been just her way of running away, too. I locked the thought away before it could do too much damage.

"Give me everything you've got, Trouble."

Lilith Caccia didn't need outsiders to protect her. They would need protection from her. I was going to use every weapon I had in my arsenal to make damn sure they knew that.

7

Lilith

Jab. Blow.
    Jab. Blow.
Jab. Blow.

Skin hit leather. Breath came and went. I let the sounds melt my thoughts away until I was both in and outside of my body. My legs were shaking. Every muscle was exhausted from push kicks, round kicks, and switch kicks. I ignored them.

In here there was only me. Only him. My fists. Striking. Striking. Striking. My breath became hot and sharp, tearing at my throat as I exhaled with each blow. Existence was narrowed down to physicality. Nothing could break me here.

"That's enough," West said, stepping away from me before I could land another blow. "You're bleeding."

I looked down at my hands. The skin had split on a knuckle, peeling away like a blister between my shifting wrist wraps. Prodding at it with my fingers, I sucked in a breath at the sting.

"We're done now," West offered as he took my hand to examine it.

"It's nothing. I'm fine."

I didn't need protection. I needed to hit something. This was the only thing clearing the fog in my head. The only thing that helped me feel like myself.

"If you keep going like this, you're going to break something."

"I said I'm fine," I spat. "Come on."

West growled his dissent as he stepped away from me, undoing the punching pads attached to his hands. Shaking his head, snarling, clearly thinking something he didn't want to say. I didn't need that. My blood simmered at the idea that I'd need protection from his thoughts.

"What?" I barked.

"Nothing," he grunted.

I shoved him. Actually shoved him. Because I needed a fight. Needed something.

"Stop it," West warned.

"I don't need you to protect me, West. Just fucking say it!"

"Fine," West snarled.

He squeezed his eyes shut like he was giving himself one last chance to reel himself in.

"Hurting yourself, driving yourself into the ground until you can't stand up, is not going to bring your sister back."

His statement punched a hollow void into my gut. I opened my mouth to speak but was interrupted by the front door squeaking as it swung open. Daniel ran into the gym, followed closely by Remus. The old bully mutt huffed as it trotted in behind him, having taken to shadowing the boy wherever he went.

"Zia, what are you doing here?" Daniel asked as he changed direction and walked over to us. West dropped the punching pads onto the ground and crossed his arms across his chest, losing the look of anger he'd directed at me to give Daniel a warm smile.

"She was working on her one-two combo."

Daniel angled his head, then looked at my wrapped hands.

"You can box?"

I shrugged and wiped my face off with a towel. A creak at the door announced Lupo's entrance. He yanked a duffle bag up under his arm and stuffed his keys into his pocket. After a glance at me that moved to West, I could have sworn a look of wariness crossed his expression.

"Hey," he grunted. "I, uh, was just going to get the kid started on footwork."

"Lupo, did you know she can box?"

The old man laughed as he hefted the duffle bag onto a chair beside his office and approached the three of us. Daniel sat down beside the bag as I started unwrapping my hands. With Daniel around, the roaring fire of rage had dimmed to burning embers.

I picked up the weighted jump rope, stepping away from Lupo and Daniel. West shook his head at me. I smiled defiantly and started hopping to burn away the anxiety building in me.

"Of course, I know that she can box, Champ. Who do you think taught her?"

Lupo mussed Daniel's mop of dark curls and looked down at his grandson. The slap of the rope against the ground drowned out the rest of their conversation.

Sweat soaked my sports bra and ran down my back. My lungs and legs started to burn. West watched me while leaning against the lockers, smoky green eyes still gleaming with ire.

"I'm going to teach you when you're old enough. For now, we're going to work on your feet."

Lupo unzipped the bag and shoved his arm inside, searching for something. I let the jump rope slap to the ground one more time before I coiled it around itself and hung it on the hook I'd retrieved it from. As he pulled his hand out, a rope ladder revealed itself. Lupo unrolled it on the ground and looked up at me.

"You want to show him how it's done?"

I wasn't sure if I nodded or not. I tried to, but my breath was still heaving. Unable to answer, I just shrugged.

"She needs to rest," West said coldly as he stepped closer to me.

I looked over my shoulder at him in surprise. He was right. My legs were useless and I could barely lift my arms. But that wasn't what jolted me. It was the way he angled his body between Lupo and me. It was the tone. No nonsense. Not an ounce of friendliness in it. He was protecting me.

"He's right," I said, trying to brush the odd moment off. "We've been here a while."

"We'll see you at home," Lupo muttered. His brow knit together as he looked down his nose at the man next to me. Like he had a bone to pick with West, too. Whatever was going on here, I needed to know.

Daniel, unaware of the shift in the room, melted to the floor from the bench to scratch Remus behind both ears. The dog's big wrinkled head split in a fanged smile.

"Right," I said. "See you at home."

After grabbing my things from the locker, I threw my leather jacket over myself. I'd shower at home. I still had several hours before I needed to meet with Dr. Forester. Lupo leveled an assessing gaze at West, who wrapped an arm around my waist as we walked toward the door. Not in a possessive or affectionate expression. It seemed almost defensive. Protective.

"TELL ME WHAT in the hell is going on between you and Lupo."

"Nothing."

The Camaro purred as we made the short drive back to the house. It seemed to like West better than it liked me, but maybe all cars liked him best. Or maybe it liked him for bringing it back to life. West shifted gears, glancing at me as he did so.

"Don't lie to me, West. I don't have the energy for it," I sighed, looking out at all the uninflated inflatable Christmas decorations in the neighborhood. It was well past the time to put them away for the year. They were all so sad and flat during the day.

West took my hand from my lap and lifted it to his mouth before kissing my wounded knuckle, drawing my attention back to him. My chest ached at the tenderness in it.

If you don't stop being such a brat, you're going to lose him. The thought made me wince.

"It's not important, Lili. Just some bullshit. Don't worry about it."

It didn't feel like bullshit. In all of the years we'd been training at the gym together, Lupo practically treated West like a son. They'd laugh together. Lupo used to talk about West to me. Brag about him. I'd never seen them argue. Not really.

The gears on the iron gate squeaked as it rolled open for us. Tires crunched into the gravel driveway. I was happy to find there were no other cars parked in it. No one else was here. The house had been teeming with people for weeks. Lanna. Clayton. Lupo. Nico. None of them were here now. It was just us.

"You need a shower," West said as he helped me out of the car.

"Oh?"

"Yup," he grunted as he reached behind the seat for my things. "You stink. I like your stink, but you still need a shower."

I rolled my eyes. Still unnerved by the new tension between Lupo, a man who was now family to me in truth when he had always been so in sentiment and West.

West, the man who I had fallen in love with. The only one I'd ever loved, really. And I trusted him. Despite everything I'd been through with every other man. Despite getting played by both Benjamin and Ethan. Benjamin almost killed me, while Ethan cheated on me with every woman he could. Being with West made all that fade away.

I had to stop behaving so terribly to him. Give him something, even if I had nothing in me but anger and despair.

Climbing the steps to what was now technically my bedroom, I drifted back to the night I confessed my love to West. He'd pushed me to do it. Knew exactly how I felt about him before I did. It seemed like he knew me better than anyone.

"You're mine. And I'm yours."

He'd done everything he could to protect me and nurse me back to health in the safety of his cabin. As I turned on the shower, our first kiss floated into my mind. Sitting by the fire in the middle of the night. His beard grazed my skin. The way my body lit up at the feel of his lips on mine. That was the night things forever changed between us.

Why did it seem like he was protecting me now and from Lupo, of all people? What the hell happened? The thought circled me like the steam that billowed out of the shower as I undressed, throwing my soiled clothes onto the ground.

Water was pouring over my face when I heard the glass door open. I wiped my eyes to see West step in and turn on the other shower. The hair that had been in a messy knot on the back of his head was loose in brown waves around his shoulders. My eyes skated over miles of sun-bronzed skin covering his well-muscled body. Hunger welled low in me. Hunger I didn't have the energy to act on.

"So?" I asked, not ready to let the issue drop.

"So what?" He tested the water with his extended hand and stepped under it, satisfied with the temperature. His face tipped up toward the showerhead. I watched rivulets of water skate over his thick shoulders.

"Are you going to tell me what's going on with you and Lupo?"

West sighed and moved his head out from under the stream. I unsuccessfully avoided watching the water coast over the rest of his body as he pushed his hands through his hair, moving the soaking long strands out of his face. The urge to close the distance between us was overwhelming.

Focus, I scolded myself.

"I told you it's not important."

Irritated with the direction of my thoughts, I returned my attention to bathing myself. Pumping shampoo into my palm, I huffed a sigh. As I lathered the liquid into my hair, I continued.

"If it's not important, then why did you hustle me out of the gym? And he seemed upset with you, too. Explain that."

West rubbed at the back of his neck, blowing out a breath at his feet. Once his eyes locked on mine, he seemed to decide on something and moved toward me. I watched him carefully as I rinsed the shampoo from my hair. In a shower more than big enough for two, I suddenly wished for more space because I couldn't tell if it was the steam or his nearness that made it hard to breathe.

"He wants me to leave you."

"What?" I snapped.

My gut bottomed out. Lupo told him to leave? That wasn't his place. He had no right. No. That was impossible.

"That doesn't make any sense. He was the one who told me to be careful with you."

West's face twisted in confused surprise.

"When did he say that?"

"When he first found out about us. At his house. He asked me what was going on between us. Told me I shouldn't play games with you."

West nodded, working shampoo into his hair as he ducked under the shower I was using. I flinched at the cold tile hitting my back.

"A lot has changed since then," he said as he scrubbed at his scalp, a note of woe entering his voice. "He said that you're vulnerable without an heir or an underboss. That you needed someone from another family to marry you to show your strength with a political alliance."

Married? My gut plummeted to my feet at the thought. Memories of my sister flashed. She was shopped around from family to family while my father tried to arrange an advantageous marriage for himself. After everything my grandfather did to make sure my sister could stand on her own two feet, I was about to lose all they had worked for.

The underboss thing wasn't an issue. Not with Nico and Damon to choose from. The Wolf was automatically an underboss. It was how I had gotten here. But I couldn't tell West what I had done. The vows I had other men swear to me. It felt like a betrayal, somehow. I glanced at the still-healing wound on my palm.

"And he thinks your being here is getting in the way of that? Like I'd just be alright with being forced to marry someone-?"

The last word evaporated on my tongue.

West sighed as he stepped further under the showerhead, closing his eyes as he let the spray wash over him.

I tried to keep my mind from racing. Tried to keep a leash on the panic that welled in me at the bullet I thought I'd dodged when our father died. Kaia was on the verge of an engagement when our parents careened off of a canyon highway. Unlucky for them. Lucky for her. Nonno had always been against arranged marriages for us and canceled the planned engagement immediately.

I wasn't cattle to be auctioned off. This was wrong. Lupo was *wrong*. My little black heart was already spoken for. I stared at West. If I couldn't get myself out of this, what good was it being the boss of one of the most notorious families in the world?

"You're not going to leave," I breathed, barely able to speak above the rush of water pouring down around us. "Are you?"

West opened his eyes. A look of anguish entered his smoky green gaze and approached me. With one hand pressed against the tile beside my head, he leaned in. Fingers threaded into my wet black strands and tugged, forcing my eyes to meet his burning eyes.

"I'm not going anywhere."

If words weren't enough, there was the way his lips sealed to mine. Angling my head with his grip on my hair, his mouth soothed the storm in me as he deepened the kiss. Tension loosed from my body like he took the weight I carried with every second. I let him.

8

WEST

The blonde man was sweating through his crisp blue button-down. Every few minutes, he pushed up his glasses. Something about her made him nervous. If they'd met before, it was for business. Knowing the business she was in, his nerves were understandable.

After our shower, Lilith told me she needed to get back to work. I didn't take no for an answer when I told her I was going with her. Her mouth tightened in a way that told me she wanted to argue but didn't have the energy. That was enough for me.

Sitting in on this meeting was not what I had in mind. Still, I wanted to know what was happening when she disappeared to this office. This family business. Clayton told me I should help her. I didn't know how I was going to do that when I was in the dark about her position.

I still remember her standing there in the middle of the living room. It had been only days since her sister passed. A tailor had come to take her measurements for the expensive suits she'd purchased from various designers. Even though they cut, pinned, and measured every part of them to perfectly fit her body, they still looked wrong.

Lilith sat back in her seat, a look of assessment on her face. I wasn't sure she was even wearing a shirt under that blazer. She'd taken her wet hair and tightened it into a knot, making her thick dark eyebrows stand out against her olive skin. The light dusting of freckles across her nose seemed to undercut the seriousness of her expression. Like a little girl playing at ruling a kingdom. But here she was. Ruling.

"I need your assistance with a complex issue. This issue involves sensitive information. Information that may involve innocent people. These people don't deserve any sort of scrutiny, shame, or ridicule from the public or government organizations. Before I go any further, I need for you to agree not to disclose anything you find to anyone but me. Do you understand?"

Her gold-rimmed irises seemed to simmer with warning. They fixed on the man sitting beside me, who shifted uncomfortably in his chair. An awkward squeak of the leather upholstery broke the silence before he cleared his throat to answer.

"Of course, Ms. Caccia. I would never-"

"Good." The word was firm and even. "While investigating another matter, I came across some emails. There is an email account I'd like for you to let yourself into. This email has attachments in several threads. Spreadsheets. In these spreadsheets, you'll find tracking codes. Find out where these shipments were delivered. Find out who they were delivered to. Can you do that?"

"Well, y-yes, of course, but I'd need to know a name and some other details."

Listening to her talk like this was making all of my blood rush south. After that kiss in the shower, I'd been aching for her. But here we were. I shifted my hips, trying to ignore it. Lili picked up a piece of paper with several lines of scribbled-down notes.

"This should be everything you need. Oh, and there's something else."

Forester stood to take the paper from her. Her painted red lips gave him a soft smile that seemed designed to calm his nerves. He reviewed the notes on the paper and nodded as he folded it up, then tucked it into his khakis.

"David," she purred.

He swallowed audibly.

"Can you get me another untraceable phone?" She asked sweetly. "I enjoyed the last one, but it was stolen from me and I need another."

"It will- yes. Yes, of course. But it will take me a couple of days."

"Fine," she nodded. "Deliver it here, please."

THE FRONT DOOR frame popped and hissed as I pushed it open. It had been almost a week since I'd been back here, but it still felt as though it had been months. Years, even.

After Lili's meeting with Dr. Forester, she'd gotten up to take some things out of the safe. Ledgers. She told me she was still reviewing her sister's estate.

"There are a lot of numbers to crunch," she'd said absently, already looking things over. I knew it for what it was: a dismissal.

Deciding to take my leave, I came here. My living room was the same. Same old brown sofa. Same pile of worn out books beside it. Plywood coffee table. I dropped my keys on the kitchen counter and opened the refrigerator out of habit. Nothing in there.

The first time I set foot in here since taking Lili to my father's cabin was an adventure on its own. While my sister was clearing out Kaia's things from the house and Lili was spending most of her day grieving for her sister in silence, I was here throwing out old food that made my eyes water. I cringed at the memory and shut the refrigerator door. There was nothing in there anyway.

With a sigh, I strode into my bedroom and slid my closet door open. My seabag was still on the top shelf, the patch stitched with HALE in big black letters facing me. I grabbed the canvas bag and threw it onto the bed.

Chirping broke the silence. I picked up my phone to see a text message from Lilith.

Where'd you go?

I typed in a quick response.

> My place. Just grabbing the rest of my clothes and some other stuff.

Three dots appeared on the screen, flashing and stopping. Flashing and stopping. As though she was drafting a long message or rephrasing what she wanted to say over and over. I watched until her response came through.

> Ok.

With a grunt, I tossed my phone onto the bed and began cleaning out my dresser. My mind flooded with what she could have to say that she was holding back. Uncertainty started to pool in my gut as I worried about the small possibility that she decided Lupo was right.

My lease would be up in a few months. I'd thought I would move in with Lili. I wanted to be near her. When things looked like we were heading in that direction, I thought a few more months would be plenty of time to decide something like that. But now it felt like too little. Was I upending my life for nothing?

The screen lit up as my text alert went off again. I stuffed more pants into my bag and glanced at the screen, figuring she had more to say. Only this time, it wasn't Lilith. It was Clayton.

> Ronan Arwan has something he wants to discuss with you. Alone.

Cryptic. What the hell would he want to talk to me about without Lili? She hadn't discussed any business with me. I knew Clayton had worked for worse men than Ronan as a mercenary. He had nothing to lose. No family. Just him. After putting my sister in danger and almost losing the woman I love, I wasn't in the same boat. Whatever Ronan had to say, it wasn't worth it.

> I'm not interested.

> You should be.

> I'm not.

Twenty minutes went by. Thirty. I was heading out the door with my bag over my shoulder when my phone alerted again. I waited until I was in the driver's seat with the engine rumbling before I looked at the phone again. Clayton.

> I wouldn't be asking if I didn't think it would be good for you, too.

> I'll think about it.

I wondered if Lili was home yet. The club was open by now. She probably hasn't eaten since that bowl of cereal I'd watched her swallow. I fought the urge to ask her if she'd eaten, instead deciding to head home and await her arrival.

I never wanted to tell her about Lupo or his bullshit belief that she couldn't stand on her own two feet. She didn't need to feel like he wasn't in her corner. And that wasn't the truth. It wasn't just the old dog who was afraid for her. As I closed the door and locked up, I knew I was too.

9

Lilith

The basement of Pal's was cold and dark. No one sat in the chair before me. No one stood under the bare lightbulb that dangled from the ceiling. But I could hear his voice like he was standing right next to me. It was filled with violence and laughter.

"Failure," he sang.

"No."

"Failure," he giggled.

"Stop," I begged.

"Failure. My little princess. Oh, my little disappointment. You failed her. You failed her son. You will fail this family. Just as I predicted. A useless, useless girl. You were always a failure to me."

A furious cackle erupted, filling my ears with its cruel echo off of every bare surface. I covered them with my hands, hoping to drown out the noise. As I looked down at my feet, there was a crack in the ground. An earthquake maybe? Another jolt sent the ceiling tumbling down. I ran for the door.

I pulled at the doorknob. Yanked and screamed for help. Begged for someone to please, please open the door.

The room rocked again. The building came down, crushing me under the weight of everything my family had built.

MY EYES BLINKED open to complete darkness. Wind whipping through the trees outside was the only sound. Even West's steady breathing was practically silent. Grateful I hadn't woken him, I set my feet on the floor and padded out of the bedroom. Careful not to let the door click, I shut it behind me as I eyed the guest room door across the hall.

Nightmares had plagued me for as long as I could remember now, but lately, they'd been getting worse. I wasn't sure if it was grief or panic, but every second spent in it felt like drowning. Focused breathing as I descended the staircase was the only reminder that I was awake. I was alright. I wasn't in danger.

The light on the vent hood was still on when I entered the kitchen, illuminating the spotless marble countertops with its faint glow. I never imagined that this would become my house. It felt too grand for me. But I guess I always assumed my life would be small and my home would always reflect that. The vast amount of square footage felt like a bad metaphor for the shoes I now had to fill. I should probably stop wearing old tee shirts and boxer shorts to bed.

My fingers wrapped around the handle on the industrial-sized refrigerator door and yanked it open. Sorting through various containers of leftovers, I spotted the last of Lupo's lasagna and pulled it free.

"What are you doing up?"

I slammed the door shut to find Lupo staring at me with tired blue eyes. His silver hair stood up with slight curls that made him look more like Daniel's grandfather than I'd ever noticed before.

"You scared the shit out of me."

"Sorry," he shrugged. "Are there any of those meatballs left in there?"

"Yeah. On the middle shelf."

He shuffled to the refrigerator and pulled out the container. I grabbed a pair of forks from the drawer beside me and handed him one. With a hop, I sat on the counter and popped open the lasagna.

"West told me what you said," I said as I stabbed my fork into the hardened brick of pasta and cheese. Lupo grunted as he sat down at the island and opened the container of meatballs. "Why didn't you come to me?"

"I figured you had enough on your plate," he shrugged, skewering a meatball with his fork and pulling it up for a bite. "It was a conversation we needed to have. Man to man."

I took a bite of lasagna and chewed on what he'd said. After a swallow and shake of my head, I yelled at him while trying to keep my voice down. An absurd whisper yell.

"So you thought going to my boyfriend and telling him I needed to get married to somebody else was a good idea? You didn't think that would cause problems for me?"

Boyfriend felt like a weird word to use for a man who was pushing 40, but whatever. Lupo looked into the container of meatballs and sighed.

"I know you remember how difficult things were for your sister when she became the boss of the family."

"Of course, I remember how it was for her," I said through a mouthful of noodles and cheese. Swallowing hard, I whisper-shouted at him. "I was here for all of it."

"Well, your sister had backup. She had Nico and you. She had an heir already. You don't have what she had and you already had to fight off a usurping piece of shit and his crew. You don't know how many of them are left. How many of them are still looking you in the eye at those meetings? I'm just trying to look out for you. I thought with the Arwans on your side, you could strike something up. Make a deal to marry the son."

The cold chunk of lasagna looked up at me from the container like even the noodles thought he was making a good point. I sliced into them again. Fuck that. Sexist freaking noodles.

"That might be the case, but I don't need the people closest to me second-guessing my ability to run this fucking family. I watched my grandfather do it for most of my life. Then I watched my sister do it. They were pretty goddamn good at it. I think I've learned enough to handle it on my own."

Lupo snorted.

"Kid, if you think you've got nothing left to learn, you're in more trouble than I thought."

"I didn't say that," I said, whisper-shouting again as set down the container of leftovers and leveled a hard look at him. "But your lack of confidence in me is insulting, Lupo."

He flinched as my statement struck him. Good. I'd been thinking about what West told me for hours. It was what bothered me the most. This man had taught me to defend myself. Had been there for me during the hardest moments of my life. To find out he thought I couldn't stand on my own two feet had been a blow I wasn't able to overlook.

"I'm not going to sell myself into marriage for a political advantage," I finished, stuffing the last of the lasagna into my mouth.

With a sigh, he stood from the stool and made his way back toward the stairs. Our conversation was over. But because I was irritated that he'd abandoned his food, or maybe because I couldn't resist the opportunity to assert my dominance, I called after him. The boss of a mafia family wouldn't put up with this undermining bullshit.

"Lupo?"

"Yeah," he said, turning back to look at me.

"Don't ever keep anything from me again."

10

West

"10-4, Blackjack is inbound with the rest of the package."

Clayton responded to our commanding officer, the feed crackling in my monitor. Our feet slapped against the airstrip, slipping on patches of sand as we hurried toward the helicopter. Our ride out of here. We were almost there.

Almost there.

Sweat stung my eyes. Coated my skin. Covered every inch of me. It was so fucking hot here. Even though we were in a seaside city, it was damn near boiling. But hey, that's the Middle East for you.

The rest of our team dispersed, moving to cover the entrance of the C-17 as embassy employees scurried aboard to safety. Popping shots punctured the air, accompanied by flashes of light in the near distance.

"Command, we've got indirect fire."

"Disco, scramble that bird. Hostiles in the area."

Blisters on my feet screamed at me as I ran. Faster. I had to move faster. The ambassador hurdled himself into the helicopter, unconcerned with his wife and child. His child, a six-year-old girl with wispy blonde hair, was safely tucked into my arms. There was no time to wait for little legs to carry her to safety. So I did.

The wife stopped short of the helicopter, almost tripping on the skid to look back for her daughter.

"I've got her," I cried.

"Mrs. Ellis, you first," Clayton shouted as he extended his hand to help her into the chopper. The buffeting of the propeller blades nearly drowned out his voice. She looked over her shoulder at her daughter before climbing inside.

A hot bolt of pain lanced into my forearm. Then the damp rush of blood. It flowed down my arm. Fire licked my nerves as I lifted the girl into the chopper. Her mother reached out to take her from me. But the girl had gone limp. Her little blue nightgown was covered in blood from my wound.

"Emmy?" The mother's voice was panicked as she tried to wake her daughter.

The edges of my vision swam in darkness. My head spun as I lifted myself inside beside her. The mother pulled her child into her arms. It was then I saw the wound. Not the one that was created by a bullet that had pierced through my arm. The one that wept blood from a hole in pale blue cotton.

A hail of gunfire was drowned out by Mrs. Ellis. Weapons discharged to defend us as she screamed and clutched her child. Her face twisted in agony. Her voice was rasping and desperate, broken as she called the child's name again and again. The ambassador shouted, begging for medics from the comfort of his seat.

"Someone, please," he rattled.

The doors slid closed. A medic checked the child, but too fast. It was too fast because then their hands grabbed my arm and began assessing me, cleaning my wound.

"The girl," I tried. How much blood had I lost? Words were slipping away from me. "Her. Help her."

"Please," the mother screamed, "help my daughter!"

The ambassador was still in his fucking seat. I wanted to get up and throttle him, but my legs felt weak. The mother was wailing and sobbing while rocking the motionless child. The medic continued working on me and spoke without looking up.

"The girl is dead."

GONE AGAIN.

Her side of the bed was neatly made when I opened my eyes. I hadn't even heard her car start when she left this morning. She must have popped it into neutral and rolled it out before actually firing up the engine. Damnit.

I couldn't shake the feeling that she was keeping something from me. The feeling crept over my bones as I thought about the way she disappeared from the house whenever she could, often working for hours on end at the club. Something weird was going on with those ledgers. She was keeping secrets. Secrets I could see behind those haunting, lovely eyes.

Padding down the stairs, I arrived to see an empty kitchen. Daniel must not have been up yet because there was no abandoned bowl of cereal on the counter as there had been most mornings lately. The coffee maker had been used, small spills and grains of sugar betraying whoever had used it last. With a glance at the refrigerator, I saw a tiny pink sticky note left by the perpetrator.

West,

Meet me at the gym at noon.

XO,
Lili

At least there was that. I fixed a cup of coffee for myself and walked around the first floor, checking windows and doors, and noticed Lupo moving around outside. A pork pie hat was perched atop his head, and it sounded like his car was running. Remus wagged his whip-like tail in the backseat as I stepped outside to investigate.

"Going somewhere?" I asked.

"I think I've worn out my welcome," Lupo grunted as he hefted his overnight bag into the trunk of the vintage brown Cutlass Supreme he was driving these days.

"That's not true."

He gave me a hard look and slammed the trunk shut.

"You need to step aside and do what's best for her now," he said as he approached me.

Old hands flexed and relaxed at his side. Once a fighter, always a fighter.

"I'm in love with her, Lupo. You know that. That didn't go away. It never will. Neither will I."

"Selfish."

The word was a growl in his throat. I took a breath, trying not to let this get under my skin, even though the idea of leaving Lilith set every nerve on edge. Instead, I reminded myself that he was just looking out for her. Trying to protect her, even if this was a fucked up way of going about it.

"No," I argued. "The selfish thing to do is leave. I may not be able to help her with the family, but she needs me."

"I guess if you're getting what you want, then what's best for her doesn't matter now. Does it?"

My blood started boiling in my veins. With a flex of my hands, I tried to breathe through the urge to scream in his face that if there was anyone on this planet who would give everything to her; it was me. Someone wanting to protect her for loyalty was bullshit compared to what I would do for her.

He watched me carefully. As I folded my arms across my chest, I loosed a sigh. It was the best I could do to avoid raging at the old man. But his next words told me it didn't matter what I had to say.

"You don't know what you're up against. This world eats people alive."

I rolled my eyes. This was going nowhere. If Lilith wanted me to leave, I would. I'd do anything she asked. But when she looked devastated at the idea that I'd leave her, I knew I sure as hell wasn't walking away.

Lupo scrubbed a hand down his face and looked back at the house. Heaving an agitated breath, he stuffed his hands into the pockets of his chinos. Remus popped up from the backseat again, his ears askew in some dog version of bedhead.

"Tell the kid he's welcome at my house anytime."

Sorrow tugged at my middle as I thought about Daniel. This wouldn't do. Not for him. Not for Lili. My jaw ached as I unwound it and rolled my shoulders. With a glance back at the house, I sighed.

"Tell him yourself. Don't go anywhere."

I THOUGHT ABOUT what Lupo had said to me the entire drive over to One Two.

"This world eats people alive."

Watching Lili take over the family had been a strange and terrifying thing. I'd never forget the woman she was that first day in the office. She'd gone in with a plan. Ozzie slowly choked to death on poison. Dozens of guns were trained on her. The Irish. In the middle of it all, she maintained her composure. Instead of the smart-mouthed girl who I'd come to love, she was a woman with a grand plan to make men suffer. No, not a woman.

A queen.

As I parked out front, I remembered that moment. She took control of the family, thinking it was temporary. Thinking she would get her sister back and things would go back to the way they were. But these days it was getting harder to get to her. I wondered if the distance between us was her grief, or if she was collapsing under the weight of her crown.

The gym was empty when I walked inside, which was curious because I saw the blue Camaro parked out front. As I dropped my gym bag and keys onto the ground, I heard Wu-Tang Clan start to pipe in from the speakers.

"Lili?"

Lupo's office door opened and Lili entered the open area where mats were laid out for training, adjusting her bra as she walked. She always trained in the same black training bra and leggings. Even if every pair she owned had faded from thousands of washes, they still showed off her incredible curves and muscles.

I kicked off my shoes, took off my shirt, and approached the mat. Lili watched me approach, tying her hair back into a ponytail with an elastic from her wrist. The wolf tattoo's eyes peeked out from a little cutout in her bra.

"Alright," I said. "Is your hand ok?"

"Yeah, it's fine. I thought it might feel good to be out of my head for a while. And I have my first big family meeting tonight. So…"

"So you want to get out of your head by beating the shit out of me for a little while?"

She bit her lip and cast her eyes to the ground with a nod.

"I think we can manage that," I said as I sat on the mat and waited for her to join me. Lili folded her legs under herself as she came to the ground.

In what seemed like a few short minutes, she had me trapped in a damn mount. We were both sweating and breathless. Straddled across my lap, it was difficult to do anything but admire the warrior she was as she looked down at me with a smirk. Sunlight filtered in through the windows, making the loose edges of her black hair look almost brown. A thin sheen of sweat coated her olive skin.

"Come on," she laughed down at me as she squeezed her thighs, her forearm pressed into my neck. "Tap out."

"Nope."

It was easy to move her arm to my chest. Easier still to buck her from her seat with a bridge position that forced my hips up from under her. With an arch and a roll, she was underneath me.

"Shit," she groaned.

"Don't be too hard on yourself," I smiled. "We haven't mat trained in a while."

And I trained for hours with men thrice her size for years before meeting her, but she didn't need to hear that. She pushed her hips off of the mat, attempting to get out from under me. It had been a while since we'd trained like this, but I relished the contact. It was only when she needed comfort from her nightmares that she'd gotten this close to me lately.

As she writhed underneath me, attempting to move me, I remembered her in a similar position in the bed we'd been sharing. It was impossible to drive away the memory of her soft moans or the way she felt squeezing around me with that tightness I'd come to need like oxygen. My cock's reaction to her body pressed against me was unavoidable.

Then my hands moved on their own. Squeezing every curve, gliding up her body until they reached her full breasts. The band of her bra was dark with sweat. My hooked thumbs lifted the material to reveal the dusky pink tips of her nipples.

"West," she breathed, licking her lips.

Fuck, I loved the way my name sounded coming out of this delicious mouth. I'd enjoyed every single time she'd panted it in ecstasy. Especially that first time with my tongue between her legs. The memory had me shifting my weight until my hips pressed against hers. With one arm holding me over her, the other was free to enjoy her. To tease one soft pink bud. Then the other.

She sucked her lower lip into her mouth and trapped it in her teeth. Arched into my touch as I continued tracing her soft curves and hard edges. A whimper burst from her as I took one nipple into my mouth and pulled gently with my teeth. Softly licked with my tongue. The sound alone was enough to send rational thought out of my mind as my focus narrowed to this. Nothing else mattered. Only her.

"Someone might see," she gasped.

"Let them."

Lili was strong in ways I was still learning. Smarter than anyone I'd ever met. She could stand on her own two feet and rule like the fierce warrior queen I knew she could be. But goddamnit, I needed her now.

Sunlight warmed our bodies as they moved together on the mat. Her hips rose to meet mine, seeking the same relief I needed as she ground herself against my erection. I freed her breast from my mouth to capture her lips and taste every delicious sound that dropped from them. The fabric separating us was hardly anything. Thin and damp. A barrier to keep me from plunging home. I wanted to tear it away. To sink into her. Make her mine, mine, *mine*.

"Hello?"

Lili let out a surprised squeak and shifted out from under me. My hand snapped out to tug her bra down quickly. She turned away to cover and adjust herself. Peeking over the elevated boxing ring, I could see someone standing at the door. A gangly blonde teen said, pushing a hand through his sun-bleached hair.

"The boxing class is at 1 o'clock, right?"

"Uh," I said, pausing to clear my throat. "Yeah. You're early. The trainer should be here soon."

I glanced to where Lili had been, only to see that she'd scurried off to the office. The door slammed shut behind her. After tucking my hard-on up into my waistband, I stood to find the teenager smirking at me with a knowing look.

Thanks a lot, buddy.

11

Lilith

My ears were ringing. Ringing. Sharp, agitating ringing repeated in my head. Wait. No, that was my new phone. It had been waiting for me at Muse this morning. Normally, I'd keep the ringer off, but I'd forgotten. I ignored it as I tried to collect myself in Lupo's office. After nearly pulling West in here to finish what we started, blood was pounding through every delicate part of me. I'd been seconds away from begging him when that boy waltzed in.

I let out a laugh at the absurdity of it. It had been so long since we'd touched each other like that. I'd become so numb to any other feeling but rage or grief. Something about falling into our old routine made me feel at ease. Or maybe that was just the effect his touch had on me.

I breathed deeply, willing air into my lungs to cool the blaze West had sparked. I couldn't touch myself in here. That would be weird. As I debated the issue, my phone began ringing again.

Nico. He'd called me three times. My stomach plummeted. Taking the call, I lifted the phone to my ear. Before I could say a word, Nico spoke.

"Boss, you need to get here. Now."

"Where? What's happening?"

His breath was ragged. He barked orders at someone nearby. I could hear screaming. And sirens.

"Muse. It's burning."

The phone case creaked as my grip tightened around it. The club. Someone set the club on fire. No, *my* club. There wasn't a fucking chance it was an accident. I spoke through clenched teeth as I acknowledged what Nico had said.

"I'll be there in ten minutes."

I threw my leather jacket over my bra, not bothering to change out of my sweaty clothes, and stepped into my boots. As I slung my bag over my shoulder and fished my keys out of my jacket pocket, I took a breath to steady myself. Then another as I flung open the door.

"What?" West asked.

People were filing in for the afternoon boxing class. West had gathered his things and waited for me. A look of concern washed over his features as he noted my hasty stride. His long legs were quick to catch me as I hurried out the door.

"What?" He asked again as we walked toward our cars, standing between my Camaro and his Bronco.

"Someone burned down my fucking club."

SMOKE AND SIRENS greeted me in the golden sunlight of the afternoon. It would have been beautiful if it wasn't devastating. I searched my mind for valuables. Inventoried the contents of the safe. At least my sister had the presence of mind to make it a fireproof safe. But that wasn't what filled my gut with unease.

"Jesus," West uttered, coming to stand behind me.

We'd both ignored the rules of the road to get here quickly, speeding through every intersection in West Hollywood. I parked as close as the fire trucks would allow. I'd only been here a few hours ago.

It was too early for most of the dancers to have arrived. I scanned the area for anyone I recognized. Close-shaven black hair caught my attention. Nico.

"Hey," he said with a nod in my direction.

I beckoned him to my car. He buttoned his jacket to hide the holster from the police as he walked past. Not that it mattered. Between his gambling debt and a mistress in San Fernando, the police chief was so deep in my pocket that he'd never see daylight. I opened the driver's side door and sat as West opened the passenger side, pushing the seat forward for Nico to take the back. As soon as the door shut behind West, Nico spoke.

"The Arawns?"

"No," I dismissed the accusation.

"This is what they do. Ronan might have fooled you. Betrayed you."

"No. He didn't do this to us. You know better than that, Nico," I breathed, trying to grasp the fraying edge of my control. He'd seen Killian show up for me when I took over the family. He'd been present for my meeting with Ronan. Apparently, that wasn't enough to trust him.

"We have dozens of businesses. There are any number of locations connected families like Ronan's could have been targeted. I imagine, thanks to recent history, that the responsible party is not trying to send me a message."

A message I heard loud and clear. Not Ronan, but someone who knew about his penchant for arson. Someone who wanted to let me know how much he knows about me and who I do business with. He was trying to smoke me out. Make me do something stupid. Something rash.

This is not going to be the only pretty Lily I put inside a box.

"Who?"

I turned in my seat to look at Nico. The Duke's mind games would remain a secret. For now.

"Possibly the men you and I have already discussed," I lied cooly. It could have been the remainder of Ozzie's men. But probably not. "Has there been any progress there?"

Nico sat back, spreading his arms across the back of the seat. West watched him in the rearview mirror. The scarred eyebrow ticked in irritation. Nico lifted a hand to scratch at his jaw. His newly tattooed hand. West's eyes flared at the marking.

A wolf.

"Yes. Damon and I have narrowed it down to a couple of crews for you. With your permission, we'd like to confirm and then eliminate them one by one. It may take some time."

"No."

Nico opened his mouth to argue. I cut him off.

"Time is not on our side, Nico," I said, gesturing toward the now-smoldering remains of the building before us. "If we're going to take them out, I propose we do it in one fell swoop. Better to rid ourselves of them now before they cause any more problems."

Before the man who'd sent my sister to her grave could use the stragglers of Ozzie's backstabbing crew against me. Loose ends like that promised my death would be close behind. No. Only a fool would leave so many enemies on the board.

"Yes, boss," Nico agreed. "So, what should we do?"

West's gaze shifted to a sidelong glance at me. Right. I had some explaining to do. Though Nico shifted in his seat to leave, West didn't move. I sighed.

"Get me a list. We're going to have to deal with this."

Nico nodded at my declaration, an uncertain look crossing his features. I gave him his marching orders, asking him to pass information along to Damon, and looked to West hoping he'd at least let the man out of the backseat before interrogating me as he so obviously wanted to do. The sound of the door closing was still rattling my eardrums when he whirled on me.

"You made Nico the Wolf? Why didn't you tell me?"

"Can you blame me? Look at this mess," I barked, gesturing toward the wreckage. "I need backup. I need protection."

"You have me."

I blew out a breath through my nostrils and looked down at my lap. My fingers wrung together. *You might as well tell him. He's going to find out anyway.*

"Nico knows everyone in this family. He can help me solve this problem and put out other fires for me," I said, glancing at the burning building before us. "Alright, that was a poor choice of words. But he's not the only one."

"What do you mean?"

"There are two. I swore in two wolves. In this family, I needed two people I could trust to do what I asked of them without question. Without worrying if they're going to betray me or not. Because I know being the boss in this family puts a target on my back. So I swore in Nico and Damon, who you'll meet, eventually."

West shifted in his seat and took my hand, but said nothing. The feel of his calluses on my skin was a strange sort of comfort. His eyes drifted away from mine. Weighing every possible response to what I'd said. His jaw tightened before he squeezed my hand and let it go.

"Let's go home. It sounds like you have some planning to do."

12

WEST

"Shit."

I hadn't realized I'd fallen asleep until the soft curse woke me. Lili stood by the dresser, bending over to pick up something she'd dropped.

"Hey."

"Hi. Sorry, I didn't mean to wake you up," she apologized.

After we'd gotten home from the club, she went straight into the apothecary to retrieve her gloves and shears. When she reappeared, it was to work in the garden. Cutting away at fluffy white flowers and stuffing them into a canvas bag. Cut. Stuff. Cut. Stuff. When she was satisfied, she stomped up the stairs to return to her apothecary. And didn't reemerge. Until now.

I turned on the bedside lamp and sat up, taking the book I'd fallen asleep with off of my bare chest and placing it on the nightstand.

"Hemingway putting you to sleep?" She angled her head with a little smile that didn't meet her tired eyes.

I thought about the worries she wanted to work off at the gym. About the fire. She was still wearing the gym clothes, though she'd thrown a threadbare white tee shirt over the black bra. The leggings rolled down her legs as she peeled them off, throwing them into the hamper when she finished.

Lupo and Daniel had been occupied with a movie and snacks in the living room, paying no attention to me as I climbed the stairs. The urge to douse myself with a cold shower to calm myself after our discussion in the car was overwhelming. Wolves. Not one, but two.

That conversation could wait. The mere sight of the woman before me was rekindling the heat in my blood.

"Come here," I beckoned, barely able to speak as I remembered the taste of her sweat I'd enjoyed only hours ago.

I hadn't forgotten the way she'd writhed and moaned as we ground ourselves into each other, aching for satisfaction. It was near enough to the fantasies I'd had about pinning her to the mat and taking her in that gym. The memory made my breath go shallow.

Obeying my command to come closer, she removed the shirt and tossed it away as she came to stand between my legs. Nibbling at her lip. Toying with her hands. She couldn't look me in the eye. She knew we needed to talk, but that sure as hell wouldn't do. Not right now.

"Lili, look at me."

My fingers caught her chin and turned it until our eyes met. The tips of them traveled down her neck, grazing her breast on the way to her waist. I watched her react to my touch. Her eyes remained locked on mine as my hand traveled up her spine to where her bra was hooked. My other hand gripped her waist as I released it, tugging the material down her arms to take in the ample mounds I was dying to taste again.

"West," she gasped.

I pulled her close to me as she let the garment fall to the floor. The feel of her body against me dissolved any restraint. Her voice, her skin, her sumptuous ass in my hands. It was simultaneously too much and never, ever enough. My nose grazed a peaked nipple. She shuddered in my hold as I followed it with my mouth. Fuck, she tasted like heaven.

"Let me make you feel good," I desperately growled against her breast, barely recognizing my own voice.

If she wouldn't let me swear myself to her, if I couldn't marry her to protect her, I sure as hell could do this. Her fingers traced the waistband of my boxer briefs, pausing as my teeth grazed her stiff peak.

"Oh," she breathed at my nip and stiffened.

For a second, I thought she would pull away. Stop this. I would. My aching cock would kill me, but I would. For her. That full lip sucked into her mouth, between her teeth as she considered. Then she seemed to change her mind.

"Yes. Get me out of my head. Please. Just for now. Please, West."

I looked up at her, unable to stifle the grin from the pure relief I felt as I thought that maybe we would always have this. Our bodies could connect when words failed us.

"I love it when you beg, Trouble."

Since the death of her sister, I'd felt her pushing me away. I hadn't known if it was from grief or something else. Other men swore themselves to her. But when she was in my arms, I could ignore all of those things. Just for now. She was mine. And there was no getting rid of me.

Lili's mouth was on mine in an instant. Somehow, both hungry and soft. Our tongues met in a caress that quickly turned ravenous. Her round, fleshy ass flexed in my grip as she pressed her thighs together. My sweet, needy girl. I turned her, yanking her toward me as I backed myself against the headboard. She followed, reclining against my chest as my hands traveled the length of her body.

Long black hair brushed against my skin as I squeezed her breasts, teasing her nipples until she was squirming in my arms. Calluses rasped against the tender peaked flesh. Her legs moved against each other, looking for pressure. Looking for the relief I was more than willing to provide.

My teeth sank into her shoulder as I dipped a hand between her thighs, tracing the exquisitely wet slit that was begging me for more. Traced until I found her swollen clit I knew ached to be touched. Her ass ground against me as she mewled, a desperate little noise. She may be the most dangerous woman in this city, but she was so sweet with my hand between her thighs. I growled into her neck, licking and biting at her like an animal. Drinking in her scent as I circled my thumb where she needed me.

"You want more?"

"Please," she breathed.

Her hips tilted as she let her head fall backward. This. Her. It was what I'd always wanted. For better or worse. From the day I met her, it was the thought that traveled through my mind in unguarded moments. Wondering what it would be like to touch her. Taste her. Love her. I'd distracted myself with other women, but they were never enough. They could never be her.

I would think about her as I lay alone in my bed some nights. When I showered. Smelling her on my clothes as I drove home after training with her every day. All I wanted was for Lilith Caccia to come for me the way I'd fantasized about. For her to burn for me the way I burned for her every single day.

"West," she begged.

Beautiful rosy lips met mine in a desperate kiss. Her tongue stroked mine as she moaned into my mouth. My thumb continued to work her clit as I grazed over her opening with my fingers. Tiny tremors shook her legs as she panted into my mouth. She was close. One finger dipped inside, testing. Teasing. Then another. We watched, relishing the sight of my fingers burying themselves in her tight opening.

They moved in her, working my thumb against her and filling her until another moan burst from that beautiful mouth. With a frantic and broken sound, her orgasm wracked her body. Drinking her moans down, I could taste the pleasure on her breath.

The desire to make this last collapsed under the urge to claim her. I pushed Lili forward until she lay on her belly, hooking my thumbs into the waistband of her panties to pull dark green lace over the round ass I couldn't take my eyes off of. Down, down, down until she was completely bare before me.

"So fucking beautiful," I praised, running a hand down her spine.

She shivered at the touch. Olive skin flushed pink with need. Gorgeous full ass. Obsidian hair spilled like oil over stark white bedding. She was. She really fucking was.

It was the work of a moment to free myself from my boxers and toss them aside. To climb over her and straddle her thigh as she twisted at the waist to kiss me. Sweet, tight heat teased the tip of my cock, mirroring the way her tongue licked at the seam of my mouth. Plunging forward, I clenched my teeth to steady myself as I sunk deep into her damp sex. She gasped at the movement, suddenly filled with me. The feel of her squeezing and stretching around my length was nearly enough to send me over the edge. It had been too long.

"West, please," she panted.

The angle of her twisted body beneath me had her hips pushing back to meet mine. My arm threaded under her and up between her breasts to grasp her throat for leverage. Skin slapped and slid as we chased release for what could have been hours or seconds. Close. The squeeze of her around me. Fuck, I wasn't going to last much longer. Her moans grew louder and quaking muscles told me she was close. My thumb found her mouth, forcing its way through full pink lips as I tried to quiet her.

"As much as I love the sounds you make, we're not alone here, Trouble. Bite down if you have to scream," I panted.

Hazel gold eyes looked up at me through dark lashes as Lili's tongue slicked along my thumb. Black hair tangled with the inked tentacles curling down my arm. Wrapped up in each other, we moved as one. Damn, I missed this. A muffled moan soon followed as her shaking thighs pressed against me. She was close.

The slide of her tongue against my callused thumb snapped any control I had left. Teeth clamped down on me as her inner muscles flexed around my cock. Her release was exquisite agony. The combined sensations were enough to destroy any resolve I had left.

"Fuck," I groaned as I let go, spilling myself inside her.

It felt endless. Like falling over a cliff into a deep and bottomless ocean. As I tightened my grip around her body, I buried my face in her dark tresses. Took in her scent and the tantalizing feel of her. The soft curves of her coupled with thick muscle. My hands greedily traveled over every inch of her delicious flesh.

She was everything, everything, *everything*.

We stayed like that for a while. Her body wrapped up in mine. Our hair a mess of brown and black, sprawled across the white linens. Heaving breaths were the only sound.

She'd told me that she loved me. Standing out in the garden just outside. She told me that she'd known it for a while. I'd known it then, too. Knew it the way I did now. I could taste it on her love as I kissed her shoulder where I'd marked it with my teeth.

Her breath was my breath. Her pulse flickered in my veins. And her fear. Her pain. It was mine too.

Once I could form thoughts again, I fetched a washcloth and cleaned her up. Pulled my underwear back on and climbed into bed. But before I could take her in my arms again, she was in the bathroom turning on the shower. Her absence was still fresh when my phone lit up on the nightstand. It was another message from Clayton.

Ronan Arwan wants to meet with you. Tonight.

IT SMELLED LIKE frankincense and cigarettes. Little hairs stood up on the back of my neck as I entered the abandoned church. Or at least, seemingly abandoned. The door was heavy and scraped against the stone threshold as I shouldered it open to find that the interior was no warmer than the frigid morning air outside.

Clayton had given me the address and meeting time. I'd been able to dress and leave while Lili was in the shower, but I wasn't sure how to explain where I'd gone. I'd decided to keep it brief and left her a note.

Clayton needs my help with something. I'll be back soon.

West

An echo of the closing door bounced off of the vaulted stone ceiling, once adorned in gold paint that had nearly chipped away. Little remnants of it winked at me as I walked down the aisle, looking for the man who'd called this meeting.

The dark wooden pews looked like they'd seen better days, but they were in much better shape than the half-rotten wood flooring that stretched all through the cavernous space. An old marble altar that would have been white if it weren't covered in dust was bathed in colorful light from the stained-glass window behind it. Aside from the narrow windows surrounding the front doors that were mostly boarded up, the streetlights blazing through the window were the only source of light. Beneath it sat three large wooden chairs, ornately carved but bare of any upholstery. In the center chair sat the man I was here to see.

"Didn't have any trouble finding the place?" Ronan called from his seat.

His black suit and shirt concealed him in the shadows. He'd been waiting for me.

"Not really," I said, with a glance around. "I'm amazed this place hasn't been torn down to make way for townhouses or something."

"Well, they'd have to buy it from me first. I'm not a very charitable negotiator."

"Why am I here, Ronan?"

He adjusted himself in his seat, letting both of his hands grip the armrests. A throne on a dais. It was an intimidating first impression. Likely a strategic one. I'd met some of the most dangerous men in the world. Ronan was as terrifying as any of them.

With a tilt of his head, I knew he was debating how he wanted to begin. The smirk that followed told me he'd decided.

"Your friend Clayton tells me you're romantically entangled with Ms. Caccia."

I said nothing as questions flooded my mind. Why would Clayton tell him that? What did that have to do with Ronan? Maybe I shouldn't have left her alone. I wondered if I should have asked Nico to come to the house to guard her. Though I didn't speak, my face must have betrayed my thoughts because Ronan continued.

"I'm not going to kill you and push my son on her if that's what you're worried about," he laughed.

My teeth ground against each other as I waited for him to continue. I certainly wasn't worried about that before. Though now...

"Not a talkative man, are ye?"

"I'm waiting for you to get to the point."

Ronan laughed and stood from his seat behind the altar, gesturing for me to continue my approach as he walked into the light. I mounted the marble steps and stuffed my hands into the pockets of my jacket. Something told me not to let him see my balled-up fists.

"Ms. Caccia and I have allied ourselves to take down this organization. The one trafficking women and children. But she and I don't share the same agenda when it comes to a particular detail."

"What detail is that?"

"The Duke. Duke Harrison Augustus-Stanley. He's the one at the top of that chain. The way Ms. Caccia tells it, it seems that old Benjamin Camden was answering to the cunt."

Ronan stepped forward, placing his hands on the dusty white altar. His silver signet ring glinted in the golden light. A skull with the letters R and A where eyes should be surrounded by engravings that looked like billowing smoke. His fingers tapped on the surface. I looked up to see his dark eyes fixed impatiently on me.

"I have unfinished business with this man. He saw fit to take something precious from me. My only girl. Thanks to you and your woman, she's been returned to me."

"Lili had more to do with that-"

"Regardless," he interrupted. "Clayton tells me the two of you have worked together before. Served together. I've purchased his services to deal with this Duke. He's told me he can't do it on his own."

Understanding dawned on me. This wasn't a message for Lili. It was a job offer. For me.

"I'm not a mercenary."

"Would you like to be?" Ronan's black eyebrows shot up at the question. The lopsided grin on his face felt like a dangerous thing. "Clayton will tell you I pay quite well, ye know. Despite appearances."

He looked around at the derelict church and chuckled. Ronan didn't have to tell me he had money. The cut of his suit, the watch on his wrist, and the shoes on his feet did that for him. He scratched at his salt and pepper stubble, awaiting my answer.

"It's not about the money," I replied. "That life's not for me."

Ronan leaned forward, his head taking on a conspiratorial angle.

"I know what happened to Kaia Caccia. I know that the Duke gave the order to kidnap her. His men killed her. Will you ever forget that? The way your woman screamed as her sister died in her arms? The way she looked kneeling in her blood?"

Tension clamped down on every nerve as the image rushed back to me. The blood. The tears. The sounds Lili made as she clutched her sister's corpse like her touch was going to bring Kaia back.

Ronan's eyes gleamed with cruel promise as his voice lowered to a whisper. The devil's offer wrapped up in a simple question.

"Wouldn't you like to make that bastard pay in blood for what he's done to the woman you love?"

13

Lilith

My cheek still pricked with the sting of it. The sharp backhand I'd gotten. He'd tripped. I laughed at him. Not even on purpose. It was a reflex! But I'd laughed at my father and paid for it. It was my fault this was happening. My fault for laughing. It wasn't the first time this had happened, but it was the first time she had witnessed it. Silent tears streamed down my face as I watched my sister scream at my father for what he'd done. Our mother monitored from the kitchen.

"Say that again!"

His voice boomed around us, filling every corner with the awful sound. My sister stood before me, a fist balled at her side as the other hand was lifted with an accusatory finger pointed directly at him. At barely fourteen, she was fearless.

"You don't touch her. Don't you ever touch her like that."

"Don't tell me what to do, you ungrateful little bitch. You don't give me orders. I put a roof over your head. I put food in your mouth. I am your father. Speak to me with respect."

"I can't respect men who hit little girls."

She spat at him. It hit his polished leather shoe. He stormed for her, raging *as he reached for her with an angry hand. Kaia moved from his grasp, ducking away swiftly before she struck. Our father collapsed to the floor.*

"YOU WANT ME to bring the kid with me to the hospital?" Lupo had asked when I begged him to keep an eye on Daniel. I knew Lanna would do it if I'd asked, but I needed someone with his set of skills. Someone who would lay down their life for Daniel, if it came to that.

"We both know this is a dangerous time. With what happened at Muse yesterday, I want to make sure he's protected. Really protected."

Lupo grunted, rubbing a hand over his face before looking at my nephew. His grandson. Remus, his dog, perked up to eye us from his perch on the sofa beside Daniel. The thought of my sister losing her shit about a dog lounging on her creamy white furniture lightened my mood a little.

"Yeah, fine," he agreed. "But I can't do it alone."

"You won't have to. Nico is busy, but Gino De Luca is on his way. He's a good guy. A little crazy, but a good guy. He'll back you up."

"I can't come with you, Zia?"

"No, buddy. I've got work to do and it's going to suck. But I promise I'll see you later."

Every time I left Daniel, I felt awful. Walking out the front door, I heard him ask the old man where I was going. It was a question I'd been on the receiving end of many times. Always about his mother. I'd tell him she'd be back later. That she'd call him at bedtime like she always did. She always put on a smiling face for him, even when I knew she was stressed by family business. It was all I thought about while driving the gleaming blue Camaro through the streets of Los Angeles.

As I walked through the newly constructed Bootlegger restaurant, I couldn't help the warm feeling that seeped into me. It was as good as new. Better than that. It walked the line between old and new again. Large, shining red tufted leather horseshoe-shaped booths lined the walls, just as they had before. The bar was beautifully crafted with deep walnut panels. Aged mirrors hung behind it.

All of it, just as it was before.

I traced a finger along the new marble bar top as I walked toward the back office. With Muse out of commission, I needed somewhere to work. Slinging my bag off of my shoulder onto the antique steel desk I'd had moved out of my grandfather's warehouse, it gave a dull thud as it connected with the metal.

I hesitated to begin working. To sit in here as if nothing had happened would be a lie. I looked around at the freshly painted walls that used to be filled with pictures. Pictures of other guys in the family. Pictures of my grandparents. A picture of my mother. All of them were gone. And now I had another place to rebuild.

Losing Muse. In truth, I didn't know how to feel. I didn't know that there was any part of me that had anything left to give. Except for the safe, everything that belonged to Kaia was gone. It was like losing her all over again. Augustus-Stanley must have known the way that would hurt me. He had to.

Pushing my hands into my pockets, I freed the card I'd kept with me for days. The one I'd found in my sister's safe. Black on black. Just an email and a phone number. The email was made up of random numbers and letters.

I opened my laptop and typed the email address into an outgoing message. Without knowing who was on the other end, I kept my message brief.

Kaia Caccia is dead. This is your new contact.

After that, I began working. First, checking my email for any updates on the Duke. I'd set up a search engine alert for any news on the man, but it had thus far proven fruitless besides the occasional fluff piece on his social appearances or engagements.

Clicking on the most recent article, my eyes began to skim for details. If I had one thing going for me, it was that very few people knew I even existed. My social media accounts only functioned as a means to stalk my targets. No one else in my life had an online presence. He'd have to mine for information on my life while I could use his status as a public figure against him. When you're a royal, almost everything is public information.

But in researching him, I'd run into several problems. The first was that with someone that wealthy, his homes were off the grid. He'd likely paid off someone somewhere to convince web map creators to lie about where his estate sat, making it seem like only protected government landscapes existed in its location. So there would be no surprising him in his territory.

The second was that his movements were documented after the fact. Never any announcement of his expected presence. Only photos or articles after the event had happened. But that was less of a problem. No. That would at least give me somewhere to start.

When I was studying biology during my graduate program, I attended a lecture on pattern recognition. Essentially, the concept boiled down to data collection and analysis. With enough information on the subject, you can look for arrangements of characteristics that yield significant data. Patterns.

Thanks to years and years of news coverage on the Duke's appearances at various events and engagements, I had an ample amount of information to analyze. If I was lucky, I could deduce the probability of where the sonofabitch was likely to appear next. And I'd be waiting for him.

HUMANS ARE PREDICTABLE creatures. We find comfort in routine. Routines we create from habit. The Duke. Harrison had a routine. Some events he attended infrequently. His schedule was hard to pin down. It only took me hours staring at a screen until my eyes felt like they were going to start bleeding from the radiant blue light to find what I was looking for.

Flora Hunter - Reservation Confirmed.

The email notification popped up on my phone as I adjusted the drip on the condenser. My mouth twitched in amusement. Oh, Flora. Flora Hunter had a passport. She had a degree in comparative literature from some obscure liberal arts college in the Midwest. She owned a cute little laundromat and liked to take pictures of food for her Instagram. I'd spent time cultivating Flora. Had started it years ago, but lately, I'd gotten more involved in creating lies as a way to distract myself. The art of crafting a good lie begins with the truth.

"Lili," West's voice sounded in the room. I hadn't even heard him come in. His eyes skated over the little brown bottles I'd lined up like soldiers. "What are you doing in here?"

"Party planning," I grumbled.

He was silent, undoubtedly counting the bottles before me.

"Is this what you were working on last night?"

I nodded, filling another bottle with the mixture I had created. With a few twists to seal the lid, I lifted my gaze to West.

"That's a lot."

"Yes, it is."

West looked at me with worry in his eyes, his jaw tightening. Whatever. I was too tired to explain myself. Before we could end our standoff, Nico entered the apothecary to find West and me silently staring each other down.

"Uh. Everything alright in here?" He hesitated.

"Fine," West said simply, leaning back against the bank of cabinets behind him. "We're fine."

I took off my gloves and safety goggles, beckoning Nico toward me.

"I've got," Nico glanced at West as he approached. "Got that information you wanted, Boss."

Nico placed a piece of paper, surely a page torn out of some small notebook, on the work table in front of me and stepped back, undoing the button on his blazer as he did so. West's fingers gripped the cabinets, going white at the knuckles, though his expression remained impassive. I picked up the small page and looked over the list he'd made up. Names. Names. Names.

"Are you sure these are all of them?" I asked.

"Yes. Every single one. Sorry, it took so long. Interrogation got a little messy."

I angled my head, reading through the list again. I could feel West tensing from across the room.

"And the others are doing what, exactly?"

"Rounding them up for you, Boss. All they know is when and where to show up."

My gut churned for a moment. Just a moment. This was the point of no return. The hard reality of who I had to be now. I could still back out. Still choose to be a merciful leader. But mercy can be more dangerous than poison.

"Good," I rasped.

I could choose to exile the men listed on this page. Let their threat fester from miles away while living on borrowed time, believing that I'd done the right thing. Then, when they came for me or someone I loved, I'd have to kill them anyway. And someone else could get hurt.

West drew my gaze as he crossed his arms. Waiting for the command I'd give Nico. Waiting to see what kind of leader I was going to be. It was my decision. Take the risk and let them live? No. Any decision that put my family at risk would never be the right choice.

14

WEST

"BANG!" Daniel shouted from behind the sofa, aiming his toy gun at me. I took the impact of his imaginary bullet and fell to the floor, grunting as I pretended to die. The small boy walked over and nudged me with his foot.

"Hey, get up!" Daniel said.

"I can't. I'm dead," I responded, looking up at him with one eye. "Dead guys can't do anything."

"But I'm hungry," he whined.

"Oh, well, in that case," I laughed as I grabbed him. He squealed as I hoisted myself up and tossed him over a shoulder. The sound made me cringe as I remembered the sick old man napping upstairs after his treatment. "Alright, what can this zombie cowboy fix for you?"

"Pancakes!"

"For dinner?" I laughed.

My growling stomach demanded something a little more substantial, but I couldn't argue with the kid. Breakfast for dinner did sound good.

"Alright. But I'm also making scrambled eggs and bacon. Scrambled eggs and bacon that you, sir, are going to eat."

"Fine," Daniel huffed.

The front door opened and shut, followed by the sound of boots clapping on the tile entryway. Lili's black hair tumbled down around her shoulders as she released it from the bun atop her head. I'd left her in her apothecary or laboratory, or whatever she called it this morning, along with Nico to plan their "party." Their planning took most of the day. At least she was finally finished preparing the wicked brew she'd been working on. At least for now.

"Zia, we're having breakfast for dinner!"

"Oh yeah?"

She winced at her nephew's shirt and hands, which were now covered in pancake batter. How that happened, even I didn't know. Kids weren't really my area of expertise, but I've always been more of a learn-by-doing sort of guy anyway.

"He wanted to help," I offered.

Lili told Daniel to wash up for dinner and headed upstairs. It wasn't so long ago that I was leading a pretty solitary life. After bringing Lili to my cabin to hide out, I'd gotten used to having her around. Having her to take care of, which felt... Now I was in this house with her and this six-year-old boy. But it was strange. It didn't seem like too much too soon, though I would never have wanted things to happen this way. For Daniel to lose his mother. Or for Lili to get hurt the way she did.

"Wouldn't you like to make that bastard pay in blood for what he's done to the woman you love?"

Ronan's question echoed in my mind as I scraped the eggs into a dish. I'd never forget the way they broke her. The sounds of her screams, as though those wails could call her sister down from wherever she'd gone. The way she fought Nico and Gino like a wild animal when they tried to pry Kaia out of Lilith's arms.

I'd known for years that Lilith Caccia existed in a world outside of the law. Had become alright with that reality as I'd grown more and more infatuated with her. She made me feel whole in a way I'd never known. Even when I found out that she wasn't just an enforcer, but a fixer. Now a boss. I could live with all of it because I loved her. But if I stepped into this world and took Ronan's offer, I'd be leaving my life behind for good.

Lili reappeared in the kitchen in one of my shirts and a worn-out pair of sweatpants. She tossed her hair over a shoulder and approached me from behind, wrapping her arms around my waist.

"Smells good," she said, her voice muffled as she pressed her face into my back. Wedging herself under my arm, she looked up at me. "What did Clayton need? What couldn't wait until morning?"

I opened my mouth to answer her question, even though I wasn't sure what I was going to say. Gold-rimmed eyes watched me, awaiting an answer. Daniel trotted in from the bathroom and took his place at the island. The little man was responsible for the rapidly expanding soft spot in me. The urge to protect him was impossible to ignore. Just as it was for Lili.

She squeezed me and walked away to pour some water for her nephew. I placed a plate piled high with breakfast foods in front of Daniel and said, "Dinner is served."

"Thanks, zombie cowboy!"

Daniel and I both laughed at the look of confusion on his aunt's face. My phone buzzed in my pocket. Lili's eyes darted to the source of the sound. I set her plate down in front of her, kissing the top of her head before moving away. The phone buzzed again, anxious to get my attention. Rounding the island, I slipped it out of my pocket to look at the message. It was from Clayton.

Ronan told me you met with him. Are you in?

Daniel poured maple syrup all over his pancakes, eggs, and bacon. Lili's head tipped back in a laugh. The sight tugged at something in my chest. I filled glasses of water for us before taking a seat at her side.

She'd sworn two men to protect her. They tasted her blood. She'd kept that hidden from me. They vowed to keep her safe. To protect her with their lives. That wasn't their promise to make. It was mine. This woman. She was mine. Mine to love. Mine to protect. For as long as I was still breathing, no one would ever hurt her again.

I'm in.

RONAN LIT A match. The light flared, turning his dark brown eyes into smoldering lumps of coal in the dim space. The tip of his cigar illuminated, causing the flame to flash and die with his breaths. An immortal god of death sitting on his throne. This was only my second time in this church and it was quickly becoming one of my least favorite places to be.

"You smoke?" Killian said from the wooden seat beside his father's.

The mirror image of his father, Killian's hair and beard, was still dark brown. I imagined it would turn salt and pepper like his father's eventually, but he was barely thirty. There was still time. He shifted in his seat as though my appraisal made him uncomfortable. I couldn't tell if Ronan's son loved holding court or hated it.

"Only to celebrate," Clayton remarked, using a casual tone he'd perfected in dealing with hostiles in the Middle East. With his close cropped hair, it was like no time had passed. "I like to keep a few Cubans around."

"What are we waiting on?" I muttered to Clayton, who stood beside me just below the marble steps of the dais.

A door obscured by the protruding altar opened, announcing itself with a loud creak. Camping lanterns were the only light, the sun having set hours ago. It was difficult to see the figure walking in. These people all seemed to love wearing black. The figure, like Ronan and Killian, was clad in black from head to toe. Except... was that a collar?

"Sorry I'm late," the figure said as they approached the third seat.

A man almost identical to Ronan, but older. If Ronan was in his fifties, this man was maybe in his sixties. His voice was thick with years of cigarettes and gave away his Irish upbringing.

"Father Brendan," Ronan said, casually gesturing with his cigar. "My brother, who seems to have forgotten the time."

"It's Sunday, brother. I had other business to attend to."

Killian waved us closer. Clayton and I mounted the steps. Only a step away from the still-dusty marble altar, I tried to remain impassive. Unaffected.

"Ms. Caccia's tech man sent over some information I thought might be useful to you lot," Ronan said. "There's a shipment due to arrive in Belfast in a few days."

"How does this help us?" Clayton asked as he rubbed at the back of his neck.

"Belfast is my home," Killian said. "Father Brendan has got resources available to help the displaced persons."

"My church will care for whomever you find and until we're able to send them home again," Father Brendan confirmed.

Clayton looked confused as he pushed a hand through his chestnut-brown hair. Taking a step toward Ronan, he argued.

"So we're supposed to just show up and spring everyone loose. That's the plan? What about the Duke?"

"The Duke is attending a large New Year's function at Parliament," Ronan responded, still puffing his cigar. "You can kill two birds with one stone."

"Someone like that is going to have security. And it's a government event in a government building. It's going to be heavily guarded," I interjected. "We're good, but we're not that fucking good."

Ronan chuckled, looking over to his son, who smirked. If I thought I was unsettled before, I was wrong.

"Don't worry about the government, Hale," Killian snarled. "We're more than prepared for that."

"I'm supposed to just take your word for it?"

Killian looked to his father, who gave him a terse nod. The man stood and picked up a motorcycle helmet that had been behind his seat. The door slammed closed behind him.

"How are we dealing with the government building, Ronan?"

"Killian will be joining you," the Irish boss declared with a growl, clearly annoyed at being questioned. "And so will the Belfast chapter of our clan. You'll have an army and everything else you'll need at your disposal."

15

Lilith

Seagulls called in the sky as our yacht carved its way into open water. I watched the wake peel away from the rear of the ship, casting white water into the broad blue expanse. Far from land, the Erebus was more than a large black yacht. It was a floating haven of luxury. But this wasn't my ship.

It was easy to call in a favor from my powerful Irish friend. Even easier to ask him to lend me some of his men to wait below deck until we dropped anchor in international waters. Ronan had laughed when I explained what would happen. Had said it was the right thing to do.

"For a wound to heal, sometimes ye have to cut away the rotten flesh," said the Irishman. "Better to rid yourself of it before it starts to fester."

"Are you sure you want to do this?" West asked, looking around at the Caccia men eating the expensive food and drinking the top-shelf liquor I'd provided.

Nico had given me a list, filled with the names of every man who had or would have betrayed me. Everyone on that list had been invited aboard the yacht. I'd told them it was a celebration of my ascension. The event was a delayed coronation, I'd said. No longer a mafia princess, though I never truly felt that way. I was the spare. Kaia had been the heir.

"Cheers, boss!"

Carlo raised a glass to me but didn't sip from it. He knew better. Gino folded his arms and leaned against the sofa, watching the others glut themselves on the provisions that would gradually destroy them. I smirked.

"Too late to back out now," I said quietly, checking my blood-red lipstick in a bit of chrome hardware.

With a sweep of my pinky, I corrected the liner on my lower lip. My black silk dress whipped and billowed in the ocean breeze, filling the temporary silence between us. Turning to let the friendly visage drop for a moment, I looked at West in the hope that he might see there was no other way.

Regret made my voice hoarse as I continued softly. "You know it has to be done."

He nodded, looking at his watch for what had to be the twentieth time and then to the horizon. It wouldn't be long now.

"Sunset?"

"Sunset."

The ship slowed, drawing toward the coordinates I'd given the captain. A clank was heard from below, followed by a splash.

Anchors away.

People act surprised when a woman lashes out. When she's angry. But they keep piling on. Turning up the temperature with every comment, interruption, condescension. Small acts of aggression that press in and burn while she's screaming with rage on the inside. And when it becomes too much, they have the fucking nerve to be outraged when it boils over.

Chatter from the men inside continued. Gossip. Arguments. Laughter. None of them had noticed Gino, Carlo, and their compatriots make their way out onto the deck.

That was when the vomiting started.

"JESUS CHRIST," KILLIAN muttered, covering his face with the crook of his arm as he picked his way through the gasping, vomiting crowd. "It's like a goddamned biblical plague up here."

Pools of vomit laced with traces of blood. Faces were drawn into twisted purple masks of anguish. It all reminded me of a medieval plot. In a sense, it was. Eliminate every traitor to the crown to ensure the safety of the kingdom.

My kingdom.

I shrugged, looking over my shoulder to the chilling bottles of champagne sitting in a shining silver tub on the table behind me. Carlo, Gino, and all the rest of my loyal Caccia family members had come to stand on either side of me. West placed a hand on my exposed lower back, steadying me against the bobbing sea.

"Let's get to it then."

Still, twitching bodies were tossed overboard by my remaining men while the Arawns cleaned up their leader's ship, ridding it of the hemlock-addled food and drink. I removed my heels and picked my way around the deck to count the bodies as they were prepared to plummet to the sea below, pulled down by the cement blocks being tied to their ankles. Say it's a cliche if you want, but it works.

Sixteen.

Sixteen men had either betrayed the family or planned to. As I looked at their faces riddled with burst capillaries from vomiting until they couldn't breathe, I ticked off each name on the list Nico had given me. Each vile turncoat with blocks of cement attached to their still-twitching bodies.

Every man who was still standing now had demonstrated their loyalty to me or my sister. Their invitation aboard this glamorous sunset cruise had been accompanied by a direct and stern warning from Nico.

Eat nothing.

Drink nothing.

Their eyes were filled with horror as they watched their traitorous brethren suffer. I hoped the message was clear. Each fallen man now headed toward the bottom of the sea had been plotting against me. They were a liability. All of that was true. The nail in their proverbial coffins, for there would be no actual coffins for them, was that they didn't use their good sense. Maybe didn't have any at all.

It was for the best.

Unobservant men were useless to me. None of them noted the absence of other crews. Gino's men. Carlo's men. Dozens of them were missing from this voyage. None of them noted that ten of them, ten of my Capos, had not imbibed nor devoured anything provided in the lush buffet spread laid out before them.

Kaia had run the family just as our grandfather would have wanted. His way. It was a good tactic. Simple. Logical. But that approach was all strategy and numbers. Bottom lines. If I'd learned anything about botany, it was that a perfect environment didn't always yield the best results. Sometimes you had to introduce a little chaos.

Yes, this was for the best. If they hadn't been readying to betray me, they were all deeply stupid and needed to be removed anyway.

Nico popped the bottles of champagne and began pouring servings into the awaiting flutes. I watched as my gut turned with the motion of our vessel still bobbing with the ocean's movement. Carlo handed a flute of champagne to me and then to West, who took it with a gracious nod.

I looked him over. Hair braided back in twisting shades of deep brown and sun-lightened wheat. Beard neatly trimmed. He wore that burgundy suit I'd come to love on him and a black shirt that only highlighted the golden undertones of his skin. Little whorls of chest hair peeked out from the unbuttoned color. At several inches above the rest of the Caccia men, he cut an intimidating figure standing beside me. As I took in the sight of him, I wondered if he knew that what had just occurred wasn't only for my benefit.

The need for a political marriage to secure my power was now irrelevant. I was allied with the other most powerful family in the city and anyone who would dare question my choice of husband was now fish food. Problem solved.

Still, a wave of unease stirred in my gut as I thought about the man by my side. Would his proximity to me be his end, as it had been for Kaia? I could never forgive myself if I failed him, too. I blew out a breath and closed my eyes, taking in the sea air to wash the thought away.

A splash sounded behind us as the last body was thrown overboard. Bags containing the contaminated food and drink were tied neatly inside, along with all that remained of the gastric responses to being poisoned. How none of them saw that coming would forever be a mystery to me, but it was no longer my problem.

"Alright, everyone," I said, raising my voice to address the ten living Caccia men as I lifted my glass. "If you're still among the living, congratulations. You've proven your loyalty."

I nodded to Nico, who picked up the steel briefcase I'd been guarding and opened it on the table behind us. West's eyes narrowed, unsure about where this was going.

"My grandfather always believed that our men should want for nothing. I don't believe that loyalty can be purchased. But I do believe that your loyalty deserves to be rewarded."

Nico pivoted the briefcase to face the remaining men. Ten men. Ten keys. I hopped up on the table to sit beside Nico, readying to distribute a key to each man. *A show of good faith*, he'd called it. I had another show of good faith waiting for him at home.

"From here onward, we're going to be doing things a little differently. I know my family has a history of generosity with its members, but I want to make things more equitable. If I benefit from something financially, so do you. We're family. You dine at my table. If I eat well, so do you. If I make millions, well. So do you. Like shareholders."

I picked up a sleek black fob, identical to the nine remaining in the case. Brushed nickel details and a shining Mercedes crest gleamed up at me.

"Gino," I smiled. "You first."

He raised his eyebrows, putting down his empty champagne glass before approaching us at the table.

"You've been to church. Hold out your hands like you're receiving the sacrament."

Gino cupped one hand under another and smirked as I placed the key into it.

"Are you serious?" He said as he examined the key.

"It's yours. Come on, gentlemen. Line up."

THE TRIP BACK to shore was far more jubilant than the false levity that had filled the air on our way out. Killian and his men sat around the now-sparkling interior of the ship with fine whiskey and champagne, drinking with my men like they'd always been allies.

"I can't believe you just gave away ten cars," West said, shaking his head in disbelief. "You keep spending like that and you won't be wealthy for long."

Feeling as though I'd dropped an unnecessary weight from my shoulders, I looked out at the approaching harbor and sighed. A refilled champagne glass came into my view.

"I'm not worried about the money," I said as I turned to gaze at him. "Kaia invested so well that our money is multiplying like it's doing cellular division in the bank. But I needed them to understand that I value them. All of them."

I didn't want to say what I was thinking to West. That they needed to operate well without my supervision. That I needed for them to be loyal while I hunted the man who was hunting me. I had a more pressing issue at hand, and these men needed to operate like a well-oiled machine in my absence. The black lily flashed in my memory again.

This is not going to be the only pretty Lily I put inside a box.

Whooping and laughter sounded from the interior as the ship docked in its slip as my men spied the parking lot lined with the black Mercedes-Benz S-Class sedans that accompanied the keys each of them had received. Each car had a tracker. An insurance policy against deceit. I trusted my men. But that didn't mean I would be foolish enough to let my guard down. Each of them would be closely monitored by me. Even Nico and Damon. They had proven themselves, but the only man I trusted completely was standing beside me.

To the naked eye, it was a fleet of cars for a driving service. West glanced at me with a knowing look, undoubtedly remembering what I'd told him when he asked me why I'd been driving an identical car not so long ago.

Nothing blends in around here better than luxury.

My phone pinged with a calendar reminder. One red-eye flight to Belfast. First class. As I looked at the itinerary again, my mind clouded with one thought. A thought that beat in my head like a drum.

Duke Harrison Augustus-Stanley. I'll see you soon.

16

WEST

I'd caught Lili packing a suitcase as I entered our bedroom, needing to shower the memory of the cruise off of myself. That was one of the more gruesome things I'd ever seen. I could still see their panicking, terrified faces. But they'd made an enemy of Lilith, and she was an unyielding opponent.

"Going somewhere?"

She glanced up at me as she stuffed clothes into her bag. Mine had been packed hours ago. It was sitting in the back of the Bronco. I knew where I was going. The crew was awaiting my arrival.

"I need to get to Las Vegas. Lupo is going to take care of Daniel until I get back, so you don't have to worry about them. We have businesses there and I need to show my face to the rest of the family. Establish myself as the boss, you know?"

Lili's sudden departure saved me from having to come up with an excuse to disappear for a few days, but she lied right to my face. Her passport had been on the bed. She moved it, thinking she'd hidden it before I could see it, but I saw the damn thing. A car horn sounded from outside. Her ride to the airport.

"I better get going," she winced.

"Have a good trip."

There wasn't a chance in hell Lili was going to Vegas. Why couldn't she tell me the truth? The question was like ice water in my veins. It flowed through me as I said my goodbyes to Daniel and Lupo. It froze my disposition to ice during the long drive to the private airfield.

She lied to me.

What was she hiding? She already named two men to be her successors without informing me. They tasted her blood. I'd noticed the small wound on her hand, but she'd brushed it off as an accident. Something she'd done while caring for her knives. Another lie.

As I took my place in a plush leather seat, I thought that maybe I was being a hypocrite. My eyes skated over a small spread of fine food. A beer tap sat beside it, made for dispensing Irish beer by the pint. I'd never been on a private plane before, but it was impossible to get comfortable because this plane belonged to Ronan and we weren't flying alone. I needed to stop thinking about Lilith and get my head in the game. My fingers skimmed over the scar on my forearm. No. Distraction was the last thing I needed right now.

"So," I said over the charging engines, turning to the only other man on the plane I actually trusted. "Are you finally going to tell me how you got mixed up in this? We have ten hours to kill."

Clayton lifted a pint of the dark Irish beer to his mouth and looked out the window, kicking off his boots. It was just like him to make himself comfortable wherever he happened to be, though the frequent glances at his phone didn't escape my notice.

"It's not important," he muttered.

The rain that had been threatening to fall all day finally started pouring, streaking against the window as the plane began its ascent through the clouds. I looked into my pint and back at him. Clayton checked his phone again, stuffing it into his shirt pocket with an air of finality. With a tired sigh, he put on a lazy grin.

"You've never done anything stupid for a girl?" He lifted a dark eyebrow and looked me over.

I was here. I was doing the stupid thing. Reckless. Sitting on a plane with one man I trusted and six I didn't. Ready to extract a man and execute him. For my girl.

"Alright, yeah. Point taken," I offered.

Killian and his men were playing a drinking game. Something loud. Something I didn't understand. I examined the Arawn smoking skull tattoo on his hand as it lifted a pint to his mouth. They all had them.

"What's the deal with the skull tattoos?" I asked Clayton.

He looked over his shoulder at the group of men behind him, then back at me with a look of surprise.

"It's kind of their sigil. Caccias have the arrow and crown, the Arawns have the skull. All that reading you do, you don't get into any mythology?"

I shook my head.

"Arawn is the Celtic god of the underworld. I'm not sure how someone ends up with that as a last name. It might not even be their original last name. But Ronan likes to lean into that whole thing. Their family crest. The tattoos. It's all creepy as hell."

If families were like monarchies, then these men were their soldiers. As soldiers ourselves, Clayton and I weren't strangers to marking our brotherhood with such things. That's what they were. A brotherhood. I could understand that. Tentacles wrapped around my arm in dark ink, leading up to the Kraken's skull they were attached to. Clayton's sprawled across his abdomen. The phrase "Memento mori" marked us both.

Remember that you will die.

When we were young and dumb, it filled us with vigor. We ran toward danger. Chewed up enemies and spit out bullets. But that wasn't who either of us was anymore. A memory of Lili tracing a finger over that tattoo washed over me as I finished my beer.

"There's a second part to this," she'd said. "Memento vivere. Remember to live."

The plane shuddered as it breached through the clouds. I blinked, handing my empty glass to the flight attendant. Once the plane crested above them, we leveled out. The loud drinking game had ended. Instead, each man was talking with another. All except for one. I couldn't tell if it was the mild turbulence or the way Killian Arawn wouldn't take his eyes off of me that turned my stomach.

17

WEST

Belfast in December was fucking cold. Really fucking cold. And wet. Our plane landed at a rain-soaked private airport not far from the city. A large private hangar containing everything we could possibly need awaited us. Along with heavily armed guards. Each of them acknowledged Killian's presence. Their commander had arrived. Though I knew Killian's men were on our team, the sight set me on edge.

"Over here," Clayton said as he gestured toward the back of the hangar. "They've got everything we need."

He led me toward a large work table pushed up against one wall, well out of sight from the entrance. I dropped my bag at my feet and looked at the array of lethal utilities. The table before me was laden with six different types of artillery. Door breaching tools. An axe or two. Plastic explosives. Kevlar for everyone.

"Jesus Christ," I muttered, running a hand over the barrel of an automatic rifle.

"They take their weapons seriously," Clayton offered as he took his backpack off and dropped it onto the table.

I blew out a breath. What in the hell was I getting myself into?

"Hey."

I looked at Clayton. Despite the long flight, he looked wide awake and ready to go. Of course, he slept for most of it. He could always sleep anywhere. Killian and his crew made me wary of closing my eyes. I'd tried. But my attempt to sleep was thwarted by the desire to listen to every word they said when they thought my guard was down. Even if it was mostly bullshit.

"You alright?"

Before I could answer, two blacked-out commercial vans pulled into the hangar. Aggressive tires. Auxiliary lights. Armored, probably. Perfect vehicles for urban warfare. The drivers got out. Killian greeted them with brief handshakes, gesturing toward the tables we stood beside.

"Oi," Killian said with a nod in my direction. "Come into the office."

Clayton dipped his chin. He wasn't worried.

"You know what I need," I said to him as I walked away. "Set me up with something effective, Disco."

"Will do, Blackjack."

Killian's men watched me follow him into the small office above the hangar. Closing the door behind us, he walked to the old metal desk and sat atop it.

"You need to understand something about my father."

I waited. I didn't know what he had to say, but I sure as hell didn't want him to know any more about me than he already did. If I'd learned anything from watching Lilith, it was that people would fill the silence with the truth. You just have to let them stew in it.

"He's asked me to make sure you follow through on your end. Deliver the Duke cunt. Alive."

I nodded.

"Not much of a talker," he said. More to himself than to me. "That's wise. Talkers are a liability."

At least we could agree on that. Turning toward the window that overlooked the hangar, Killian watched his men gear up for the night ahead.

"My men are ready. Are you?"

IF WE WERE going to intercept the Duke from this event, we'd need to know the exit and entry points of the building. Killian ensured his men would be discreetly monitoring all possible exits. Some were dressed as security. Some were dressed as waiters, milling through the room. Clayton was running surveillance, speaking to all of us through the monitors in our ears.

"Blackjack, this is Disco. You ready to party?" His voice piped into my ear.

His ability to hack into anything amazed me. I'd spent the last six years training Lili to fight and bouncing assholes out of the strip club while he'd been honing more useful skills. Between intricate security systems and diabolical mercenary jobs, Clayton was more dangerous than he let on.

"Romeo," I affirmed as I watched guests enter the grand marble hall.

Glittering guests entered the event through a security checkpoint at the main entrance. Tuxedoes with various heads of hair walked in with their dates. Some were old. Some were way too young. Some alone. Still no Duke. From the ventilation system I'd had to crawl into, I swept the room with a glance downward, in case I'd somehow missed him.

Then my eyes snagged on an ocean of black hair swept up into some simple hairdo. A red dress that exposed her toned back and highlighted that glorious ass. I ground my teeth as I watched Lilith, *my* Lilith, make her way into the room like a wolf in sheep's clothing, a dangerous smile painted on her crimson lips.

"Head's up, Disco. We've got a bogey."

"Little Red Riding Hood. I see her."

Even at barely over five feet, she walked taller than half the men in the room. I watched her strut through the perimeter of the hall, Clayton's feed swapping perspectives just to keep an eye on her as she took in her surroundings. She swigged back the flute of champagne a waiter offered. The urge to go to her was overwhelming. But from this vantage point, all I could do was watch.

"Blackjack," Killian snarled. "Is she with you?"

"Nope. She shouldn't be here. Little Red Riding Hood-"

"Disco, tally. Alfa Sierra."

One of Killian's men made the call we'd been waiting for. AS. He was here. My attention returned to the feed. One of Killian's men approached, taking the empty glass from her hand. I watched it happen. Watched her head turn. Watched her hands ball into fists. Watched Lilith Caccia's eyes fix on the man responsible for her sister's death.

18

Lilith

Swelling strings filled the large marble lobby of the Parliament Building. Strange. So strange to be surrounded by government workers who all looked like they'd rather be home. Stuffy aristocratic types looked like this was just another excuse to get together and congratulate each other on being better than everyone else. Jerks.

People milled about a table stacked with tiny beige food. Waiters in white coats and black bow ties circulated with silver trays of champagne. The last time I'd worn this dress, it had been to a similar event, surrounded by similar people. On the arm of Benjamin Camden.

This time when my thigh flashed from the slit in the floor-length skirt, it wouldn't be smooth olive skin people would see. The still pink scar from my bullet wound had made me cringe as I'd dressed myself. Absently rubbing at my leg, my eyes skimmed the crowd for the man responsible.

Still not here.

Instinct forced my fingers to touch my hair and make sure my chignon had held. Despite the raging headache I'd have later, having thick hair was good for some things. My fingers found the hard edge of the vial I'd tucked away, much to my relief.

"Champagne?"

A tray of champagne flutes entered my vision. I took the flute and smiled blandly at the server. The sparkling wine popped and sizzled on my tongue as I swallowed it down. I went over the list in my mind. Everything that awaited the Duke.

A sedative. The one I'd carefully packed inside of a travel shampoo bottle. Then mixed in my hotel room. A syringe that was hidden in the lining of my clutch. And the thin blades holding my hair in place. Smaller than what I'd normally use, but they'd have to do with so much security. They'd been dismissed as an accessory by the hapless guards.

Corner him. Sedate him. Get him back to my room. The room with a large bathtub. A bathtub big enough to disassemble a grown man and drain away all of the life inside of him. Pack him away in a suitcase and dispose of him like Henry Johnson. Easy peasy.

"Lass?"

Blinking the thoughts of a gruesome murder away, my eyes refocused on the waiter before me.

"Can I take your glass?"

Something tugged on my memory as I looked at him. Scratched at my mind like a wool sweater. As he took the glass from me, I saw it. A familiar tattoo. Smoking skull on the top of his hand. Arawn. There had to be an explanation for his presence. But I was too preoccupied to care about that right now.

"Thank you," I muttered absently.

Familiar sandy red hair announced his arrival. A security team of two flanked him, one on either side. One with sparse blonde hair and a retreating hairline. The other's head gleamed like a greased-up volleyball. Light glimmered on his shiny bald dome. But the man between them had my fists balling so hard, my nails dug into my palms.

Duke Harrison Augustus-Stanley. He'd had my sister kidnapped. Kept her like bait, waiting for me to come to him. I'd fallen into his trap and my sister paid with her life. Red flashed in my mind. A blood-soaked tee shirt.

Light leaving her warm brown eyes. The look on Daniel's face when I told him his mother was dead. All of it washed over me like ice water.

Slowly, as subtly as I could manage, I moved through the crowd in his direction while fighting the torrents of rage inside me. He was glad-handing other guests. A smile here. A wave there. Acting like the very picture of dignified aristocracy. I wondered if they knew he sold women and children.

"Excuse me!" An older woman scolded me. Had I bumped into her? I looked down toward my heel, tugging through the tulle skirt of her periwinkle gown.

"Oh. Sorry, I-"

My eyes drifted back to my target. To his security. The bald security guard by Augustus-Stanley's side whispered in his ear. My target's eyes locked on me.

Shit.

They moved to the side. Discreetly and quickly. He recognized me. Damnit. My Louboutins clacked loudly on the marble floor as I followed them to the door they had disappeared behind. One of my sister's remaining pairs. Beautiful, but not great for speed. This was officially the first and last time I'd let fashion decide for me. Carefully, I tried to tug a spike from my hair. Another door slammed closed ahead of me.

No, no, no!

My hands left my hair, giving up on the spike as I tried to push open the heavy steel door. These heels had no traction. I cursed the red-soled shoes. It was their fault he was getting away. Into the cold wet night, Duke Harrison Augustus-Stanley had disappeared.

The cobblestone street was empty of any other cars. Dim street lamps were my only source of light as I scanned my surroundings. Before I could turn back to the door, pain flashed through my skull. I threw an arm up out of defensive reflex, fast enough to block the next blow.

"Caccia," the bald security guard grunted in a thick Scottish accent.

He'd been out here waiting for me. That fucking prick Duke knew I'd follow him out and left one of his men behind. Warmth trickled down the side of my face. I didn't lift a hand to check the fresh wound. I knew it was there.

"You shouldn't put your hands on a lady without permission," I drawled as I dropped my bag and put up my fists. My feet wobbled as I took a defensive stance. I'd never had to fight in stiletto heels before.

He was tall. Though he was still shorter than West. The bald man tried another strike as he lunged toward me. His reach missed as I danced backward. Another lunge forward brought him close enough for my elbow to connect with his nose. Tears flooded his eyes and I drove my knee into his gut.

"Bloody," he gasped, "cunt!"

A barking laugh escaped me as he collapsed to his knees. I would have left him there and returned to the party. Would have turned and walked right back into the building if it hadn't been for my damned shoe. That damned high heel stuck between the cobblestones. The phrase "fashion victim" flashed through my mind.

I freed my foot with a yank, but the freedom was short-lived as an arm wrapped around my waist. My attacker's hand circled my throat. Squeezed. My feet lifted from the ground as I thrashed in his grip, losing a shoe as I kicked. No. I would not let this bald piece of garbage kill me. Absolutely not.

The stiletto heel slammed down into his thigh, piercing the flesh in a sickening squish. He screamed into my ear as he dropped me, my other Louboutin sticking out of his now bleeding wound. I hit the ground with a yelp. The bald man removed the shoe and threw it to the ground. Breath sawed through his clenched teeth as he staggered toward me. Towered over me as I crawled backward.

And just as I hadn't seen the bald man awaiting me, too blind with rage at losing my target to fully take in my surroundings, he didn't see. Didn't see the man who had charged from behind him. Rushing on quiet feet despite his mass. Appearing as if from nowhere out of the night dressed in black tactical gear and a familiar skull gaiter. Slamming him into the side of the building. And breaking the trachea of my bald attacker before he could let out a scream.

19

WEST

I'd trained her well. Well enough to hold her own in almost any situation. I would have trusted that training. If it were anyone else, I would have. But I was rounding the building when I saw her go down. I heard the sound she made when she hit the ground. And every rational thought fell out of my head.

Cartilage collapsed under the heel of my palm. But it wasn't enough. Not enough. Images of Lilith's limp body as she was dying in my arms ambushed my mind. The woman I loved almost slipped away from me. Never again. With my arm pinning him to the wall, I struck again and again. Until my knuckles ached and there was nothing left of his face. Then the attacker wasn't a random goon, but a billionaire who'd deserved more than a bullet to the head for what he'd done to Lilith.

"West?"

Some part of me was aware of the sticky slide of his blood on my glove. Bits of bone. The way his eyes went empty. Gone. I'd killed dozens of men. Insurgents. Terrorists. Whoever I was told. But it never felt good. Not like this. As I took in the pulped crevice where the man's face used to be, I felt a rush of satisfaction. Especially as he crumbled to the ground beside her.

"How did you find me?"

Those beautiful gold eyes took in the body of her attacker and the pulp where his face used to be. Then turned to me. She pulled her shoe from the dead man's thigh and slipped it back on her foot. Before those red lips could utter a syllable, I heard Clayton's voice on my monitor.

"Blackjack, Irish goodbye. Now."

One of the Arawn vans appeared on his command, the door sliding open as two men lept out. I looked down at Lilith, who had put on her shoes and brushed her hands off as she stood up from the damp asphalt. Like hell I would leave her here.

"Hey!" Lili yelped as I threw her over my shoulder and carried her to the awaiting van. Though I'd surprised her, she didn't fight.

She'd lied to me. Lied to come here. As her weight bounced against my shoulder, my blood boiled. She'd put herself in danger. Without any backup. Without any exit plan. Letting her need to avenge her sister cloud her judgment.

The Arawns would make quick work of disposing of those remains, I had no doubt. Two men jumped from the open van door and walked toward us with a black bag. Past us. Lili stiffened on my shoulder. Watching. Assessing. She knew I was here. Now she knew who I was with.

"You've got to be fucking kidding me," she grunted as my shoulder bumped into her belly.

I climbed into the van, threw her down on the floor, then knelt in front of her. My blood-soaked gloves slid over her skin as I searched her for wounds, bruises, or any sign of injury. Before I could finish, she grabbed the gaiter covering my face and angrily pulled it down my neck.

She's fine, I told myself. *She's not hurt.*

"So, are you going to tell me what the fuck you're doing here?" She demanded, pursing those red lips at me in anger. "With Arawn men?"

Adrenaline was still riding me hard, stifling my ability to say the right thing. So I kept my mouth shut. I could taste all the wrong answers waiting on my tongue.

Saving your ass.

Stopping you from making a big mistake.
Protecting what's mine.

A scoff answered from somewhere. This wasn't a two-person conversation. Clayton's voice sounded in my ear.

"That's pretty rich, coming from her. Driver, route to the Vagrant."

"Copy," the driver said from up front.

"Well?" Lili's voice was sharp. Irritated, but shaky. Still wound up from what happened. "I'm assuming it has something to do with the Duke."

I lifted a hand to the wound on her head. She flinched away.

"I'm keeping you alive. That's all you need to know," I uttered through gritted teeth as I tugged an orange bag with a big red cross on it toward myself.

First aid. Alcohol stung my nostrils as I opened a package of cleaning wipes. I took her jaw in my hand so I could wipe the blood away from the wound near her temple. She flinched again. Swatted my hand away like I was the one in the wrong here. Unbelievable.

"Stop that!"

I grabbed her chin again.

"Let me clean it, Lili."

Still flinching away, I tried cleaning her wound as she ducked the swab.

"We could have questioned that guy. With you here, we could have learned something valuable. Why did you kill him?"

Because he touched you. He hurt you. He deserved worse.

"Her gratitude is fucking astounding," Clayton interjected sarcastically, knowing only I could hear his side of the conversation. I snorted in agreement.

The urge to shout at her rattled my bones. Instead, my teeth ground as my grip on her chin firmed. I tugged her face back toward me and finished cleaning the wound. It wasn't bad. Bad enough to break the skin. Not enough to do any real damage. Like he'd been too far from her to make a proper strike, but threw a punch anyway. The urge to tear his spine out brewed in me as I cleaned the small wound.

WHETHER SHE WOULD admit it or not, my girl had expensive taste. Lili strutted through the lobby of the grandiose hotel, red silk floating behind her. We walked through archways lined with gold, surrounded by black columns, under a gilded chandelier toward the small elevator. She looked like an unforgiving goddess in that dress. No one gave me a second look as I followed closely behind. I supposed that by her side; I looked like a bodyguard.

"Come on," she sighed as she stepped into the small mirrored box.

The elevator seemed only large enough for one. I squeezed in beside her. Her lavender and vanilla scent enveloped me as she pushed the button.

"I'm not going to ask how the driver knew where I was staying."

Everything I wanted to say to her still thrummed in my blood. I gripped the straps of my vest to keep my hands from shaking. I could have lost her. If I'd been a few seconds too late. A minute. I would have found her dead on the ground. The words were there, salting my tastebuds.

How could you be so reckless?

Don't you ever fucking do that to me again.

You're everything to me.

She'd lied about where she was going. Let me believe that she'd be safe. Then put herself exactly where I didn't want her to be. I was going to kill her. If that red dress didn't kill me first.

20

Lilith

West looked around the room as we entered my suite. Seeing it through his eyes, it was more grand than I had initially noticed. Red and gold baroque curtains surrounded the large windows that looked out onto the streets of Belfast. Blood-red rugs covered the dark polished wooden floors. This had to have been some lord or king's room. A long time ago. When this was a stone manor belonging to some royal. It was still decorated that way; I supposed.

I watched West disarm himself and place his guns on the table between the two silk-upholstered armchairs that faced the large four-poster bed. He hadn't said anything since we'd been dumped behind the hotel. But I had felt the anger emanating off of him like waves of heat. Still in his tactical gear, he crossed his arms over his broad chest and glared at me. A dark monolith in this red room. Even with his gaiter pushed down around his neck, he seemed ghoulish.

"What?" I asked, letting myself sit on one of the chair's rolled arms. He was not going to intimidate me. Nope.

"Explain," he barked, a dark strand of hair coming loose from the knot he'd tied it into.

"I'm not the only one with explaining to do here, West."

A knot twisted in my gut. Why did I have to explain? He sure as hell hadn't told me why he was here. He and Clayton were with a team of other men. Arawn men. It wasn't hard to deduce who their target had been. My target.

I crossed my arms and practically snarled at West. With an aggravated sigh, he approached the chair I'd perched on and continued to glower at me as he towered over me.

"Well?" He snapped.

I'd never seen him like this. He'd beaten the hell out of rowdy frat boys at Muse. He'd defended me against people who tried to end my life. We'd even argued before. But not like this. Never like this.

I glared up at him. Our dueling tempers were two animals circling each other. If he thought he could overwhelm me with silence, he was mistaken.

"You know exactly why I'm here," I seethed.

The admission spilled out of me, stinging like acid. Maybe that was my eyes. My rage flooded them with tears. Breathing became difficult. I hated that this happened when I was angry. Grinding my teeth together, I forced myself to focus.

Do not cry.

"You were just going to take him down by yourself? With a whole security detail by his side? What were you planning?"

"Unrelenting agony. Hours of it."

A disappointed sigh loosened his shoulders as he lifted a still-gloved hand to my cheek and wiped away a tear. His glove was cool against my hot flesh. I sucked in a breath and looked away. I didn't need his approval.

"Do you want to explain what you're doing here?" I practically spat the question at him.

A muscle ticked in his jaw. It was the only way to bite back the irritation that flared in his eyes.

Good, I thought. *Let's both be angry, then.*

"I work with Clayton now," West said as he stepped away from me, toward the window. "Clayton works for the Arawns. But I'm not getting into that tonight."

I snorted. I had to answer his questions, but he didn't have to answer mine? I didn't answer to him.

"Why?"

"Because you lied to me. You lied and you need to be punished."

The small hairs on my arms raised at his declaration. I... What? He yanked the thick gold rope holding back one of the red brocade curtains. What the hell does that mean? The rope unfurled as West walked toward me.

"What are you going to do with that?"

"Stand up."

Was he going to hit me? My stomach tightened with worry.

West shook his head gently, noticing what must have been a horrified expression on my face. I stood facing him. Leather-covered knuckles gently grazed the curve of my jaw. Then drifted lower, to the closure of my dress at the back of my neck.

"This is coming off."

Red silk spilled to the ground, pooling around my heels. West's eyes remained on mine as I stood there before him in my bloody heels and underwear that was barely more than a scrap of black lace. Darkness flooded his features as he made his next command.

"Hands behind your back, Trouble."

Obeying his order, my fingers laced together at the small of my back. Even as I told myself I could trust him, I began shaking. He'd never given me a reason not to trust him. Not until today. Not until he'd kept this from me. But I'd lied, too.

West allowed himself a look downward toward my breasts, their peaked nipples, and the wolf tattoo between them. He stepped into me, blazing green eyes locked on mine as the rope dangled from one hand. He circled around. I wasn't sure what he was doing until I heard him sit on the bed behind me. Silky rope wound around my wrists, the length of it gliding against my ass in a sensuous slide as he fed the line over itself. When he stopped, I tested his work. The bind was firm.

West's hands pulled me backward. Toward his lap. Except I wasn't positioned to sit in his lap. I was being bent over it. The silky soft duvet grazed my cheek as his palm smoothed over my ass. I went rigid as I realized his intention. Oh. Oh no. Oh *hell* no.

"Don't you fucking dare," I hissed.

Too late. The hard slap of his leather glove made the skin on my ass sting. I bit down on the yelp.

"Feel that?" He growled. Another slap landed hard on the other side. "Does it hurt?"

My teeth sank into my lip as I writhed and bucked in his hold. I wouldn't scream. Wouldn't give him the satisfaction. He was spanking me. Actually fucking spanking me! His hand slapped against my bare skin again. The other arm pressed me down into his lap. I felt his elbow pinned between my shoulders while his hand gripped my bound wrists. My skin heated at the humiliation of it.

"Do what you want, Trouble," he panted as he struck again, alternating sides until my skin was screaming. "Do anything you want. I'm not going to stop you. But my girl does not ever fucking lie to me. You hear me?"

While my face burned with embarrassment, other parts of me seemed to awaken. Writhing against him turned from resistance into something darker. Everything became sensitive. My thighs squeezed together, trying for pressure, trying for anything that would help sate the need that surged at every rough slap. Again and again.

"Say it."

"Yes," I cried out.

Ignoring the urge to examine exactly why this was getting to me, I squirmed in his hold. Just as I was starting to let myself enjoy it, he stopped. The hand that had struck me until my ass was raw and stinging began gently working each mound, massaging the aching flesh. I whimpered at the relief.

"You will not put yourself in danger like that again. And you will not lie to me," he snarled, the darkness in his rough voice betraying what I already knew from the press of his erection into my belly.

West's fingers threaded beneath the waistband of my panties. Cool metal slid against my skin. One cut here. Another there. A hard tug at the fabric between my legs. I squeaked. The black lace landed in my eyeline a few feet away. I was still looking at it when I felt his touch slide down my exposed slit. He'd taken off the gloves. A rough laugh rasped out of him at the wetness he found at my opening.

"You never stop surprising me, Trouble."

He's surprised?

A moan escaped me as his touch grazed my center again. Then again. Not enough. No. It wasn't enough to take the pleasure I needed. Just enough to torture. I pushed my hips backward to seek more, more, more.

"Please," I rasped.

A soft slap landed on my still-aching ass. I whined.

"No. I told you, this is punishment. I'm not going to reward you until you show me how sorry you are for lying to me."

You lied to me, I wanted to say.

His arm released me and I sat up to glare at him. Those smoky green eyes were radiant with heat. The broad chest clad in Kevlar heaved with each breath. Except for the blood-covered heels, I was bare before him. He leaned backward on his hands, looking me over as I adjusted myself to sit beside him on the bed. Even the silky duvet felt torturous against my newly inflamed skin. He smirked as if he knew it.

"Untie me," I bit out.

If I wasn't getting anything else from him, I sure as hell wasn't going to sit here tied up like some prized hog.

"No."

That was his favorite word tonight. I huffed and tried to stand, only to find his hand snapping to my wrists to keep me down. Gold rope chaffed against my skin at his hold.

"I'm not done with you yet."

Sitting upright again, the hand that wasn't holding me in place thoughtfully rubbed at his beard. He hadn't thought this through. Hadn't planned what he would do to me. But he had ideas. I knew that much. Especially when amusement danced across his features.

"Get on your knees, Trouble. Beg for my forgiveness."

West took a fluffy throw pillow and tossed it to the floor between his knees. Jerked his chin toward it. My teeth sunk into my lower lip, holding back the sarcastic remark that had been my first instinct.

"Untie me," I snarled again.

"No. Kneel."

Anger and need warred under my skin as I went to my knees before him. He was still fully clothed. Still in his black tactical gear. Kneeling on the pillow in nothing but the heels I'd had on, I was completely exposed. But that was the point, right? If it were anyone else, I'd feel humiliated. He gripped the shoulder straps of his vest and looked down at me expectantly.

"West, I-"

"No, no. Trouble," he scolded. He tsked as he let go of his vest and swiftly undid the button and zipper of his pants. "Beg me with your tongue. Your lips. And your throat. Not your words."

The length of him sprang free as he pulled himself from the fabric. Shifting his hips forward until I only needed to sit up on my knees to wrap my lips around it. I didn't.

He leaned forward, bracing an elbow on his knee as his other hand captured my chin and pushed it upward until my eyes met his again.

"What a gorgeous mess you are," West rasped as he reverently brushed his thumb over my lower lip. His eyes dipped down to my peaked nipples. "Do this for me. Do this and I'll let you come, Trouble."

My thighs squeezed together at the offer. He tracked the movement and smirked. Sitting up straight, he watched as I examined his exposed cock. Fine.

A low curse burst from him as I took his head into my mouth and sucked hard. Unable to use my hands, I let my tongue explore his thick length. Lapped at the tip that was already salty and wet with need. Alternating soft and hard pulls of my lips, my efforts were met with groans and gasps. Almost as if he were savoring me, humming with approval as I licked, sucked, and nibbled as I gazed at him through my lashes.

"Your mouth," he sighed. "It's fucking magic."

I continued tasting and pulling, this time gently, attempting to torture him. The fact that his punishment had turned me on was a complete surprise. Sucking him was also torturing me, but that was no shock. It made my body vibrate with desire. My torture seemed to be working on West as he shifted his hips to aid my mouth. My lips and tongue wrapped around him for another hard suck when his hands braced on either side of my head. His hips arced up, thrusting into my mouth as he watched.

West was all done with torture. Each thrust matched the movement my hips made as I ground my thighs together, begging for release. With his head tipped back, the strong column of his throat worked around each panting breath. He may have been punishing me, but I had all the power. I moaned desperately around him.

"Fucking hell," he groaned. "Get up here."

His hands moved from my head to my underarms as he pulled me up into his lap. My knees settled on either side of him as I sank onto his cock, crying out at the sensation of being so full of his thick length. Unable to hold on with my wrists still bound, West cupped my ass and rocked me against him.

"That's it," West growled as I moaned into his neck. "My girl's doing such a good job."

The feel of his gear against my bare skin made me weak as I drank in his praise. Gritty fabric brushed against my peaked nipples. The ripstop material of his pants, now halfway down his hips, was coarse against my soft inner thighs. Shuddering breaths sawed out of me as he moved my body on his.

"I'm sorry," I gasped as every muscle in my body began winding up tight as a bowstring, ready to be plucked.

Release aimed itself at me and I could hear it cocking like a pistol. I wanted to pull the trigger. Every cell in my body was screaming for it. For him. I couldn't take much more of this.

"Do you love me?" He snarled through gritted teeth. A knife grazed the skin at my wrists, freeing them from the bind. I wrapped my arms around his neck. *Close. So fucking -*

"Yes," I sobbed as my orgasm shot through me like a bullet. "I do."

"Then I forgive you." The words were still hot against my mouth as he pressed a kiss to my lips, hands plunging into my hair. His tongue was commanding and insistent as he emptied himself inside me, chasing my climax with his own.

I rested my head on his shoulder, letting my fingers wrap around the straps of his vest to steady myself as I let the welcome silence flood my mind. Sweet, serene dopamine. Large hands cupped my jaw, forcing me to collect my shattered thoughts. Wrath and ire had faded from his beautiful eyes, replaced with that look. The one that made my chest ache. West kissed me, lazy and sweet.

"Don't you ever fucking lie to me again," he breathed.

After a punishment like that, I wasn't sure I could make that promise.

21

WEST

Every cell in my body was still on fire for her. My gloved hands made strokes down her back as she trembled in my lap, her eyes closed as she collected herself. My girl. My Trouble. Lili and I were still breathing shared air when my phone chirped from inside my pocket. I ignored it. The outside world could wait for a damn minute.

"Do you need to get that?" Lili whispered between breaths, her forehead still pressed against mine.

The ringing stopped. Before I could summon my rational mind and speak to her, it began again. I groaned, lifting her off of me to access my pocket. The screen confirmed what I'd suspected as righted my clothes and stood to take the call.

"Everything secure at the hotel?" Clayton started.

"Yeah, I don't think we were followed."

"Good. I need you at the shipyard. Lili, too. There are thousands of containers. We need all the eyes we can get to sort this shit out."

Lili sighed as she rolled over and stretched out across the foot of the bed. It was a rare, beautiful vision. Sated and smiling. Smudged red lipstick. Smeared mascara. I noted all of the places where the rough material of my pants and Kevlar vest had reddened her soft skin. The smirk that bloomed on my lips was involuntary. It was satisfying to know that I'd marked her.

Enjoying the view, I knew all I wanted to do was stay in this room and use my mouth to worship every inch of that sumptuous olive skin. Unfortunately, I also knew that she would never want to stay put if she knew some women needed help. A shipping container full of them.

"We'll be there."

Lili twisted onto her side and propped her head up on the palm of her hand, night-dark hair tumbling into her eyes. I watched her full breast obscure part of the wolf tattoo, then noticed her furrowed brow.

"We'll be where?"

"Do you have anything more practical than that?" I asked with a nod toward her discarded red silk dress.

"No," she said dryly, rolling her eyes. "I came to Ireland in the middle of winter with a cocktail dress and nothing else."

I gave her a flat look.

"Where are we going?"

My hands set my clothes to rights and checked for everything as I watched her watch me. Gold-rimmed eyes narrowed, waiting for an answer.

"Put on some warm clothes and comfortable shoes. It's going to be a long night."

ONE THOUSAND CONTAINERS was an understatement. The shipyard was filled with storage containers. Clayton assured me that the newest batch from the cargo ship we'd been tracking unloaded in only one area and had only dumped half of its load. So, only three thousand containers to search.

Fantastic.

Arawn men, Clayton, and the two of us. We all broke into teams of two. Each of us had the tracking number for the container, lifted from Forester's hacking. Thanks to his hard work, we would be getting information like this fed to us with regular updates. Arawn's men and the Caccia men would be dispatched to different locations to intercept every shipment we could. Belfast had been our turn. And even with a group of eight, this promised to take all night.

Lili stalked down an aisle of containers, black hair piled high on her head, nearly invisible in her black clothing. I was beginning to understand why almost everything she owned was black. In black jeans, black boots, and a black leather jacket, she was just another shadow. Even the gun I'd given her disappeared into the night.

Puddles rippled under her careful steps, followed by my own. She pulled out her phone, using the flashlight to examine the tracking numbers painted on the side of the next row of containers, glancing at the series of digits she'd written on her wrist. A disappointed sigh wooshed from her as she turned and approached the next stack. I should have left her in that hotel, safe and warm in her bed.

"I should have eaten something," she grumbled.

"Go back to the hotel," I offered. "I can handle this."

"No."

She rolled her shoulders and started checking the stack in front of her. I focused on checking my sections, all while keeping her in my line of sight.

Never giving up. Never letting jet lag, hunger, or the exhaustion of the last few months wear her out. Even when it was practically freezing on the other side of the world, she soldiered on like any good recruit. Looking at her, I knew that my girl may have lost some battles, but Lilith Caccia would never lose a war.

Two gunshots popped. I was too slow to grab Lilith as she loped toward the sound.

"Lili!"

We rounded the corner to find Clayton and the lean Arawn man checking containers, two bodies being dragged off by other Arawn men.

"Have you cleared these?" I asked.

"All except for this stack," the lean man said, fatigue slackening his posture.

Without a word to either of them, Lili moved on to continue checking containers.

"They couldn't have moved it already," Clayton said with uncertainty in his voice. "But that wouldn't make sense. They just unloaded. It's only been a few hours. Besides, those two were clearly guarding something over here."

A clanging sound drowned out his next words. I looked around for the source to find Lili trying to open a container sealed with a large lock.

"Lili, wait," Clayton hissed as he turned to the lean man. "Get the pick set."

The lean man ran off in the direction of the Arawn vans parked on the other side of the yard. Lili watched him go, then looked around the ground. Searching. Something caught her eye. I approached the container, trying to tell her to wait. Tell her that help was coming. I should have known better, as she breezed past me and walked back to the door with a crowbar.

"Lili!" I barked.

With the bar wedged into the lock, she put all of her weight on it. Tried to pry it loose. The shackle loosened but didn't release. She adjusted herself and tried again. A high-pitched groan sounded through her teeth as she pulled. Then another. I opened my mouth to admonish her when a crack rent the night. Bits of padlock fell to the ground at her feet.

"She's going to get us killed like that," Clayton muttered. "Those guards can't be the only two here."

"We're here with an army, Clay. Let them try."

Lili shifted her weight, pushing the bar up to unlock the door panel on the container. Creaking hinges pierced the air as the panel swung open. My gun stayed trained on the darkness within.

"Oh fuck," Lili gasped and placed a hand on the door as she stood in the opening and beheld something none of us could see.

I hurried to enter beside her. Still too worried about her safety, I didn't consider my own. Didn't think about what I might see inside the container. Or who I would see staring back at us.

22

Lilith

Children.

I'd known. Informed of what they were doing when the Duke mentioned children to me in his villainous monologue. He'd threatened my nephew with this. Still, when horrible things are happening in the world, it's easy to feel removed from it. A horrific nightmare. Not real. Not real like the sets of large eyes, wide with fear, that were now focused on me.

I stumbled back. Nausea hit me hard and fast. My hand reached for something to steady myself as my stomach plummeted within me. West's arm. He took a step forward, placing a hand between my shoulders to guide me in.

"No one is going to hurt you," he said, his voice calm and soothing.

Even to an adult, a massive man like West dressed in tactical gear and armed to the teeth would be intimidating. I couldn't imagine how he looked to these children.

"It's alright," I cooed.

A small blonde girl who couldn't have been more than six was closest to us. Still in sparkling pink leggings and glittery shoes to match, the white puffy coat she had on was marred with dirt. She scooted away as West stepped inside.

It was fast. A reflex. West looked down in surprise at the arm I'd thrown in front of him. No. These kids didn't need another man invading their space. Not right now. I stepped in before him and knelt. The girl made another backward move, smaller, but looked me in the eye.

"Hi," I said gently, scooting closer only slightly. "I'm Lili. Like the flower. What's your name?"

"Ainsley," the girl whispered, a soft English accent in her voice.

"Ainsley is a very pretty name."

I looked back at West, who had pulled off his mask and stuffed his hands into his pockets to lean back on his heels. Casual. Non-threatening. Without asking, I knew he was waiting for my permission and would only enter when I said it was alright.

"It's nice to meet you," I continued. "My friends and I want to get you all out of here. First, we'll go somewhere safe. Then we'll get all of you home. But you have to come with us now, alright?"

Ainsley shook her head. Smart enough not to take someone at their word.

Good girl, I thought.

Looking around at the other children, I tried to count again. Seven. Seven children, including the brave little girl before me.

"I'll make you a deal. If I do anything you don't like, if you feel unsafe at any time, tell me. I'll make it better. But you're all going home. All of you. I promise."

I held out my hand to her. Not my hand, exactly. My pinky. I'd done it a thousand times with Daniel. He made me swear over and over for big and small things.

"Promise, Zia," he'd demand, holding out his pinky to me. The way I held my pinky out to Ainsley now.

She eyed my hand. Then looked up at West. Seeming to decide something as she took him in. I didn't dare take my attention off of her. A moment passed. And another.

Then she locked her pinky with mine.

FILTHY AND COVERED in heaven knew what, it was a sight that would have wounded even the coldest hearts. Hauling seven children away in a van felt awful. I would have complained, but I was already imposing myself on Arawn's men. West and I sat in the back with the children. Ainsley remained closest to us. She fiddled with her shoelace but kept glancing at me. Making sure I would make good on my promise.

West's legs were braced against the floor of the van on either side of me, allowing me to relax a little as the van bumped along what seemed like a dirt road. We'd left the city a while ago. I'd noted the transition from pavement to, well, not pavement. Aside from my body leaning against his, we weren't touching. His hands rested on his knees. Mine were relaxed on my thighs. Seeking any more comfort from him felt wrong surrounded by so many watchful eyes.

As we felt the van turn, I looked at the children. Some seemed to stiffen at the direction change. After spending who knows how long in a shipping container, a thought that still sickened me, any type of transportation would feel jarring. Terrifying, even. I looked up at West.

"Where are we going?" I asked quietly.

Not for me. For them.

"The Arawn hangar. There's a house on the property. We can get them bunked down for the night and fly them back to their homes tomorrow. Clayton has an intelligence contact who can help locate their families."

I arched an eyebrow at him. Maybe it wasn't the first time they'd seen something like this. Removed children from a dangerous situation. There were so many stories I didn't know. Missions. I wanted to ask. Later. I'll ask later.

The brakes squealed as we finally rolled to a stop. Our driver and Clayton both hopped out. With a click, the lock on the door disarmed and it slid open. Clayton's frat boy smile greeted the children.

"Who likes pizza?" He grinned.

No one answered, but a few hesitant smiles crossed their faces. Even I smiled. His energy was infectious. Positive and unassuming. I wondered if it came to him naturally or if this was a personality he'd crafted for situations exactly like this. West squeezed my shoulder, urging me to stand so we could disembark.

Without thinking, I took Ainsley's hand in mine and led her out of the van. Clayton helped two of the smaller children down. West helped the others. I was grateful the rain had held off. A large grey hangar sat with its doors closed. Ronan Arawn's secrets were safely locked away from prying eyes, at least for the night.

"Come on," West nudged me with an elbow, now holding a small boy.

The child's dark eyes were locked on West, wrapping his arms around the thick column of his neck. My eyes danced over the forearm positioned under the child. In the darkness, I couldn't see the scar there. But I'd felt it. Traced it. I remembered the story he told me about the little girl that had died in his arms. Remembered, as we walked around the hangar, that he was haunted by it, and was still broken when we met.

Even in the dim glow of the hangar security lights, the white brick house set behind it seemed to glow. It was surrounded by a low stone wall and a dark green painted wooden gate that creaked as we opened it. I could smell the damp grass as we walked the stone path to the front door, which was also painted green.

West put the child down and opened it before us. Glancing at me, to us, he cleared his throat.

"This is a safe place."

I wasn't sure if he was trying to reassure me or the children. Neither was convinced. As the door swung open, we were met with booming laughter and the smell of pizza. My mouth watered. I looked at the children gathered around us. All of the expressions ranged from terrified to hopeful. Hungry.

West ushered us inward toward the smell. I was grateful for our shared instinct. Feed them. Help them feel human. Help them feel safe. Well, safer, at least.

As we entered the kitchen, I wondered how long this house had been here. If maybe it predated the hangar. Based on the look of the stove that had been shoved into what looked like an old hearth, I bet it had. Even though the stove itself looked like something from out of the 1950s.

"Welcome," said a deep Irish voice I was coming to know well. "To my home."

Killian emerged from behind the small refrigerator door as he closed it. In a white tee shirt and jeans instead of his usual button-down and slacks, his arms revealed thousands of dollars worth of tattoos. A step forward made me tense, even as I reminded myself that we were on the same side. Ainsley squeezed my hand, more afraid than I was. I loosened my stance and tried to stay relaxed as the large, dark Irishman approached.

"They're making up beds by the fireplace so all of ye can get nice and warm. But first I think ye need to fill 'yer bellies, aye?"

His smile was broad and kind. So different from the cold expression I was usually greeted with. Our families had been rivals for as long as the two of us had been alive. Maybe longer. This truce hadn't been in place for long, but it was quickly becoming one of the best decisions I'd ever made.

It was strange to see one of the most dangerous men I'd ever met go all soft and gooey for a bunch of kids. Killian walked to the large wooden kitchen table and flipped open the pizza boxes sitting atop it. The children looked at each other. Ainsley let go of my hand and sat at the table. The tattooed gangster carefully placed a plate in front of her and gestured to the box.

Watching Ainsley take a bite of pepperoni pizza, my shoulders relaxed. Soon, all seven of them had seated themselves, taking pizza after Killian's men presented them with plates. Cups. Juice. Smiles.

The scene kindled something in me. A small offering of kindness to these children made my problems seem so small. West stepped to my side, his boots heavy on the wooden floor. I loosed a shaking breath. An arm wound around my waist as he pulled me close and kissed the top of my head. The smoky green eyes I'd come to know as well as my own were soft as I turned to look at him.

"You did good, Trouble. Really good."

23

WEST

The next twenty-four hours seemed to go by in a blink. Though for Clayton, I was sure it felt much longer. I'd sat down on Killian's sofa, watching over the sleeping children in their little makeshift beds. After washing each child as much as they'd let her with washcloths and a bar of soap, Lilith curled into my side, watching them with me. Sleep soon claimed both of us.

But not Clayton. He posted up at the kitchen table, laptop surrounded by empty pizza boxes. As the children ate their dinners, he'd questioned them. He'd gotten their names and any other information they could remember about their homes and families. He was at that table when my eyes closed. He was still there when they opened several hours later.

Lilith was sprawled across the loveseat, head in my lap. I pushed her night-dark hair away from her eyes and covered her ear with my hand before speaking.

"Hey," I whispered.

Clayton lifted his gaze from the screen to look over at me. I had no idea how he managed to look so awake with no sleep. He gave me a nod and looked back at the computer.

"I'm almost done here. Just having a little trouble with one of them."

I shifted my hips and lifted Lilith's head gently, trying to move out from under her without waking her. She tucked an arm beneath her head, mumbling something I couldn't quite make out as I stepped away.

"What do you mean?"

Clayton pointed to the notepad beside the keyboard. Thanks to years in the field together, I could still read his chicken scratch handwriting.

Ainsley Boroughs. Jersey. February 14th. Lives with mother. Father unknown.

"You can't find her family?"

"That's not it," he said, taking a sip from his coffee.

"What do you mean?"

"I can't find her. Ainsley. It's like she never existed. No birth record."

My palms covered my face, rubbing at my tired eyes as though that would make any of this make sense. She didn't have any reason to lie to us. At least, it didn't seem like it. Before I could utter a syllable in response, Clayton continued.

"I've done image searches. I've searched through missing person reports. School records. I've even searched every morgue in the United Kingdom. Nothing. She's a ghost."

"Ainsley."

Lilith's voice was soft and sweet. I looked up to find her crouching beside the little girl's bed. Her hand patted the girl's stomach gently, trying to wake her. Though I wished she had kept sleeping because she needed the rest, I was grateful for her help. How long had she been listening?

"Ainsley, wake up. We need to ask you some questions, alright?"

Small blue eyes opened, glazed from sleep. A yawn followed. Despite her drowsy state, Ainsley still looked frightened. In a strange place, surrounded by strange people, miles from home. I couldn't blame her for that.

"It's alright. Remember me? You're safe," Lilith purred. "We just need to know more about you so we can get you home."

"Yes, ma'am," Ainsley warbled. My heart tugged at the polite response.

"Do you want some breakfast?"

The little girl nodded at Lili's question. With a hand extended to her, Lili stood up and guided her through the array of sleeping children like they were walking through a minefield. Their feet snaked through the small walking path toward the kitchen. I pulled out a chair for Ainsley as Lili headed to the refrigerator to hunt for food.

"I think all we have is leftover pizza," she muttered, her mouth twisting to one side as she assessed the situation. "Is that ok?"

Ainsley nodded again as she sat down beside me.

"Do you want it hot or cold?"

"Cold, please."

Lili smiled as she pulled a box out of the refrigerator and set it on the counter. Hunting through various cabinets around the kitchen, she grunted when she found what she was looking for. Lili retrieved two plates from within, plating a slice of pizza on one and two on the other. She moved toward the table and set a slice down in front of Ainsley. Then she pulled two glasses off of the drying rack on the counter, pouring water into them before coming back to the table.

"I like my pizza cold, too," Lili said as she sat down.

"Animal," I teased.

Lili snapped her teeth at me, winking at the little girl. Ainsley picked up the pizza and took a small bite, chewing as Clayton worked silently on her other side. Lili began eating but watched the girl carefully. I wondered how she would approach questioning a child when her usual tactics of interrogation involved methods banned by the Geneva Convention.

"So," Lili said, her mouth half full of pizza. "We just wanted to know a little more about you so that we could find your mom and get you back to her. Can you tell us her name?"

Ainsley put her pizza down. The little girl rolled her lips in and thought hard for a moment. At no more than six, I doubted she used her mother's name very often.

"Her name is Emily," she said.

Clayton's fingers flew over his keyboard, adding this new information to his search. Emily Boroughs. Jersey.

"And her last name, is it Boroughs, like yours?"

She nodded.

Clayton sucked in a breath. Lili stiffened. She heard it. Before I could glimpse what was on his screen, he minimized the tab and looked at Ainsley. His voice was thick as he addressed her.

"Do you know your grandparents? Or maybe an aunt or uncle?"

Lili gave Clayton a sharp look. His mouth tightened as he gestured with his eyes toward the girl sitting beside him. Whatever he had found about Emily Boroughs, it had not been good.

"No. Mummy said her parents died before I was born. She said since she was an only child, like me, we are all the family we need."

A muscle flickered in Clayton's jaw as he nodded. I tapped his shoulder, getting up to step outside. The sharp bite of winter greeted us as we stepped into the garden, closing the door as quietly as we could.

"What did you find?"

Clayton blew out a breath. As it fogged between us, he gave me a grave look.

"Her mother, Emily Boroughs, is dead. Died a few days ago in a traffic accident, it looks like. That kid is all alone in the world now."

The front door opened and Lili appeared. Whatever warmth and kindness she'd summoned for Ainsley disappeared in the winter air.

"What's the deal with her mom?" She said abruptly.

"Dead," I responded, still looking at Clayton. "With no other family, she has nowhere to go."

Lili rubbed at her temples, squeezing her eyes shut for a moment like the action would bring about a solution to our new problem. Her mouth pinched to one side as she opened her eyes and looked at Clayton thoughtfully.

"OK. Let's DNA test her. She has to have a father, right? She didn't know his name, so we can find him that way."

"Sure, but there's just one problem with that," Clayton interjected. "A DNA test is going to take weeks. Even if we get the results, there's no guarantee the father would even take her in."

The icy wind whipped through the small garden as we stood there, each of us in thought. Lili wrapped her arms around herself, fighting off the cold. As she surveyed the thistle bushes growing around us, I could see the gears of her mind turning over, looking for a solution to the problem.

"I need to talk to Killian," she said, more to herself than to us. Turning on her heel to go back into the house, I wondered if the Irish mafia had much experience with childcare.

DAWN SPREAD OVER the waking city of Los Angeles as Lili and I made our way home from Ronan's private airstrip. Lili's solution to Ainsley's problem was to get Killian to care for the child in his home until they could find her father. The man had agreed to the arrangement, stating that the elderly caretaker of the property would be happy to add a little girl to her regular duties. When I saw that the caretaker looked like a kindly teapot, my worries about leaving Ainsley behind ebbed.

Lili arched her back as her arms stretched over her head, pressing her ample chest forward. She tilted her head from side to side, seeming to work out the kinks in it as she squirmed in the passenger seat.

"Do you want to stop for some breakfast?" I offered.

She angled her head, weighing her options. Before she could open her mouth to respond, her phone pinged in her pocket. She pulled the device out and typed in her code to look at the new message.

Lili's face drained of color as the phone dropped into her lap. She swallowed.

"We have to get home. Now."

24

Lilith

The image on my phone was as clear as day. A picture of Lupo and Daniel, sitting in the living room from an unknown number. They were watching television and laughing together. Completely unaware that they were being watched by someone who wanted me to know. Someone who was about to hurt me.

By hurting *them*.

The glove box flew open as West reached over me. A 9mm pistol and two clips of ammunition awaited his grip. Unclipping my seatbelt, I turned in my seat to fish around in my bag.

"Got what you need?"

I grunted my ascent as my hand connected with the wrap containing my knives. Righting myself in the seat, I strapped the holster to my thigh. Arriving at the house sent my nerves into freefall. My mouth went dry as I tied my hair into a ponytail.

The gate was open.

"Get everyone into the panic room. I'll sweep the perimeter," West said as the Bronco skidded to a stop on the gravel driveway, shooting rocks everywhere. I made to turn and leave.

"Wait."

I looked back toward West, who grabbed my jaw with one hand and pressed a hard kiss to my mouth.

"Come back to me, Trouble."

Fear that had been welling in me expanded as I looked into his face for what could easily be the last time. I wasn't sure of what I was walking into. Neither was he.

As soon as my feet hit the ground, I sprinted toward the door. No signs or sounds of distress. Inside, I heard laughter. Cartoons. Remus walked up to me, the bull terrier mix wagging his whip-like tail. Unable to worry about the peace I was disrupting, I shouted for them as I hooked my finger through the old mutt's collar to usher him to safety.

"Lupo, Daniel, come here now!"

Shouldering open the panel beneath the stairs, I did my best to conceal the keypad as I punched in the code for the concealed steel door behind it.

0903

Kaia's birthday. Metal scraped and a loud beep sounded as Lupo and Daniel came to stand behind me.

"Get in," I said, nodding toward the small space inside. More than big enough for two. Plus a dog. I pushed Remus in by his backside, who resisted even as he waddled in.

"What about you?" Daniel asked as he looked up at me with wide, wet eyes.

"I'll be fine. Get in," I barked. There was no time. No time for this. Whoever sent that photo was here.

"Come on," Lupo said to Daniel.

Lupo and Daniel entered the panic room. That thing could withstand anything. They would be safe in there. Daniel's eyes remained on me, gleaming with fear. Shouting sounded from outside, followed by a gunshot. My gut turned while I said a silent prayer for West.

"Kid," Lupo said, turning to me. "Get in with us."

I didn't answer. Lupo gave a terse nod as I shut the door in his face and sealed it, the lock clicking as it slid into place. With the panel shut, you'd never know they were there. At least, that was what I was counting on.

Kicking off my boots and shrugging off the flannel shirt that could hinder my range of motion, I walked on light footsteps through the first floor. My hand skated along my holster, counting each blade. Six. Six throwing knives were at my fingertips. The hunting knife remained clipped to my jeans at my back.

Crouching down behind the sofa, I slowed my breathing and waited. I tugged my socks off and stuffed them under the sofa as I listened. The sticking squeak of a rubber sole neared me. A large man in tactical gear turned as my face and arm appeared over the sofa. He was too slow to stop the knife that pierced his throat, replacing his ability to scream with the sound of a choked gurgle.

One down.

My other hand unclipped the hunting knife, keeping it ready for close combat. Ready to defend. My dominant hand was free to be used for throwing. Careful steps lead me around the sofa. Toward the kitchen island. I glanced at the first man I'd downed. Kaia's creamy white Persian rug was ruined with his blood. A dirty white tee shirt stained red with a bullet wound flashed into my mind. I blinked.

Gravel crunched outside. It was followed by the pop and hiss of the front door opening. My hand grabbed another knife from the holster. These men were in tactical gear. Undoubtedly Kevlar. I'd have to keep risking the trickier shots to down my targets. I shuffled around the island as I heard the intruder approach.

More shouting came from outside, easier to hear their accents with the door open. Scottish. Definitely Augustus-Stanley's men, then. Frantic steps pounded the gravel driveway.

"Just get the bitch! She's not alone. She -"

A gun cracked. A thud sounded.

Quick steps hurried away from me. Toward cover from the outside threat. His head angled, peering out the front door. Looking for West. Exposing his carotid artery like the juicy target that it was. Not aware of the threat closing in on him.

Bingo.

I'd thrown the knife as hard as I could. When I heard it pierce the wall, I knew my sister would have been proud. There was choking and the clunk of his gun hitting the ground as he lost control of his hands. They twitched. Once. Twice.

Two down.

The backdoor opened and I scurried up the stairs. Into my bedroom. Breathing was a dangerous giveaway I couldn't afford. I schooled my traitorous lungs into slow, even draws. Childhood games of hide and seek now turned into a deadly reality. Being caught meant death.

A stair tread creaked. Someone was coming. Coming for me. The creaking floors hinted at someone with a heavier stride. Someone big, then. Hope that it was West carefully searching for me died when I heard him speak.

"I can smell you," the man growled. "Come play with me, little flower."

Shaking fingers circled another knife. Then a second. I hid behind the bed as best I could. A snort came from the doorway. He was here. I weighed my options. I could risk a blind throw. Or give myself away and possibly take a bullet.

I threw my blade.

It landed. But the man smirked at me, eyes cold like a shark. I was right. He was big. As big as West. Wild red hair. Cold green eyes. A scar through his lip. And a nose that had been broken many times over. He'd managed to block my throw to his neck, instead taking the blade in his forearm.

He charged me as I threw the second knife. It embedded in the wall beside his head, and I attempted to sprint away, only to be tackled to the ground beside the bed. I screamed in surprise as the air whooshed out of me. Pinned under him, I tried to pry myself free. Thought left me as I took a rock-hard fist to the gut.

Then another.

Wheezing, and panting, I coughed. Air. There was no air. I couldn't breathe, couldn't breathe, couldn't breathe! My attacker mounted my legs, knees straddling my own while his feet tucked beneath them. The weight felt like too much for my aching joints to bear. He ran an appreciative hand over my body. I tried to shove his hands away as my lungs fought to breathe. I was still seeing stars. He grabbed one wrist and twisted as I wheezed another scream.

"Pity," he grunted. "You're built for fun."

My twisted wrist was pushed above my head. I tried to shove him away as he leaned in close enough for me to smell the stale coffee on his breath. His free hand circled my other wrist and pinned it to join the injured one. I jerked upward, my forehead colliding with his nose. He laughed. Actually laughed as blood welled where my forehead had split his.

"Oh, this will be a real shame, little flower. But orders are orders. Business first. Fun second. You'll still be warm."

His words made my stomach turn. The pain shot down my arm as he gripped my wrists tight. A zip tie bound them together. I tried pushing up my hips, but it was impossible with his position on my thighs. Tried shifting myself with what little freedom I had left. It was no use. I sobbed. The man loosed what looked like a coil of wire from his vest.

Fuck.

His forearm oozed blood from where my knife had pierced it. It slid down, down to where his hand now gripped my jaw. I felt the wire circle my throat.

"No last words for you, pretty girl."

A guttural snarl and spit loosed from my clenched teeth as I fought again to free myself from his grasp. His hand pulled at the wire, the garrote tightening around my neck like a snake.

Squeezing.

Squeezing.

Squeezing.

No.

Tears stung my eyes as I wriggled and fought. The edges of my vision began to darken. Daniel was safe. That was all that mattered. And West...

Red mist clouded my vision as my attacker's face went slack. Large hands gripped the man's vest, throwing him off of me. My vision was patchy, but I knew that was the shape of West was standing over me. He emptied his clip between the man's unseeing eyes.

Coming to his knees beside me, West slipped two fingers beneath the wire around my throat, pulling slowly to loosen its merciless grip. Once the wire was free from my neck, his knife went to my wrists and cut the zip tie. I coughed and gagged, my fingers rubbing my neck as I fought for air. Why do men always go for the throat?

Dusky green eyes filled with rage and panic as they searched me for injury, landing on my swelling wrist. A large hand gently traced the sprain as his other arm scooped me up toward him.

"Lupo and Daniel are safe?"

I nodded weakly. The tears in my eyes welled and fell as I let out another sob. West made soothing sounds as he clutched me to his chest, gently kissing my brow.

"You're alright."

He repeated the phrase in whispers against my skin as he rocked me in his arms. I wasn't sure if he was talking to me or telling himself. But I let myself weep anyway.

25

WEST

"I feel like we just did this."

Lilith dropped her bag on the floor, looking around the living room in casual assessment. I looked back at her. Lupo had wrapped her wrist, able to stabilize the sprain. She'd still insisted on carrying her damn bag.

"Yeah," I sighed.

Of course, the last time we were in hiding it was at my cabin in the mountains. Just the two of us locked away from the world. It was at that cabin that our friendship died and whatever we were now was growing in its place.

I'd almost lost her. Again. As I had crept up the stairs, his plans were clear. Kill her. Then do what he wants with her. I glanced at the burn mark the wire left on Lili's neck. Thirteen bullets weren't enough.

"Zia, can I go outside?" Daniel interrupted, planting his face on the large glass window to gape at the pool.

Lilith rubbed her eyes with her thumb and index finger, then looked to me for a second opinion. I answered her silent question.

"It'll be fine, Lili."

"Fine," she agreed with a nod. "But take Lupo and Remus with you. And no swimming! It's too cold."

His reply disappeared with him out the door as he ran to get the old man and his dog. I looked over at Lili, who rubbed at the bruise on her neck as she watched the little boy.

A small part of me wondered if Daniel would ever know what she went through to protect him. Only a few feet above him, she had been on her back with a garrote around her neck and seconds away from death. The memory started to tangle with all of the other times Lili almost died in front of me. Like a fucking nightmare I could never wake up from.

I had to remind myself that Nico and Damon were at the house, disposing of what was left of the Duke's men. I had shown them the men I'd taken care of outside. Nico thanked me for being efficient.

"So this is Clayton's house?" Lili asked as she let out a low, appreciative whistle at the open floor plan laden with expensive furnishings.

I laughed. Clayton made a ridiculous amount of money as a mercenary, but he would never spend it on a mid-century mansion in the Hollywood Hills. I supposed being a mercenary meant I was making that kind of money too, now.

"No. This house belongs to one of his clients. Clayton said they're out of the country, traveling the world for like a year or something. We're free to use it for the foreseeable future."

Lili walked to the sofa table, picking up a framed picture of strangers to examine it. Her worn black combat boots squeaked on the polished wood floor as she pivoted toward me again.

"Well, I don't recognize any of these people. That's a good start."

I chuckled as I leaned against the kitchen island and watched as she continued to explore the living room. At first, I thought she was making herself at home until she started picking up decorative objects, looking under them, and moving other photos around. My head tilted to one side in confusion as she looked behind the television.

"What are you doing?"

"I'm looking for hidden cameras."

"Oh. They're not hidden," I said, pointing to the tiny black dome camera mounted in the ceiling. Lili's face twisted in disgust.

"That's creepy."

I shrugged.

"Clayton installed it. He installed all of the security here. It's not as discrete as your family's house, but it's effective and, more importantly, off the Duke's grid."

Lili opened her mouth to respond, only to be cut off by the sound of a loud splash. We both ran to the window overlooking the oversized pool. Daniel was still dry, as was Lupo. The small boy was laughing his head off as Remus swam around, happy as could be.

Her hand moved to the glass, fingers curling on the windowpane as melancholy swept over her features. The sleeve of her flannel slid down to expose her freshly wrapped wrist.

"I feel like I ruined his life," she rasped.

"Hey," I said sharply, pulling her small frame into me. She clutched my shirt and looked up at me with those gorgeous, sad eyes. "None of this is your fault."

She made a face, ready to argue.

"None of it, Lili," I barked.

I knew what was down that road. The road your mind travels down when you replay every bad thing that's ever happened to you. I walked that road for years. It didn't lead anywhere good. And I'd be damned if I'd let her see what was at the other end of it.

"Come on," I said as I moved her away from the window. "Let's check out the rest of this palace."

AFTER A DINNER of terrible delivery pizza that tasted like cardboard and an animated movie to put Daniel at ease, Lili and I excused ourselves to the bedroom we'd claimed on the other side of the house. It was nice enough. Simply furnished with walnut furniture. Wheat-colored linens that seemed soft and luxurious. A small wave of relief washed over me at the sight of the California king bed.

Lilith poked around the room, no doubt checking for more cameras. She disappeared into the adjoining bathroom to continue her search. I was ready to get started planning our next move with this fucking Duke when I heard the shower turn on.

"Lili?"

I rounded the corner, wondering if she was drowning a camera.

"Are you getting in?" Lili asked as she bundled her hair atop her head in a loose knot.

It was an effort to peel my eyes away from Lilith's lithe waist and the curving swell of her generous ass to examine the shower. Simple, like the rest of the house. Dark grey marble everywhere. Black fixtures. One built-in bench against the wall opposite a frosted glass window. It even had a steam feature.

I kicked off my boots and lifted my shirt over my head. Shucking my pants and boxers down, I smirked at her. Lili stood inside the open shower door, bracing herself against the glass. Her cheeks flushed with color as she eyed my body. My girl was so fucking transparent.

"How's the water?"

She turned and lifted a hand into the stream. I'd scold her for taking the wrapping off later.

"Perfect."

"Good."

Our voices barely echoed off of the walls. I was grateful for that. Grateful for a moment alone with her. Fuck it. I was going to enjoy the hell out of this. Enjoy tasting her.

You almost lost her today.

Lili stepped backward as I entered the shower, hands twisting together in front of her. I let the thought melt away under the warm water. I knelt on the floor, pressing her backward so I could better access her. She gasped as the cold marble hit her back. The back of her thigh was firm with muscle, though the skin was slick and velvet-soft as it slid against my palm. I lifted her knee and grazed the knuckles of my other hand against her sex. A soft mewling sound came from above.

"Use your words, Trouble. Tell me what you want."

Her eyes squeezed shut as she frowned, brows knitting together.

"I just. I don't," she stammered, exhaling through her teeth as I nipped at her inner thigh. "I want you. Everywhere."

Fine. I could do that. She'd told me she was worried she'd lose me. That she'd somehow caused all the pain in her life.

"The things I love have a way of getting destroyed because of me."

Watching her sister die in her arms was just a confirmation of that fear. I could understand her desire to pull away from me. Pull away because she was afraid of more loss. That didn't mean I was going to ignore the barrier she liked to throw up between us. It had started to crumble, but I knew today would set her off. I saw that tension rise in her from the moment we vacated the house. There wasn't a chance in hell that I was going to let it keep me out forever. Not when I craved the reassurance of her body. She was here. She was fine.

With a nip to her other thigh, I teased her entrance, sliding one finger into her. A soft yelp from above echoed off of the marble walls. My tongue skimmed over my fingers, licking and tasting with gentle sweeps. Lili's hands slapped against the wall, steadying herself with panting breaths.

Moving her knee to rest atop my shoulder, I took her ass in my hand and squeezed. Her hips jerked as I beckoned my finger inside her, but she was soon grinding herself into my tongue. One hand moved from the wall to plunge into my hair, using the thick mass to angle my mouth where she wanted it.

Yes, I wanted to say. *Use me. Take what you want.*

I tried to remember how many times I'd fantasized about this. A hundred? A thousand? But those fantasies felt empty now. They could never capture the feel of her. So soft. Or the taste. Sweet like caramel. I savored it as I watched her bite back a scream as she came undone.

So fucking sweet.

"You alright?" I asked as I set her leg back down. A half-empty nod was my only response. With all of the blood in my body rushing for my cock, I wanted to tell her the feeling was mutual. *Very* mutual. Instead, I stood and pulled her toward me as I sat on the bench, turning her body to face away from me.

"We're not done yet, are we?" she smirked, looking back at me as she rubbed her ass against my erection.

"I'll never be done with you," I said, barely able to get the words out. Her entrance grazed the tip of me, wet and beckoning. I wrapped an arm around her waist and tugged her toward my lap. "Grab that."

Lili looked at the sprayer nozzle attached to the wall, a long hose dangling from it close enough for her to reach. Her fingers wrapped around and pulled, the sprayer falling into her outreached hand.

"Turn it on and give it to me," I ordered. I wanted her to get out of her head, so I was going to do my best to shatter her mind. The spray sputtered on and she placed the handle in my palm, turning toward me with a conspiratorial grin.

Maybe it was from training with her for years. She learned my tells and I learned hers. Our bodies had a way of speaking to each other, with no need to say a word. It was why I knew she loved me before she ever voiced it. It was why I knew she was trying to numb herself to the pain she was feeling. And it was why she knew exactly what I planned to do with her.

Lili rocked her hips as she placed her hands on my thighs, steadying herself. I focused the sprayer on her breasts, moving it with idle strokes. The arm I'd circled around her pulled her flush against me. I put the sprayer in that hand. My free hand moved up to cup her cheek, forcing her to look at me.

"Ready for more, gorgeous?"

"Yes," she sighed.

I rolled my hips against hers, gliding myself through her core. Our water-slick bodies slid together as she undulated against me.

"You know what to do."

With one more movement of that perfect ass, she reached down and notched my cock at her entrance. I plunged inside her. Exactly where I wanted to be. She writhed and clamped around me. A muffled moan sounded behind the pink lip she bit into with ferocity.

Angling the small sprayer against her clit, I felt her inner muscles clench as she whimpered. The hand I'd had on her cheek dropped to her breast. Lili's hands moved from my thighs to tangle into my hair again, fingers curling to grip the strands as she rocked her hips.

"Come on," I gritted against her neck, barely holding onto the threads of my self-control. "Let me hear you."

My lips traveled over the bruise the garrote left behind. Her head fell backward as she let out a gasp, as if holding it up was too much effort with everything else she was feeling. Hell, with the tension building low in my core, I wasn't sure if I could hold out much longer.

"West, please," she panted, her voice cracking and shaking with the rest of her. "It's too much."

"You can take it. You're doing so well," I praised as my climax threatened, building with every move of that glorious ass. "Show off for me. Come on."

I felt it before she buried her face in my neck and cried out. Every little muscle in her body tightened in a wave as she arched against me, panting and quivering with her orgasm. My release was close behind. So close that I wondered if her pleasure was all I needed. If she was everything I'd ever need.

I turned off the sprayer and wrapped my other arm around her. Our kiss was lazy and lingering. Her mouth feathered against mine as her breath began to even out. Lili pulled away and looked up at me with heavy-lidded eyes.

"There better not be any fucking cameras in here."

26

Lilith

Scientists observe patterns. They use that information to form a hypothesis. To ask questions about the world around them. Fractals. Seasons. DNA. They all involve patterns.

"I don't mean to brag, but this is a perfect Bistecca alla Fiorentina," West said as he picked up a plate and brought it to where I was sitting. "Should we wait for Lupo?"

"No, he ate with Daniel," I said absently as I poured him more wine.

"Find anything?" West said. I looked up to see him setting his plate down beside mine as he examined my screen.

My mouth watered at the late evening dinner he'd prepared for us.

"No," I huffed, stretching as I rolled my neck to loosen the muscles that had wound up into knots. "Sort of. Nothing useful yet."

"You should take a break. You've been at this for hours. At least stop to eat."

Actually, I'd been at it for six days. Almost a week since we'd left the house to find safety in this mid-century mansion in the hills. After establishing a guard at the house to mislead anyone still looking for us, I'd resumed researching the Duke. Looking for patterns. Checking gossip magazines and newspapers.

Part of me felt guilty for upending everyone's life. This was my fault. They were in danger because of me. My need to track down the Duke was amplified by the desire to give them their lives back. Even if it was at the expense of my own.

It felt like a fine layer of stress was tightly wound around me, like a vacuum bag sucking out all of the air. But then I found it. Not a pattern in words or money. It was in photos. Photos of someone else.

Lifting the glass to polish off the wine inside, my eyes drifted back to the screen of my laptop. The glass fell from my lips, clacking with the countertop on the way down.

"Who the fuck is that?" I said aloud, pushing the glass away. Then grabbed the laptop to pull it closer to myself.

"Who?"

West stood up from his seat. He braced his hands on the chair behind me, leaning so close his beard grazed my neck. I moved my finger over the different photos of the Duke at various events.

"Right there. There's a woman in every photo. The same short auburn hair. The Duke is always alone in the formal shots. Red carpets and whatever. But she's always next to him in the candid ones. See? These are all different events all over the world. And she's there. By his side."

"Maybe a girlfriend?"

"No," I said. "She's wearing a wedding ring."

"He has a wife?"

"No. He's not married. But she's important to him. And we need to find out why."

Technology is a beautiful, terrifying thing. Did you know that you use images to search for the information you want? That's what I did. Found images where I could see this woman's face and then digitally snipped her out of them so that only her likeness remained. A few image searches brought up the identity of the mysterious red-haired woman by the Duke's side. American heiress Helena Allerton.

Born and raised in Manhattan, she was the picture of generational wealth. Ivy League education. A body earned by a personal trainer and diet curated by a private chef. Her home was featured in Architectural Digest. It looked like something from out of an Agatha Christie novel.

She was always standing next to the Duke with a bland look on her face or casually angling her body toward him like she was going to say something to him. If she was important to him, it was a functional relationship. Not a romantic one.

Benjamin had told me that he'd been born poor. After everything he'd done to get into this man's good graces, it struck me that Benjamin was just one of the Duke's many implements in his organization. Helena Allerton was another one of his tools. Useful enough to keep around, but for what?

"LOOK AT THIS," West said, pushing his phone toward me.

After discovering the identity of the mystery woman, I asked West to contact Clayton and Dr. Forester to find out what he could about the woman that wasn't public information.

"These are all owned by her. Well, Clayton says it's a shell corporation that she owns and all of these businesses are subsidiaries. But look at this one."

A list of business names, some familiar and some obscure. West's finger hovered over a nonsensical name. I read it aloud.

"Enterprise Realty Organizational Syndicate."

Syndicate? I cringed at the name. What horrible cumbersome Wall Street bullshit! It sounded like they picked the name out of a hat filled with business jargon. I guess her Ivy League education didn't include any courses in creativity.

I clicked the link for more information. A list of office locations. I supposed that made sense for what might be a real estate company. My thumb swiped up through the list. Amsterdam. Belfast. Singapore. Rio De Janeiro. California. West let out a laugh that sounded more like a snort.

"What?"

His beard grazed my ear again as he leaned closer and scrolled the screen back to the top with his index finger.

"Look at that name again. What do you see?"

Enterprise Realty Organizational Syndicate.

"EROS."

COLD WATER STUNG my flesh as I stood in the too-large shower. After hours of research, we'd come up with a loose approximation of a plan. Chasing the Duke had kept me wired. The hunt for him occupied my mind enough to ignore the loss I'd been trying to avoid feeling. It ebbed and surged in me, turbulent like a stormy sea.

In the small hours, I was too tired to run from it. Too weak. My eyes felt heavy with a lack of sleep. I let them fall shut and braced my palms on the wall, leaning into the spray to let the icy water wash over me.

As I stood there with my eyes closed, I saw all of the times I found my sister still awake at her computer. Still at the club, working in her office. Showing up for her son when he needed her and stealing hours of rest away from herself just so everyone in her life was satisfied. The role of a mother and a boss. Guilt had been circling me for days. Now it dug its claws into me as I remembered all of the times I made her life more difficult.

I should have helped her more. Should have shown up for her more. Should have taken away her burdens, not added to them. Even when I thought I was helping, I could have been better.

A metal squeak sounded and the water began to warm on my skin. I opened my eyes to find West standing in the open shower door, looking at me with tired eyes that mirrored my own.

"You'll catch your death like that."

I just stared at him.

West stepped in and began washing himself, casting sidelong glances at me as I just leaned back against the wall. Closing my eyes again, I listened as the water splashed against the tile floor as West bathed.

Instead of letting the sounds drown out my thoughts, they crashed down on me. I imagined the man seconds away from killing me only a few days ago. The look on Daniel's face when I opened the panic room to retrieve them. Utterly petrified. It was my fault. My actions and stupidity had dug this hole and now everyone around me was paying for it.

Your fault.

Your fault.

Your fault.

"Kaia should be here. Not me."

The water turned off and I opened my eyes to see West before me. He pressed a palm to the wall beside my waist, the other hand moved to my cheek to brush away a wet tendril of hair and stayed there.

"Don't say that."

I took a gasping breath. The kind that doesn't quite feel like you can get any air down when grief's fingers are wrapped around your throat. My voice shook as thoughts tumbled out of me.

"It feels like when I slow down, even for a second, everything rushes in. All the ways I let my sister down. The way I let Daniel down. I failed them. I had one job and I failed. If it had been me, she would still be here. Daniel would still have his mom. It would be easier if I had been the one to...to go. Everything would be fine."

"I wouldn't be."

West looked down at his arm, the one that brushed against my bare skin as his thumb made soothing sweeps against my cheek. I looked, too. With his gaze fixed on the ink, he spoke.

"Clayton and I got this after our second tour. Everyone in our unit did. The Kraken was Clayton's idea. Frogs are more common for SEALs. He said it was legendary. That we were legendary. But we got it because we lost a team member. We wanted to honor him. Clayton chose the image. I chose the words."

My eyes shifted from West's face to the tattoo. The words were almost lost in ink-black tentacles. Memento mori.

"*Remember you must die.* It's supposed to remind you to live. To remind you that you're still here. Life is still stretching out ahead of you. You have to remember that because if you act like it's over, you might as well be in the ground."

West moved closer, pulling my body against him as he coiled around me. I let myself get wrapped up in him. He cradled my head in his hand, letting his other come around to my back.

"Remember what you told me? Memento vivere."

Only a few weeks ago, or was it a month now? I couldn't remember. Time felt like an imaginary thing now. But I remembered that. The night I gave my heart to him, I reminded him of those words because he made me feel alive.

Memento vivere. Remember to live.

I nodded weakly. West kissed my forehead, then leaned back to look down at me before pulling me in again. We stood in silence for one breath. Then another. And another. Until I realized he was silently commanding me to breathe by breathing with me.

27

West

Butter sizzled as I dropped it into the hot skillet. Lilith sat at the island with her laptop open, working hard. Her dark brows furrowed in concentration. She looked up at the sound; I smiled at her.

"So we need to find this Allerton woman," she sighed.

The light had returned to her eyes. A little. But I would take it for now.

Grieving doesn't happen in a straight line. I know that. After losing our father, Lanna and I learned that the hard way. My sister looked so much like him that sometimes the loss of him still hit me. With everything happening around Lilith, it didn't surprise me that grief was crashing over her in waves. But last night, her admission scared me.

"Kaia should be here. Not me."

Imagining my life without Lili in it was impossible. Not when we were just friends. Certainly not now. She came into my life like she'd fallen out of the sky. She was the first person to make me laugh, really laugh, since I left the military. I didn't want to know a day without her.

I used to think love at first sight was an idea for idiots in made-for-TV movies. I'd watched so many of them while crashing on my sister's couch after being medically discharged. I knew it was time to get out and do something when I started seriously entertaining the idea of becoming a Christmas tree farmer.

That was the day I met Lili. Bruised and laughing. Fighting. Looking at me like I was someone other than a discarded serviceman. Suddenly, I wanted to be someone again. Because I knew, somehow, that being someone to the girl with golden eyes was important.

"Is there any more coffee?"

"Almost done," I said, glancing at the bubbling pot.

She didn't cure me. I know that's not a thing. She was just there while I worked on myself. Every time I got to work out with her or laugh with her, I wanted to be here a little more. It was like a reward for sticking around. I sure as hell wasn't going to let her fall apart when I could be there for her now.

The batter sizzled as I poured it into the pan and let it cook as I peeked over the rim of her empty coffee mug. The vintage-inspired coffee pot almost intimidated me into going out for coffee. I pulled the pot from the heating plate and poured. Lili gave me a grateful look as I refilled her cup.

After setting the pot back in its place, I rounded the island and stood behind her to take her in my arms. Her hands fell away from the keyboard as she leaned backward into me.

"We'll find her," I said into her mess of black hair that smelled of the shampoo in the shower. Mint and rosemary. It filled my senses as I relished the feel of her. My wolf. My wildflower. My deadly, beautiful thing.

"The pancake is burning," she replied.

I released her and returned to the range to flip the slightly scorched pancake. Daniel laughed so loudly at a cartoon that I almost missed my phone chirping on the counter. It chirped again as a text message from Clayton appeared on the screen.

> Come to my place this afternoon. We need to talk.

"CLAY?" I CALLED from the center of the space. He'd let me up, so I knew he was here.

Clayton's loft smelled like incense. Incense and cleaning products. And there was actual furniture in here. I walked in and could see the polished concrete floor. And the expensive rug now covers it.

I'd made Lili promise to stay at the house while I met with Clayton, explaining that he'd had some mercenary shit he wanted to discuss with me. She only nodded and joined Daniel in the living room for what looked like a movie marathon involving superheroes leaping around in colorful outfits.

The door to a balcony I didn't know existed opened. Clayton appeared with what looked like a watering can.

"Hey man," he said casually. "Beer?"

"It's barely noon."

"Right. Beer?"

I let out a laugh and nodded. Clay set the can down on a small table beside the door and passed me to grab a pair of Pacifico bottles from his kitchen.

"What happened to all the boxes?" I asked, remembering the city of cardboard that had been here since he moved in.

"It was pointed out to me that with all the money I make as a mercenary, I could probably afford a storage unit."

"Pointed out to you by who?"

Instead of answering my question, Clayton opened his beer on the edge of the black countertop and took a swig. Message received. For a talkative guy, he was becoming incredibly private.

"I got the results of Ainsley's DNA test."

I used the bottle opener on my knife to crack the beer and sat down on the couch.

"Is that why I'm here?"

Clayton grabbed his laptop before sitting down. He set the computer down on the coffee table, a new modern industrial-looking thing that was far nicer than the giant construction spool he had before.

"I need to talk to you about what it means."

I let out an uncomfortable laugh.

"She's not somehow mine, is she?"

Clayton didn't so much as smile. That alone was enough to make me nervous. Before I could ask what the hell he found out, he gave me a grave look.

"You need to promise me you're not going to tell Lilith about this."

Irritation stirred in me. Keeping anything from her wasn't an option. Instead of agreeing, I said, "Just tell me what you know, Clay, and we'll deal with it."

Clayton opened his laptop, clicking through countless open tabs until he found the information he wanted. He hesitated for a moment, then turned the laptop until I could see the screen more clearly.

Before me was the breakdown of everything that the DNA test had discovered about Ainsley Boroughs. More elaborate than anything available to the public, Clayton had sent the sample to friends in forensic intelligence. Though the reports were wordy and filled with jargon I didn't quite understand, the results were clear.

Fifty percent of her DNA came from a man of Scottish descent with some other things thrown in here and there. Someone who'd participated in countless charity events, including blood and plasma donation.

"Almost everything about her mother has been erased from public record. However, after finding out who the father is, I was able to dig through his records for her name and figured out that she worked at his foundation. As an intern. She was let go shortly after she started, presumably went back to Jersey and that's all I know."

I sat back and took a drink from the bottle in my hand, unsure of what to say. Lili had a soft spot for this girl. But the boss of the Caccia family, I didn't know what that woman would do when she found out whose child this was.

My hand flinched as I remembered the sting of a bullet and a girl going limp in my arms as her mother screamed beside me.

Because Ainsley Boroughs was not an orphan. She had a father.

"Harrison Augustus-Stanley."

28

Lilith

Daniel's breathing was soft and even. He'd finally passed out after the third movie in a row where the world was about to end because of some calamity that could only be solved by the miraculous existence of someone with superhuman abilities. Halfway through the second movie, I wondered why so many aliens from across the galaxy had beef with Earth. Grateful for the break, I shut the television off and carried him to his bedroom.

With Lupo had turned in for the night and West was still at his meeting with Clayton. For the first time in ages, I was alone with nothing to do. Not really. I'd hit a dead end with Helena Allerton. If I were at home, I'd be working in the garden or the apothecary. Muse was being rebuilt from a pile of ash, so I couldn't go work there. Oh, and let's not forget that I was in hiding anyway, so all of my usual haunts were more likely to get me killed!

With nothing available to occupy me, I wandered around the borrowed house and let my mind turn over. While Daniel watched his films, I'd scrolled through countless articles about Helena Allerton on my phone.

This Allerton woman was a public figure like the Duke. A socialite. But she wasn't born into aristocracy. She was a wealthy American. Helena Allerton looked like the kind of girl who made fun of girls trying to pledge her sorority. The shade of red on her pin-straight hair was probably some proprietary blend that her colorist was paid handsomely to never use on another patron. Her eyes were brown. Just brown. Void of any warmth or wisdom. Similar to that of a scavenging rodent.

It amazed me how different brown eyes could be. Kaia's eyes were brown. Even though this woman and my sister shared that trait, their brown eyes were worlds apart in appearance. I wanted to kill Helena Allerton just for that. For having the nerve to walk the earth wearing eyes that were a mockery of what my sister's used to be.

Getting to Helena Allerton would be a challenge. Fortunately, I'd spied a familiar face in an older photo. Benjamin Camden. Though my sort-of ex-boyfriend was killed by my current boyfriend, this revelation could be useful. Getting to Allerton might be as easy as troubling an old acquaintance for a favor. If I hadn't already worn out my welcome.

Returning to the kitchen from my walk about the house, I grabbed my laptop. The door hissed as I opened it and stepped outside to take up a lounge chair beside the pool. Covering myself with a blanket, the ambient landscape lights gave the crisp night a sense of peace. I settled in, propped the laptop on my lap, and began typing.

A response to my email arrived within moments.

Dear Ms. Hunter,

I so appreciate your continued interest in my career. Our last conversation was illuminating. I would love to meet with you and continue our discussion regarding an opportunity with your organization. Please let me know when and where would be best.

Respectfully,
Juliet Ambrose

A familiar rumbling engine followed the squeak of the security gate rolling open. After typing a quick response with the meeting details, I closed the laptop and watched as West pulled into the driveway. He parked the Bronco and met my gaze. Though he smiled at me, his eyes seemed strained. Something was bothering him.

West jumped out of the truck and crossed the pool deck in a stride that was hurried but attempting to appear casual. A nervous ache swirled in my gut. Whatever his business was with Clayton, he didn't want me to know.

"Alright," he started.

West looked down at me as if he were deciding something as he spoke. He took a step toward me. Then back. Then stuffed his hands into his pockets. My nerves had turned the ache in my gut into nausea. I swallowed a mouthful of saliva. He noted the bob of my throat and ran a hand down his face before taking a seat beside me on the lounge chair.

"I need to talk to you."

West sighed through his nose and looked around, no doubt searching for our other house guests.

"They're both asleep inside."

He nodded.

"It's about Ainsley."

I sat up.

"Is she alright? Did Killian do something? I thought she would be fine but-"

"She's fine. She's safe. It's just... Clayton got the DNA results and he knows who her father is."

I smiled and let out a breath of relief.

"That's great! So we can get her-"

"Lili, it's complicated. It's... I need you to promise me something."

I lurched backward, surprised at his interjection. How could it be complicated? And why did my reaction to this news matter? The nausea that had left me only moments ago flooded like a returning tide. My hand went to my stomach, trying to ease the discomfort.

"What?"

The question popped out of my mouth in a quiet breath. West took my other hand and squeezed, looking down at my palm in his. I studied his face. It was tight with worry. West avoided looking me in the eye as he made his request.

"I need you to promise me that this little girl is going to be safe. It's not… I don't think you'd do anything, but this information is incendiary."

My jaw clenched. Incendiary? I tried to remember the little girl's features. Nothing about her was familiar. She likely favored her mother in appearance, but clearly, her father was someone I knew.

"West, who is her father?"

He finally looked me in the eye, worry filling his smoky green gaze. If he was about to tell me he somehow had fathered this child, I was definitely going to vomit.

"Her father is Harrison Augustus-Stanley."

I pulled my hand away from his and placed it in my lap. Blinking in surprise, I scooted away from him.

"Lili," West started. A note of warning sharpened his voice.

"Do you honestly think I would do something to a child to get back at their parent? Is that the kind of person you think I am?"

"No, but I know what he did to you. He's still trying to hurt you. Clayton thought that you might use this information to get back at him."

He'd been afraid to tell me because he thought me capable of hurting a child. He thought I could look at a girl like Ainsley and blame her for her father's wrongdoings. If she was responsible for his terrible deeds, I couldn't imagine the kind of hell I was in for with a father like mine.

"You dumped sixteen men into the Pacific like a week ago. I'm not allowed to be a little concerned?"

My hand stung with the impact. West rubbed his face where I'd slapped him. I stood up, staring down at him as fury surged like fire in my blood. Harrison Augustus-Stanley. The Duke. The fucking Duke. I wanted to scream at West, but my voice remained low as I growled a response to his implication.

"I would never punish a little girl just because of who her father is."

"Lili, wait!"

I picked up my laptop, making to storm back into the house. The macaroni and cheese I'd shared with Daniel was about to make a reappearance and I had to get to a bush or a bathroom. Frantic steps toward the house carried me away from West.

But in my anger, my mind cleared. A realization snapped into place. The need to vomit was gone, replaced with understanding. I stopped two feet from the door and walked back to where West was still sitting, watching me.

"You and Clayton are both idiots."

His eyes narrowed, waiting for me to go on.

"All evidence of her mother has been erased. Her mother died while Ainsley was captive in her cunt of a father's human trafficking ring. Do you think that's a coincidence?"

He opened his mouth to respond, but I cut him off.

"That little girl is a liability to him and he knows it. She exists despite him. I'm not going to put her in any more danger by letting him know she's still alive. We are going to find her a safe place to live. As far as he knows, she's disappeared and I can't imagine that he even gives a shit beyond losing the money he was going to get selling her to the highest bidder."

My stomach lurched again at the thought. I remembered my father trying to sell us off for better connections in the family. Almost twenty years later, the idea still frightened me. But the Duke wasn't going to be allowed to treat his daughter how he wanted, just because her existence was an inconvenience to him.

"Lili," West said as his hand shot out to grab my hip. "I'm sorry."

"If you think I would ever hurt a child, maybe you don't know me as well as you think."

I brushed his hand off of me and walked back toward the house. Being touched by him was the last thing I needed. Remembering my email exchange, I winced. No matter how I was feeling about him right now, going anywhere alone would be incredibly stupid. I turned back toward West, speaking over my shoulder as I opened the door.

"I have a meeting in Westwood tomorrow. You're coming with me."

WEST DIDN'T COME to bed. When I got up from our empty bed to look for him, he wasn't even in the house. After I got out of the shower, I found him in the kitchen making breakfast for Daniel. Neither of us said a word to the other.

The ride into town was silent. West kept glancing at me, thinking I didn't see his head turning as I forced my eyes to remain forward. The air between us was thick with all of the things I wasn't saying. Thoughts like a bad pop song you can't get out of your mind. Stuck in there on a loop.

Every bad thought I've had about myself. Every time I felt like I wasn't worthy of him. Maybe I really wasn't worthy of anyone. But he'd told me he loved me. After everything he had seen me do. I was reminding myself of that fact as I relived our conversation from last night.

This world was new to him. He'd already seen the worst of me. He watched me kill and torture. I had to remind myself of that, too. But if his concern for Ainsley was understandable, why couldn't I understand it? I rolled down the window, anxious to give my spinning mind a break with some fresh air.

"I still think about her every day."

I turned from the open window to look at him, but he stared at the road ahead as he continued. He tapped the scar on his forearm.

"The little girl that died because of me. I still think about her every single day."

I opened my mouth, unsure of what to say to that, but tried to summon a response. He continued.

"I guess I just couldn't live with another child getting hurt because I didn't do my job. My reaction wasn't about you. It was about me."

My lips clamped shut as I remembered what he'd told me about the embassy extraction gone bad. The family he'd shepherded to a waiting helicopter. The sniper whose shot had pierced his forearm and the little girl he'd been trying to carry to safety, killing her and wounding him.

"I'm sorry I slapped you," I offered, filled with shame at my lack of self-control. We were both imperfect people in a completely fucked situation.

"I deserved it."

"No, you didn't," I muttered.

We both went quiet. I didn't want to say that he'd still judged me. Deemed me to be a danger to that little girl. I huffed a sigh. This was exhausting. He pulled the Bronco into the parking lot. His scarred eyebrow shot up as he gave me an incredulous look.

"Why are we going to the movies?"

29

WEST

Peaceful pop music piped in through the speakers as we sat and waited for the film to begin, interrupted only by the occasional crunching by my side. At noon on a Wednesday, the theater was empty except for us. Lili scooped up another few pieces of popcorn and popped them into her mouth.

"You're going to finish all of that before the movie starts."

"You know we're not actually here to watch a movie, right?" She muttered, annoyed. "Besides, the guy said it was bottomless. If I run out, I'll just get more."

I snorted. Both our heads turned at the sound of the theater door opening. A blonde head bobbed into view. Lili nodded in confirmation but turned forward in her seat again as if this young woman was of no consequence. Merely another moviegoer. In a suit.

The blonde moviegoer sat behind us. I almost turned to look at her, but Lili pinched my arm. Lights dimmed and trailers began, filling the theater with a cacophony of sound effects and voiceovers.

Fine. I could play along. I reached over the armrest and took Lili's hand. This was the closest we'd probably ever get to an actual movie date.

"Thanks for meeting me here," Lili said, eyes still trained on the screen ahead.

"How could I say no?" the woman behind us responded with a breathy laugh. "This is a bit cloak and dagger."

"I think we both know I have a flare for drama," Lili said, smirking like a cat as she dug into the popcorn again. "There's someone I need more information on and I think you may be able to help me. Do you know a Helena Allerton?"

There was a small intake of breath behind me. Then she let out what sounded like a resolved sigh.

"Of course I do. She's on the board of EROS."

An incredibly loud action trailer started. I wasn't sure if Lili was deciding on what she was going to say to this woman or if she was just letting the trailer play out. She took a sip from the gigantic iced coffee she ordered, still quiet. The trailer ended, and Lili began speaking again.

"Tell me where she's going to be next."

Not a request. A demand.

"What are you going to do?"

The woman sounded scared. Whoever she was, she knew exactly what my girl could do.

"I can tell you, but you won't like it."

Dramatic music boomed from the speakers around us as the movie started. I'd forgotten what the hell were we seeing. A desert landscape filled the scene.

"What happened to Benjamin?"

Lili turned only slightly in her chair, not enough to look at the woman behind us but to ensure her response wasn't heard. Her voice was low and clear.

"You wouldn't like that either."

On the screen, people were chanting in a fictitious language for their newfound leader. I returned my attention to the conversation happening beside me. Lilith knew this woman and this woman knew Benjamin. I'd not met her before, but this had to be his former assistant, Juliet.

"He's dead, isn't he?"

Without seeing her face, I couldn't tell if her statement was an emotional one or not. At barely a whisper, it sounded more like a confirmation of a conclusion she'd come to on her own. Lili picked up her bag of popcorn, digging another handful out to stuff into her mouth.

"Yeah," Lili chomped casually. "But I didn't kill him."

I did.

From a hundred yards away, I put a bullet in his head. I'd wanted to do more. Make him suffer for almost stealing her from me. I'd lost so much sleep watching over her unconscious body, hoping she'd wake up from the overdose he'd dealt her. She'd discovered his secret and he almost killed her because of it.

My hand squeezed Lili's, a small reminder that she was here. She was fine. She threaded her fingers through mine and rubbed her thumb along the back of my hand. After we argued about Ainsley, I was grateful for the gentle, soothing touch.

"Good."

Lilith's resolve crumbled as she turned to look at Juliet with a look of surprise.

"That selfish prick always screwed me over when it was time for a promotion. Said he didn't want to lose a perfectly good assistant. Why do you think I answered those fake recruiting messages so quickly?"

My girl turned back around with a lupine smile. Something about that grin always heated my blood. She brought her coffee to her lips as she spoke.

"I guess don't be too good at a job you don't want to do?"

We'd stayed for the rest of the movie to avoid arousing suspicion. Juliet left, promising she'd get Lilith the information she needed as soon as she could. It seemed strange to me that she'd leap at the opportunity to help. I wasn't sure how the woman benefited from this relationship.

The question of Juliet still troubled me as I stepped outside, having had enough of the third round of Daniel's superhero movie marathon. As the door clicked shut behind me, the sound effects stopped and were replaced by the sound of chirping crickets. The faint sound of metal scraping stone met my ears as I stepped further into the open yard.

"I'm over here," Lili said, though I couldn't see her in the dark.

Ambient lights surrounded the pool, which meant she was in the landscaping somewhere. I followed the sound of the knife sliding against the whetstone.

"Marco," I called.

"Polo," she chuckled.

I found her sitting beside a pond that had been hidden by hedges. The faint sound of trickling water and light reflecting on the surface told me there was a water feature somewhere.

The tension between us had returned on the ride home. In the long, uncomfortable silence, I meditated on the state of things. Her grief and my desire to protect her. I'd told her I wasn't going anywhere and that was true. But what if she wanted me to leave?

Lilith had a habit of pushing people away. She thought that being alone was better for her. She'd told me so. The argument about Ainsley had been valid. But it could also be an excuse. A tactic to create distance between us. I'd assumed the worst. That was true. I let my bullshit cloud over what I knew of the woman I loved. Because I did love her. I always would.

With her knives laid out on a piece of fabric beside her, Lilith sat with her bare legs tucked underneath her on a small patch of grass and pushed her knife against the stone. She'd showered after dinner and come out here.

As I looked down at her, I wondered if she had anything on beneath the red flannel she'd thrown on. My flannel again. Even when she was irritated with me, she still wanted my comfort. It was something, at least.

I sat on the ground in front of her, soft grass meeting my palms as I steadied myself.

"Preparing for battle?" I joked awkwardly.

Lili snorted. With a glance at the knives beside her, she returned to her work.

"Just staying busy."

I nodded. Lili examined the knife she'd been sharpening, tucking it into its sheath beside the others on what I could now see was her roll. The new throwing knives had joined the set. She took her hair out of the messy knot atop her head, night-dark waves tumbling down around her shoulders. The idea of sifting my hands through it made my fingertips tingle.

"You know I don't like being cooped up," she sighed.

Lilith leaned back, setting her palms in the grass to hold herself up as she stretched her legs out in front. My eyes skimmed the floral tattoos on her hip, peaking out from under the shirt that barely covered them. She was beautiful like this.

I moved forward, crawling toward her. She remained propped up on her elbows, watching with guarded interest. With a kiss inside one knee, then the other, I hoped she'd let me show her how I felt. Words were failing to do the job. I spread her thighs and ran my fingers over the muscle and soft skin banded with small stretch marks. Tiny tiger stripes I wanted to worship with my tongue.

"Lili," I paused. "Let me."

The cautious expression she wore softened, replaced with understanding. An apology. That's what this was.

"Someone's going to see," she warned.

"No, they won't," I said as my fingers pulled aside the scrap of cotton to expose her. "I could barely find you out here."

"They'll hear us."

I licked her exposed flesh in a teasing stroke. Lili squeaked at the contact.

"Then I guess you'll have to be quiet."

The distance between us was too much to endure. Her grief. The family. This thing with the Duke. Every time I felt her coming back to me, something pushed her away again. I wanted to remind her that I was here for good. That I was hers. I wanted to get that hurt look on her face out of my mind.

When I told her about Ainsley, I didn't want to upset her. But it was hard to know where she drew the line now. She'd killed sixteen men on the open sea. Then saved half a dozen children from being trafficked. Between Lili's grief and her need for vengeance, I was unsure of how far her mercy extended.

Then she slapped me and I knew my fear had been for nothing. She treated the children we found with dignity and grace. Made sure each of them was bound for their homes before setting foot on a plane home. Ainsley didn't know her father. Her father didn't want her. Lili knew that.

I licked her again and again. Teasing her bare skin with taunting touches until I saw the way she gleamed for me. Her soft breaths clouded the night air. I planted a kiss at the apex of her, taking her soft bud into my mouth. She gasped.

"Quiet," I said against her. Lick, kiss, suck. "Someone will hear you, Trouble."

As I took her in my mouth again, her hips rocked against me. So responsive, my girl. I relished the feel of her soft thighs in my hands. The sweet little sounds she made. Lilith eased back onto the grass, panting softly at every touch. Every taste. Her back arched as I sucked and plunged my fingers inside of her.

"Shit!"

The word was an explosion of breath as it burst from her lips. I couldn't help but laugh. My eyes drank in every movement of her body. Her hips bucking against me. The way her hand plunged beneath the fabric of my shirt to touch her breast. Fabric gaped, exposing the wolf tattoo against her olive skin that was nearly white in the light of the half-full moon.

As she came for me, I didn't think of the uncertain path ahead. Or the things we'd endured together. Only that I didn't want her to push me away again. She was the sun. I couldn't exist without her light. I didn't need protection from the world she lived in. None of that mattered when I'd given her my heart. Every beat was for her.

I'd fantasized about making this woman my wife. Always when she was smiling and laughing with me on days that felt so far away now. Before losing Kaia, she'd pushed me away, but the distance felt navigable. Now, each time she pulled away, it felt a little further. An ocean between us that grew larger with her fear. It was only now that I worried that my dreams of our future together would be drowned in it.

30

Lilith

The backseat of the Bronco was surprisingly comfortable. West picked blades of grass out of my hair as my fingers danced along the trail of hair below his navel. Silky hairs grazed my skin, creating a tingling sensation. He was so soft here.

It felt like I could never get enough of him. By the pond, he'd made me feel desired. Swearing vows to me with every stroke of his tongue. With every touch, he silently conveyed what I needed to hear.

I'm yours.

Before West, so much of my life felt like doors closing behind me. I was so aware of how short my life would likely be. There was no ending for me that included a happily ever after. I was just one wrong move away from ending things forever. I accepted that.

I'd kissed him hard, tasting myself on his lips, and got up to run to the Bronco. He picked me up before my bare feet could hit the gravel driveway. Once inside, our fingers frantically pulled at buttons and zippers until we were skin to skin.

As he looked down at me, breathing hard after our frantic coupling, I felt it. In the shadows of his dusky green eyes, I saw everything that he wanted.

When I was a child, marriage felt like a death sentence. It was a threat. Being shackled to a man was something to be feared. My father wanted to sell my sister and me into matches that would be advantageous for him. Matches that would have likely been similar to the marriage between my parents. A powerful man and his wife, who was nothing more than a political trophy.

A living nightmare.

After my sister and I were orphaned and went to live with our grandparents, I'd forgotten all about marriage. My grandfather wouldn't let any man near us. Until college, when men became nothing more than a distraction. I fooled around with them, but nothing ever came of it. A few years later, there was Ethan, the cheating EMT, and my only serious relationship.

I'd known West then. Maybe that was why he'd kept his distance. Kept his feelings for me to himself. As my fingers played along his happy trail, I remembered watching other women watch him. As his friend. Getting irritated with their attention. As his friend. Wondering what he would feel like inside me. As a friend.

I was such a blind idiot.

Then he saved my life. In a cabin a hundred miles from here. All the noise of real life was gone. No more bullshit to hide behind. The night he kissed me, I was terrified. I still am. Maybe because he won't let me hide from him. Even if I still wanted to sometimes.

"What?"

I blinked at him in surprise.

"I can see the gears turning behind those eyes. What are you thinking about?"

"So much has changed," I said. "Do you ever wonder how we got here?"

West dropped a blade of grass into the small pile he'd been making on the floor. I hadn't realized I had that much of the lawn in there.

"Sometimes."

I shifted on my side, pulling his flannel shirt over me in a makeshift blanket as I looked up at him.

"What does the future look like to you?"

I don't know where the question came from. West's eyes went to the roof of the Bronco as if searching his mind for what he wanted to say. I tugged at his beard. He chuckled and took my hand to press a kiss in my open palm before placing our joined hands on his chest.

"The future," he started, hesitation crossing his dark green eyes as he looked at me. "I honestly don't know what it looks like."

He took a breath, his broad chest rising with the deep inhale, and removed his hand from mine. The edge of his thumb was gentle against my cheek as he took my face in his hand.

"But you know I want a future with you, Trouble."

It was impossible to mistake the hesitation in his gaze for anything else. Afraid to admit the full truth of what he wanted to me. Scared of what I'd say to him. Shame washed over me. I'd put that fear there. I felt my cheeks flush as I nuzzled into his hand, unable to say what I wanted.

I want that, too.

Tears welled in my eyes. I rested my head on his chest and fought the urge to cry. Anger boiled in my center. Anger at myself. What I wanted felt impossible. I tried to ignore my inner critic as West quietly ran his hand over my body. But even as I drifted off to sleep, I knew why I still hesitated. Our argument served as a convenient cover for my fear. Fear that whispered of loss. Of pain. Blood-soaked memories that kept me from reaching for the things my heart needed.

Pushing West away was about survival. Because everything I love gets taken away from me. Losing Kaia almost killed me. I wasn't sure I would survive losing him.

UNABLE TO SLEEP, *I climbed downstairs. Past my sister's closed door. Then my grandparents. I could hear the persistent beep of my grandmother's heart monitor through their door. As my feet padded down each wooden tread, I prayed a creaking step wouldn't give me away.*

Cold night air licked at my skin as I stepped outside, toward the garden. The grass was cool and soft beneath my feet. As I reached for my discarded tools waiting by the garden gate, a clicking sound cut through the thick quiet.

I searched for the source to find the garage door open. Carefully, I crept toward the open door. A bulb hanging from overhead lit the space, barely. Its light was partially obscured by the open hood of the Camaro. I rounded the car to see my grandfather limned in golden light.

"What are you doing out of bed, Mia Principessa?"

"I can't sleep," I said.

He stood up, the light behind him surrounding his salt-and-pepper hair. Grease-covered hands cleaned themselves, then placed themselves on his hips to give me a look of appraisal.

"Neither could I," *he sighed.* "But that's what grief does to us. It steals our peace with memories and broken promises."

"What if I can't fix it?"

Tears welled in my eyes. It was only then that I truly heard myself. I'd been speaking with not a child's voice, but a woman's. With a woman's hands, I wiped the tears from my eyes.

"It is not a thing to be fixed. What was broken cannot be undone. But you can decide."

My grandfather opened his arms, waiting for me to accept his embrace. I did so without hesitation. The familiar scent of his expensive cologne and gasoline hit my nostrils, forcing more tears from my eyes.

"What?" *I asked, my voice muffled by the cotton of his undershirt. He rocked me gently, patting my back in a rhythm I'd almost forgotten.*

"You can decide to forgive yourself. And become the woman you were always meant to be."

I OPENED MY eyes. The room was quiet. Morning had come, drenching our bed in its butter-colored light. West lay beside me, one arm bent beneath his head, watching me. Even before I let myself love him, I liked him best in the sunlight. It was as if the sun was created just for him. His bronzed skin looked like soft velvet stretched over thick muscle. The ends of his long hair glinted like gold.

West's other arm extended toward me to push loose strands of hair out of my eyes.

"You slept all night," he marveled.

I sighed, rolling onto my back to stretch my arms above my head. My toes pointed as I let my muscles bend and move for relief.

West picked his watch up off of the nightstand and looked at the time.

"Actually, almost all day. It's after two."

"Really?" I sat up in disbelief, clutching the sheets to cover myself. Clamoring for my phone, I looked at the screen to confirm the late hour for myself, as something else captured my attention. It was a message to Flora Hunter from Juliet on the job board site.

> Dear Ms. Hunter,
>
> I hope this information aids your head-hunting efforts. You will find the attached document contains links to each mentioned event where you may have the opportunity to confer with potential candidates. I hope you find who you are looking for.
>
> Juliet Ambrose

I opened the PDF to find a calendar filled with Camden Industries events. While it was crowded with various gatherings, only a few contained links to event information. Events that the EROS board would be attending. Oh, she was good. She was very, very good.

"Everything alright?" West asked as he got out of bed. I barely registered the movement.

Calculations and variables turned over in my head as I clicked through each event. If I was going to get what I wanted, I needed a big event. Somewhere someone wouldn't notice the disappearance of an attendee or two.

"Lili?"

My head snapped up.

"Is everything alright?"

I looked down at the phone, then back at him. Two weeks. It wasn't enough time, was it?

"What is it?"

I took a breath. Sorted my thoughts. After sending a polite thank you note to Juliet, I looked to West.

"Call Clayton. We have work to do."

31

WEST

The Chancer was almost empty on a weekday morning. Folk music and the scent of fried onions were floating in the air. Lilith shrugged off her jacket, exposing the dark green sweater she had on beneath it. Because I was eyeing her ass in those black jeans, I didn't see Casey standing behind the bar until Lili chirped a greeting in the redhead's direction.

"If it isn't the big bad boss of the Caccia family," Casey grinned.

Lili snorted.

The last time I'd seen the brown-eyed bartender, she was still recovering from her time in the Duke's trafficking ring. No light in her eyes. No color in her cheeks. An empty expression on her too-thin face.

That wasn't who was looking back at us now. I walked up behind Lili, trying my best to appear pleasant and friendly. For someone with Casey's past, being around men couldn't be easy. As she gave me a polite smile, I felt too aware of my size. Even if she was a few inches taller than Lili, I still towered over her. I returned her smile.

"We're here to meet Clayton. Is he here?" Lili asked.

Casey picked up a tumbler and started polishing it with a red cloth. Lili waited for her answer as I looked around the bar. No sign of Killian or his men. No sign of Clayton either. I returned my focus to Casey, who picked up another glass and got to work.

"He's here," she said, addressing the glass.

"He is?" The question popped out of my mouth before I could stop it.

"In the back. With my father."

"Oh," Lili said. "Well, we'll go back there in a minute, then. Are you doing alright?"

Casey sighed and set down the tumbler she'd polished until it gleamed brightly in the sunlight pouring in through the glass front door. Her red curls bounced as she shrugged casually.

"I'm alright. This place is keeping me sane, I think. Except for breaking up the occasional fight or brushing off a dirtbag here and there, the routine is pretty peaceful."

I nodded.

"It's nice to have a little bit of normal to lose yourself in sometimes," Lili agreed.

I put a hand on her back. Normal. I couldn't remember the last time things were normal for us. It had been weeks. Months, even. Lately, I never knew which version of Lili would show up. This morning she was pleasant enough, but how long would that last?

A pleasant silence settled between us as we watched Casey go about her work. Of course, Lili broke it only a moment later with a request.

"Is there any chance the kitchen could whip up some breakfast? I'm smelling food and it's killing me."

Casey's brown eyes lit up with her smile.

"Always thinking with your stomach. Yeah, I'll send some food in there for you two. And coffee. My father is more of a tea-in-the-morning type of person, so I'll get some coffee brewing for you."

"You're the best," Lili winked as she pushed off of the bar and started toward a door in the back of the bar.

Strolling through the space, I took in the wood paneling and cream paint. Several large leather booths with dark wood tables. Antique mirrored signs hung around the place, reflecting the sunlight coming in through small transom windows. It felt like Ronan had picked up a pub in Ireland and dropped it down in the middle of Los Angeles.

If it weren't a hideout for one of the scariest men I'd ever met, I'd drink here. Pleasant fiddling replaced the folk singers on the speakers. Lili pushed open the door. Laughter tumbled out. Ronan and Clayton sat at the end of a long table. The Irish boss sat at the head, Clayton to his left. A simple porcelain tea service sat between them.

This room seemed less worn in by daily use. Everything still smelled clean and the wood was gleaming with polish. A large black fireplace was behind Ronan's seat, though no fire was burning within it.

"Mr. Wrigley told me you two would be coming by," Ronan said.

"Hey guys," Clayton greeted us from his seat.

Ronan's three-piece grey herringbone suit was freshly pressed. The white button-down shirt he had on was nearly blinding. Lilith noted his clothing, taking up the seat on his right.

"So you always dress like this, then?" She said, glancing at Ronan's obsidian tie.

He took a sip from his teacup and set it on the saucer.

"You never know when you're going to meet your maker, Ms. Caccia. I'd like to look my best when that day comes."

Lili glanced down at her outfit as I sat down beside her. She shrugged.

"I've almost died a few times now. It didn't occur to me to be worried about what I was wearing."

Ronan laughed. The door swung open and a lean ginger young man entered, balancing a tray on one arm and holding a carafe in the other. Our host waved him in.

"I see my daughter has not lost her sense of good hospitality."

The ginger waiter rounded the table, setting two plates of food before Lili and me. As it was set down between us, I could smell the hot coffee steaming inside the carafe. Lili reached for the cream and sugar in the tea service and started fixing herself a cup.

"So," Clayton started. "I filled Ronan in on this Helena Allerton person."

Ronan's jaw tightened beneath his salt-and-pepper stubble. Lili stabbed one of the two eggs on her plate with her fork and scooped it up with some of the crispy hash.

"A woman is running the Duke's operation," Ronan growled. "You'd think she'd have a problem with selling out her own sex."

Lili huffed a laugh, washing down her bite with a sip of coffee.

"If I've learned anything from these people, it's that human decency can be forgotten for a big enough bottom line, Ronan."

He smirked at Lili. After hearing so much about the rivalry between these two families, it was strange to see them becoming friends. But I wouldn't begrudge my girl one more friend in the world, even if it was someone as frightening as Ronan.

"A couple of criminals like us becoming arbiters of human decency. What is the world coming to, I wonder?"

Lili snickered and took another bite of food. I glanced down at my plate. A matching serving of eggs, potato hash, and bacon stared up at me. Worried about offending our murderous host, I started eating and let them continue.

"If she's running things, then she has all the information we need to make the organization crumble," Clayton observed.

"Yes, and no," Ronan interjected.

Lili took a bite of bacon and sat back in her seat.

"This business of theirs earns almost one hundred billion dollars a year. That's not the kind of income anyone would give up easily. There's a reason she's trusted with this kind of information. Even if you're able to get close to this Allerton woman, she won't be easy to break."

Out of the corner of my eye, I saw Lilith's hand flex. I'd watched her chip away at Benjamin Camden. Her years of experience with extracting information would make her an expert, according to some. I've had captains who were less intimidating than my girl when she wanted to make someone crack. This Allerton woman would break. Lili would make sure of it.

"Under normal circumstances, I'd tell you I've got it covered. But in my experience, women have a higher pain tolerance than men. It's harder to get them to spill their guts. I'll just have to get creative."

Ronan let out a dark laugh and moved to refill his teacup. Clayton cleared his throat and lifted a hand.

"I hate to interrupt, but we do actually need to plan how we're going to get close to this person."

"People," Lilith corrected. "She and her husband both."

I twisted in her direction. Ronan nodded as though he already knew what she was going to say. She glanced at me and continued.

"He's always at the events with her. If she goes missing, he'll notice. If he notices, we're screwed. The whole operation will go off the radar and we'll have to start from zero. So we need to take them both."

Clayton let out a small hum and bent over, picking up the laptop I hadn't noticed before. Ronan's eyes shifted in his direction. Lilith shoved another few forkfuls of food into her mouth before Clayton spoke again.

"This schedule you sent over, that's confirmed?"

"Mm-hmm," Lili said into her cup as she took a sip. "My contact said the RSVPs are finalized for the next three events."

Shutting his laptop, Clayton looked to Ronan and then Lilith. With a half-cocked grin, he sat back in his seat.

"Let's crash a party."

32

West

A flower print sofa with ornate wooden legs faced a set of matching chairs. Pleasantly plump pink roses on gold silk sitting on what looked like possibly cherry wood. I tried to focus my attention on those details instead of the caskets lining the walls. Lili's eyes caught mine. Her eyebrows raised in amusement.

"Do funeral homes freak you out, Hale?"

"You're not uncomfortable right now?"

She shrugged and picked up a matchbook from the crystal bowl on the coffee table in front of her, reading the tiny silver letters on the small blue box before stuffing it into her pocket.

St. George Mortuary.

"When you grow up in a," she paused glancing to the door of the office our host had disappeared into. "Family as big as mine, you spend a lot of time at funerals. I think I went to two funerals a year. Kaia and I eventually started a drinking game. Drink every time someone disrespected the dead."

After our meeting, Ronan suggested we visit this establishment. With so many enemies in the world, visiting any of our usual haunts had the potential to be a death trap.

I opened my mouth to ask her how many funerals ended with her being blind drunk when our host reappeared. The statuesque woman, who must have been in her early fifties, walked back into the room and straightened her dress. The cut of it was modest. Not showing much skin. But the look of it was expensive. Paired with her flaxen bob haircut and well-tailored clothes, she looked completely at odds with the showroom decor. It was clear the granny furniture was a front, not an aesthetic preference.

We'd arrived twenty minutes ago to find her with clients. A weeping old lady and a man who looked like her son. Our host greeted us and we told her Ronan had sent us. After a curt nod, she'd asked us to wait and disappeared into her office with the mourning pair.

"Follow me, please," she said, her London-accented voice light and pleasant. Lili smirked and followed her toward a door marked with a small brass sign that read "no admittance" in black letters.

A dark stairwell greeted us as the scent of chemicals stuffed itself up our nostrils. This was definitely still a mortuary. My gut turned at the thought of what awaited below.

The click of our host's expensive heels down the metal stairway sounded ahead until they hit the tile floor. Buzzing filled the room as she flipped a light switch and fluorescent fixtures dangling from chains flickered on.

"Right," the woman said, clapping her hands together. "What can I do for you?"

"We were told by our mutual friend that you could help us acquire some," Lili paused, uncertainty splashing across her features as she searched for how to ask for what we needed.

"Supplies," the woman inserted. "Ronan told me you might be coming round."

She walked toward the wall of stainless-steel cabinets I'd been trying to ignore until now. Pale pink fingernails glinted in the fluorescent light as they pulled at a handle of a drawer near the back wall. I glanced at Lili, who watched the woman pull a steel slab out.

"I've taken the liberty of curating a small selection," she said as she tucked a short lock of smooth white hair behind her ear. "Please don't be afraid to ask for anything you don't see here."

We stepped forward to examine what lay on the slab. A black velvet cloth covered most of the steel tablet. On top of it lay several types of weapons. Pistols, rifles, and what looked like smoke bombs littered most of the surface. Lili examined the array of knives on one side. It didn't take long for a set of throwing knives to catch her eye. Smaller than what I'd seen her use. These blades looked more like spikes. She ran a finger down one edge.

"Ah, the bo-shuriken. Excellent choice."

"May I?"

The woman lifted her hand toward a corkboard mounted to the wall across the room. Lili flipped the knife in her hand, testing the weight. A teapot calendar, which appeared to be several years out of date, was the only item mounted to the board. It made a perfect target.

Her throw was quick. I was examining the illustrated teapot adorned with flowers when the blade penetrated a painted fat pink daisy. Lili turned back toward the display, gesturing at the rest of the set.

"I'll take those."

After choosing a small arsenal of weapons for ourselves, we walked toward the stairwell. Lili approached the corkboard and yanked the spiked blade from her makeshift target.

"Sorry about this," Lili said, wincing as she gestured toward the pierced paper calendar.

"Oh please," the woman replied with a laugh. "I think you've improved that ugly thing."

Lilith went quiet on the way back to our temporary home. It wasn't the normal, contemplative silence she sometimes dropped into. I knew she wasn't considering our plans. She'd been thinking of something else as her gaze fixed on the middle distance.

"Are you alright?" I asked.

She hummed but didn't respond.

"Lili," I pushed.

"What?" she snapped.

My skin tightened in irritation. It had been like this for weeks. Every time I felt like I was getting her back, she would shut me out. She'd done this before. When she was worried that she'd lose me. Now that she'd lost her sister, the shifts in her were so severe that I didn't know which Lilith I was going to get.

Grief doesn't happen in a straight line, I told myself again.

Sometimes grief looks like anger. I knew that. But I wasn't sure how much longer I could ignore the growing space between us. I could feel her distancing herself again. Giving me hope in one moment, then holding me at an arm's length from within. I loosed a sigh through my nose. There was only one thing left to do.

33

Lilith

It felt strange to be alone at the house again. This stranger's home was becoming more comfortable, but not having a constant eye on Daniel was a source of dread. I fought the urge to check my phone for the twentieth time for a message of distress from Lupo or Nico, who'd been assigned to watch them whenever they were out of my sight.

"Where's Daniel?" West said, walking into the kitchen with his sweats slung low on his hips. With all of his tattoos on display, I still couldn't take my eyes off the Kraken.

"At the hospital with Lupo. He's got a doctor's appointment today. I sent Nico with them."

West grunted as he braced an arm on the frame of the refrigerator door. I'd poked around for some breakfast but found nothing. When he looked at the empty shelves inside, he heaved a sigh.

"We'll have to do it hungry, then."

"Do what?" I smirked, grateful at the opportunity to sidetrack my anxiety for a bit.

"Talk."

He closed the refrigerator and braced his hands on the island between us. The dark mop of hair tied atop his head bobbed as he looked down at the counter.

"I don't really know how to start."

Fuck. It was going to be one of *those* kinds of talks.

Suddenly I wished I was wearing pants for this conversation. Pulling the flannel shirt I'd thrown on closed, I started buttoning it up just to collect my thoughts. Whatever he was about to say hung in the air like smoke.

"You've been through a lot. In the last few months, it's been a lot. I get that. I really do. But I thought things changed between us."

"They did," I countered, my voice wobbled with anxiety.

Damnit.

My throat tightened as a pit opened in my stomach. I didn't need this. Not right now. I'd done everything I could to avoid having a conversation like this. What was I supposed to say? I felt like I was standing on a cliff's edge as I spoke again.

"They did. You're here, aren't you?"

West huffed a humorless laugh and stood to look me in the eye.

"I'm here. And I told you I'm not going anywhere. But you're pushing me away, Lili. I can fucking feel it. Again. It's like this dance you do. One second, I think we're fine. The next, I can't feel you. I thought we were done with this shit."

"Yeah, and then my sister died," I shouted it.

It was the only way to say it aloud. It felt like frost on my tongue. Cracking the layer of ice that had been building around my heart. Flowing through my veins. I said it again, quieter to myself.

"My sister is dead."

"I know."

It was a matter of fact, the way he said it. Not cold. Not angry. My fingers knotted together in front of me. I stared at the twisted digits, unsure as to what to say.

"Her being gone doesn't change anything between us. You have to know that."

"It changes everything. I told you that people get hurt because of me. She got hurt. Daniel's life is in shambles because of me. I can't let you... It's better if you just go."

West recoiled as if I'd struck him. I looked away, unable to stand the sight of his hurt. I hadn't intended to say that. It came out of my mouth before I had a second to think about it. As I stared at my feet, I thought it was for the best. Rip it off like a bandage. Even if every part of me wanted him to stay.

"No."

I looked up.

"No. You're not ending this. I'm not going anywhere."

I looked away, anxious to hide the tears threatening to fall. His footsteps were swift and angry. I could feel him drawing near.

"You're going to stop using me to feel better and then slam a door closed when I try to get in."

When someone calls you on your shit, your first instinct is to disagree. But I had nothing. No way of arguing. Of course, I'd been aware of the wall between us. I was the one who laid every single brick.

Wet splashed my toes as I gasped for air through my tears. Putting distance between us was easier for me. Easier if he wanted to leave. If he decided this truly was too much to endure, I could make myself understand. I tried to take a deep breath. Tried to stuff down the fear. To shut the yawning pit of anxiety and sadness.

"Hey."

The word was soft as fingers tucked beneath my chin to tilt it up. West stood over me. We'd stood beside each other dozens of times, but in this moment I felt smaller than I ever had. His eyes were soft. Pained.

"Whatever it is, say it," he rasped, sliding his hand to cup my jaw. His eyes lined with tears. "I've been taking what I can get with you because I know how hard everything has been. But you can't push me away again. You can't. Please. Let me in."

I squeezed my eyes shut and took a shuddering breath. An arm wrapped around my waist, pulling me toward him. Cedar and fresh laundry. Soap. West.

"Just let me in, Trouble," he begged into my hair, voice breaking.

"I'm sorry," I whispered, opening my eyes to find him again. "I don't know how to do this."

His eyebrows furrowed. Green eyes flashed with anger. Or maybe that was fear crossing his face at whatever he thought I was about to say. Pain lanced in my chest, aching to make that look go away.

"I mean that I don't know how to explain how I feel." I wound my arms around his waist and sucked in a breath. Tucked myself into him. His scent. His warmth. The tightness in my throat forced everything out in a whisper. "I'm yours. I told you that. But I…"

One more breath. I had to take in one more breath to say the thing I never dared say out loud. Ever. To anyone. Not even Kaia.

"I'm scared. I'm not scared that you'll walk away. I'm scared that you won't."

With the caution you would use to approach a wild animal, his arms coiled around me. I felt the rumble of his voice as he spoke, sifting a hand into my hair to smooth the strands. His question was patient. Quiet.

"What do you mean?"

"So many bad things have happened to me that whenever I have something good, I'm just waiting for it to be taken away or destroyed. Everything is always destroyed. It always is."

I took a shuddering breath. West huffed a breath, waiting for me to continue.

"It's like if I let myself have you, really have you, then it's only a matter of time before you're taken away from me. And I don't want to lose you the way I've lost everyone else. I can't take it. I can't."

Each sentence pulled at the stitches over old wounds. Bleeding aches that forever lived inside of me.

"I can't," I whimpered.

"Lili," West sighed. "I understand. But you have to stop shutting me out when you get scared. Stop pushing me away. Please."

The scar tissue in my heart burst open. In his arms, I ruptured. Shuddering sobs sawed out of me as I wept. Wept for Daniel. For my sister. For myself.

When I had finally calmed enough to breathe at a steady pace, West lifted my face with his large hands, wiping tears away with his thumbs.

"Give me everything. All that pain. I can take it," West said as he pushed black strands out of my eyes. "You gave me your heart. That means it's mine to protect. But that grief you feel. That pain? Let it be a stone. Sharpen your anger against it. And use it."

I don't know how long we'd stood there. West released his grip on my face and let me press myself into him again. In his arms, I'd always felt small. As his hand combed through my hair, I let out a shallow breath. His other hand made soothing strokes down my back.

"Alright," he said after a while. "I want to keep talking. But you're useless when you're hungry."

My laugh in his chest was thick with tears. The kind of laugh that rubbed up against the raw parts of my soul. West pulled back and kissed my eyes before looking into my face with a soft smile.

"I'm going to go find us some food. Then you and I aren't leaving this house until we're on the same page," he said, letting go of me to walk toward the bedroom.

As he returned and grabbed his jacket off of the coat hook, he opened the door and paused with his hand on the knob to look back at me.

"I'm never going to stop fighting for you, Lili."

Waiting for him to come back, I pulled on sweatpants. Looked around the house for cameras. The entire time my mind turned everything over and over again like a pestle grinding on stone. Just thinking. Thinking about what I was willing to lose to my fear. To my grief. I'd already lost so much. My sister. My grandfather. Trying to push West away because I was afraid to lose him was an insane thing to do.

The logical side of my brain knew that didn't make any kind of sense. Throwing something away because I was afraid to lose it? And he was right. It was a pattern with me. But I was also someone who walked into situations faced with almost certain death to fight for what belonged to my family. I'd taken over the Caccia family because it was mine by right. Mine.

"I'm never going to stop fighting for you."

The door creaked open as West pushed through with bags of groceries. As he placed the bags on the counter and began putting them away, something clicked inside me. I'd been willing to put everything on the line for my sister. I fought for Kaia. I fought for Daniel, too. I'd almost died for them. For my family.

He looked around the kitchen for something and pulled a skillet out from under the cabinet. As he turned on the stove, we watched each other in silence. I had to stop. Stop running away. Stop being afraid. It wouldn't change anything. I could borrow tomorrow's problems and suffer without him. Or I could do what I do best. For West. The decision was simple. I could never promise to be perfect. I could only be what I am. For him. This man. He was mine. He was mine and I was his.

I would fight for him, too.

34

WEST

We'd spent three days locked up in that house. During that time, she told me everything. Every single thing. Every man she'd ever been with. Every wound that was inflicted by her father. On her. On her sister. And all of the fears that came with them.

The nightmares she had started to make sense. The anxiety. So many of her little behaviors. If the man wasn't dead already, he'd be in a body bag by now.

"Good morning," she said, rolling over to face me.

I'd been awake for hours thinking about, well, everything.

"Good morning, Trouble," I said, returning her smile.

Our talks were only interrupted by the presence of Lupo and Daniel, the two of them joining us for meals or movies. Watching Lili smile and laugh as she played checkers with him filled me with a sort of hope. Hope that things will get better. The thing about hope is, though, it doesn't mean anything unless you're willing to work for what you want.

I was willing to work for her. For us. For the future that I knew was possible with her. Settling down with a mafia boss certainly hadn't been in my life plans, but settling down with Lilith Caccia was. Waking up to this woman by my side was enough reason to fight through anything.

She hummed as she stretched. Still sleeping in one of my tee shirts, it bunched around her waist as my arm hooked around it. Pulling her toward me for a kiss, I relished the feel of her against me.

"You feel so good," I sighed, squeezing her ass just to feel more of her.

Lili's hand traveled down between us, nails softly grazing my length before curling around it. She laughed at the push of my hips into her hand as she stroked me.

"Oh, you're in trouble now."

A knock on the door interrupted the plans I had for this morning, as a small voice called through the wood.

"Do you guys want pancakes?" Daniel shouted.

Clearing my throat, I shouted back.

"Yeah, buddy. Give us a few minutes."

Lili's laugh was a soft, beautiful thing. I eyed the way she bit into her index finger, stifling more laughter at what had to be a pained expression on my face. Sitting up, she pushed her hands through her hair and yawned.

"Hey," I grumbled. "Where do you think you're going?"

"Breakfast?"

"Fine," I sighed. "But I want to talk to you about something. An idea."

She turned toward me, crossing her legs beneath her. I had her full attention.

"It's about Lupo and Daniel. I think you should tell Daniel what you know about his father. Both of you should. Together."

Teeth sunk into her lower lip. Dark brows bunched together, considering. I reached out and twirled a lock of night-dark hair around my finger. Fuck, she was beautiful in the morning.

"Yeah," she breathed, not making eye contact with me.

I sat up and took her jaw in my hand, only satisfied when her eyes locked onto mine.

"Whatever you're afraid of, tell me."

"What if he's angry at us for lying?" She said her voice barely above a whisper.

"Then keeping it from him any longer won't make it any better," I countered.

Lili nodded, her chin dipping into my palm with the motion. I pressed a kiss to her mouth, the feel of her lips rekindling my need for her.

"I was thinking we could go to Laundrette today. Pick up some cash?"

"Sure."

The change in subject wasn't surprising. She needed to think about what I'd said. But I had no doubt she'd arrive at the same conclusion.

PANCAKES, LAUGHTER, AND Lili's lips wrapped around me in the shower. I couldn't ask for a more perfect morning. I was basking in the perfection of it for the whole drive to Lilith's laundromat, Laundrette.

She'd revealed this business to me in a moment of desperation. I wasn't sure even her sister knew about it. We pulled up to the building. The first thing I noticed was the sign.

"You had it repainted?"

"Yeah," Lili laughed. "I couldn't leave it like that."

Admiring the hand lettering that now read "Open 24 Hours," I followed her inside. The long black ponytail she wore swished with every step, almost grazing the top of her black jeans. Before she could ask, I hoisted her up. She squealed at the contact, but then shifted a ceiling tile to find what she needed. The lock box containing her set of keys was still there.

We opened the coin deposits for washers, dryers, vending machines, and change makers. Thousands of dollars in bills and change later, we stuffed the money into discarded detergent boxes and started loading it into the back of the Bronco.

"Is that the last of them?" Lili asked from the doorway.

"Yup. Four boxes," I said, heaving the last box into the cargo bed.

"Great, I'm going to finish closing up."

Turning to head inside, I watched her walk away.

Stars burst across my vision as what felt like a fist connected with my cheekbone. Then another hit struck my side. A foot kicked my knees forward, forcing me to the ground. It all happened fast. Too fucking fast.

"She just went inside," my attacker grunted. "Find her."

Bile rose in my throat as I thought of Lili being ambushed. Two men disappeared into the doorway. Cold steel pressed into my temple as a man tied my hands together behind my back. Maybe she'd gotten away. That's all that mattered.

He hauled me to my feet and pushed me forward, attempting to walk into a small alleyway. If I was going to get away from this guy, the smaller space might work to my advantage. As we passed a dumpster, I planned my escape.

"Don't worry," the man said, his voice thick with the cigarettes I could smell on him. "You'll be reunited faster than you think."

"Well, you're right about that."

Lili stood behind us, her small stature obscured by the dumpster. How she was so quiet in those combat boots, I'd never know. The men he'd been with lay dead at her feet. Sharp spikes protruding from their necks. Her cropped white tee shirt was splattered in a red mist. A matching spike was in her hand, carefully scraping under her nails. Cleaning them like she hadn't a care in the world, even though her chest still heaved to take in air.

She must have seen them. I saw them and went out the back door to hide behind the dumpster. I wasn't sure if it was the blow to the head, but I couldn't help marveling at the woman before me.

"Don't make another move, sweetheart, or I'll splatter him all over the ground."

My captor, the last man standing, pressed the pistol to my side. I'd been in situations far worse than this. Been injured worse than this. This man would soon be dead, just like his friends. He just didn't know it yet.

"Drop the knife," he said, pressing the weapon into my side.

His voice was shaking. Maybe he did know.

Her full lips lifted at the corner. Any other man would ignore it. Think it was a laugh. They'd think she didn't understand the situation she was in. I knew it for what it was. A snarl. A warning.

I shoved my body into him, pushing him off balance. The blade whipped past my head. Into his eye.

"Fuck!" He cried. "Fuck."

The second word was soft. Falling out of his mouth. A gasp. The mouth that started to gape and twitch like a fish out of water. I'd barely seen the guy. A blonde man a few years younger than me, dressed in street clothes. Someone I wouldn't have taken a second look at. The other two men were dressed the same. Just another couple of guys. I cursed myself for the oversight.

But she'd seen them coming.

Lilith bent down and picked up a gun from one of his dead partners. Releasing the safety, she squatted down and pushed the barrel beneath his still-gaping jaw. Her gold eyes went cold as she bid him farewell.

"Tell your friends I said hello."

35

Lilith

He knew everything about me. That Duke. I cursed him as I worked at the stain in my tee shirt. They had to have staked out my laundromat, but how did they find out about it? It wasn't in my name. It belonged to Flora Hunter.

I cringed as realization washed over me. Flora Hunter. The name I'd used to check into the hotel in Belfast. The name I'd used to book my flight to Ireland. Whatever resources he had available to him, he'd used them to figure out my alias.

After checking on Lupo and Daniel, I barricaded myself in our bedroom. I was grateful for the black stone shower as I washed blood off of myself. I kill people for a living. Or, I used to. I'm not allowed to have a hangup about blood. I'm just not. Once the scorching water had blasted off the last of it along with what felt like my last layer of skin, I wrapped myself in a towel, rushed to my bedside table, and threw the top drawer open.

West entered, still on the phone with Clayton. I pulled out everything I had in Flora Hunter's name. Credit cards. Passport. The only thing missing was her birth certificate and Social Security Card. Both forgeries were locked away safely in the house.

"What are you doing?" West asked, pulling the phone away from his ear.

"My alias is compromised. So is everything attached to it."

After grabbing the other thing I needed, I scooped up the tainted items and strode past him into the bathroom. He followed me in, watching as he listened to Clayton. I picked up the metal trash can and placed it in the center of the shower. Each item clanged as I tossed them into the can.

"Lili?" West asked as I pulled open the little blue matchbook. Silver lettering glinted in the light. St. George's Mortuary. I struck a match and dropped it into the can.

"Until this is fixed, Flora Hunter is dead."

IT WAS DARK. So dark. Still, I moved forward. My feet slipped, even as I took careful steps. Black. My eyes struggled to see in the oppressive darkness.

"Hello?"

My voice was foreign to my ears. Unsure that anyone had heard me, I tried again.

"Hello?"

Faint light seeped from an open door ahead of me. My unsteady feet carried me through it. The scent of flowers stuffed itself up my nostrils. I looked around for the source. Glistening black gravel lined either side of the walking path ahead. It nearly disappeared beneath the blooming lilies that stood up like birthday candles.

I bent over to examine them more closely. The black petals. The green stalks. But instead of a stamen, burned a flame. Each flower flickered with its own light.

The flowers provided enough light for me to see what surrounded me, just as that light had guided me forward. Ahead of me, the small room was lined with black stone boxes. Black engraved plaques labeled each one. I took another step forward.

Water. It felt deeper than before. The door slammed shut behind me. I continued on the path ahead. Water pooled around my feet. Up my ankles. The little flaming lilies were doused. The room became dark and cold. The water was so cold.

It crawled up my neck. I strained, balancing on the balls of my feet to keep my head above the water. Cold. Black. Alone.

"Hello?" I called, my lips and nose barely peeking through now. The darkness seemed to swallow my voice. I tried once more. A desperate last whisper before fear and cold swallowed me whole.

"Hello?"

THE FOUR OF us sat in the living room. Daniel laughed quietly at the morning cartoons on the TV. Lupo, West, and I exchanged tense looks. After dinner last night, we'd spoken with the old man and decided it would be now. Today.

"He needs to know that he has more family in the world. It'll help him," West reminded. "It's better than living with a lie."

Lupo gazed down at the picture cupped in his hands, still worn around the edges from the inside of his wallet. Dante. Daniel's father. My sister's secret romance. I reached over and squeezed his arm. We could do this. We'd behaved like family for decades.

West picked up the remote and muted the TV as soon as a commercial came on. Daniel's head snapped in his direction.

"Hey, buddy," I interjected. "Can we talk for a second?"

"About what?" Daniel twisted in his seat, pulling his little legs under himself as he faced me.

"Well, do you remember when you and your mom talked about telling the truth?" I asked, remembering Kaia's struggle to break him from lying for fun.

"Yeah," he said, hesitation in his voice.

"You're not in trouble, it's not that," I said, trying to ease the tension we were certainly all feeling.

"What she's trying to say is that we have to tell you the truth now," Lupo said, photo face down on his lap.

"Oh."

I examined Lupo, who returned my gaze. Now was as good of a time as any.

"We want to tell you about your dad."

Daniel's eyes went wide. I remembered being asked about his father a dozen times. He'd always wanted to know. But I couldn't tell him what I didn't know. Now that I did know, it didn't feel like my business. Lupo cleared his throat.

"Your dad," Lupo started. "He was a good man. A strong man. His name was Dante. He worked for your great-grandfather. Protecting him. Like your Zia protected you and your mom. He was very good at it."

"Was he a boxer?" Daniel asked, a note of excitement entering his voice.

"Oh yeah," Lupo chuckled. "Knocked me on my ass a time or two."

I laughed. Maybe from nerves. West reached out, placing a big, warm hand on my back. Of all the situations I'd been in lately, this one was making me sweat.

"Wow," Daniel said, a note of awe in his voice.

We all went silent for a moment.

"Did you know him?"

Lupo sat back on the sofa, looking down at the picture in his hand. For a moment, I thought I glimpsed tears in his eyes. He let out a sigh, deciding to charge forward with the plan. Our plan. Make it easy. Make it tangible.

"Yeah, I knew him," he said, moving the photo to show Daniel. "This is a picture of me, Nico, and him. Nico is his brother."

Daniel thought for a moment. Calculating. Dark brown eyes fixed on me. Smart kid.

"That means he's my uncle, right?"

I nodded.

"But you're Nico's dad," he said. "Does that mean you're his dad, too?"

West and I both looked at Lupo. He was silent for a moment. Tears now rolled down his stubbled cheeks. I moved my hand to his and gave it a squeeze.

"I'm his dad," he said quietly. He took a deep breath. Then another. "Which means I'm your grandpa."

The little boy's eyes went wide again.

"I have a grandpa?"

For most of his life, it was just me and Kaia. We did everything for him. Took him to the beach. The mountains. Even Disneyland. We were his whole world. But now, with his mother gone, he deserved more. Lupo lifted his head, finally looking Daniel in the eye.

"Is that ok?"

"I have an uncle and a grandpa," Daniel said with a smile.

He scooted awkwardly toward Lupo, looking up at the old man. That guy faced down the scariest mafiosos in Los Angeles for over twenty years. This was the most frightened look I'd ever seen on his face.

"Can I call you Grandpa now?"

Lupo started laughing, thick and loud through his tears. He wrapped an arm around Daniel, pulling him into his side before tousling his dark curls.

"Yeah, Champ. You can call me Grandpa."

I leaned into West's side, grateful for this light moment amid so much darkness. Lupo handed his grandson the picture he'd shown him. Daniel looked at it, carefully cupping the picture in his hands like a baby bird.

"He looks like me."

36

West

Sitting at the bar, I glanced at my phone again. No word from Lili. She'd instructed Nico to go into her apothecary and meet her with every item on a list of ingredients and equipment she'd laid out for him. Supplies for tomorrow.

They'd decided to meet at a neutral location. Even though it was a terrible idea, I offered to cancel on Clayton and Ronan and go with her. She refused. So now I was sitting here sipping the beer Casey had poured me, waiting for Clayton, hoping she was safe. Nico would tell me if something happened. Wouldn't he?

The door of the Chancer swung open. Clayton walked in, horn-rimmed glasses perched on the end of his nose. His black sweater was pushed up above his forearms. I noted the motorcycle boots peeking out from under his jeans. He rode the Triumph here.

"Hey," he nodded, pushing a hand through his wind-swept hair.

I wasn't sure if he was talking to me or the red-headed bartender behind me.

"What can I get you?" Casey asked all business.

He gestured to my pint of beer.

"One of those, please."

Though the words were casual, his request was soft. Tentatively, he approached the bar. Casey grabbed a glass and pulled on the tap, waiting for the dark Irish beer to reach the proper height before stopping the tap. The three of us existed in tense silence as we waited for her to finish to top it off. Perfect. The pint had a beautiful head of foam atop the sea of dark beer as Casey approached us with it in her hand.

The glass slammed onto the bar top. Foam spilled over the rim. Without a second look, Casey walked away. Clayton reached over the bar to grab some cocktail napkins, cleaning up the mess.

"What did you do to her?" I asked.

"Nothing," Clayton responded. "Come on."

Striding toward the back room, I spotted Killian and his men sitting around the table beside the door.

"Blackjack," Killian nodded at me with a smirk. "Why do they call ye that?"

"Because his hits never miss," Clayton interjected, patting my shoulder as he opened the door. "Don't give him a reason to shoot you, Killian."

With a tattooed hand, Killian raised his pint to me and laughed. I shook off the odd toast and entered behind Clayton.

The fire roared in the fireplace behind Ronan. Its light flickered off of the whiskey glass sitting before him. Just him. The room was in near darkness except for that. Clayton went to flip the light switch.

"Don't," Ronan growled.

I cleared my throat and took up a seat beside the Irish mob boss. Clayton had told me their last name had something to do with the Celtic god of Death. Tonight, Ronan looked the part.

Wearing a smoke-colored suit, Ronan's signet ring flickered in the light as he flipped his lighter open and closed.

"I know you two have got plans for tomorrow. But I need your assistance with something tonight."

Clayton took the seat at his other side, lacing his fingers together in front of him. Ready for orders. I tried to keep my expression neutral.

"What's the job?"

THEY ALWAYS SHIT themselves. My eyes teared at the stink the bodies created. For what Ronan was paying us, this was easy work. But as I hauled another body into the oil barrel beside me, I wondered if it was worth it.

"Is that the last one?" I asked, watching Clayton drag a man from under his arms toward an empty barrel.

"Yeah," he grunted. "This is the last of them."

Blue eyes pinned open, the man's forehead was still leaking blood from the bullet wound. I pushed his eyelids shut as Clayton closed the barrel lid.

"This is not how I was expecting this night to go."

I let out a chuckle. Things definitely took a turn.

As the man who was paying for our services, Ronan decided that our assistance wasn't optional. While his men were still searching every shipping container they could find with the tracking numbers Lili had provided, the Arawn clan was spread thin. That was where we came in.

"There's an auction tonight. I need you to disrupt it. Killian and his men will assist you."

Half a dozen identical office buildings surrounded us. Each of them looked like a cement brick with small rows of windows. A business district in the middle of the suburbs. That's where this auction was going to be held. Or at least, where it was supposed to be. With the few very wealthy attendees, their security seemed comedically small. Equipped only with pistols and earpieces, I wondered if these mall-cop-looking bastards even knew what they were protecting.

The auction, as it turned out, was for children. Children like Ainsley. Like Daniel. I shuddered, thinking about the men who wanted to purchase them. It wasn't hard to execute every last one.

Our targets had entered a conference room that looked more like a lecture hall, ready to start their bidding on the small selection of children. While Killian's men found and moved the children, Clayton and I stood by in the shadows of the lecture hall as the customers waited for the auction to begin. They weren't kept waiting for long.

As Clayton had informed Killian, my hits never miss. Between the two of us, six men were dead within seconds.

Killian backed the flatbed truck up to where we'd been loading deceased customers into barrels. Clayton and I hefted barrel after barrel onto the flatbed. When the last one was secure, Clayton left me to sweep the building for any last scrap of evidence that we'd been here. I approached Killian, who sat in the idling truck. There was one thing I had to know.

"How did your father know about this?"

Killian's dark eyes were as cold as his father's as he looked me over, uncertain about sharing the answer with me. With a shrug, he spoke.

"I keep forgetting that you're new to all of this. Our family is well known around the docks. We've got our hands in importing and exporting goods. One of our associates got wind of what was happening here. Found the organizer and turned him over to us. After some face time with my father, the man was amenable to giving us the details."

I didn't need much more of an explanation. Ronan didn't seem like the understanding type. When I didn't speak, Killian went on.

"Much like your woman, my father has a gift for encouraging conversation. She uses her poisons and blades. He uses... other things."

The building's steel door slammed shut. Clayton twirled his finger in the air, a signal to get going. We were all clear.

"Oi, Blackjack. Disco. It's payday," Killian laughed, calling out the window as he pulled away. "See you boys around."

As we walked away from the building and down the street, Clayton lifted his mask off of his face. I followed suit, rubbing my face to relieve the sensation of my beard being compressed beneath it.

"How are things with you and Lili? Any better?"

A half-cocked grin crossed my face. Better? That was a word for it. We were the best we'd ever been. As though my expression was answer enough,

Clayton slapped me on the shoulder. I repositioned the gear bag I was carrying.

"See, man? That's what I'm talking about. You two have got something. It's rare."

"Yeah, I know."

Unlocking the Bronco, I tossed the gear bag in the back seat and hopped in. With the key in the ignition, I glanced at Clayton who climbed into the passenger seat. A contemplative countenance had taken over his previously jubilant face. It didn't take much work to figure out why. Spilled beer and an angry redhead.

"You know," I started. "I knew right away that Lili was it for me. But it took over six years to get where we are now."

Clayton grunted. I shifted into gear and went on as we headed back to the Chancer.

"All I'm saying is that for the right girl, the wait is worth it."

For a long while, things were silent. I turned on the radio. My thumbs were drumming a beat along with the Stones when Clayton finally spoke.

"How do you know she's the right girl?"

I glanced at him. He turned to look at me, street lights flashing off of the glasses he'd put back on as he waited for my answer. With two fingers, I tapped my chest.

"Here, man. You know it in here."

37

Lilith

Convenience. It will kill us all. Or at least, it will kill the wealthy. People to drive your cars. Care for your children. Make your food. Pour your drinks.

Helena Allerton and her husband Frederick were attending a charity event. It doesn't matter what for, the organization probably spent most of its donations on the champagne bar. The hotel's pristine view of the Los Angeles skyline couldn't be beat and the organization had likely paid a pretty penny for that as well. Not to mention the heating units they'd placed all over the terrace.

I poured another glass for a glittering socialite as I watched Helena and Frederick walk over to the glowing marble bar. Speaking in low, harsh voices. People like them ignore waitstaff. Things just appear. So when they approach me, they continue the conversation as if I'm not even there.

"She's dropping out? After everything I did to get her into that program in the first place, that ungrateful little bitch better kiss her trust goodbye."

Lovely. Suddenly I wasn't feeling so guilty for separating this girl from her parents. She might enjoy the reprieve.

"Helena, that's hardly fair. She got a job offer and she's taking it. It's a great opportunity. That's what college is for, right? Great opportunities."

Helena gave her husband a flat look. An *I create our daughter's opportunities* look. I popped a new bottle of champagne and poured a glass, sliding it across the glowing bar top to Frederick. I poured another and slid it to Helena. They continued their conversation. I assumed it was about their perfect pedigreed daughter. The one who'd been to boarding school in Switzerland where her roommate was a literal princess. The one who'd been in the middle of getting an Ivy League education, which she wanted to quit.

Frederick looked beaten down. Tired. His brown eyes were kind. Almost kind enough to make me forget how he and his wife paid for their daughter's expensive education.

"I've had enough of this. Let's go home."

I glanced at my phone. Two text messages awaited my reply.

> **NICO:** The meeting went well. Everyone is on board with the new directive.

> **WEST:** Driver paid. Security dealt with.

I sent West an immediate response.

> Be out front in five.

I topped off Frederick and Helena's glasses with the dregs of the champagne bottle I'd left open and reserved for them. The bottle I'd avoided reaching for every time I poured a glass for someone else. The bottle I'd added just a touch of a powerful sedative to. They both toss back the remainder of their drinks and head for the door.

"That's not going to kill them, is it?" West asked as we worked in the dining room at my makeshift apothecary.

"No," I promised. "They'll pass out pretty quickly, though, so we have to move fast."

At six feet, Clayton stood about four inches shorter than West. He's more easily ignored than West. Just another man in a uniform. At least, that's what I wanted the Allertons to think as they got into their car without looking at the driver who held the door open for them. It would be only a minute or two before both Allertons blacked out completely. Clayton winked at me as he opened the driver's side door.

A nondescript black Mercedes pulled up to the curb behind their Maybach. I hopped in. West had the driver's seat pushed back, possibly as far back as it could go. The white button-down shirt he'd been wearing was rolled up to the elbow, exposing the black tentacles coiling down his muscular forearm. His hair was braided back, holding all of the tendrils that usually fell out of his bun.

As we pulled away from the curb to follow the Maybach, I started undressing.

"This goddamn catering uniform doesn't breathe," I explained as West arched his eyebrow at me.

"What have I told you about doing that while I'm driving?"

"I ignored you then. I'm ignoring you now," I grunted as I tossed the shirt into the backseat and pulled a tee shirt over myself. "You didn't want to change?"

He shrugged, turning as we made a right toward our destination. Miles away from the upscale hotel the Allertons had been residing in for their trip. The hotel they'd unknowingly checked out of when they left for their evening out. I looked down at my phone, hoping for an update on that situation, and was greeted with a message from Nico.

All clear. Everything has been moved.

I thanked him, firing off the message as our car arrived at the Pal's parking lot. West pulled the car around back. The entrance used for deliveries and immediate basement access was dimly illuminated by the small, dim security light overhead.

The Allerton's Maybach pulled in behind us. Clayton hopped out of the car, tossing the driver's hat inside behind him with a flourish. I chuckled.

"Your guests are unconscious. Still breathing, though."

West opened the rear door, peeking in at the Mr. and Mrs. With a grunt, he stood. I strode to the back door and unlocked it.

"This will be quite a step down from their luxurious accommodations for the evening, I fear."

West hefted Frederick Allerton over a shoulder. I cringed as he shifted the lean man. At close to six feet, he was probably not light. Between him and Clayton, I felt grateful not to be on my own anymore.

38

WEST

Little iridescent beads caught the light as Lilith's luscious form moved through the dark hall. Her night-dark hair was in loose curls around her shoulders. The makeup she wore only highlighted her natural beauty. She was a goddess tonight. The long, sheer fabric of her dress grazed the floor as she and Benjamin Camden passed me.

For him.

She'd gotten all dolled up for him. Just as she had every time she'd been out with him. Logically, I knew this was part of the act. But logic didn't keep the sour taste of jealousy off of my tongue as I watched Benjamin Camden and Lilith go into a small room together.

I'd tucked myself away in a corner. Just an observer of the bacchanal that surrounded me. Bodies writhed together. Sounds of ecstasy drowned out the angelic tones of various stringed instruments. But it wasn't them I watched.

It was the door.

She was in there. With him. Alone.

It didn't take much imagination to picture what they were doing in there. If it were me, I would have taken her into that room, so I didn't have to share her pleasure with anyone else. I sighed through my nose as I reminded myself that it was not me locked away with her. It was him.

But then Benjamin and a large bald man came out. Another man. Which meant he'd been waiting in there for them. For her.

Panic flooded my veins as I waited for them to get out of sight. Camden looked ruffled, taking out a handkerchief to dab at his nose. He'd taken a blow. He'd come out without her. She put up a fight and he'd won.

Benjamin and the bald man disappeared around a corner. As I opened the door carefully, only one thought filled my mind.

If my Lili is dead, I will rip Benjamin Camden's spine out through his goddamned throat.

I cringed as the door slammed closed behind me. This was not a room designed for pleasure. No. It was a utility closet. A bare bulb dangled from the ceiling. Shelves had a few cleaning supplies here and there. And Lili... Her head was angled back, lips parted as she breathed shallow breaths. Her hands were tied behind her back, her body looking broken, limp in the chair she was bound to.

"No, no, no."

She whimpered as I knelt beside her, taking her head in my hands for a closer look. A bruise bloomed on her cheek.

I am going to end that fucker.

"Stay with me. Eyes open. Come on, Lili. Look at me."

Her eyes fluttered. Gold and gorgeous, they locked on me. Just for a moment. Her lips formed a silent word. West. Then her eyes closed again. Fuck.

"I've got you. Eyes on me. Please, Lili. Please, don't give up on me."

I cut away the binding from her wrists and ankles, careful not to let her slide to the ground. She was heavy in my arms. Deadweight, yes, but not dead. I wouldn't let her die. Not here.

Hefting her into my arms, I pushed my way out of the room. The surrounding people were too lost in their revelry to pay any mind to a man carrying out an unconscious woman.

Unconscious, I told myself. Not dead.

Two waiters with white feather masks pushed into their hair shared a cigarette in the alley. Each of them looked barely old enough to drive, let alone work a party like this. One of them eyed me warily as I carried Lili to my SUV.

"Too much to drink," I tried to laugh casually.

The other waiter got impatient and nudged him for the cigarette. His attention returned to his coworker, both of them too occupied with stealing time away from their jobs to pay any more mind to the man loading a girl in his passenger seat. They continued to ignore me as I sped off into the night.

I knew exactly where to go. I fired off the text message, sure she was there. She better be there.

Lanna was waiting in the parking lot with a medical bag when I arrived. As I had asked, she helped me pull Lilith into the backseat, examining her as best she could in the minimal light.

"She's got a pulse. Barely."

I could do nothing but watch and hope as I knelt beside them. Hope that I haven't gotten there too late. That I hadn't failed the woman I... I'd been too big of a coward to confess anything to her. That day in the gym, I'd had an opening and couldn't say the words. I'd just made her cry and felt like an asshole. What was all of that worth now?

"She's getting cold," Lanna said. She lifted Lilith's hand and examined her nails. "They're blue. Looks like an OD. What did she take?"

"I don't know. She was barely conscious when I found her. I think they poisoned her. She was all tied up. She didn't do this to herself."

Lanna searched through her bag and pulled out several objects. A needle, a small bottle, and a bag of what looked like saline. My sister started searching through her bag again, speaking to me as she did so.

"Talk to her. Give her something to fight for."

I took Lili's hand in mine, squeezing, trying to rouse her. Something to fight for. The words were on the tip of my tongue. Instead, I just begged.

"Come on, Lili. Stay with me. Open your eyes!"

A twitch of her fingers told me she'd heard. She heard me. For just a second, her eyes opened. Glassy and unfocused. Until they found me. And closed again.

"No, no, no. Lili, come on. Come on, gorgeous, stay with me."

Lanna pillaged through her medical bag and cursed.

"I need some cord or something."

"For what?"

"I need to hook her up to a drip. She needs fluids and an antagonist now or we're going to lose her."

I suddenly regretted not wearing a tie. My hands searched my person until I looked down at Lili again. It was a shame to hurt something so beautiful, but I ripped a strap from her dress, pulling the silk fabric away for a makeshift tourniquet.

Lanna tied the strap around Lilith's arm, pulling tight. A light tap of her fingers told me she'd found a vein. I could feel myself wince as I watched the needle plunge into smooth olive skin and administer the antagonist. My sister sat back and looked at her watch.

"Now what?" I asked.

"Now we wait."

Wait to see if we were too late. To see if I'd well and truly failed her. As Lanna and I sat in silence, watching Lilith for any sign of life, I decided. I kissed her forehead and whispered against her skin.

"If you make it out of this alive, Trouble, I'm never letting you go."

THE CLICKING OF a twisting ratchet filled my ears, drowning out my thoughts. I'd dreamt of Lili near death again. The memory exhausted me. Watching her barely cling to life wasn't a memory I would forget soon. The seven-figure payday I'd found in my accounts certainly didn't do anything to calm me down. Working on the engine of the Bronco was enough to center me. At least for the time being.

"I'm sorry."

I leaned out from under the popped hood. Lupo stood there with his hands in his pockets, squinting at the work light I had attached overhead. Somehow at night, he always looked a little bit older. A little more tired, maybe. He peered over his shoulder, probably making sure Lili was still inside with Daniel.

Searching around for a rag to wipe my hands on, I came up short. Lupo handed me a bandana from his back pocket.

"Thanks," I said as I cleaned the grease off of my hands.

"I helped raise that girl like she was one of my own. I'd never do anything to hurt her."

Lili. He looked back at the house, like he could see her inside reading with Daniel in his temporary bedroom.

"I know," I offered.

Leaving the bandana on the roll next to my tools, I leaned back against my truck and gave Lupo my full attention. The old man took a breath, then brought a hand out of his pocket in a beseeching gesture.

"I'm not so good at apologizing. But I'm glad you're here," Lupo said, adding with a rough laugh, "I'd probably be dead now if you'd listened to me."

He was trying. I'd known the man for long enough to understand that this was the best he could do. With a sigh, I folded my arms and gave him a smile.

"As you've told me a dozen times, I'm a stubborn bastard."

A chuckle rumbled in his chest. He moved closer, placing a hand on the Bronco to look over its engine.

"Something wrong with it?"

"It was built in 1973, Lu. There's always something wrong."

He nodded. A sideways glance in my direction. An arched grey brow. He cleared his throat to say something but seemed to be hesitating. Our conversations always started like this. Bullshit first. Real shit second.

I still remember the night I told him I was in love with Lilith. He didn't mince words then.

"Don't tell me. Tell her."

Lupo picked up a pair of pliers, feigning interest for a moment. We could be here all night. I cleared my throat. He spoke, still not meeting my gaze.

"I need your help."

I arched a brow, waiting for him to elaborate. He set down the pliers and looked at me. If it weren't for the work light, I wouldn't have seen the tears lining his eyes.

"There's something she needs to know."

39

Lilith

Eventually, you learn what a lie sounds like. The sentence might be completely ordinary coming out of someone's mouth, but the words. The words sound wrong. Only a trained ear can sort them out. I've had years of experience.

Perched atop the worktable, I surveyed my tools as my captives watched me with horrified interest. Nico had done a wonderful job of getting the space ready for my work. Though he'd offered to do the job, I'd told him I was itching to get my hands dirty.

"Do you know why you're here?" I asked.

I picked through the bag of trail mix for a piece of chocolate candy and popped one in my mouth. West was insistent on buying healthy snacks since we had Daniel to think about but this trail mix was just fodder for the trash can. Wistful thoughts of my sister's secret stash of candy bars floated through my mind as I crunched loudly.

"Well?" I pushed, tossing the remainder of the trail mix away.

Helena Allerton gave me a disgusted look. Her husband muttered something around his bowtie. They'd only been here for twenty-four hours and I'd had enough of his whining already.

"You tell me."

"Oh, come on. You know. You're here because you ruin lives. You take something that doesn't belong to you and sell it. Them."

Helena gave a pointed look around the space. The drain. The hooks. The worktable filled with instruments of pain.

"I suppose you think you're some kind of saint."

"Hardly," I mocked, hopping off of the table with a pair of needle-nose pliers. "But I don't hide what I am."

Sauntering up to the husband, I tucked a finger under the improvised bow tie gag and pulled it down.

"Anything to contribute here, Freddy?"

"Please. Our daughter," Frederick started.

"Ugh. Don't worry. I don't prey upon innocent women and or children. Unlike your wife," I said, returning my attention to the woman in question. "I just want to know how you sleep at night, Helena."

Frederick's eyes narrowed, as though he was trying to understand what I'd just said. I asked myself if it was possible he didn't know. Surely he must.

"If I had to guess, I'd say I wasn't the first person locked up in here. How do you?" Her question was sharp. She must be hungry.

"How do I do what?"

"Sleep."

The pliers felt heavy in my hand. I shoved down the urge to use them. Questions first.

"I ask the questions, Helena."

She smirked at me. I imagined that smirk as she watched someone in customer service get fired for her superfluous complaint. That kind of smirk was practiced. It was the sort of thing someone cultivates from years of getting exactly what they want. The smirk of a house cat after it knocks a vase off a table.

The thought made the scent of her perfume turn rancid in my nostrils.

"Ballet Dancer?" I asked.

"What?"

"The color on your nails. That soft, pretty pink. It's called Ballet Dancer, isn't it?" I took her nails in my hand to examine them more closely. Her hands flexed against the arms of the chair they were bound to. "It's a lovely shade."

"Stop it."

"No."

It was my turn to smirk.

Index fingers stick out more than thumbs. Thumbs are filled with muscle. Strong from our dependence on them. They curl in as a reflex. We protect them instinctively. But the index finger sticks out. It was easy to rip the almond-shaped nail from its bed. Helena tried and failed to pull against my grip with a scream that sounded like it came from her gut. Too bad.

Metal screeched on the floor as Frederick tugged against his restraints, trying to get to his shrieking wife.

"Stop! Don't hurt her!"

"Helena, look at me," I cooed. "Answer my questions and this stops."

"You didn't ask me any questions," she spat.

"Please! We don't know anything. You've got the wrong woman. She didn't do anything."

Still holding his wife's hand in mine, I looked up at Frederick. His face, which was handsome in a bland way, was now leeched of color. Terrified.

"I asked you three questions," I corrected her.

"No, you didn't!"

"Count again."

She was quiet for a moment, looking down at her bare feet as she tried to recall our conversation through the fog of pain.

"Oh, sorry," I continued with a laugh. "I almost forgot. That was three questions you didn't answer. That means I get to do this."

The middle and ring fingers lost their nails next. It was only fair. Helena's screaming was starting to pierce my brain. Frederick's frantic jerks in his chair accompanied the sound.

"Stop! I'm begging you, please!"

With a constitution like that, I was beginning to understand why Helena hadn't let Frederick in on her secret. Too bad, though. This would be going a lot faster.

"You know, normally, I wait to use force to get information from my guests here. I like to let them marinate in their solitude for a while. It tends to be more effective. Besides, sometimes they can't help it. The situation they're in."

I tossed Helena's fingernails into the metal bucket, each making a small plinking sound as they went in. With a hand pressed to my heart, I continued.

"I'm sympathetic to that. Not to you, though. You answered my question with a question, which means you were trying to buy yourself time. Because you think I'm going to punish you. I am going to punish you, Helena. But before we get to that, you're going to tell me everything that you know."

NOTHING. THE BITCH gave me absolutely nothing. Which, weirdly, I sort of respected. I wasn't sure I could stand having every acrylic nail ripped from my hands and remaining silent as the grave. But she did. And then she passed out.

"It seems I know your wife better than you do, Freddy."

Frederick Allerton had watched with wide eyes as I left him with those words and exited the basement. I kept thinking about that look as I drove the Bronco back to the house. There wasn't much open at three in the morning, which was how I found myself at a convenience store to pick up snacks. While debating between a honey bun and a sleeve of chocolate-covered mini donuts, I felt a tap on my shoulder.

"Hi."

If I had seen Dolly Parton herself, I would have been less surprised. As if the universe felt the need to pay me back for what I'd just done to Helena, the man who'd destroyed me with infidelity and gaslighting stood before me with a smile on his face.

"Hi, Ethan," I croaked. It had been years. What in the hell was I supposed to say to him?

"It's nice to see you."

He looked me over. I took the opportunity to return the favor. Now a paramedic instead of an EMT, he was still in a uniform. But now he was wearing a wedding ring. My gut twisted.

"Married, huh?" I asked, my voice sharpening.

He rubbed at the back of his neck with a bashful grin on his face. Sandy blonde hair dipped over his brow. Time was doing nothing to that handsome, chiseled face. But the nights I'd spent crying over him made him repulsive.

"Yeah, uh. For a couple of years now."

I nodded absently. The math was mathing. His wife was undoubtedly one of the nurses he'd been sleeping with behind my back. Had to be. Desperately, I scrambled to keep my thoughts from registering on my face. The last thing I needed was to feel like this guy knew he had ruffled me. Again.

"You guys have kids?" I grabbed the honey bun as I asked the question.

Mounting discomfort forced my feet into motion toward the refrigerators for a beverage. Helena's unanswered questions left an electric current of violence in me that was possibly going to strike Ethan if I wasn't careful. This conversation needed to be over before I got myself arrested.

"Yup," he whipped out his phone to show me a blonde boy clutching a golden retriever as his lock screen. "That's Braxton. He just turned two."

My fingers flexed around the apple-shaped bottle of juice I'd picked up. Not only had this guy cheated on me repeatedly, but he'd apparently knocked up one of his conquests. Instead of coming clean, he gaslit me. Then, when I confronted him about his cheating, he verbally berated me for what I did for my family after I told him about my life in confidence. Called me trash.

It was because of Ethan that I'd been so easily duped by Benjamin. In a roundabout way, my sister was dead because of him. Sort of. Alright, that wasn't fair, but I wasn't in the mood to be charitable. Screw it. Rolling my shoulders, I turned toward him and let my pleasant face drop. Let him see the snarling beast I'd always tried to hide from him.

"You need to leave."

And he did. Maybe he remembered what I did for a living or that my family was connected because he didn't even pay for the coffee he'd picked up. I did. That night Ethan went home, presumably to his wife, and the little boy he'd fathered while pretending to be in love with me.

Seeing Ethan had destroyed my appetite. I tossed the cinnamon bun on the kitchen island and put the apple juice in the refrigerator. All I wanted to do was climb into bed.

Trash.

That's what I'd believed for so long. But as I pulled back the covers and slid into bed with a slumbering West, I realized I didn't believe that anymore. And when he reached out and pulled me into his warmth, I understood why.

40

WEST

It was a strange and comfortable thing, being in this house. It wasn't the gigantic Caccia mansion. It wasn't my little one-bedroom apartment. Like neutral territory. I'd gotten up early and cleaned my weapons. Checked every clip and magazine. While Lili was in the shower, I started brewing coffee. It felt like a glimpse into what things could be if we had the chance at a future together. A home. Our home.

"What were you doing with Clayton the other night?"

I hadn't heard her enter the kitchen. Her hair was damp, dripping into the shirt she'd pulled over herself. I could smell the fresh rosemary scent of her shampoo from here.

"Well," I weighed my options. Telling her the truth was the best path. With a heavy sigh, I poured a cup of coffee and slid it toward her. "There was this auction. For children."

Lilith set the cream down on the counter as horror crossed her features. She blinked and resumed doctoring her coffee.

"Ronan needed Clayton and I to break it up. Killian and his guys got the kids out and we did the rest."

She took a seat at the island and stared down into her cup. Thinking that would be the end of it, I took waffles out of the freezer and popped them into the toaster oven. Leaning back against the counter, I put a hand in the pocket of my sweats and drank my coffee.

"How did Ronan know about it?"

"Killian told me they found out through their contacts at the docks. And that his father got the information out of the organizer. He didn't elaborate."

Lilith seemed amused and sipped from her coffee. I pulled the waffles out of the toaster and drizzled some syrup on them.

"What?"

"Nothing, it's just," she paused, considering. "Ronan has his own way of doing things. It's not pretty."

I gave her a flat look, sliding the cooked waffles toward her. I'd seen what she's done to people. That certainly wasn't "pretty." I took a page from her book and waited for her to elaborate.

"Well, you've seen what they do to buildings and such. The fire. Their emblem is a smoking skull."

She raised her eyebrows, waiting for me to catch up.

"He burns people?" I asked.

She nodded.

"That's it?"

She scoffed.

"When the Caccias and Arawns were at each other's throats, things got ugly. Men would come back with horrible burns if they came back at all."

I rounded the island and took a seat by her side. When I didn't speak, she went on.

"These are not the kinds of burns you get from a stove. Or a match. He uses all sorts of chemicals and implements. He lets them heat up with a gas torch. Then he brands them. Burns them. Or they would restrain them and pour gas on different parts of them to let them watch that part burn."

Stuffing down my horror, I reminded myself that this man was on our side. Lili stabbed her fork into her waffle and dragged it through the maple syrup pooling on her plate. She chewed, then licked the syrup off of the fork and shrugged.

"Like I said. It's not pretty. But I guess it's cleaner than what I do."

I cringed. That was true. During our long talks, she'd described what it was like to flay the skin off of a man.

"It's sort of like ripping off a long piece of packing tape."

That description took me a while to shake off. I'd never look at tape the same way again. I let out a sigh and took a sip from my coffee. Lili chuckled and continued eating.

"What's funny, Zia?" Daniel said, walking in from his bedroom.

"Nothing," she laughed, mouth half-full of waffle. "You ready to start school today?"

He nodded.

"Awesome. Your grandpa is going to help you with your assignments, okay?"

"He's still asleep, though," Daniel complained.

"Then I guess that leaves time for breakfast," I interjected. "You want some toaster waffles?"

"Yup," he said as he hopped up on the stool next to Lili.

She mussed his dark curls and gave him a look of reproach. He sulked at her silent correction.

"Yes, please."

"That's better."

I stood and started preparing Daniel's breakfast. It was hard not to laugh at the absurdity of it. My girl had skinned men alive. But at least she had good manners.

THE GARAGE WAS as good a place as any to get in a workout. I'd stolen some mats and pads from the gym, but it still felt like it wasn't enough. I took in a deep breath, grateful to smell the sea air. This was much better.

We'd spent the day conversing with Clayton, who assured us that his security feed in Pal's was still operational. Then Lilith set up care for her captives with Damon. He assured her that the Allertons were receiving their food allowances and bathroom breaks.

After doing some research on Lilith's second Wolf, I decided it didn't surprise me that they wouldn't try to escape. The boxer was someone even I would think twice about getting into a scrape with.

A glowing orange horizon and a sliver of bright light were all that was left of the sun's presence as Lili and I ran down the spit of beach. Her footsteps were a steady beat behind me, breath pushing out of her with every other step.

The last time we'd run on the beach, when things had still been relatively normal, I'd been close to spilling my guts to her. After she asked me why I didn't have a girlfriend, I thought about it. I thought about telling her that every time I went on a date; it ended terribly because they were never enough. They were never her. Setting aside the fact that a lot of beautiful women had a problem with my past and the fact that I was a bouncer, the ones who could overlook that were always missing something.

Instead, I'd just said it was complicated and we moved on. Until I had to watch her get close to Benjamin Camden. Watch him touch her. Taste her. Make her crawl for him. And then I had to save her when he decided he was done making her his doll.

Lili's footsteps halted behind me. I stopped, checking to see that she was still there. She'd laced her hands together atop her head, staring out at the still-setting sun. Her breath stuttered. Heaving. A tear rolled down her cheek.

"Are you alright?"

Obviously not, but what else do you say to someone who looks like that? Another tear ran down her face. She sniffed.

"All this running. I just got lost in my head for a minute. I'm fine."

I watched her. My body tightened as I braced for it. Braced to be cut off from whatever she was dealing with. Begged her internally not to shut me out again. She took a shaky breath. Then another.

"I feel like my heart is bleeding and it won't stop."

"It will," I offered.

Her eyes hardened as more tears spilled from them.

"Every time I start to feel better, I feel guilty. I feel like I shouldn't be allowed to be happy. That I shouldn't feel good without her here."

She sniffed, wiping the tears from her face with both hands. I nodded, trying my best to show I understood. I hadn't lost a sibling, but losing men I'd served with on missions they should have walked away from felt similar. Some of those guys had wives. Some had families. I was just me. It was a familiar ache.

I closed the distance between us to wrap my arms around her, blocking her from the cool evening air but also trying to focus her on the crashing waves before us.

"Look at the water," I said quietly.

She took a breath. I watched her watch a wave roll toward us and then recede.

"When I lost my father, sometimes I needed to come here and look at the ocean. When I had pain that felt so large, it would swallow me whole... I came to the beach, just to set eyes on the water."

Lili looked over her shoulder at me. Her voice was almost drowned out by another crashing wave.

"Why?"

"It reminded me that I'm just a man. Just one person in a world so much larger than me. I can't control what happens any more than I can control the tide. I can only control how I react to it. Because no matter what happens, that world will go on."

She sighed, shoulders dipping with whatever she'd decided to release.

"So I don't have to feel guilty for it?"

I put my hands on her waist, turning her to face me. The gold lining her hazel eyes still glinted with tears. I wiped them away with my thumbs.

"Guilty for what?"

"For wanting a future," she breathed. "For enjoying things. Enjoying things feels like I'm betraying my sister's memory somehow. Because being with you makes me happy."

Her brows furrowed as she let out a little laugh.

"That's stupid, isn't it?"

"No," I said, pressing a kiss to her forehead as I pulled her against me. "It's not stupid at all."

41

Lilith

Another night. Another bust. Helena Allerton was wearing me thin. Her lack of response to my normal techniques was agitating. I'd told myself I couldn't do too much damage to her physically because if I needed her to work for me in any capacity, she couldn't appear permanently damaged. But damn, I wanted to tear her apart.

So I started pulling teeth. The molars were the easiest to begin with. No one could see that they were missing. But the thing about pulling teeth is that people don't feel like talking much after that, so you have to be judicious with it. You can't just yank every tooth out of their skull, as tempting as that thought may be.

But when I asked her for her contacts, she spit at my feet and smiled. Red and awful. My blood boiled at the sight.

I was running out of ideas. Deciding to go home, I left them with the lights off. Let them sit in darkness while I tried to work this shit out.

Damon was at the entrance, food in hand for the captives.

"Let them starve," I growled.

My generosity was coming to its limit. I huffed, rolling my shoulders. I was supposed to be in control and this bitch was winning. There was an angle I wasn't seeing. There had to be something she valued.

"Let them relieve themselves and then bind them up again. Give them water and nothing else."

Without another word, I left Damon to his task. The deli had been closed for hours. Deciding to exit through the shop instead of the back door, I strolled through the kitchen. A few stray boxes of colorful lemon knot cookies had been left on the stainless-steel counter. I picked them up, tucking them under my arm.

I eyed the rainbow dots covering the glazed cookies, tossing them onto the passenger seat of the Bronco before heading back to the house. My grandmother's recipe. I'd sneak them out to my grandfather whenever he was working on his car. I missed driving the Camaro, but it was too identifiable. After being resurrected from the warehouse, it sat in the garage at the Caccia house. Untouched again.

My phone pinged with a text notification. West.

> On your way back?

I stared down at the screen. It was late. I should have already gone back to the house. Climbed into bed with him. Slept it off. But I felt restless. Unsettled.

> Going to the warehouse.

The door rolled up easily enough. As wide and dark as it had been when I'd discovered the treasure trove of my family's past only months ago, the warehouse sat awaiting my perusal. Kaia had locked away all evidence of my grandparents' existence when she became head of this family.

Now it was all mine. All of the ornate antique furnishings. Every box of carefully wrapped crystal barware. Sterling silver services. All mine.

This was where my family had come to rest. Not in the cemetery where their bones were buried. Here.

Atop a gold-accented credenza sat a musical figurine my grandmother cherished. A scene of lovers mid-waltz. The sweeping blue skirts of the woman's gown had faded with time. Her lover's face was still gazing at her. Like something from out of a fairytale. I picked it up and cranked the key. The room filled with a tinkling, metallic melody. Chopin.

I wandered further in, letting my hands meet with things as I passed. Until I got to the fainting couch that had once graced my grandparents' bedroom. I sat down and surveyed my surroundings. My heels thunked as they hit something solid below. With a groan, I bent over to pull out a white file box. It was labeled in a scrawling black marker.

Matteo Caccia. Office.

I hefted the box up and set it beside me. The lid had warped with time and what looked like a little water damage. Still, it lifted off easily enough.

Files. Loose papers. Notebooks. Envelopes.

"Fuck," I muttered, immediately annoyed with the complete disarray.

As I shifted things around, my fingers stilled. The stirring papers released a scent. My grandfather's cologne. This was all that was left of him. The contents of his mind were in musty papers and old leather-bound notebooks.

For a second, I didn't feel alone. I didn't feel their absence. My sister. My grandmother. My grandfather. Or even my mother. That feeling was enough to force me to my feet. To cover the box and carry it with me to the Bronco. And go home to the family who was waiting for me.

WEST CAME BACK to the sofa with a fresh mug of coffee for me. Daniel had been sequestered to his room, busy with assignments Nico had been picking up for him. It had been easy enough to explain to the school that his mother had passed suddenly and we would be schooling him from home for the time being.

I took the coffee from him and reclined into the soft cushions of the sofa. West told me that Lupo needed to discuss something with me. He sat down beside me, choosing a place between me and the old man.

"So there are no more secrets," he'd said as he served me breakfast. "There's something you need to hear."

French toast had been awaiting my consumption this morning. Something West told me I had to earn. So whatever Lupo was about to tell me was not good.

"I, uh...," Lupo started, staring down into his empty mug.

It felt like everything was happening to me at once. Lupo looked down at his shoes. Then at his mug again. Then at his hands. Everywhere but in my eyes.

"Old man. What do you have to tell me?" I sighed, forcing a kindness to my voice that I didn't feel.

Without meeting my gaze, he began again.

"Do you remember the night your parents died?"

Was he serious? When a twelve-year-old loses both their parents, they tend to remember that. Pouring rain. My grandfather's pained face as he woke me in the middle of the night. Yeah, I remembered. I swallowed down my irritation and blinked.

"Yes. It was my parents' anniversary. It was raining. They died in a car accident."

Lupo cleared his throat and flexed his hands.

"It didn't exactly happen like that."

A cold slab of anticipatory dread slid over my gut. The urge to go back to bed hit me hard. I wasn't sure I could take any more surprises.

"Lupo," I said as evenly as I could, the tension in my gut gnawing a hole through me. "Tell me everything. Now."

Finally, his eyes met mine. A pleading expression had covered his face, but not his eyes. That was regret lingering there. I knew what he was going to say before he even opened his mouth.

"That night, your mother was supposed to go home on her own. Your grandfather called your father away for family business. She insisted on going with him because Matteo called Raoul to the house."

"Because Kaia and I were there," I added.

His chin dipped in conformation.

"It was raining. Your mother and father were coming through the canyon back from Malibu. I was waiting for him to pass me. I was parked in the dark on the side of the road. Matteo and I agreed that I was going to shoot out the tire. It had to look like Raul blew a tire, lost control, and drove off of the highway. It's what was supposed to happen."

Matteo and I agreed. The phrase sucker-punched me.

"What happened, Lupo?"

Blood rushed into my face. Into my ears.

"She was never supposed to be in the car with him. A driver was supposed to bring her here in the car Matteo sent for her later."

My hands started shaking. I wanted to vomit French toast all over the table. Scream at the top of my lungs. Beat Lupo within an inch of his damned life. I hadn't noticed the tremor in my hands until West took one in his and stroked the back with his thumb. The feeling brought me back into my body.

"Go on," West gently urged Lupo to continue. "Finish the story."

"I missed. He hit the turn too fast and I missed. Hit too high and too far to the left."

I shook my head. He went on.

"Your mother was killed instantly. Raoul pulled the car over onto the ridge. Jumped out of the car and ran to her side. I put a bullet in his head while he was standing there. Pushed the car off the side of the road. Your grandfather paid off the police and the medical examiner to cover my mistake."

"No," I breathed. "I don't believe you."

"Your grandfather ordered the hit. But your mother. It was my mistake, Lili."

I squeezed my eyes shut, trying to process everything. And I thought of the Camaro. The car he'd been working on instead of attending my parents' wake. Not because he was filled with grief. But perhaps because he was filled with guilt.

"Bambina, I'm sad for you. My heart breaks for you and your sister."

The look on his face as he sat beside me. It was not only sadness there. I took a deep breath. Then another. I tried calming myself as I looked around the room.

"Lili."

Blue rug. Green vase. Pink flowers.

Breathe.

It wasn't working.

"I need for you to leave, Lupo."

"Lili," West said again.

"No. Actually," I freed my hand from his. I couldn't do this. Not now. If I stayed here, I wouldn't be able to take back what I wanted to say. Or do. "I'll go. I can't believe I'm about to say this, but I think I understand. I just can't look at you right now."

Lupo's head fell as his shoulders began to shake. West was silent, but I could feel him watching me.

"I need to go," I said, standing suddenly. "This is too much."

"I know," Lupo whispered through his tears. "I'm sorry."

"Yeah," the agreement that came out of me was half-empty.

It didn't change anything. My mother was dead. My father deserved to die. At least Lupo and I had agreed on that. My grandfather's role in all of it was something I'd need time to wrap my head around.

Lupo sat on the sofa, unmoving. West sat beside him, watching me as I retrieved my knives from the bedroom and went outside. I needed to put my steel in something.

42

WEST

Her grandfather had his own son killed and her mother had gotten caught in the crossfire. To go from believing your parents were killed in an accident to knowing that they'd been murdered was something anyone would have a hard time with.

"This is too much," she'd said.

Yeah. Too much was right. This was definitely too much. When Lupo told me he'd had something to tell her, I wasn't told every detail. Just that he'd need me there. To support her.

I did my best, but I didn't see that coming.

Lupo sat on the sofa for hours. He didn't move or speak until Daniel emerged, looking for his help on a homework problem. When the boy resumed his work in his bedroom, I spoke.

"She just needs time, man. It'll be alright."

He gave me a nod. I went outside to look for Lili. She hadn't left the property. I knew that because I would have heard the gate open. Especially with as quiet as things had become since she'd walked out the door.

Blades glistened in the morning light as they whipped through the air. One. Two. Three. Fast and brutal into a wooden pallet she'd dragged out from the garage. It wobbled with every blow.

Long black hair was pulled back in a sloppy ponytail. The early spring air was warm with sunlight. Sweat dampened her brow. Still in the tee shirt and boxers she slept in, except for the holster she had strapped to her bare thigh. Her hand went to her side, searching for another blade, only to find none.

"Hey," I said, trying not to startle her.

She put her hands on her hips, turning to face me.

"You should come in for a shower."

"I need to get to Pal's."

"After you shower."

She grunted. Her fingers flexed and relaxed, like claws retracting on an animal. Gold eyes fixed on me. Wild and beautiful.

"It shouldn't matter what happened. They're gone," she huffed, wiping her face with her forearm. "But after everything that's happened. I don't know. Why tell me now?"

I approached her with careful steps until I was standing before her. She placed her hands on her hips again, looking up at me and squinting into the sun.

"You told me your father was," I paused, looking for the right words. "Difficult."

"That's a nice way to put it," she frowned.

"Right, well. It sounds like they were trying to protect you. You and your sister."

Lili sighed, turning away from me to stomp toward the pallet and retrieve her knives. One, two, three, until all six of them were sheathed at her side. She took up her stance and threw one knife. Hard.

"That means my mother is still dead. Because of my father. She never escaped him. She was always his victim."

She pivoted, her boots crunching in the dirt as she turned to look at me again.

"You want to know something? When I was killing people for the family before, it always made me sick. I'd get the job done and then puke my guts up. It was like some part of me couldn't live with what I was doing. I was worried I was becoming like my father. But he killed people for fun. What I did was just business. Except," she paused, turning back toward the makeshift target.

"Except I don't do that anymore. I have everything my father ever wanted for himself. Boss. Money. Control. I have it all. At the cost of losing my sister, yeah. But also, maybe that little bit of humanity in me is gone, too."

I shrugged. Lili angled her head at me in surprise.

"That's all you've got?" She asked.

"Yeah," I said, approaching her again as I stuffed my hands into my pockets. "Your past isn't what defines you. It isn't your parents, either. You get to make that call."

She snorted, looking away from me as she fought tears. They'd been coming so easily lately. I tucked two fingers under her chin, bringing her gaze back to mine.

"Only you get to define who you are."

In a blink, the tears were gone, replaced by the hint of a smile. She stood on her toes to plant a kiss on me, short and sweet.

"That's a little cheesy, but I like it."

We walked, hand in hand, back into the house. The living room was empty. That was for the best. I turned on the shower. Shucking off my sweatpants to join her under the spray, I thought that I'd probably done the Allertons a service by calming her down.

Lili stood under the water, letting it flow down over her. She looked so small like this. I wanted to shield her from any pain. From heartache. She was strong and incredibly intelligent, but she was also so fucking breakable.

Loving Lili felt like jumping out of an airplane. You have to throw yourself into it completely. Without hesitation or else you'd get hurt. I would leap for her. Every goddamn time. Even if sometimes I worried I wasn't going to land on my feet.

43

Lilith

"Still nothing?"

"I'm sorry," Dr. Forester said. "There's nothing here. I've swept their deleted files, their emails, and the geo-markers on their phones. There's nothing here to show that they're doing anything other than what's here. It's all somewhat normal."

I chewed on the edge of my thumbnail. My plan to set up Dr. Forester at a luxury hotel nearby to crack the Allerton's phones was not going as I had hoped. I'd put the doctor up in a suite for thousands of dollars a night in case their devices were being tracked by the Duke's people in an effort to buy ourselves some time. Time to dig for information. But it was all for nothing.

"Alright," I huffed, trying to stuff down my frustration. "I'm going to send someone to escort you home. Give him the phones."

His agreement was cut off when I hung up. I was getting nowhere with the Allertons. If it wasn't for Helena's open defiance, I'd think I had the wrong people. Someone innocent would proclaim it to their dying breath. She proclaimed nothing. She said nothing.

Frederick was the one who proclaimed their innocence. He was insistent that we had the wrong people. It was obvious that Helena's ties to the

Duke's organization were unknown to him. In a normal situation, I'd let him go. But without the two of them together, there would be no doubt that Helena was abducted. Then the rest of the organization would go into hiding.

I couldn't have that.

Scrubbing my thumb and forefinger over my eyes, I took a breath. This was all so exhausting. If it wasn't for Nico running the family in my absence, I'd feel too overwhelmed to go on.

"Everything alright?" West asked as he entered the kitchen.

Showered. Dressed in jeans and a flannel. In those brown work boots, he looked like a friendly lumberjack. He ran a hand over his beard as he leaned back against the countertop. I cocked an eyebrow at him.

"Where are you going?"

"I'm going to the airport. Ronan's airstrip, actually."

I blinked.

"To fly where?"

"Nowhere."

I rubbed my hands over my face. Alright, clearly my brain was starting to melt because this conversation wasn't making any sense.

"Ainsley is being flown in. We've found her a home, and I thought it would be good for her to see a familiar face."

"Oh."

I'd forgotten about her. I stood from the stool at the island and walked toward the hallway.

"I'm going with you," I said over my shoulder. I didn't give him a chance to refuse me as I shut the bedroom door and began dressing myself.

AINSLEY BOROUGHS AND I had something in common. The Duke wanted us dead or disappeared. I was a loose end. Something to be clipped. Burned. Disposed of. An inconvenience. And so was she. But here we both were. Unclipped. Unburned. Still breathing.

The little girl shifted in her seat. After such a long flight, I was amazed she had so much energy, but nerves would do that to anyone. Casey set a tumbler filled to the brim with chocolate milk down in front of her and took a seat opposite the little girl.

"Thank you," Ainsley said politely.

I tried to imagine being in her shoes. No mother. No idea who her father was. No family out there looking for her. She might as well be a ghost.

Ronan entered the back room of the Chancer, unbuttoning his dove grey suit jacket before taking his seat at the head of the table. Killian was nowhere to be seen, likely off handling some aspect of Arawn business as Ronan's heir.

Ronan scratched at his salt-and-pepper stubble and looked at the little girl seated beside him.

"They said to bring her to the Chancer," West had said. "She's supposed to meet her new family there. Killian set it up."

Without Killian here, I wasn't sure who to ask when I looked around for the little girl's new guardians.

"Was your flight alright?" Casey asked, breaking the silence.

"I've never been on a plane before," Ainsley said, nodding as she picked up the glass and carefully brought it to her lips for a sip.

"Did you like my plane?" Ronan chimed in, grinning at the girl. "It's quite comfortable, isn't it?"

She nodded.

"The lady on the plane was nice. She made me my own bed and let me watch a movie."

Ronan gave a wink to the girl as he glanced at his daughter, then looked back to Ainsley.

"You know that your mother is no longer with us."

Ainsley's eyes saddened as they cast downward. She nodded. I patted her slight shoulder gently. There wasn't much else to do. This was how he was going to tell her about her new family?

"No one can find your father," he said matter-of-factly.

I breathed a small sigh of relief at that. She didn't need to know that her father had tried to get rid of her. The man didn't deserve to know this girl.

"So you need a new family."

A waiter entered, bringing over trays of food to set on the table before us. Fish and chips. Bangers and mash. Chicken fingers. Plates were set before each of us. Ronan waved his hand over the spread, inviting us to partake as he continued.

"This is my daughter, Casey," he said, gesturing toward my red-headed friend sitting across from Ainsley.

She gave her a kind smile.

"You've already met my son, Killian," Ronan continued. "I know they're quite a bit older than you, but they've agreed that they'd love to have you as a sister."

I felt my eyebrows shoot up my forehead. Unable to resist, I glanced at West for his reaction. Outside of a twitch of a scarred eyebrow, there was nothing. No surprise. Just acceptance.

"I don't have a wife, but I do have a large home with plenty of space for you. If you'll have me for your father, that is."

"It's a nice home," Casey added. "I live there, too. There's a pool and a big garden. It's pretty. Like a castle."

Ronan put an elbow on the arm of his chair, resting his chin on his fist as he let his daughter speak.

"I know what happened to you was scary," Casey continued. "It happened to me, too. It was very scary for me. I think it would help me to have someone around who understands."

I swallowed hard, picking up the water glass in front of me to take a drink. Remembering the men who treated Casey like something to be used and thrown away. I'd heard it happen. Seen the empty look in her eyes when they were done. That there was any brightness in her face now was a testament to the woman she was.

Ronan's voice was rough as he spoke, as though he too now thought of everything his daughter had been through in the last year.

"I promise you'll always be comfortable and safe so long as I'm around. No one will do you any harm," he offered.

My heart thundered in me as I waited for her response. This man had threatened my life. He was one of the most frightening people I'd ever met on this planet. But maybe for the right person, he could be soft. Even if that person was a girl with soft blonde curls and eyes like blue marbles.

If there was anyone who would protect this girl, this loose end, with their lives, it would be Ronan. He extended a hand toward her but didn't touch her. Instead, he let it rest atop the table, palm up. An invitation, but no more.

We sat in silence as Ainsley considered. West pushed food onto my plate from one platter. I was unable to eat as I waited for her to say something. Then it happened.

A delicate hand reached across the table to rest inside the leader of the Arawn family's offered grip. As his tattooed fingers closed around hers to give a gentle squeeze, I realized that this was the moment Ainsley Arawn was born.

44

Lilith

Entertaining the most powerful people in the world in my little basement hideaway was becoming a regular thing. Benjamin Camden, the billionaire playboy dirtbag, had been kept down here for long enough. I wondered if I should redecorate with marble instead of cement and subway tile to make them all feel more at home.

But getting blood stains out of marble would be such a bitch.

Ronan tapped the ash off of the end of his cigar into a steel basin on my worktable. I'd decided to call in another expert at extracting information since I was getting nowhere with these two. After watching my work on the cameras Clayton had installed, Ronan agreed so long as he was allowed to see a live performance.

"Show me what you can do, love."

Frederick Allerton had witnessed his wife lose fingernails. Lose teeth. Dry drown. And she didn't break. It had been eating at me for days. This woman could withstand the type of pain that would have sent most men to their knees. She could withstand fear. But Lupo's confession had made me realize something. I wasn't hitting her where it hurt.

"Tell me, Frederick," I knelt between his legs, tracing my palms up his thighs as I let my voice go soft and inviting for him. "How many women have there been? How many have you sold?"

"I-I don't know. I don't sell people. I'm not involved in anything," Frederick stuttered, watery eyes watching my hands as he trembled.

Helena whispered her husband's name.

"Uh-uh," I scolded as I unfastened his pants. Tugging the material down his thighs, I continued. "I'm not talking to you, Helena. I'm talking to Frederick. Now, Frederick, I think you and I can be friends. You know, I'm really very good to my friends."

Now stroking his bare skin, I let one hand drift to my back. To where the serrated hunting knife waited. My thumb unclipped the closure. Helena gasped but said nothing.

"Wouldn't you like that?" I purred. "Don't you want to be my friend Freddy?"

Frederick nodded. My skin felt drawn to the hilt of my knife. Magnetized to it. As my grip closed around it, I glanced over my shoulder to West. Behind me, Helena was cringing away, trying not to watch as I worked. I couldn't have that. I'd told him exactly what I planned to do, why I needed his sister here, and had given him only one direction.

"Make her watch."

West moved to stand behind Helena's chair, turning her chin to face toward her husband. His green eyes were cold. Ready for what was coming next. I returned my attention to Frederick.

Years of training had made me quick. Hours of studying had made me precise. The knife pierced the thick flesh of his thigh with ease. Slowly, surely, I drove it in until I hit my mark as Frederick Allerton screamed and sobbed in anguish. She shrieked at the wound I'd inflicted on her husband as blood welled up around the blade.

My father had done this. Strapped another man to a chair in the attic of the Bootlegger. Threatened his life. He wasn't careful or intentional with the placement. But he didn't know what I knew.

"How long have you and Freddy been married, Helena?" I asked as I stood, leaving the knife jutting from Frederick Allerton's thigh. The look on Ronan's face could only be described as bemused. He tapped a bit of ash off of his cigar and leaned back against the work table.

"Please," she whispered.

"How long?"

"Twenty-two years."

"Wow," I whistled. "That's a long time. Do you remember your vows?" She nodded frantically.

"Good. So you remember the end, probably. *For as long as you both shall live*. Well," I lifted my wrist to look at a non-existent watch. "I'd say he has about six minutes."

As though on cue, blood started to patter onto the floor. It pooled beneath Frederick and slid toward the drain. Toward Helena. Reaching for her. Like even Frederick's cells couldn't stay away from his wife.

"Unless," I purred as I bent down to look Helena in the eye, taking her chin in my hand. "You're a good girl for me."

I straightened and turned to see Frederick's head loll back as he whimpered in pain. Ronan took another drag from his cigar, smoke billowing out through his nose as he exhaled and looked at his watch. Helena didn't take her eyes off of her husband as we sat in silence for a minute. Her eyes were heavy with worry, but gears turned behind them. Weighing. Measuring. Another minute passed. A tear slipped down her elegant cheek.

"Four minutes," Ronan drawled.

"Please," Helena whispered as she watched the thick red liquid approach her bare feet. "I'll do whatever you want. Please. Just help him."

I nodded to Lanna, who stepped forward with the tools I'd laid out for her. As she worked quickly to dress the wound I'd inflicted, I looked back to West. His eyes were on his carefully disguised sister. He'd insisted that letting Freddy live would be a more effective negotiation tactic than making Helena watch him die.

"If you kill him, she'll take her secrets to the grave. She'd have no reason to help you," he'd suggested.

As it turned out, he was right. I folded my arms across my chest and looked down my nose at Helena.

"I'm no economist, but I understand the concept of supply and demand. Tell me everything about EROS and your buyers. Now."

45

West

As we entered Clayton's loft, I heard Lili curse softly. It was still clean, still well decorated. And now it smelled like... herbs. Or lemon. Or both. She looked around, dragging a finger along the entryway table, because he had a damn entryway table now. Lifting it to inspect the lack of dust, she blew out an impressed breath.

"I know, right?" I muttered. "It's like he changed into a different person."

"I'll be out in a sec?" Clayton called from his bedroom. "Get whatever you want out of the fridge."

Lili made her way to the kitchen and pulled out a pair of Topo Chico bottles, cracking one open, and then handing it to me before opening hers. She took a sip from her bottle and set it on the counter, surveying the residence again.

"Maybe he decided to improve his lifestyle," she said, angling her head at me.

"For what?"

Lili gave me an incredulous look and reached for a little rock garden sitting on a brand new credenza, picking up a pink crystal from the center of a swirl of sand ripples. She smiled at the stone as if the answer was obvious.

"For a girl."

For a girl. We all did crazy things for the people we loved. I decided when she was torturing the man who nearly killed her that I wouldn't judge her. Watching her almost end Frederick Allerton's life hadn't gotten to me. It was all just a part of who she was. After all of the people I'd killed in my career, it wasn't up to me to judge her. My heart wouldn't let me anyway.

Carefully, she set the rock back in its place and went to the living room to sit on the brand-new sofa. I sat beside her, watching as she put her bottle down on one of the coasters that was definitely new. Our host emerged from his bedroom a moment later, hair still wet from the shower.

"Sorry," he huffed as he hurried toward us.

I thought about our conversation on the plane to Ireland.

"You've never done anything stupid for a girl?"

He was one of the least stupid people I'd ever met. He and the woman who sat beside me. She gave Clayton a smile and relaxed in her seat. This woman could weave tangled webs designed to trap even the most cunning prey. But love could blind her easily. I'd seen it happen with her sister. Love made her question herself. Maybe it was the same for him.

"Alright," Clayton started, grabbing his laptop from where it rested on the television stand. "What do we know?"

"Settle in. This is a lot."

At my warning, Clayton nodded.

"Don't worry, I already ordered in food. I know she doesn't like to work hungry."

Lilith chuckled.

"No, she can. She's just not very useful."

She swatted my shoulder and then began speaking.

"Allerton laid out the inner workings of EROS. It's complicated. But I think we can dismantle the structure of it fairly easily."

She paused, taking a sip from her water. With a glance at me, she went on.

"The problem is that there are so many heads. Like a hydra. If something happens to one of them, the others will be warned off and protected before we can get to the rest."

Clayton clicked away on his laptop, listening while he searched through the list Lilith had sent his way. Each person Helena had named.

"These people span the globe. How are we supposed to get to all of them?"

"We'll need to get them all in one place," Lili answered. "And we need to make it look like Helena dropped off of her own volition so she'll draw out her associates without arousing suspicion. Get her to work with us."

I thought of the near-fatal wound Lilith dealt to Frederick Allerton. After something like that, I doubted the woman would be feeling charitable toward us, but maybe she'd keep up her end of the bargain if his life was in danger.

"I don't know how much more Frederick can stand," I argued. "You might kill him if you try anything else."

"What I'm going to try next won't be physical," Lilith countered.

Clayton arched an eyebrow at her, gesturing with his free hand for her to go on.

"They have a daughter. I heard them talking about her at the party. We use her as leverage until Helena comes through on her end."

I did my best to hide my surprise. She'd told me off for thinking she might use a child against the Duke and now she was offering this? A knock at the door shook me from my thoughts.

"That's the pizza," Clayton said, pointing to his screen and the security feed he was watching.

I stood to retrieve the food, one hand on the pistol tucked into the back of my pants. Clayton and Lilith quieted. I didn't need to look over my shoulder to know they were watching me. Armed and ready for the poor kid who brought us food.

With one hand still on my weapon, I opened the door and gave the kid a friendly smile. He handed me the pizza boxes, returning my smile with a nod. I kicked the door closed, locked it, and grabbed some plates off of a shelf in the kitchen. Clayton resumed the conversation with a question, taking the plates from my hand to set on the coffee table.

"What makes you think she'll go for it?"

Lili bared her teeth in a grin, as though the next part of her plan made her salivate. She shrugged, snagging a slice drowning in various meats from a box. Clayton handed her a plate.

"She might not," she said casually, taking a bite before continuing. "But she loves Frederick. And Frederick loves their daughter. She'll do whatever it takes to save her so long as she doesn't disappoint Freddy."

"But we don't know where she is."

"Yes, we do."

Clayton blinked. I must have, too, because Lilith looked at me like I'd contradicted her out loud. At least, I didn't think I'd said anything.

"Don't look so surprised. She's an influencer. People are easy to track when they can't help but document their entire lives. I've been keeping track. I know what she had for breakfast this morning. Between that and the regular credit card charges that come through on her mother's card, which come through like clockwork on her phone, kidnapping her would be a cakewalk."

Lilith took another bite of pizza, chasing it with her water. It wasn't adding up, though. This plan. Kidnapping wasn't exactly under the radar. At least not for these people. With an influencer who posted things so regularly, people would notice if she went missing. Probably.

"We can't kidnap the daughter without raising any alarms. Won't that just alert the rest of them, too?"

She set her plate down on her lap and gave me a pitying look like I'd missed some key detail.

"We're not actually going to kidnap the girl. We're not going to do anything to her. We're just going to let the Allertons know that we can. Threaten them with the idea of losing their darling only daughter."

"And then she'll tell you who the buyers are? What about the Duke? Isn't he going to get wind of this?"

Lilith sighed and plopped backward on the sofa.

"I don't know what to do about him."

Clayton took a swig from his bottle and plated another slice of pizza for himself. Lilith picked up the slice from her plate and took another bite. He watched her, then laughed as he sat forward again.

"Can I ask you something?"

Lilith swallowed, shrugged, then took another bite. Clayton studied her for a moment, then spoke.

"Why exactly are you chasing someone who's trying to hunt you down?"

Her swallow was hard. She blinked. Clayton shrugged and sat back again. I knew exactly what my girl was thinking. She didn't need that kind of encouragement. Not knowing where she was for days as she sat in a trailer in the middle of the desert, taken away from me. I couldn't bear that again. Clayton ignored the daggers I stared at him. He didn't need to say it. But he did.

"Let him catch you."

JUST BECAUSE IT was the right solution to the problem didn't mean I had to like it. I fucking hated it. The elevator down to the street felt too small. My blood curdled at Clayton's suggestion. Lili's agreement had only made it worse.

"I'm not doing this again."

The doors slid open. I soldiered forward through the lobby. Lili chased after me, trying to keep up as she spoke.

"It won't be like last time. First, you'll be in contact with me the whole time. You will. Second, I won't be unarmed. I just need to get close to him."

I threw the door open. She followed.

"How do you even know that they'd bring you to him? What if they just kill you on the spot?" I barked.

Lili snorted, tugging her jacket around her to shut out the brisk air as we strode toward where I'd parked the Bronco. I slowed as it came into view around the corner.

"Because his ego is larger than his good sense. He'll want me to know he bested me. He'll want to rub it in my face."

I stopped, opening the passenger side door.

"From the other side of the world?"

She climbed in, resting her hand on the handle as she paused to answer my question.

"No."

"No?"

I let out a cold laugh. Unbelievable. She was unbelievable. Storming around the front of the Bronco, Lili watched me as I let myself in. Before I could get a word out, she explained.

"There's a polo event in Santa Barbara. The royal family goes to this thing. Everyone with his kind of money goes to this thing. It's in a week. He might be there. We have until then to figure our shit out."

I shook my head in disbelief, staring down at a small hole in my work pants. She couldn't believe I'd be alright with this. Putting her in danger again went against every instinct in my body.

"If you think I'm endorsing this, you're insane," I said, hearing the rough tone of fear that had entered my voice. "You don't even know for certain if he's going to show up himself and not dispatch someone else to take care of you."

Lili's voice took on a desperate note. Anxious.

"This is what I have to do, West. Either he's going to kill me or I'm going to kill him. I can't just let it drop. This isn't over until one of us is gone."

"You don't know that."

She twisted in her seat; her face contorted in anger.

"He promised to put me in a box, so I'm pretty sure that I do know that."

"What."

If my blood was boiling before, now it was ice cold. I'd known he was trying to get to her. That he'd gone after her after Belfast, but this?

"After Kaia's funeral, I got a package. It was a flower. A lily. In a long black box. It came with a note."

"What did it say?"

I shifted to look at her only to find her eyes cast downward.

"It said," Lili sniffed, voice trembling. "This is not going to be the only pretty Lily I put inside a box."

Lili roughly wiped her cheeks and puffed out a breath.

"So the attack on the house wasn't payback for going after him in Belfast?"

"No."

"And Muse getting burned down wasn't some mafia retaliation, either, was it?"

"No."

I stabbed my key into the ignition. He wasn't fighting back. He was hunting her. Hunting Lilith. *My* Lilith. The urge to break every bone in the Duke Augustus-Stanley's body warred with a general sense of irritation at being lied to.

Again.

Squeezing my eyes shut, I tried to calm myself before starting the Bronco. Lilith's lip was pinched between her teeth when I opened my eyes. Staring down at her hands, knotting her fingers together in her lap, like she was expecting me to scream at her.

No.

I knew exactly how I wanted to repay her lies.

46

Lilith

A metallic ping sounded in the still night air. The rickety pallet I was using for a target wobbled at the impact. It wasn't perfect, but it would have to do. At least my throwing skills weren't getting rusty. I rolled my shoulders, taking my next blade in hand to aim for a small imperfection in one of the slats.

Ping!

West hadn't spoken to me for the drive back to the house. I should have told him the whole truth from the first moment. About everything. I knew that from the moment I burned the box. The flower. The note.

Ping!

When the people you love are in danger because of you, do you keep the truth of that danger from them to protect them? Or do you tell them so that they're able to protect themselves?

Ping!

I had been so sloppy when I hunted for Casey and Isabelle that I didn't see Benjamin closing in on me. When I was looking for my sister, I was distracted by the fear of losing her.

Now she was gone.

I had let fantasies of revenge, of killing the fucking Duke, cloud my judgment. I thought about Kaia and what she'd say about my carelessness. She would have told me to focus. And that a dead wolf was of no use to her.

"It's alright to make mistakes," she'd say. "So long as you learn from them."

I had West. The family. Clayton. And even the Arawns. I didn't need to shoulder this burden alone. That's what he'd wanted. The Duke. He wanted me to feel trapped and alone. I'd gotten caught in his snare when I burned all evidence of his threat. But at least this time I'd learned from my mistake before it was too late.

"Come on."

West was standing behind me, tying his hair back in a knot atop his head. In only his workout pants, I knew exactly where this was headed. He nodded his head toward our makeshift gym in the garage.

"We've been slacking. If you're going to get captured, you better be able to fight your way out."

The night air seeped into the small space, chilling the garage. But that wasn't what set the hairs on my arms standing on end. West waited for me to change and meet him inside, arms folded over his chest, with something dangling from his fingertips. A blindfold?

I arched an eyebrow at him.

"What are you planning to do with that?"

"You need to fight with your instincts. Make choices from here," he said, tapping his stomach.

"Oh," I laughed. "I thought we were going to have some fun."

"We are," he said, grinning at me in that West way that made my knees wobble. "But first we're going to fight."

The black fabric was silky against my skin. West's fingers slid the blindfold in place, nestled beneath my ponytail. Warmth emanated from his body. He pressed something into my hand. Cold swept in as he stepped away. My fingers traced over the object he'd given me. A rubber training dagger.

"Ready?"

"Ready," I said, taking my defensive stance.

Shifting the fake blade in my hand, I waited. My ears twitched at every sound. I listened for anything. Grit twisted on the mat from behind me. A shift in his footsteps.

An exhale that preceded a strike.

I felt his knife at my throat.

"And now you're dead," he said, lips grazing my ear.

"And so are you," I smirked.

He felt my knife at his crotch. West's laugh was hot against my neck.

"It's not nice to hit below the belt, Trouble."

His blade grazed my neck, as if in warning. My skin pricked, goosebumps following the sensation. I tapped my blade against the space behind his manhood. Coupled with an elbow to his gut, it was easy to remove myself from his hold.

"If I'm fighting for my life, the crotch is not off-limits."

"Fair enough," he chuckled. "But you forgot one thing."

"What's that?" I said, lifting the blindfold from one eye to look at him.

Rubber clattered as it hit the floor and West's hand shot out. Not to grab me. But to balance himself. Because he'd used his long stride to trip me and take me down. A simple leg sweep I hadn't been expecting.

"Never let your guard down."

Flat on my back, I looked up at him, feigning defeat. West offered his hand to help me up. I grabbed it. Then yanked it toward me, pulling his body to the ground and straddling him. The rubber dagger was angled at his throat. I grinned in victory.

"I'll try to remember that."

West shifted beneath me. I squeezed my thighs tighter to restrict his movement. Leaning forward, I brought my mouth within a breath's distance of his.

"I thought you said this would be fun."

His dark green eyes flashed with wicked intent. With my eyes on his, I hadn't noticed his hand. Not until it crept up my thigh. His long fingers curled, tucking themselves into the space between us. They grazed over the fabric of my leggings, drawing a gasp from me.

West's other hand squeezed my ass, pulling me against him. I could feel every inch of his desire as it built between my thighs. Then his hips shifted up, pushing me off of him. I was pinned face down on the mat.

"Hey," I barked in surprise.

He straddled my thighs, tugging my leggings down until I was bare before him, but only just. The waistband and his stance bound my thighs together.

"I had no idea you were into this kind of thing," I said, my cheek pressed against the mat.

I could feel the heat building in my core. West shifted his hips, leaning forward to take my wrists. Pinning them together behind my back, he leaned down to growl in my ear.

"I've imagined all sorts of things when it comes to you, Trouble. But that's not what we're doing."

"What?"

A hand smoothed over the curve of my ass.

"You lied to me. Again."

47

WEST

Lilith lowered herself carefully onto the stool at the kitchen island. Her eyes went sharp as I snickered at the sight. She may be dangerous, but she didn't scare me.

"Are you hurt, Zia?" Daniel asked around a mouthful of French toast.

"I'm fine," Lili gritted through clenched teeth.

I fixed a cup of coffee and slid it across the counter to her. She lifted the cup for a sip. A plate piled high with bacon and French toast followed it. My peace offering.

"She's just a little sore from training, buddy," I added, grinning into my coffee.

And the ten-minute spanking I gave her. I had warned her about what would happen when she lied to me. Only this time it wasn't followed by anything but a shower and a massage. She was too pissed at me to let me do anything else.

Lili rolled her eyes and drank her coffee. Lupo just shook his head and continued reading the news on his phone.

"Mind your business, Champ."

With a bite of bacon, Lili shifted in her seat and cringed. Maybe I went a little too hard, but how else was she supposed to learn?

THE DINING ROOM in this house looked like a glass box compared to the rest of the space. Large windows bathed Lili in sunlight as she sorted through a box of goods. The light illuminated the parts of her that were exposed in the cropped white tank top she wore. Her black waves hung over her shoulder in a sheet like the ocean on a moonless night. The gold in her eyes looked more hazel today as they searched for something.

"What's all this?" I asked.

She lifted a big stone bowl out of the box and placed it carefully on the large wooden dining table, then shifted to adjust her grey lounge pants.

"Nico brought over some things from my lab. He's going to come by with the rest later."

I sucked on a tooth, leaning against the wall as I watched her unpack item after item. This could only mean one thing.

"So, are you going to be making some of that vomit poison for the Allerton people?"

I tried to shake the memory of men vomiting all over Ronan's yacht. It was a hard image to forget.

"No," Lili smirked as she pulled out a glass bottle and unwrapped it from brown paper. "I think we can agree that was pretty unpleasant. Not something I'll be doing again."

"You want to get them all in one place. I'm assuming there's a plan related to all of this," I said, jerking my chin toward the table.

She didn't answer my question, instead she went back to digging through the box as if whatever she needed was eluding her. A satisfied grunt and a rustle of paper later, she pulled out the pestle.

"Lili?"

She blinked.

"What?"

"What are you planning?"

Lili paused, her hand on the pestle, and angled her head. It was a small motion that happened as her eyes went glassy. Distant. Weighing what she wanted to say. I waited. The information was a series of moving parts shifting around to give her an answer. After a beat, she blinked. Back in the room.

"I have an idea."

"Any chance you're going to share that information with me or am I going to be subjected to some grand reveal?"

She snorted. A pair of notebooks slid out of the box. Lili opened a black leather-bound one that had band stickers and worn corners, thoughtfully flipping through the pages as she chewed a corner of her full pink lips.

"I have to figure out how to make it work, first."

"And none of this is for the Duke tomorrow?"

Lili's fingers flexed around the notebook. She didn't lift her gaze from the pages as she answered me.

"No. I want to make him bleed."

RONAN LEANED AGAINST the marble altar, content to watch me walk the length of the church before speaking with me. I'd called this meeting, but he'd named the place. Before my boots hit the bottom steps, he spoke.

"Do you want to tell me what this is about?"

I paused. If he wanted to talk like this, we could talk like this. All that mattered to me was the favor I was about to ask.

"We may be able to get our hands on the Duke."

"Yes, Mr. Wrigley filled me in on the details of your venture out to Santa Barbara tomorrow. Did you need some polo tips?"

I blew a breath out through my nose. He was going to make me beg. Fine. I could beg. For Lili.

"I'm here to ask-"

"To borrow a suit."

This fucking guy.

"To ask-"

"To see my barber."

"To ask for your help!" I barked.

"Ah," Ronan said with a satisfied smile and a nod. "That. I had a feeling you'd be looking for help here."

"You hired us to get rid of this guy. We need your resources to do it."

Ronan checked his pocket watch. A gold antique I hadn't seen before. He looked up through dark eyebrows at me.

"You need my resources to protect your woman."

"Yes."

Yes, I needed his resources. Lili was going to walk into the lion's den tomorrow. She was going to make it out. No matter what I had to do. No matter who I had to make promises to.

Ronan looked me over, seeming to consider my request. Letting me stew. He picked a bit of fuzz off of his black wool suit jacket.

"Sadly, we won't be joining you tomorrow."

"What."

My jaw tightened, the word barely passing my lips. Every muscle in my back went tight. I needed them. She needed them. I opened my mouth to argue, and Ronan went on.

"I know your woman has got a team to take care of her business while she's on this mission of hers, but I've got other ventures that require my attention."

Ronan stepped off of the dais. Though his body aimed forward to leave, his head turned toward me. Darkness and something like pity warred in his expression.

"So, what does that mean?"

The smoking skull on his tattooed hand gave my shoulder a reassuring pat. Then he walked away. His black-booted footsteps echoed in the sanctuary as he raised his voice to answer me.

"That means, Mr. Hale, that you're on your own."

48

Lilith

Thundering hoof beats and polite applause were drowning out my racing thoughts. He should be here. Duke Harrison Augustus-Stanley had to be here. My heart thudded a steady beat as I stepped gingerly onto the field adjoining the pitch.

Polo players walked through the crowd in their tight white pants and high boots. Willowy women in pastel-colored dresses watched them with interest while sipping from glasses sweating with chilled rosé.

At least I'd gotten that much right. My hands smoothed over my dress, gliding easily over the pale yellow silk. Thin straps, a gentle sweetheart neckline. Simple in design, this dress was one of my favorites. My time with Benjamin Camden had taught me about what little luxuries I enjoyed. Silk dresses happened to be among them.

High pitched whining and buzzing sounded in my ear. I flinched, approaching the bar to grab a drink before beginning my search. If the Duke was here, this seemed like a good enough place to start.

"Have you spotted the big bad yet, sunshine?" Clayton's voice was muffled in my earpiece, like he was chewing on something.

"No," I muttered as the bartender approached me. "Not yet."

"I'll give you a minute," the bartender said, thinking I'd been addressing him. Forcing a polite smile onto my face, I thanked him and picked up a menu off of the polished bar top. Pretending to be undecided on a cocktail would be enough reason to stand here for a minute.

"Well, well. I haven't seen you around here before."

Long tan fingers wrapped around the menu and tugged it away. I looked up to see one of the green-shirted polo players standing before me. He was a conventionally attractive sort, if you're into that Ralph Lauren look. His scruff was trimmed around his neck. Slightly overgrown brown hair in loose curls that definitely had some product in it to highlight the calculated "messiness."

Unnaturally white teeth greeted me with an easy smile. I returned his grin and gave a little laugh.

"This isn't my usual crowd," I said.

"Let's get you a drink and I'll keep you company, sweetheart."

I batted my eyelashes at him, trying to think of a nice way to tell him to buzz off so I could stay focused. The polo player leaned onto the bar, stuffing one hand into his spotless white pants. While trying to get the bartender's attention, he gave me another easy smile.

"You know," I started. "I really shouldn't."

The polo player reached out, attempting to take my hand in his. I backed away a step.

"Have you got a boyfriend, sweetheart?"

"Yes," I said.

"And he's armed," West growled into the receiver.

I had to bite my lip to keep from smiling. Taking my amusement as a sign to keep trying, the polo player leaned forward to speak into my ear.

"I won't tell him if you don't."

Polo players don't wear cups. Or, at least, this one doesn't. His soft nether regions were completely unprotected from my knee as I drove it into them. Tears flooded his eyes as he bent over, bracing one hand on the bar as he grunted.

"No means no, pal," Clayton laughed.

Several onlookers turned to see the commotion. As the crowd parted to see what had happened, I saw him. Sandy red hair and blue eyes. A breezy cream linen suit and an expression to match. Harrison Augustus-Stanley. The Duke was here.

"I see him," I said, walking away from the bar.

"Careful," West warned.

A small group of men had gathered to chat with the Duke. Each of them looked like they were immersed in whatever story he was telling. The smile he wore was charming. It sickened me as I remembered the way he smiled at me all those weeks ago.

"Goodbye, Caccias."

Boisterous laughter erupted from the group of men as I circled them. His security seemed to be hanging back. Or they were dressed like the other guests. I wondered who amongst this group was ready to strike at the first sign of trouble. All I had to do was get into his eyeline.

"Get him to follow you," Clayton instructed.

It was all part of his genius plan. I had to hand it to him; it wasn't a terrible idea. But using myself as bait was risky. It wouldn't be the first time I tried such a thing, but it still made me nervous.

Don't get too close, I told myself. *Just close enough for him to see. Close enough to know it's me.*

"Excuse me for a moment," Augustus-Stanley said in his gentle Scottish accent.

The group of men began to disperse. As they cleared from their cluster, he spotted me. The congenial mask he wore dropped. And I started walking. Weaving through bodies and cocktail tables, I headed for the exit. With a glance over my shoulder, I checked for followers.

Two.

A short, dark man and a tall blonde man moved through the crowd in a pace that gave away their pursuit. They each wore suits that were just a bit too cheap to be considered part of the crowd. I cursed myself for not seeing them before. Especially as I noted the outline of pistols at their khaki covered hips.

I swerved, plunging through a crowd of chattering older women. I didn't want to lose my tail. I just needed to buy some time.

"They're following me," I confirmed to Clayton and West, who'd been listening from our rendezvous point.

"Who's following you, dear?" One woman asked.

"That short man. He's my ex-husband," I lied breathlessly. "He followed me here."

"Don't worry, honey," another woman said. "Go. We'll stop him."

I hurried toward the exit. Not far now. A flurry of feminine voices swelled behind me. All of them fussing over someone. Without looking, I knew those women had given me the delay I needed.

My hand plunged into my tiny purse, searching for the key to Nico's Mercedes. There. Lights flashed as I clicked the unlock button, searching for the car in a sea of almost identical vehicles. Heels ground into the asphalt as I trotted through the parking lot.

Another glance over my shoulder. The tall blonde man wasn't far. Maybe twenty yards back. The short one emerged from the exit. I stepped into the driver's seat and put the car in drive, peeling away like I was in a hurry. They loaded into a car as the short one lifted a phone to his ear. His smile was a rattlesnake's warning as I passed them.

49

WEST

She'd let them follow her. Here.

A shiny black Mercedes plowed up the dirt driveway. They wouldn't be far behind. Tucked away in the hills of Santa Barbara, we'd chosen this house carefully. Let them think she'd absconded to this farmhouse after the attack on her home. Let them think she'd been stupid enough to come straight to her safe house.

Lili threw the door open and began running on high heels to the large garage. Long black hair trailed her. In the late afternoon sun, she was a golden goddess. Though I was tempted to help her, I knew they wouldn't be far behind. I shoved the bundle of clothes toward her from the shadows.

"Disco," I called. "Disco, ready."

"They're right behind me," she shouted, kicking off her shoes as she entered. Lili yanked up the pants I'd thrown at her. Stuffed her feet into her boots and zipped them. Clayton didn't answer from his position in the attic of the house.

An engine roared. Tires crunched on the driveway. Lili pulled a shirt over her head. I tossed her the hunting knife. She clipped it to the back of her pants, pulling her shirt down to cover it. The throwing knives were in my hand as they pulled into the drive. We'd run out of time.

"Disco. Disco. Where the fuck are you?"

Sharp ringing blasted into my ear. Then nothing. Great. Comms were fucking dead. I moved toward the back door, ready to come around and eliminate the Duke's security while Lili lead him into the house.

A black SUV and a matching Rolls Royce plowed up the drive. Lili pivoted, ready to run. Except the SUV didn't stop. It pulled around back. Back toward my exit. Fuck. The driver of the Rolls Royce stepped out of the vehicle with a gun trained on Lili as he opened the rear door.

"Ms. Caccia," Harrison Augustus-Stanley said as he disembarked. "Lovely to see you."

I aimed my weapon at the driver. Lili took cautious steps backward, raising her hands above her head as the Duke and his driver approached. A gun pressed into the side of my head.

"Put down the gun," a voice said beside me.

I feigned surrender, re-holstering the pistol. My knife pierced his boot as he fired into the ground. He screamed as I ripped the blade from his boot. I'd been ready to gut him when a gun fired at my feet. The driver.

"On your knees," another voice behind me commanded, kicking my legs out from under me. Lili glanced back at me. Her eyes were wide, conveying everything she couldn't say to me. This wasn't how this was supposed to go.

"Who's this?"

The Duke turned his attention to me as the man with the bleeding foot limped toward Lili, taking her in hand. My blood boiled at the way his fingers dug into her skin. She threaded her fingers together as she put her hands behind her back in feigned submission. Good girl.

"Someone important to you, I gather," the Duke continued. "Take that horrid mask off, will you?"

The man behind me tugged the gaiter down to reveal my face.

"Ah, yes. Mr. Hale. Or should I call you Lieutenant Commander Hale? Does that still apply when they cut you loose?"

His eyes wrinkled as he grinned. The Duke reached out and tugged my beard playfully. The bastard was enjoying this. At least Lili had been right about that.

"Leave him alone," Lili snarled, voice trembling.

"Oh dear," the Duke said, tsking her as he returned to her side. "Didn't you learn anything from our last encounter? Your sister's grave is still fresh. Never let an enemy know what you value when it can be so easily taken away."

My blood boiled at the way the Duke grabbed her face, pinching it as he jerked it in his direction. She struggled against him, ready to take him down in a moment. Until the driver's gun cocked and she halted her movement. But it wasn't aimed at her.

The Duke looked at her. Then at me. And laughed.

"Well, Ms. Caccia, while I've got you here, I might as well ask. What have you done with the Allertons?"

"I don't know what you're talking about," she replied cooly, leaning into the man behind her.

"Don't play stupid," the Duke scoffed. "It's so irritating."

"They're on vacation. I haven't touched them," she smirked, batting her eyelashes at him. He placed his hands on his hips and backed away a step.

"On vacation," he repeated her answer, as if trying out the word for the first time. "That's clever."

She shifted against her captor. The knife. She had to be angling for her knife. I quickly calculated the odds of the two of us leaving here alive, then decided I hated statistics and would rather just get lucky. After all of this, we were owed a little luck.

The Duke unsheathed a pair of sunglasses and perched them on the tip of his nose. Looking over the top of them at my girl, he tapped her nose like he was scolding a dog.

"You've killed several of my men now. Turnabout is fair play, Ms. Caccia."

The Duke nodded at the driver. He looked at me.

And pulled the trigger.

50

Lilith

West wasn't moving.

"Oh, quiet, sweet girl. That's how louts like him are meant to die."

Acid pumped through my veins. Hot tears spilled down my cheeks.

No.

I blinked them away.

No.

All of my fears. Everything I'd let myself stop thinking about for a moment. It all came rushing back at the sight of the body splayed on the ground.

"Put this bitch down, Mr. Ellison. I've had enough of her bite," the Duke said, addressing the man behind me.

Clayton burst from the house, firing his weapon at the Duke and his driver. The man behind me fumbled for his gun as Harrison Augustus-Stanley and his driver hurried for his car. Bullets pinged off of the sides, ricocheting into the house's wood siding. Of course he had a bullet-proof car. It disappeared down the driveway. Any hope I had of catching him disappeared with it. But that didn't matter now.

West wasn't moving.

Rage crackled in me like lightning. I could taste its ether on my tongue.

I hadn't tried anything because I thought they would hurt West if I did. I'd been trying to go through my options because I thought I could find a way out. Spare him. Now that they'd put a bullet in him, they'd unleashed me from any inner restraint.

Because West wasn't moving.

One. I had one knife. The hunting knife. The one I'd carried since the day West gave it to me. It felt like a part of me as I palmed its grip behind me. Made to struggle against the man who'd held me back as they shot West. I fought against the guard with everything I had. Stepping down hard on his bleeding foot to loosen his grip. And spilled his guts from between his legs.

The man who'd held West captive only for him to be shot by the driver lifted his gun in my direction. He fired at me as I charged at him, his shots hitting the ground. The gun clattered on the concrete as Clayton put a bullet in him, sending the man into the puddle of gore left by his partner.

The goddamned Duke had left me to die. Wanted me to watch West die first. Wanted me to watch him die the way I'd watched Kaia die. And he got away.

Again.

Clayton was speaking to me. But I didn't care. I didn't hear him. Not as I heard the man I loved rasp a shallow breath.

"West?"

His name was a whimper as I fell to my knees at his side. My eyes went to his chest, where I thought they'd shot him. There was no wound. No blood. But they shot him and he went down. Where was he shot?

"Fuck," West coughed. "I forgot how much that stings."

Slow blinks followed as West roused. He looked up at me, splattered in the remains of Augustus-Stanley's men, and frowned. Wet drops darkened his shirt as I began weeping.

"Lili, I'm alright," he wheezed and coughed again, lifting his shirt to reveal a small bulletproof vest. "I just got the wind knocked out of me. And I blacked out when my head hit the concrete. But I'm alright."

West eased himself up to a sitting position and examined the bodies on the floor.

"Did you stab that man in the-" Clayton interrupted, examining the mess I'd left behind.

"Perineum," I sniffled.

"Yeesh."

West wiped the tears away from my cheeks, his fingers cool and calm against my hot skin. He moved me into his lap. Arms wrapped around me, pulling tight until I was pressed against his chest. Breath sawed out of me in sharp fragments. Even my bones shook with rage.

My hands left bloody prints on his shirt. I could only imagine what he saw when he looked down at me.

"Baby," he whispered in a voice so gentle it cracked my heart in two. "Don't cry. I'm alright."

"I thought," I choked out, unable to finish the awful truth as I released a sob.

"I know."

West kissed the top of my head, rocking me in his arms as he worked to soothe my trembling. It was unfair. Unfair that I had not learned the Duke's true weakness and he'd found mine so easily.

Lupo and Daniel were my family. They meant everything to me. And my friends, because I did have friends now, they held pieces of me in their hands. But this man. He'd put me back together. He knew the topography of my heart. Every dark valley. And he loved all of it.

THE BRUISE ON West's chest was ghastly. An angry black splotch spider-webbed out from where the bullet hit his vest. His pectoral muscle was half covered with it. I winced at the sight of it.

"At that range, I'm lucky it didn't penetrate."

Lanna sat back, finished with her examination. West pulled his shirt over his head and tied his hair into a knot.

"Well?" I asked, chewing on the corner of my thumb.

"He'll live."

West's sister gave him an irritated look. My racing thoughts distracted me from the bruises that were certainly forming on my aching body. I sipped from the wine I'd poured, hoping it would take the edge off. It didn't.

"Want to explain to me why you were shot today?"

He cocked an eyebrow and smirked. Lanna flicked him in the nose. I bit down on my lip to stifle a laugh. The sight made my chest ache. Made me remember that my own sibling was gone. West's attention shifted to me, but he spoke to his sister.

"Can we have a minute?"

"Sure," Lanna grumbled. "No funny business. You're still injured."

She stood from the bed, passing me in the doorway on her way out. I stepped inside and shut the door behind me.

"Come here," West said.

It was only a few small steps to close the distance between us. I came to stand in front of him. He took the wine from my hand and set it down on the nightstand, then put his arms around my waist. I looked him over again. Searched his face for any sign of pain.

"I'm fine, Lili."

One hand left my lower back as the other moved beneath the soft cotton of my tee shirt to stroke the skin beneath it.

"I'm sorry," I whispered, pressing my forehead to his. All of this. His injury. It was my fault. If he had died, that would have been my fault. My fault.

"I'm not."

I opened my eyes and frowned at him. His expression was soft and warm. So thoroughly him. Any fraying edge of my worry was beginning to ease with that look.

"Are you sure?"

He kissed me gently, taking one of my hands in both of his. Turning it over, he looked at it thoughtfully.

"There is not a single thing that would make me regret any of this."

West took a shaky breath. I tried to focus on what he was saying, but worry again overtook me, the fear that his sister may have missed some lingering issue. I looked at the half-open medical bag that still sat beside West on the bed.

"That bullet knocked me on my ass today, but it was a good thing."

"How?" I said as I choked on a laugh.

"Well," he said and cleared his throat. "It made me realize that we're living on borrowed time. All of this could be gone tomorrow. And we've wasted so much time already, Lili. Six years. I wanted you. Loved you. From the moment I met you, and it took six years for us to get here."

He took another shaky breath. His hands were trembling. Was he nervous?

Then I felt it. A sharp sting in my palm as he opened the skin with a knife. My knife. The one that had been strapped to my lower back. The one he had given me.

"What in the hell are you doing?" I barked.

He took my wrist, pulling my hand toward the nightstand. With a squeeze, drops of blood fell from my fist into the glass of wine. I stared at him, dumbfounded, as he picked up the glass.

"I will walk beside you in the dead of night. I will stalk your predators among the trees. I will know no peace if your enemies roam free. For their blood is my wine. Their souls are my fee."

And then he drank.

"I'm not swearing a vow to the family. Just you."

"West, I," I started, then winced as a bolt of pain shot through my hand.

"Wait," he interrupted. "There's more."

He took my injured hand in his and began to clean and dress the wound he'd made with his sister's medical supplies. When he was finished, he stared down at his work.

"You swore that vow to your sister because you love her. You know that I love you. I wanted to swear to you to show you I'm not going anywhere."

West held my hand in both of his, examining his work. His thumb coasted over my knuckles as his eyes met mine again.

"I want you to know I won't run. As long as I'm here, you will never be alone. So I'm not asking you now because it's not a question. It's a conclusion. Marry me, Lili."

My throat worked as my eyes filled with tears. Not because I was angry or even because I was in pain. No, I could handle pain. It was the idea that someone would choose this life. The idea that West would choose me.

"I..." I gasped, struggling for breath around my tight airway. I felt my lip wobble.

It was easy. So easy to form the word. The answer, because I only had one answer for him. One word. Three damned letters that would change my life forever.

"Yes."

His smile was a broad and open thing as he slipped a ring onto my finger, the tears in my eyes preventing me from actually looking at it. Folding me in his arms as I climbed into his lap, I lost myself in the feel of it. The feel of him. As I always did. I took a deep breath. Then another. Pain disappeared and fear melted away.

It felt like home.

51

WEST

*M*ine.

The tips of my fingers tingled as I held her. She said yes. She's mine. Blood pounded in my ears. I couldn't tell if I was shaking, or she was. Maybe we both were.

"West," Lilith groaned into my shoulder. "West, you're squeezing me too hard. I can't breathe."

I pulled away to look into her gleaming golden eyes. Happier than I'd seen them in months. She laughed and wiped away her tears. The motion seemed to remind her of what now rested on her finger. Lilith flattened her hand in front of her and angled it as she thoughtfully examined the new addition.

"Two stones?"

Leaning back on the bed, I took her hand and pointed with my thumb to the two different stones on the golden band. With gold ringed irises, I would never have given her anything else.

"This," I said, indicating the first iridescent pear-shaped stone. "Is opal."

She smiled and bit down on her lip, waiting for me to go on as she stared down at the ring I'd had made for her.

"And this," I continued, moving my thumb to the emerald-cut diamond.

"Is obviously a diamond. Opal for October. You. And a diamond for April. Me. You and me."

Lifting her hand to my mouth, I placed a kiss on her knuckles. I released it to cup her face. This Lilith. This new beauty. Her happiness was a light within her. I took her mouth, savoring the feel of her as I tasted her tears of joy.

"You and me," she repeated quietly against my lips. She sat back and took a steadying breath. "I don't understand how you had this ready so quickly."

Examining the ring on her finger, she looked up at me. Of course, she didn't miss my wince. Watching people was her business, and I'd just given myself away. Angling her head toward me for more information. I'd made her promise not to lie to me. I couldn't lie to her. Not now.

"It, uh, wasn't that quick."

Her silence was as good as asking the right question. Ever the patient interrogator.

"I'd had it made, then Lanna was holding onto it for me. I asked her to bring it over on our way back from Santa Barbara. She snuck it into the bag here," I said, patting the medical bag beside me.

Lili blinked at me. Still silent. Waiting for me to go on.

"When Lupo told me you needed to get married, I sort of panicked. I had it made for you. Was ready to ask you then. But then I realized how stupid that would have been."

Lili flinched.

"I just mean, it was stupid of me to think that marrying you would help you. That you needed me like that. So I didn't ask. Not then, anyway. Because you didn't. You don't."

Her expression softened as she sat backward, looking into my eyes with a mixture of love and an emotion I couldn't identify. Combing her fingers through my beard, she looked down at me as I tilted my chin up toward her.

"You don't need anyone," I said. "You're everything you need. I asked because I want you. Every part of you."

She squeezed her eyes shut. A tear rolled down her perfect olive cheek.

With another sigh, she opened her eyes to look down at me like the queen she was.

"You're wrong," Lili whispered, her voice strained by the tears lining her eyes. "I need you."

CLAYTON AND LANNA were in the kitchen together, bickering like siblings over what to order for dinner. Lupo sat at the island, rolling his eyes at their argument when he noticed Lili and I emerge from the bedroom. Lili tucked herself under my arm, careful to avoid touching the bruise burning in my chest.

"Took you two long enough. What do you want to eat?" He said, obviously hoping to end the debate.

Lili sniffled, wiping her eyes.

"What is that?" Clayton said, pointing at Lili. "What is that on your hand?"

Lanna gave him a shove.

"That looks like," Lupo said, trailing off before clearing his throat. "Well done, kid."

Lili looked up at me, grinning. I cupped her cheek and kissed her forehead. She returned her attention to Lupo and sighed before she spoke.

"I know it's fast," she started.

"Six years ain't fast. I watched you two make goo-goo eyes at each other every day."

"Can I be a bridesmaid?" Clayton joked. Lanna shoved him again.

"What's a bridesmaid?" Daniel's small form climbed onto the back of the sofa.

"That's someone who stands up with you when you get married, buddy," Lanna said.

The small boy looked thoughtful for a moment, digesting the information before he dismounted from the sofa. He approached Lupo's side and looked up at him, his face full of questions.

"Who's getting married?"

Lupo pointed at the two of us. Lili went still.

"Those two. West and Zia Lili are getting married."

"Is that okay?" Lili asked, her hand fisting in my shirt. With all of the change happening around him, I decided it was natural for her to be worried.

"If they get married, that makes West your uncle," Lupo added, as if trying to sweeten the deal.

Daniel looked at me. I nodded.

"And then I'll be your aunt," Lanna interjected.

The little boy looked at her. Then me and Lili. Then Lupo. Lili breathed a sigh of relief as the boy smiled.

"My family is getting so big."

52

Lilith

The basement at Pal's was beginning to stink. Helena Allerton, the old money socialite, was beginning to stink. I glanced at Frederick. Lanna had come with me to check his wounds. She changed the dressing. Cleaned it. Examined her stitches. She'd done good work healing him.

He watched her carefully. The masked woman who cared for him. I'd never let them see her face. She had a normal life to go back to. A normal job. Being associated with me would end her career.

"What do you want from me? I've given you everything," Helena warbled.

After all the hell I'd put her through, it was delicious to see her finally broken. I angled my head, but remained silent. The next part of this plan hinged solely on Helena's idea of me. A monster who would make her life pain. A relentless source of destruction.

"What do you want?"

She screamed the question at me. I pulled my phone out from the pocket of my leather jacket. Opened an app. Began scrolling. After finding what I was looking for, I waited.

"Is he healthy?" I asked Lanna.

The good doctor gave me a thumbs up as she listened to Frederick's heartbeat. No words. I'd told her she would not be allowed to speak in this room.

"Good. Freddy? Are you listening? I'm going to need your attention for this."

He blinked lazily at me. Still groggy from the pain meds Lanna had generously dosed him with.

"Blink twice if you understand me, Freddy."

One. Two. Good.

"Perfect. Your wife has generously given me the names of all of her buyers for her little side project. And I know you said you didn't know anything. But here's the thing. It's not enough."

I glanced at Helena, whose eyes had gone wide. She was afraid of me now. Wonderful.

"Now, I know what you're thinking. *She's going to nurse me back to health just to break me again.* Yes. I would do that. But I also get bored easily. So, I started looking for a new toy."

Hopping down from my perch on the work table, I strode toward Frederick until I was behind him. Lowering my phone to his view, I showed him exactly who my next intended target was going to be.

"No."

His protest was a whimper. I smiled, turning the phone so Helena could see it.

"It's been so easy to keep track of her. You should really warn her not to post her location on social media. It's dangerous. Anyone could find her. She doesn't have any tattoos, either. No identifying marks."

I closed the app and pulled up a piece of audio. This took some doing. Some audio manipulation from her vlogs made it easy enough for Dr. Forester to create what I needed.

"Help."

Kennedy Allerton's voice echoed off of the tile walls of the basement.

"Someone help me. Daddy. Please."

Frederick loosed a sob. Helena seethed in her seat. Oh, this was just too good. I dismissed Lanna with a wave, giving her a signal that I'd need just a moment.

"Now, I promise not to hurt your little girl if you do one thing for me. You do this one thing for me, and I will set her free. You will never see me again. Understand?"

THE DINING ROOM of our borrowed house had gone completely unused. Until now. Large glass windows looked out over the pool. A beautiful, live-edged wood table. A custom light fixture. It was all lovely. Even if I was too busy to appreciate it.

Sunlight filtered in through the beakers, jars, and bottles. Their reflections cast light onto the opposite wall in bright bursts. Flower petals filled the room with color as they dried on their racks.

"What is all of this for?" Lanna asked as she entered with a cup of tea in her hands.

Dark brown hair and eyes. She didn't look much like her brother in coloring, but their facial expressions matched. After staying to keep an eye on West, I was grateful to have her around for Daniel, too. I surveyed the plants, petals, and potions bubbling before me.

"There are some bad people in the world. The ones I had Helena call today? We're going to get rid of them."

We had watched Helena call every one of her buyers and explain that she and Frederick had gone off the radar for a little quality time with each other. I couldn't see Lanna's face then, but caution flooded her expression now as she sat at one of the leather dining chairs. She looked at each ingredient I was preparing, then at the notebooks I had splayed open before me.

"That's the recipe?"

I nodded.

"Something new I've been working on using some ingredients I already had. It has to leave the bloodstream quickly, so I'm playing with some elements here and there."

Lanna sipped her tea as I poured dried petals into the mortar bowl, watching as I ground them into a fine powder. Cupping her mug in both hands, she blew on the liquid.

"Tell me about these people."

I looked up from what I was doing, giving her my full attention. Her face held no judgement. Genuine interest.

"Did your brother tell you about what we found in Belfast?"

"The kids," Lanna nodded, a note of disgust entering her voice. "Yeah, he told me."

"Well, we're going to be taking care of that problem. At least for a while. I know nothing I can do will eliminate this completely. But I can do this."

I gestured toward the boiler that was waiting for my powdered petals. Lanna's lips became a thin line as she nodded again. Then she stood and left the room. Maybe that would be something she'd never get past. That her future sister-in-law happened to enforce her own form of justice, messy as it might be.

The petals in the bowl turned from a mixture of indigo and pink to a startling purple. Beautiful and deadly. I picked up the funnel and fed it into the distiller bottle's neck. Lanna re-entered the room in an apron, tying her hair back into a bun with gloved hands.

"Teach me."

I arched a brow at her as I carefully dumped the powder into the funnel. Free help? I'd take that.

"What do you want to know?"

"All of it. I want to know what you know."

IT SHOULDN'T HAVE surprised me that a doctor who worked in internal medicine would be a quick study, but Lanna took to the material quickly as soon as I explained my process. There was no sense in hiding this from her. She was about to be family, after all.

"This needs to distill for how long?" She asked, adjusting the burner below the bulb.

"Until we reach this volume," I pointed to the number in the notebook. "Then we can blend it with this oil."

I nodded toward the condenser in front of me. Lanna adjusted the burner again and stood, taking off her gloves to look over what we'd accomplished together. I couldn't help but smile a little. Her feminine energy was a nice break from being surrounded by men all the time.

West walked in from the adjoining kitchen, crossing his arms over his broad chest before speaking.

"What have you two been doing in here? It's been hours."

I glanced at Lanna. He wanted to spend his life with me, but was his sister off limits? I didn't know. My lips popped open, but it was Lanna who answered.

"We're making a sedative. A powerful one. She came up with it."

"And she needed your help?" West asked, a look of faux reproach crossing his face. My lips fought a smile. Maybe I didn't need to be worried.

"Actually," I offered. "Yes. I did. It's new. She's helping me with the dosage."

Lanna pushed her safety glasses up her face. After planting her hands on her hips, her stance went defiant.

"I volunteered. She's teaching me."

"Why?"

The question lacked judgement. Perhaps he'd made his peace with his sister getting mixed up in these things. Looking to Lanna, I waited. I wanted to hear this explanation, too.

"I've seen what she can do with these things. It's incredible. But she can't do it forever. She's the boss now. She needs help. We're family now. I want to help."

West uncrossed his arms, stuffing his hands into his pockets as he entered. He knew not to touch a damn thing without gloves. I'd warned him a dozen times. Daniel was banned from the area completely.

"Alright," he said carefully. "Before we sit down for dinner away from this toxic laboratory, can you explain what exactly this is supposed to do?"

Lanna looked to me, confidence waning. She was getting the hang of the chemistry, but maybe brutality was just beyond her scope. She spent most of her days treating people near death. Ushering them over the edge would be a difficult transition. I told myself that might be a good thing.

"It'll sort of be like anesthesia," I said. "Conscious sedation. Except instead of removing one's ability to feel, they'll only lose the ability to move."

"Meaning what?" West asked, his eyes going wary. He knew the answer.

I had the idea in the middle of the night. After waking up from yet another nightmare about my father. Unable to stop him from hurting me. From doing the worst. I had to take it. Every second.

"Meaning they'll feel it all," I said. "They won't be able to do anything about it."

53

WEST

The coffee table was littered with books. Half of them were scattered, pages splayed open. Others had notes jotted into the margins. What had once been a clear table now reflected what I could only imagine was happening inside of Clayton's mind.

He shifted on the sofa, turning the monitor towards me. A book fell off with the motion. I glanced at the cover. *Unboxing Complex PTSD*. He picked it up and put it back on the table.

"Helena gave us the lay of the land. Blueprints and everything from their custom architect. This place is huge. Who the fuck needs two kitchens?"

The Allerton estate was all the way out in Montecito. Its architecture seemed totally out of place with the rest of Santa Barbara County, it was entirely in character for the woman who had money to burn. I wondered what it would be like to swim in a pool that big as I looked the place over.

"Did Lili say what exactly the plan is going to be?" Clayton asked.

"She has a few ideas. Ronan and his crew will be joining us for the big event."

I looked around at the books again. He'd always seemed fine. But a lot of people always seem fine until one day their friends are left wondering why they ended it all. If Clayton was starting to deal with the shit we went through, I couldn't blame him.

"I started working through my shit a few years ago if you want my therapist's number."

"Huh?"

I wasn't sure why I'd said it, but maybe he didn't want to ask for help. I sure as hell hadn't wanted to.

"The books, man."

Clayton looked around as if seeing the books for the first time.

"Oh, uh. No. I mean, thank you. But no, that's not. That's not this."

I shrugged.

"Alright. Offer is on the table, if you're ever interested."

Clayton gave me a terse nod. He'd figure it out. Whatever it was. As one of the smartest men I'd ever worked with, I was confident he'd find his way through. I just hoped I'd be there to help him if he couldn't.

THE WOMAN WHO was going to be my wife slept soundly at my side. I'd left Clayton's to bring her dinner. Though I'd felt bad leaving my friend alone, I knew there were some boundaries you shouldn't cross with a friend. Not until they're ready. Whether he wanted to share with me about what was going on was up to him. But he knew I was ready to listen. For now, that was enough.

Miles of smooth, mouth-watering skin on top of a feather soft bed. Lilith Caccia in my arms. I'd never tire of the sight. After dinner, we came to our room and made use of the oversized bed. I could still taste the wine on her tongue as I made her moan for me.

Her breaths were soft as she slept, head propped on my chest and one leg draped over mine. I stroked her thigh. For the first time in a long time, I couldn't sleep from sheer joy. From excitement. The hand that rested on my chest bore the ring I'd had made for her. She never took it off.

"It's the most beautiful thing anyone has ever given me," she'd said.

The night Lupo told me that she needed to get married, I went to my apartment. I cleaned out my safe and went to a jeweler. Dropped thousands of dollars in their hand and told them what I needed. I knew that she deserved everything. And the thing that bothered me most was knowing that no one would love her the way that I could. She deserved that. Someone who would do anything for her. Someone who would kill for her. Die for her. Walk through fire for her.

Then I spent the rest of that night thinking. Lilith was the one. The only one for me. There was never any doubt in my mind about that. She stirred against me now, eyebrows drawing together. I threaded my fingers through the dark tangle of her hair, doing my best to soothe her back to sleep.

Asking Lilith to marry me was not something I wanted to be pressured into. It's why I decided not to. She didn't need me like that. Asking Lilith to marry me was something I wanted to do because I felt it. I wanted to do it right. Not that I had to get on one knee. She didn't need that when she knew I'd crawl for her.

"West," Lilith purred, half asleep. "You're still awake?"

"Go back to sleep, Trouble."

She smiled into my chest and shook her head. Her thigh slid over my hip as she climbed atop me and looked down, still smiling, at the ring on her hand as she placed it over my heart.

"That's Future Mrs. Trouble to you."

"That's a little cumbersome, but I like it."

Lilith bit down on her grin as my hands coasted up her thighs. A soft moan fell from her lips as her head tilted back. Her hips began to roll against my length. I laughed.

"As much as I want you to keep doing what you're doing, I'm afraid I might need a little more time before I can properly... uh, rise to the occasion."

"That's a shame," she smiled.

Shifting to remove herself from me, I stilled her with my hands on her hips. Lili stopped and arched a playful eyebrow at me. I lifted a finger to my lips and tapped.

"Get up here."

"I'm too tired to hold myself up. I'll smother you to death," she giggled.

God, I loved to hear her laugh.

"What a hell of a way to die," I grinned.

54

Lilith

A pot of water simmered in a rolling boil on the stove. I dropped a fistful of spaghetti into it and returned my attention to the cheese grater, glancing at the clock before again grating the Parmesan and the Romano into fine little shreds.

"I thought you didn't know how to cook."

"My grandma used to make this for me," I said with a quick look up at him. "Cacio e Pepe. It means cheese and pepper. Whenever I was sad or missing my mother, she'd make it for me. Then my sister started making it after she passed. Kaia was a good cook when she had time to actually do it."

Now was as good a time as any. Lupo and Daniel were out of the house. He and I had some time to talk. If he really wanted to marry me, he deserved to know everything. I focused on my tasks, moving from grating cheese to searching for the pepper grinder.

"Kaia did a lot of things very few people know about. She was a good mother. She took care of Daniel. Before that she took care of me. I swore my vow to her because of it. And it seems like she wanted to make sure I was taken care of even if she wasn't around. Daniel, too."

Placing a skillet on the stove, I turned it on and let it heat. West's eyes narrowed, going from moderate interest to outright intrigue. I took a breath and went to pull butter from the refrigerator.

"And?" West demanded.

"And," I continued. "She was good at that, too. Good at accounting. Good at investing. Good at money."

"Lili, if you're about to tell me you're wealthy, I guessed that from the gigantic family home we were living in and the S-Class Mercedes you used to drive. The jig is up."

I laughed. Wealthy was a bit of an understatement.

"We've been getting mixed up with these horrible people. These people with more money than most could ever dream of. They're truly awful people. I know how that sounds, coming from me," I said. Rambling. I was rambling. I spooned pasta water into a cup and set it on the counter. "Shit."

I hurriedly picked up the pot and dumped the spaghetti into a waiting colander in the sink. West followed me to the sink and drizzled olive oil over the top, tossing the noodles with a pair of tongs. I slapped his hand away.

"Let me do this!" I barked.

Putting his hands up in mock surrender, he let out a laugh and leaned against the counter to watch me finish the cheesy concoction in the pan before adding the noodles to it.

"Alright," West said. "So what?"

"So, I've been trying to just wrap my head around it. And I wanted you to know everything before you decided you wanted to be with me forever. And I wanted to do something for you, because I wanted you to know that it means something to me. That you would ask me to marry you, I mean."

After sprinkling extra cheese and grating pepper on top of one portion, I handed him a bowl full of noodles.

"Go sit," I nodded toward the table.

I carried my bowl to the table along with a bottle of white wine from the refrigerator, thankful for the screw top since I had no idea where these people kept their corkscrew. Plopping onto the stool, I opened it and poured a glass for the two of us. West tapped his glass against mine and took a drink.

"Tell me whatever it is you need to tell me."

Fuck it.

"West, Kaia left me over a billion dollars."

He coughed on his wine. For a moment, I just sat there, letting him catch his breath. When he took another sip and set his glass down, he took my hand and squeezed it.

"I'm not sure why you think that's a bad thing, Lili."

"Money is," I sighed. "What if it makes me worse than I already am? What if I become like Benjamin or the Allertons?"

"Money doesn't make people who they are. It just amplifies it. If you're a bad person, money won't make you any better. You're a good person, Lili. You're a little more violent than most people, but you're good."

West pulled my stool toward him, earning a cringe from me as I thought about the legs dragging on the hardwood floor. With both hands, he cupped my face. A smile danced across his lips, adding a brightness to his dusky green eyes before he leaned in and kissed me.

"Is that everything?" He asked against my lips. I nodded my confirmation. Yes, that was everything. "Good. Can I ask you something?"

"Yeah," I muttered.

"Marry me?"

I exploded with laughter.

"ARE THOSE TWO ever coming back?" West laughed, looking at his watch.

"Nico said they were going to go to the house for some of Daniel's books after they went to the hospital to pick up Lupo's meds. With traffic, it might take all night," I joked, setting my wine down on the coffee table.

"That gives us some time, then."

"For what?"

"For this."

West circled an arm around my waist, pulling me beneath him. I squeaked in surprise. He braced one hand on the arm of the couch, working to keep his massive form from overpowering me. The other hand moved up my body until his fingers closed gently around my neck. Dominating and possessive, but affectionate.

"Whose are you?" He lowered himself until his nose grazed mine, his green eyes burning with intent.

"Yours."

"Who do you belong to?" He smirked as he rolled his still-clothed hips into mine, a torturously decadent movement that stole my breath as I felt his stiff length behind the zipper of his work pants.

"You. West, I'm yours." My voice was nothing but soft sounds between panting breaths.

"That's right."

West's hand pulled away from my neck, skating down my body as he kissed the sensitive skin beneath my ear. Warm breath rasped against it. I shut my eyes, taking in all of him. His scent. His touch. His love.

"I need you," I whimpered.

With deft movements, he eliminated every article of my clothing that stood between his hands and my skin. Treating them like offending obstacles, he threw them across the room until I was completely bare beneath him.

"Tell me," West said as he knelt on the sofa. I pushed up the cotton of his black tee shirt, anxious to get my hands on more of him. Sitting up so I could better reach him, I traced a line with my tongue down the patch of hair beneath his navel and smiled at his shuddering breath.

"Tell you what?"

My question was hot on his skin as I bent to kiss the tempting space between his navel and his pelvis. One. Two. West smirked skyward, releasing an amused grunt, and began unfastening his fly.

"Tell me," he tried again.

I slid his pants down, moving my mouth down his taught stomach with licks and kisses until my tongue traced along his length.

"Fuck, never mind," he groaned.

The sound of his whimpers as I took him into my mouth was so sweet. I relished them. To have such a powerful man utterly at my mercy was like fire to the gasoline in my blood. West tenderly thumbed my cheeks as he watched every move I made.

I could have finished him. If I had gone on any longer, I would have. I was certain of it. But West slipped his grip to my chin to stop me. He stood up, sliding the rest of his clothes off and sat down beside me.

"Come here," he beckoned, palming his cock.

I moved, straddling his muscular thighs so his arousal was pressed between us. Those dark green eyes took me in, quieting every negative feeling threatening to voice itself in my mind. Through his eyes, I saw a woman worthy of being cared for. Someone who could be worthy of being his. Someone powerful.

"West," I started as I pressed my hands to his chest, feeling his thundering heart beneath my fingertips. Opal and diamond.

You and me.

Even as I looked down at the ring and thought about what it represented, I knew I needed to say it. Leap and give him everything. "Love is too small a word for what I feel for you. But I can't think of a better one. I love you."

Large hands cupped my jaw, thumbs coasting over the apples of my cheeks. He looked at me with a smile that was so happy I'll remember it until my last breath.

"I know."

Callus covered palms trailed down my body, rasping over my furled nipples and the plane of my stomach. I watched his face as his hands continued moving down. Down until they smoothed over the curve of my ass, then gripped it to pull me against him.

West nipped at my jaw, his beard grazing my collarbone. He leaned closer to rake his teeth over my neck. I arched and exposed my throat to him. An offering. He understood my offering for what it was as his teeth gently closed around the exposed column. A submission. Only for him. Only ever for him.

My core tightened, aching for more of him. All of him. I squeezed my eyes shut, pushing away the insecurities that hounded me. They howled and barked, demanding I remember I may never feel truly worthy of his love. No. With him, I could be anything. Worthy. With his love, I was infinite. Yesterday, today, tomorrow. I'd take it for the rest of my life.

"Open your eyes."

At his command, I did. Opened my eyes to find him grinning at me. The sight tugged at my heart, the heart that was already racing with cresting anticipation.

West lifted me until he prodded at my entrance. I steadied myself, bracing my hands on the sofa behind him.

"Lili," he breathed my name, soft and sweet. He leaned forward to kiss me, letting his mouth move gently against mine before speaking again. "I love you, too."

With a swift tug downward, he thrust upward until he buried himself in me. I cried out at the sudden stretch of him. His hands were still controlling the movement of my hips, moving my body against his until I facilitated the motion.

"That's it. Ride me, gorgeous. "

Every stroke of him, every swirling motion of my hips into his, narrowed my senses to the feel of him. I felt my brow furrow as he nipped at my lip, pulling it between his teeth gently as a hand moved between us and began tormenting the sensitive bud between my legs. A sharp inhale escaped me as I bowed forward, pressing my face into his shoulder.

"You can do it. Give me everything."

I whimpered. It shouldn't have surprised me, but it somehow always did. We'd trained together for years. Learned each other's strengths and weaknesses. It seemed like West knew my body better than anyone could. Knew exactly what to do to make me submit. He was the only person who could earn my submission. Make me come undone. Make me his.

"I've got you," West's voice was a dark rasp as he thrust upward into me. "I've got you. Let me hear you. Finish for me. I know you want to."

The words seemed to summon the action as a gasping wail flew from my lips. My nails pressed into his shoulders, marking him.

"Don't stop," he groaned.

My body moved at his command, still riding through the electric bolts of release coursing through every nerve. The hand on my ass squeezed, pulling me down in desperate strokes that matched the breath sawing out of him.

"Fuck it," he growled, twisting, throwing our joined bodies around until my back was pressed into the seat of the sofa and he was above me.

One hand shoved under my knee, pressing my leg out to better angle himself between them. I arched against him, letting my other leg come around his waist. Sweat dripped off of the tip of his nose onto the wolf tattoo between my breasts as his thrusts became wild and urgent.

"Touch yourself. I want," he breathed, stopping to lick my throat and lavish my mouth with a kiss that seared my soul. "I want to hear those pretty noises."

My hand went to the apex of my thighs, stroking and circling where he commanded. Every inch of my skin was on fire for him. West pressed his forehead to mine, watching me with those smoky green eyes. I knew he could feel my legs shake around him. A smile spread across his mouth as I whimpered and panted, so close to release again.

"One more," he gritted out. "Come on. One more for me, Trouble."

A surprised sob wracked my body as I came again. For him. For that smile. For the man who held my heart in his large, callused hands. West's eyes burned into mine as he imprinted himself upon me with a growl.

I slumped back onto the couch, his weight pressing into me with the exhaustion I knew we both felt. We were both thoroughly drained. West's throat worked, swallowing before attempting to speak through frail breaths.

"I can feel you," he breathed.

"You're still inside of me," I laughed. "I should hope so."

"No," he smiled and slid the large hand between us up over the wolf tattoo. "In here. I can feel you."

West sat up, pulling me into his lap again. He palmed my tattooed sternum again, looking at it with sheer awe. I covered his hand with mine and sat backward, bracing my other hand on his thigh so I could look into his eyes. So filled with joy. Soft and open for me. I took a breath and smiled. Let him see what he made me feel. And I'd let him hear it, too.

"It's yours, West. It's damaged. But it's yours."

West's face was a thing of beauty. The face that was flush with color, glowing with the reflection of everything I felt for him. His fingers curled around my hand and lifted it briefly to his chest.

"You've always had mine, Lili," he said, moving my hand again to kiss my fingertips. I opened my hand and shifted to curl into him as I cupped his jaw, and he leaned into it, nuzzling as he looked down at me. "Every second of every day. You always will."

"I know."

We sat on the sofa, still tangled up in each other until West began... laughing. I reared back and angled my head at him, confused. What was so funny?

"I fucking forgot."

I shook my head, still confused. West pulled a throw blanket from the arm of the sofa, lifting me off of himself to wrap it around me. Then, without warning, picked me up and threw me over a shoulder. His free hand lifted a middle finger in the air.

"The cameras. I forgot about the fucking cameras."

Night evaporated around us. I disappeared into West. Worries slipped away with every minute spent next to him. Under him. On top of him. Until I couldn't move. Couldn't keep my eyes open for another moment. And slept more soundly than I ever had. Knowing that I belonged to someone who would never break me.

West's warmth surrounded me as the sun poured in through the windows, coating us in soft morning light. His chest rose and fell beneath my head with a gentle snore I'd learned to appreciate. I couldn't help but feel that this was the dawn of something more extraordinary than I could have ever imagined.

With him, I felt safe and whole. The snarling, angry thing inside me finally curled up and closed its eyes. For the first time, I understood what I was running away from and cursed myself for letting fear make me so incredibly stupid.

55

WEST

Chairs were turned up on tables. The Chancer smelled like lemon and cleaning fluid. One of the waiters was mopping the polished floor. As if the young man had been expecting me, he dipped his chin in greeting and kept working.

It was a different place after all the drinkers had gone home for the night. No music in the air. Only the sound of glasses clinking against each other as they were loaded into the dishwasher.

The door to the back room opened. Killian stepped out. Clad in a black tee shirt, jeans, and motorcycle boots. This was the most casual I'd ever seen him. I wondered if the matte black Indian Scout Bobber parked beside Clayton's Harley outside belonged to him.

"Come on, Hale. You're late."

I followed him through the door, where his father was waiting in his usual seat at the head of the table. Clayton sat at his side, his laptop casting his face in a pale blue glow. He looked at me over the bridge of his glasses as I entered and returned his attention to the screen.

"Good evening," Ronan said as he scratched at his jaw. "I see you made it out of that scrape in Santa Barbara."

"No thanks to you," I growled.

Clayton's fingers stilled on the keyboard. Ronan laughed, lifting a pint of dark beer to his lips. Though the lights were low, I noticed the bruises and scrapes on his knuckles. I recognized that sort of injury. The big boss of the Arawn family had fought someone.

Killian returned to the room with two pints of beer, setting one down in front of me before rounding the table to sit beside his father.

"Regardless," Ronan smirked. "I apologize for the late hour. Mr. Wrigley was able to make some progress on our problem and we have an opportunity that we'll need to move on quickly."

I glanced at Clayton. Even though he technically worked for Ronan, hearing information like this second hand still chaffed. He remained focused on his laptop, avoiding meeting my eye. Ronan continued.

"Harrison Augustus-Stanley made a mistake. And now he'll be paying for it."

The mistake had to be huge if we needed to meet in the small hours of the morning about it. I glanced at Clayton's laptop. Three windows were open. One with a scrawling feed of letters and numbers that seemed to be constantly updating. One with a stationary image of what looked like a topographical chart. The other with a satellite feed that was gradually rendering an image.

"Clayton tracked him from Santa Barbara. All the way to his home in the middle of unmarked territory in the lush hills of Scotland. Luckily for us and thanks to Ms. Caccia's research, we know he has engagements in the area for the two weeks."

Suddenly the pint of beer before me didn't seem like enough. The Duke's home. His real home. Not the ancestral one that gave him his title, but the one where he hid out from the world. No longer off the map, according to the work my friend had done. No wonder Ronan had been in the mood to let my comment slide.

"What are you saying?" I said before slugging down a few gulps of beer to quell the building anxiety in my blood.

"I'm saying keep your bag packed because I'll be needing your services. We depart in four days."

I SLIPPED MY boots off, trying to avoid letting them clunk on the floor. Moonlight poured in through the window, illuminating the sleeping woman I was anxious to crawl into bed next to.

My shirt still smelled of Ronan's cigar. I tossed it toward my bag on the ground. My pants followed it. No sense in doing another load of wash. Not when we were going to be getting out of here.

On careful footsteps, I came to the bed. Sleeping Lili was a vision few would ever get to appreciate. Rippling black tresses spilled down her back. A few wisps of black obscured her face, pressed into the pillow she clutched. The neck of my shirt was stretched, exposing an expanse of skin. I crawled over her, pressing a kiss to her bare shoulder. She murmured an unintelligible response.

The mattress shifted with my weight as I settled behind her. My hands went to her waist, pulling Lilith into my body. I'd been sleeping better these days. Since I began sharing a bed with her, sure, but that sleep had improved further still when she agreed to marry me.

I kissed her in greeting. In her half-asleep state, her mouth lingered on mine. Her lips tasted like toothpaste. Soft hums and sleepy kisses from the most powerful woman in the city. But to me, she would always just be Lili. *My* Lili.

She shifted in my hold, her sleep-addled gaze fixing on me.

"What did Ronan want?" She rasped.

I kissed her again, trying to buy time to answer. She didn't need to know about what was to come. There was no danger in it. Not for me. Only for the man who hurt her.

"He has some business overseas he wants Clayton and I to deal with."

A little line appeared between her dark brows as she frowned at me.

"What kind of business?"

I nudged her nose with mine and reclined, squeezing her side as I nuzzled into the lush black tresses rich with her scent. This woman. A small part of me still couldn't believe she was going to be mine forever. My wife.

"It's nothing to worry about, Trouble."

She gave a tired hum, scooting backward to press her body to mine. I adjusted my position, temporarily bringing my lips to her ear as I asked the question I'd been thinking about the whole drive home.

"Do you want to go home tomorrow?"

"Home?" Her voice was clearer now.

"Sh," I said. "The house. Ronan assured me it would be safe now."

She made a noise half between a laugh and a hum. A more conscious Lili would ask follow-up questions. Sleepy Lili was only thoughtful, considering. Without answering, she shifted against me. A small, delicate hand found mine at her waist. She threaded our fingers together and nuzzled into the pillow again. For a while, there was only silence. Then, with a press of her lips to the back of my hand, I had my answer.

We were going home.

56

Lilith

"Come on, buddy," I said as I opened our front door.

"I want people to stop calling me 'buddy.' My name is Daniel."

Lupo insisted that Daniel looked just like Dante. Maybe that was true. But that kid sounded more and more like his mother every day. The thought rubbed up against the ache of her absence.

West's hand went to his back as he passed us to walk upstairs. If anyone was lurking in a dark corner, my fiance would find them. With the house under near-constant guard by the family, I was sure that wasn't the case, but having an ex Navy SEAL secure your home after you've been away was a comfort I couldn't pass up.

Daniel flopped onto the sofa as if no time had passed.

"Grandpa," he called from his seat.

"Yeah, Champ?"

"Is there still ice cream in the freezer?"

Lupo chuckled as he placed his bag at the foot of the stairs. Remus trotted in behind him. The grey mutt kept moving past him. Daniel gave the space on the sofa beside himself a small pat. That was all the permission Remus needed to hurl himself onto the sofa beside the boy.

"I think I've been replaced," Lupo muttered.

The dog glanced over at Lupo, then settled his head on Daniel's lap. I gave Lupo a tight smile and walked outside to retrieve more of our things.

"WHAT'S THAT?" WEST asked, pointing to a piece of blue paper sticking out of the file box I'd hauled into the bedroom and plopped onto the dresser, abandoning it to start a load of laundry.

I'd been sorting through the box, reading my grandfather's old notes. His ledgers. Thoughts on adjacent families. Movements I hadn't been aware of as a child. It was a window into the man he was beyond caring for my sister and me. But some of it was just plain junk. I wasn't sure why Kaia had kept some of it.

"Yeah, it's a flyer for a garage sale from our old neighborhood. I don't know why he kept it," I laughed as I fished it out to hand to West and resumed folding laundry on the bed.

"Lili, this isn't just a flyer."

I looked over my shoulder to find West reading the back of the flyer with furrowed brows. Tossing the shirt I'd been holding to the bed, I remained still. Waiting.

"Adriana," he said, with a note of confirmation in his voice.

"That's my mother. What does it say about my mother?"

My fingers shook as I took the blue paper from his hands.

"It looks like a letter. From your mother."

On the back of a flyer? That didn't make any sense. Why would my mother send anyone a letter on the back of a flyer? My stomach knotted as I flipped the paper over and back as if it would answer any of the questions swarming in my mind, ready to sting me with their answers.

"This is the week they died," I said as I eyed the date. With a deep intake of breath, I sighed through the dropping sensation in my gut as I began reading.

Dear Matteo,

Your son has been monitoring every phone call I make. Every message I send. I've sent this letter with Kaia, who has been instructed to hand-deliver it to you. I trust her to keep this request quiet. One that I must now ask of you.

When I first met Raoul, I thought we would have a lot in common, as two only children in powerful families. But I soon learned he had no interest in loving me. For years I fooled myself into thinking his affection for me would grow, and out of that misguided hope, I was gifted two daughters. And he cursed me for it. A fact that you well know.

Matteo, you have been kind to me ever since my family was joined to yours. Your generosity to my parents while they were still living will never be forgotten. You've been more like a father to my girls than your son ever could. You've loved them from the first moment you held them. But that is not the case for Raoul. I'm not sure he has ever loved them. I've done my best to shield them from his horrors, but I fear it is not enough.

He will not let me leave. He will not let me know peace. And every day his rage brings new terror into our home. I am wracked with guilt because all I can do is stand by and watch as he hurts my daughters in ways I could never have imagined.

That I could not act. Could not defend them from the wounds and fear... That is a shame I will carry with me to my grave.

I ask you now to do what a father must do. Not for Raoul, but for Kaia Mia. For Lilith. They deserve to know a life beyond the shadows of their fear. They deserve real happiness. I have seen the way they light up in your presence. They feel true safety in your home.

I beg of you, Matteo. Please help them. End their suffering. And give them a wonderful life.

With Love and Gratitude Always,
Adriana

Bile rushed up my throat as I ran for the bathroom. She knew. More than that, she asked for it. My mother's letter to my grandfather lay on the carpet, the soft blue sheet of paper like a fallen bird on a dark sea. West picked up the letter and folded it, placing it on the dresser before walking into the bathroom to kneel behind me as I emptied my stomach into the toilet.

West's hand made soft circles on my back as the vomiting eased. Tears pushed out of my eyes as I squeezed them shut. Collapsing under my weight, under the weight of everything I had learned, I fell backward only to be caught by strong arms. They steadied me as I tried to find my breath through sobs that had begun without my knowing.

"She knew," I hiccuped.

The thought started another bout of tears. I summoned the ability to speak, barely. But I went on.

"She knew. The letter. It asked my grandfather. She asked him to do it. He was supposed to cause an accident. She got in the car. He shot her but it didn't matter. She wanted to die."

A hand sifted into my hair and did so over and over again, calming me before another word was spoken.

"She was protecting you."

A strangled sob was my only response. West made quiet, soothing noises as he continued feeding his fingers through my hair.

Soft knocks on the door shook me from where I'd started to drift off in West's arms. The weight of my grief had pulled me down into unconsciousness. He was there to catch me, as he had been for months. Maybe even longer than I knew. But when I woke a short while later, he was there. Waiting patiently.

"Is everything alright?" Lupo asked from the bathroom doorway. "I thought I heard someone getting sick in here."

He glanced at me, then at West. A look of discomfort washed over his features. I rolled my eyes.

"It's not that," I said. "I'm on birth control. I was just upset. I get sick sometimes when I'm upset."

Lupo nodded his understanding. I thought about the letter. About what he had told me. He'd thought it was an accident. Something for which he'd blamed himself for years. Decades, even. Guilt over my sister still gnawed at me. I couldn't imagine how it ate at him. It wasn't his cross to bear.

"Actually," I sniffled. "I need to talk to you."

West helped me to my feet, then stood up himself and went into our bedroom. I followed, as did Lupo.

"She was protecting you."

That's what West said. My mother. She left my sister and I behind. After my parents were killed, Kaia and I had a good life. It was full of love and laughter. We didn't have a monster waiting at home for us. Instead, we felt safe in this house. This house was more my home than the haunted old house I used to walk by on sleepless nights.

My mother gave us that life by giving up her own. If she had lived, she would have been sold off in another political marriage with someone like my father. We would have been pawns in whatever scheme his replacement had in mind. Instead, she eliminated the complication of her survival. A sacrifice for us.

"She was protecting you."

And she did.

How could I fault Lupo for that?

"I'm not angry with you about it. About what happened with my parents," I started. It was true. It had been true for days. I had been sad. But not angry. "And I know you're in remission."

Lupo nodded. He'd come back from the hospital with no signs of active cancer in his test results. West had almost squeezed the air out of him in a celebratory hug.

"Daniel needs a parent in his life. As much as I love the kid, I can't be that for him. But you can."

West watched from his side of the bed, folding clothes and tucking them away in the dresser. I glanced in his direction.

I'd been thinking about it for weeks. With everything going on, I'd barely spent time with the kid. It ate at me with every passing hour. He had to miss school because of me. Miss seeing his friends. Daniel deserved a normal life. At least, a semi-normal one. Lupo could give that to him in a way I couldn't.

"I don't know," the old man said, gazing down at his boots.

"Kaia provided for him in her will. For him and his guardian. That money would be yours."

"Raising another kid," he said with a heavy sigh. Callus-addled hands scrubbed over his face.

"Raising your grandson," I added.

Maybe someday I would show him the letter. Free him of the burden of my mother's death. But I didn't have that in me now. All I could offer was this. It was enough.

He laughed and lifted his blue eyes with a nod. They were damp with unshed tears. He cleared his throat. Still, his words were barely more than a whisper.

"Thank you."

57

Lilith

Cooking was never my strong suit. But I didn't need to be professional to accomplish what I needed. The Bootlegger chef had been more than happy to lend me his services for the evening. He'd gone about his business and not noticed the drops I added to his finished plates.

To the naked eye, it was nothing. On a single plate, it was nothing. Harmless.

"After tonight, Frederick and I are free to go?" Helena asked as she adjusted the lace gloves that covered her nailless fingers. Frederick appeared behind her, dressed in an immaculate tuxedo.

"Yes," I grinned. "After tonight, you and your husband will be free."

"And you'll release my daughter."

I never had her daughter to begin with, but she didn't need to know that. "Yes."

She'd swept her hair up on one side with a pearl encrusted tortoiseshell comb. I eyed it, wondering if it would be bad form to keep it for myself. The color of her sea-foam green dress complimented it nicely. Helena unsheathed a Valentino lipstick and painted her lips in the reflection of one of the glass kitchen cabinets.

"I have your word?" She said, eyeing me from the glass.

"You do. Just get through dinner and I'll handle everyone from there. Your guests will meet their maker afterward."

Helena shuddered, re-sheathing the lipstick and setting it on the counter in the butler's pantry. I'd been in here pouring champagne after dropping a mild sedative into each crystal glass when she entered. She picked up a glass and threw back the contents. I refilled it with the remainder of the bottle.

West entered and picked up a silver tray loaded with champagne glasses. God, he looked good in a catering uniform. Okay, all uniforms. I, however, felt like one of those penguins from Mary Poppins. Then I loaded a tray for myself.

"People are starting to arrive," he said mildly. I smiled at him.

"Your guests await, Mrs. Allerton."

West and I handed glasses to each guest who arrived. Some hugged Helena, asking where she's been. Telling her how refreshed she looks from her holiday. Hug, sip, slurp. None of them bothered to look the waitstaff in the eye. One woman cast West an appreciative glance. I shoved a glass into her hand.

Each of them was dressed in formalwear that whispered of their wealth. Dazzling diamonds. Sparkling jewels. Even their perfume and cologne hinted at their inflated bank accounts. I remembered Juliet telling me that we'd have to change my scent when I had started my erroneous relationship with Benjamin. She was right. People do notice that kind of thing.

AS I WATCHED Helena's guests seat themselves around the table, directed by little handwritten seating cards, I wondered how many of them had children. How many had daughters old enough to be targeted by the very system they supported? How many grandchildren were the same age as Ainsley, the little girl we'd freed from what was certain to be a life of horrors? How long would that life have been if we'd never found those children?

They tucked themselves into their seats and emptied their champagne flutes. West and I watched, collecting each empty glass. Some sneered at the polished silver flatware. Others laughed as if they hadn't a care in the world. I'd never done this many at once before. Each of them was within roughly the same body weight range. The doses Lanna had measured out would work. The old me would have second-guessed herself. Wondered if she was making the right decision. But as a man who looked to be in his late seventies grimaced at the smile of his far younger wife, I decided I didn't care.

It was difficult not to glance at West across the table as we served course after course. I'd already spilled a bit on my white serving coat. Ice-cold salmon tartare and sea urchin. Charred octopus with chorizo mousse. The chef from the Bootlegger had outdone himself. I made a mental note to hire the chef for a date night at the house. Even knowing what I'd dosed the food with, every plate looked tempting.

They talked with each other and became gradually less inhibited. Just as the first course was meant to. Completely unaware of the food that slowly betrayed them. Bite by bite, they swallowed down the cocktail of drugs I'd crafted. Each element unfolding in their bloodstream like notes in a glass of wine with every course set for the evening.

"Is this ready?" I asked as I examined the dessert.

"Yeah," the chef said as he picked up the server and began portioning it onto delicate little plates. "Thanks again for helping with the frosting."

"Of course," I smiled. "Listen, once you finish cutting these slices, you're done here. Head home and my team will take care of everything else."

No need for him to see what would happen next.

Fat slices of Brooklyn Blackout cake, the Bootlegger's special dessert. Each slice was sitting up like a soldier. I carefully placed a drug-soaked maraschino cherry atop each serving. Gleaming and beautiful. For a moment, my mother's bright smile in a photo forever lost to fire flashed through my mind. I dragged a finger through the frosting and almost sucked it away. Then thought better of it and wiped it on the kitchen towel beside me. Too tempting.

No one says no to dessert.

Who could say no to this chocolate cake? Every plate was set before them with a tiny silver fork. A mockery of an instrument compared to a serving so large. Ready to devour. China coffee cups were set beside the plates, filled from the polished silver coffee pot Helena had said was a "family heirloom." Conversation had halted completely as cherries popped into their mouths. It went silent the way every dining table goes silent when the food was as good as this cake always was.

It didn't take long. I walked around the table with the polished silver coffee pot. Checking the guests as they slid down into their chairs, or off of them. Some were laying on the table. One pretty face stared blankly into the frosting that coated her cheek. Each of them was unable to move. All of them were aware of my presence.

Breathing. Alive. Trapped.

Just as they should be.

"Coffee?" I lifted the pot cheerfully, offering it to Helena as I came to her side. Slumped in her chair, her eyes slowly shifted to me. The look of betrayal was sweeter than the cake she'd polished off only moments ago.

"A firing squad," I'd told her. "Each of your guests will get a wonderful last meal. Then they'll face the firing squad."

I angled my head at her and smiled brightly. She'd been foolish to trust me. After every cent she'd earned thanks to someone else's pain. Every lie she'd told to get her greedy little hands on more money. Did she really think the woman who kidnapped her would tell her the truth? Would she really think that woman would tell her the lion's share of the paralytic had been in the frosting?

"All of you are probably wondering who I am. You ignored me all night, which isn't a surprise. No one asked my name. My first name is Lilith. I used to absolutely hate my middle name. It's so cumbersome. Difficult to spell. People always mispronounce it. Rhamnusia."

I looked down at Helena as I filled her cup with coffee. She narrowed her eyes at me. I was sure she would scream at me if she'd had the ability. Oh well.

"It's an old name. Based in ancient mythology. The goddess of retribution. I'm here to collect. I've been subjected to awful speeches from people who thought they were about to kill me, so I know how boring they can be. All I have to say is this. You know why you're here. You know what you've done. This is nothing less than you deserve."

West, Clayton, and the rest of the Caccia men circled the table as they poured alcohol all over the expensive furnishings around the dining room. It was almost enough to disguise the scent of gas coming from the kitchen.

"Don't you think cake is a wee bit on the nose?" Ronan said as he sidled up beside me, the Zippo lighter in his hand flipping open and closed. He was ready and so was I. "Eliminating the aristocracy is a very French Revolution thing to begin with."

"Well, it was either this or a guillotine," I laughed.

A horrible, tragic accident. That's how news networks would report on it later. A dinner party and a gas leak. They'd all dosed themselves too heavily with the prescription drugs from bottles planted in coats and handbags they'd handed over so readily. Then they'd burn to death. No one knew until it was too late.

Our men exited the building, having done one final sweep of the house. Ronan and I walked out onto the terrace. I looked back at the table filled with paralyzed men and women. Then I stuffed the rag into the bottle of vodka and handed it to Ronan. He nodded his thanks to me as I took West's hand and walked away.

I'd ushered these people to the threshold of eternity. Ronan would see them through the flaming gates of hell.

58

Lilith

I stood in the bathroom of my office, staring at my reflection. Red lips. Well-tailored suit. Hazel eyes that were more gold than green or brown. My long wavy black hair was tamed into a ponytail, highlighting the cheekbones my sister and I shared. Even if my jaw was always a bit softer.

Opening the medicine cabinet, I pulled out the tube of lipstick to reapply and shut the mirror-covered door. Kaia stared back at me from the other side.

Her pin straight hair was pulled back as mine was. Lips as red as mine. Brown eyes stared at me, pained and filled with regret.

"It wasn't supposed to be me."

No. It wasn't supposed to be her. I'd vowed to give my life for hers.

"I know," I said.

She shook her head. No. She looked at me again, this time enunciating every word.

"No. It was never supposed to be me."

"I know," I said again, anger creeping into my voice. "Don't you think I know? I did everything I could to stop it. Everything. I'm sorry."

Kaia lurched forward, wrapping her hands around my shoulders. Squeezing tightly, she smiled. Her brown eyes, our mother's eyes, softened.

I saw everything. Every time she stepped in front of my father's fist. Each *battle for my benefit. Every time she lent me a sympathetic ear. Each time she guided me gently instead of reprimanding me. Every single choice she made out of love for me. As if her touch had allowed me to do so.*

"No," she said quietly. "I did everything I could."

Leaning backward, she straightened my jacket. Brushed the shoulders gently, smoothing away wrinkles.

"This. It was always supposed to be you."

WHEN MY SISTER took over the family, she changed this club. Made it her own. I'd never expected to be in this position. In her shoes. But when the club burned down, it felt like a sign. To accept the loss of what once was and rise from the ashes to start anew.

Nico informed me that the reconstruction of the club was complete. From the pyre, a new Muse had emerged. Not much had changed on the outside then. That wasn't the case now. Now there was a bigger, flashier sign. New brick siding instead of stucco. Two steel doors instead of the single one that West used to guard. What once was a villa was now a fortress.

I'd seen the place for myself already. In a quiet moment of the early morning. It forced tears to my eyes. The contractor worried he had done a bad job. I waved him off. Told him they were tears a joy. An easy lie. The place looked beautiful. Everything was exactly as I wanted it. It rubbed up against the hollow ache in me. One more place where I could no longer feel my sister.

Muse had always been the nicest gentleman's club in Los Angeles. Now it could rival clubs around the world. West let out a surprised breath as he took in the club that I'd carefully redesigned with the help of a professional. I approached the new, much larger stage and started explaining the changes like a tour guide.

"So, the main stage is bigger. Now we can have more than one dancer working at a time. And there's a new stage upstairs in VIP. It's small, but the VIP is now one large booth with a bar top surrounding the stage. It's going to be like a neon fever dream in here. Don't even get me started on all the upgrades to the Champagne Room."

West followed me to the new bar area, passing through all of the dark green velvet barrel chairs at every new table. While the bar layout was similar, all of the finishes were new. Black fixtures had replaced chrome. Glowing white marble replaced the original bar top.

"This is all very nice, Lili," West chuckled as I pointed out detail after detail, like a child on Christmas showing off her new toys.

"Wait until you see the office," I beamed.

He pulled me into him, allowing me to circle my arms around his waist. That cedar and fresh laundry scent seeped into me with his warmth. I didn't miss his wince as I pulled away, remembering the fresh wolf tattoo on his ribs.

"Sorry," I winced.

Taking my hand in his, he squeezed.

"Show me."

It smelled like fresh paint and leather. The carefully curated feminine aesthetic my sister had surrounded herself with was gone, replaced by a minimalist dark twin. A small black sofa sat where the chestnut leather sofa had been and matching leather chairs faced the new black marble desk. After dreaming of her last night, it felt like I had her blessing.

"It's smaller," West remarked with surprise.

I smirked and approached the large black bookcase that now took up an entire wall. Carefully, I selected the green fabric-covered book I was looking for and pulled. A clicking sounded from behind, followed by metal on metal. I stepped back as the two center bookcases pushed forward. Slowly, they split apart to reveal the new hidden space.

My steps were casual as I strolled in. West followed, curious about the new addition.

"What is this?"

As if answering his question, lights slowly illuminated each of the displays surrounding us. The lights were warm and soft, like the items they limned were works of art. I ran a finger down the blade of one such masterpiece.

"An armory?"

"*My* armory," I corrected.

My knives. Kaia's knife. The throwing spikes and everything in between rested on deep olive velvet, awaiting my touch. West approached the opposite wall lined with matte black firearms of various types.

"The drawers below are stocked with ammunition. Guns aren't really my thing, but it felt foolish not to have them. Obviously I prefer these," I said, gesturing to the wall of knives behind me.

"What's in there?" West asked, pointing to a set of doors that remained locked.

I arched a brow at him and moved toward the doors he indicated. Pressing my thumb into a pad beside them, a beep chirped as the doors unlocked. Blue light washed over us as I revealed the hidden gem.

"I should have known," he said as he picked up a small brown bottle to examine it, eyes passing over the word *Lullaby*. He nodded in confirmation and set it down again.

"I did say it was my armory. Why leave out my most effective weapon?"

His fingers drifted over a dark green bottle. Lifting it to read its label, he gave me a confused look. My eye skimmed Lanna's hand-written letters.

Nemesis.

"It worked so well on the Allertons and their friends. Lanna thought I should keep some around. Just in case."

West stuffed his hands into his pockets and left the hidden room to examine the rest of the office. Running a hand over the olive-green velvet arm of the sofa, he circled the piece of furniture and took a seat. I returned to the bookcase and pushed the book back in, resetting the doors to the concealed room.

"What book did you pull?"

"The Language of Flowers."

He huffed a laugh. The black tentacles on his arm shifted as he beckoned me to the sofa. I crawled into his lap. Maybe it was the soft velvet upholstery. Maybe it was that I decided to ditch the suits forever and wear clothes I was comfortable in. Or maybe it was the man whose lips were soft as they wandered down my neck.

Maybe it was all of it. But this office, this luxurious haven hidden away in a strip club, finally felt like it belonged to me. As West brushed his hand through my hair to wrap it around his fist, I tipped my head back. My eyes drifted to the safe and the picture that covered it. To the woman who put me here.

59

WEST

Mid-morning sun poured in through the gym's large windows, filling the space with light. As I stepped in through the front door, I noticed the scent of fresh paint in the air. Aged beige walls were painted with stark white paint.

Half of the walls were covered with mirrors, while the other half was lined with black protective mats. I continued walking into the gym. Everywhere I looked, there was something new. New punching bags. New boxing ring. New speed bags. Even the lockers had been replaced.

"Do you like it?"

Lili stepped out of the office, the paint chipped old door replaced with one made of stark black metal. It clanged as it shut behind her.

"When did this happen?" I asked.

She approached me. I noticed she was not dressed in her usual black workout clothes. Though she was still in a sports bra and leggings, these were dark green. Lili smiled brightly as she pushed her hands through her long black waves. It was heaven to see her smile again.

"Over the last couple of weeks. It didn't take much time."

I observed the freshly painted logo on the wall behind her. Black dangling boxing gloves with the name "One Two" above them.

"That's a nice touch," I said, pointing at the logo.

Lili looked over her shoulder at the mural, then back at me.

"I thought you might like that. But you didn't answer my question."

I arched a brow at her.

"Do you like it?"

She bit a perfect pink lip, her golden eyes becoming two beaming orbs as she looked up at me. I shook my head, confused.

"What does it matter if I like it?"

"Well," Lili sighed, finally releasing me from her stare. "It would be really awkward if you didn't. I'd have to start all over again."

I braced my hands on her shoulders, rubbing my thumbs over the bare skin. As I leaned back to examine her face, she gave me a sheepish grin.

"It's a wedding present."

"Overhauling the gym?"

Lili harrumphed and gave me a flat look. Whatever she was trying to say was going right over my head. She reached into her bra and pulled out a set of keys. A shiny black tag dangled from them.

"The gym. The gym is the present."

She grabbed my hand and yanked it toward her, dropping the keys into my open palm. I blinked.

"Read the tag," she smiled, bouncing on her feet.

I lifted my hand closer, examining the gold lettering etched into the black plastic tag. A logo matched the painting on the wall with the addition of the words "boxing" and "MMA" in small print below.

"Flip it over," Lili said, looking at the tag in my hand.

Obeying her command, I flipped the tag. I nearly dropped the keys upon reading the inscription on the other side.

West Hale. Owner & Manager.

I looked up from the tag to see her beaming at me, bouncing on her feet again.

"What about Lupo?" I asked.

"With Daniel to take care of, he wants to retire. He doesn't need the money anyway. I mean, he'll probably be back here all the time to tell you you're doing things wrong."

I laughed. Unbelievable. This woman was unbelievable. With an outstretched arm, I pulled her against me and buried my face in her mop of black hair. She nuzzled into my chest and sighed. After a moment, she looked up at me.

"I guess you do like it," she smirked.

A yelp popped out of her mouth as I pinched her side.

"I love it," I grinned. "I love you."

"Oh!"

Lilith slipped out of my arms, shouting over her shoulder as she ran back toward the office.

"I almost forgot. Come in here!"

I couldn't help but laugh as I followed her toward the brand-new black door. She paused with her hand on the knob, grinning from ear to ear.

"You can change it if you don't like it. I mean, I hope you do like it. But you can. I mean. Change it."

I raised my eyebrows, indicating toward the door. She rolled her eyes and opened it slowly. Except, unlike everything out here, the things in here weren't brand new. They were old. They were mine.

My books. The shadow box with my badges. Photos of my unit. It was all here.

My legs had turned to jelly. Sitting down on the leather sofa, one of the new pieces of furniture in the room, I picked up the first book I saw and started flipping through the pages. The feel. The smell. Nothing could replace that.

Lili sat on the desk, placing her hands on either side of her. I took her in. This woman. It only took six years for us to get here. In only a few months, she'd be my wife. Lupo was right. *Six years ain't fast.* But every second was worth getting to this point.

"So, are you going to sit here and read, or are we going to work out?"

I laughed. Soon I was going to be winging my way across the Atlantic Ocean. I sure as hell wasn't going to spend my remaining time with her reading.

"No, no. We're going to work out. Since it's been a while, I was thinking we could start with body weight. Let's warm up. Then you're doing push-ups."

Her whine was like music to my ears.

60

Lilith

My immaculate new office was silent. Silent except for the sound of a ticking old clock from my grandfather's warehouse and the keys clicking on a keyboard only a few steps away from me. I glanced up from my ledgers to observe my new employee typing away. Working hard. Just as I had expected.

The door to the small antechamber between Muse and my office, our office, opened. Nico poked his head inside. I waved him in as the typing continued on the other side of the room.

"Here for your next assignment?" I asked.

"Yes, boss."

Nico entered and approached my desk. As he strode toward me, he looked around the new office. His head whipped back in the direction of my new employee.

"Who is this?" He asked quietly, no doubt trying not to offend me or the other person in the room.

"Ah," I smiled. "This is the new Chief Operations Officer of Caccia Enterprises. Juliet Ambrose, meet Nico Ricci."

Juliet, ever the polite professional, stood from her seat and smoothed her hand down her pink tweed dress. Then approached with her hand extended in greeting. So well mannered, too.

"Hello," she said sweetly. "It's a pleasure to meet you."

Nico looked her over. Not so professional.

"Yeah," he stammered. "Uh, nice to meet you."

He took her hand to shake it. Tattooed fingers wrapped around perfectly manicured ones. They stood there, shaking hands as the clock ticked on. It seemed only I was aware that time was passing.

"Nico," I interrupted. "We should let Juliet return to her work."

Nico cleared his throat. Slowly, he released her hand. Juliet gave him another sweet smile and turned, walking back to her desk. He observed every step.

After she took her seat, Nico turned back toward me and approached my desk. I gestured toward one of the two guest chairs. Apparently aware of the other woman in the room, Nico shrugged off his suit jacket and rolled up his sleeves to show off his arms. Not something he'd normally do. Certainly not for my benefit. My suspicion was confirmed as he strutted past Juliet's desk to hang the jacket on the coat hook beside her. The COO glanced up at him then back at her work, the apples of her cheeks now matched her dress.

"Comfortable?" I asked.

He cleared his throat and moved toward me, standing at attention before my desk. Instead of ordering him to be seated, I opened my desk drawer and withdrew an envelope. Nico took the item from me and opened it, glancing at the information tucked away inside.

"Six guys?"

Typing stopped. Juliet was listening. If she was going to be a part of this family, she would have to learn how we operated.

"Thanks to recent distraction, we've not been keeping an eye on our investments. Unfortunately, they have not been keeping up with their payments. They must know there are consequences to their actions."

"Yes, Boss."

"Oh, one more thing," I added, opening the drawer again. Slipping the black business card I'd discovered in my sister's desk between two fingers, I held it up for him to see. "Put this number into your phone. If you make a mess, be sure to text them. I'll text you the code words."

Nico dipped his chin, taking the card from me to add the number to his contacts. He then exited, but not before pausing beside Juliet's desk to retrieve his jacket.

"Nice to meet you," he said roughly.

"And you."

The door clicked shut behind him. It was quiet again for all of one minute before it swung open with gusto. I looked up from my work to see Sophie striding in.

"Lili! I am so glad you're back. Look, the new dressing room is fantastic, but I had some thoughts about the lighting. It's not doing us any favors. Maya says that if her contour looks like trash one more time, she's going to lose it."

I blinked.

"Alright, first, hello," I laughed. "Second, tell Maya that I'll get it taken care of right away."

A gentle throat cleared from across the room as Juliet stood up. Sophie whirled around, realizing we were not alone. Juliet extended her hand to the dancer, whose matching lounge set looked as carefully selected as the pink dress my COO was wearing.

"Hi there," Juliet said. "Your name is?"

"Sophie," the dancer said carefully. "And you are?"

"Juliet. Listen, I know how important good lighting is for makeup. I can have the proper lights ordered and delivered today, but probably it'll take a little while for them to be installed. Is there anything else you or your coworkers need?"

I sat back in my chair. Juliet Ambrose. Problem solver. She'd helped me through small things and big things. I'd learned she effectively ran Camden Industries as Benjamin Camden's assistant for a quarter of what I offered to pay her. Watching her handle this problem without hesitation made me wonder if I was paying her enough.

"Actually, there are a couple of other things," Sophie said as she pulled out a pink piece of paper from her pocket.

Juliet took the paper and skimmed the contents.

"This is all perfectly reasonable," Juliet said. "I'll take care of it. Please feel free to come to me if you need anything else."

Easy. Polite. Exactly what this organization needed. Juliet smiled at Sophie and returned to her desk. I did not doubt that whatever had been requested was being taken care of.

"Is there anything else, Sophie?" I asked.

"Nope," she said, the word coming out with a pop. "Just, uh. Welcome back! And nice to meet you, Juliet."

Sophie gave me an impressed look before leaving the room.

When my sister took over, she ran things the way our grandfather had. Afraid to rock the boat when she was already met with so much resistance from being a woman in charge. As a result, things had always felt very masculine around here.

I returned my gaze to the list in the ledger before me. Every female member of the Caccia family. Every mother. Every daughter. Every sister. They were an untapped resource. Some were in college. Some were wives and mothers. Some were merely waiting to be married off for some alliance.

If that was what they wanted, fine. I wasn't going to force anyone into this life. But we weren't going to overlook someone who would be of value to us.

This morning I pulled on my jeans, made sure my boots were tied, and shrugged my jacket over an old tee shirt. I decided that if I was going to keep my seat at the top of this family; it meant I was going to do things my way. No more suits. No more outdated rules. I was finally ready to become the woman I was always meant to be.

61

WEST

Things are different for the extremely wealthy. Homes feel different. They're removed from maps online. You wouldn't know they exist. Miles away from other homes. Isolated. Practically in a different atmosphere. Even the air smells cleaner.

The sprawling estate nestled in the Highlands of Scotland had looked large in Clayton's surveillance footage and photos, but paled in comparison to the real thing. Rich hardwood floors lined every room, covered in luxurious carpets, and illuminated with large windows. It was probably someone's entire job to keep them clean.

I picked up a brass duck figurine that was resting on the mahogany desk beside me. The man's office was lined with books. But above those books were dozens of heads. Heads of animals, both rare and commonplace, all stuffed to regard whoever sat behind the desk. No ducks were amongst them. I wondered if he had a soft spot for ducks or just couldn't hit one to save his life. The brass duck thudded as I set it down again. It's amazing the things that people collect when they're wealthy.

"Hale," Killian grunted from the doorway he'd been monitoring, his brown eyes wild with anticipation. "He's here."

While plans for retaliation and cruelty were his father's specialty, Killian was unpredictable and wholly dangerous. If his father was a honed blade, he was napalm. It took some convincing for them to accept my plan for the order of events. I still wasn't confident they'd follow through.

The approaching sound of opening and closing doors was accompanied the steady beat of footsteps. It was easy to hear someone coming in the large marble halls. Especially when they wore expensive shoes. Not like the rubber-soled boots each of us wore as we stood in the ornate office.

All of us except for Ronan. We'd arrived here only minutes ago. Clayton had tampered with the Duke's security system enough for it to appear as though no one was here. Not that it mattered. The Irish boss had dealt with the security team, telling them he'd be happy to pay them for their trouble or make them pay with their lives. After that, he'd made himself comfortable at the desk and waited.

The Duke Harrison Augustus-Stanley appeared in the doorway. His security team had let him enter his home, the Duke having dismissed them, assuming he'd be safe within his home. He'd been wrong.

He looked around, spotting the team of men awaiting his arrival. Killian gave him a crocodile grin as he and his men stepped forward.

"Get the fuck in here!"

Of course, he didn't know his security team would not be coming to help as he shouted for them. The cry for help was desperate and impatient as the Arawn men tugged him into the room and slammed the doors closed behind him.

"I'm afraid your security has left you."

"What do you mean? Who the fuck are you?" The Duke questioned Ronan as he eyed all of us. He straightened the lapel of his navy blazer and threw his shoulders back, as though his attitude and appearance could save him from his fate. I couldn't help but note the flawless black three-piece suit Ronan wore. Even his crisp black shirt seemed to laugh at the Duke's overstuffed ensemble.

"I mean that your security is currently being buried on your property. They couldn't be paid off. I'm a rich man, but apparently not quite rich enough. So they paid with their lives. A debt you owe me as well," Ronan sneered as he reclined in the Duke's overstuffed leather desk chair.

Metal scraping on itself sung as Ronan cut the tip from the cigar he'd been holding.

"A debt? What do you mean a debt? I don't even know you. Who are you?"

Ronan chuckled and stood, buttoning his jacket as he did so. The rest of the Arawns surrounded him. Clayton remained by the door behind the desk. I stayed beside the glass door leading to the terrace. The Duke would not escape. Not today. Not ever again.

"You may not know me, Augustus-Stanley. Horrible fucking name, by the way. You may not even know my daughters. But you hurt my daughters. My girls. And we know you've hurt many others."

Clayton's jaw tightened at Casey's mention. I wondered if he'd remembered the haunted look on her face the day he met her. The way she shrunk away from the touch of any man, even when it was to help her escape. His hand flexed at his side.

He remembered.

"You don't seem to be the noble type," the Duke said as he eyed Ronan's tattooed hands. "I'm sure we can work something out. You don't have to kill me. I have connections. You can benefit from my friendship."

"I'm not going to kill you."

Ronan held the cigar cutter between his fingers. Examined the elegant brushed steel. His eyes went dark as he set the cigar down on the desk. An unsettling sight. If my girl was a dark angel, then Ronan was the Devil himself. As I watched him evaluate his captive, I remembered his request as we arrived at this godforsaken place.

"I trust, Mr. Hale, that you'll remember my generosity when I require your assistance in the future."

Watching him now, I wondered if I'd been a fool to agree. But I also knew that crossing Ronan Arawn was a reckless mistake you make only once. Remaining in his good graces would be more useful than death.

"Get on your knees and beg me for your life."

"You just said you weren't going to kill me."

"I said I wouldn't. That doesn't mean you aren't going to meet your maker."

Killian shifted, a look of discomfort passed over his face at his father's demand. I wondered how much of his father he had in him and what set him entirely apart. One of his men shoved the Duke to his knees. His blandly handsome face was twisted with distaste at the motion. He'd probably never begged for anything in his life.

"Please," he said hesitantly. Annoyed. Like a child being forced to remember their manners at the dinner table. "Please don't kill me."

"Oh, that was quite pathetic, wasn't it?" Ronan laughed, a gleaming smile of delight spreading across his cruel mouth. Scratching his salt and pepper stubble, he growled. "You'll have to beg harder, I expect, when justice comes for you."

I'd heard it dozens of times. Men pleading for their lives. Pleading when the barrel of a gun or the edge of a blade was poised to end their existence. They knew. They all knew that their time was over. I could hear it in their voices. That tone of desperation was missing from the plea I'd just heard. I knew that even now; the Duke seemed to think he still had the upper hand.

Ronan nodded at the man on the Duke's right. He grabbed his arm and wrenched it up. Killian's pistol cocked as he pressed it into our captive's skull. The other man's hand circled the Duke's wrist and held it. Pushed up the Duke's thumb. The polished gold signet ring on it glinted in the light.

Then the Duke screamed. A violent and desperate scream. It rattled the windows. Rattled my damned brain. Ronan smiled as the Duke stopped screaming. He fainted. Went down like a collapsed marionette in bespoke clothing on his plush area rug.

His thumb and signet ring lay beside him. Ronan untucked the blood red silk from his pocket and bent down, picking up the severed appendage and unsheathing it from the gold ring. The thumb was wrapped up in the silk, which was tucked away again.

A glint of gold flashed as Ronan dropped the ring into his pocket. I wondered which daughter would receive this trophy. And what exactly he planned to do with the thumb.

62

Lilith

My skin prickled at the bite in the air as I walked toward Pal's entrance. Sun-warmed days had evaporated into a crisp spring night. I pulled my leather jacket around my ribs, cursing the thin material of my t-shirt.

In the middle of the night, Los Angeles could be dark and quiet. Pal's was empty. Dried meats hung from their hooks behind the deli counter. Delicate Italian pastries looked out from behind the glass case, packed in containers for preservation.

A sense of anticipation washed over me, worried at what I might find in the secret basement below the deli. I'd been summoned here. Though the trust I had in this man had no limit, the last six months had made me wary of surprises.

"Hello, gorgeous," he said, smirking as he laid eyes on me.

West stood in the center of the basement, waiting patiently in a pair of wrinkled green work pants and a black henley t-shirt that told me he'd come straight from the airport. I fought the urge to pounce on him. His absence was short, but it felt far too long. When he'd asked me to meet him here, I didn't hesitate. Even if I did wonder what he could possibly want with this space.

It wasn't the most romantic location. But he'd been gone for almost a week and I would have done anything to see him. As I pressed him for more information, he only told me that he had something for me. That "something" was sitting in the chair beside him with a black hood covering his head.

"What's all this?" I asked casually as I descended the small wooden staircase, down to their level. My boots squeaked as my feet finally hit the concrete floor.

"A gift for you."

Without further explanation, West yanked the black hood off of his captive's head. Duke Harrison Augustus-Stanley. Beaten. Bleeding from what looked like a twice-broken nose that was bruising purple under his eyes. And tied up like a present. The gag in his mouth was soaked with saliva. Despite the obstruction, the Duke tried his best to say something to me. Maybe plead for his life. Maybe curse the man beside him. Or me. I chuckled at the useless effort.

On the worktable against the wall sat my assortment of knives and other little tools I'd acquired for extracting information. All freshly sharpened. Gleaming. Waiting. My finger dragged along the serrated edge of the hunting knife West had given me ages ago. I examined a curved blade that had belonged to Kaia as it rested on its red velvet wrapping. A blade she rarely used. A gift from our grandfather. Pure poetry in its craftsmanship.

West's sense of justice was poetic. It was impossible not to appreciate it. I took off my engagement ring and placed it beside the array of knives. A fresh box of black latex gloves awaited my hands. My hand dipped into the box of gloves and pulled out a pair.

"For me?" I purred.

"I couldn't think of a better wedding present. Besides, as your newest Wolf, I felt it was my duty."

My teeth sunk into my lower lip as I bit back my smile. The wedding present I'd had in mind for him wasn't bad. That would take his breath away to be sure, but this was so much better. I stood up on my toes and kissed him. West's palm cupped my jaw as he deepened the kiss. The feel of his lips on mine sent a flutter through me. He was mine. I was his. He didn't just accept the darkness in me. His love was the starlight in my pitch-dark soul.

"Make him bleed, Trouble," West whispered into my ear before giving the lobe a tug with his teeth.

We both looked at the Duke, watching us with disgust from the chair. I sighed. Like he had any room to judge.

"Well, I guess there's no sense in ignoring him any longer."

I picked up my sister's curved blade and cut off the gag. The spineless bastard didn't waste any time. Words flew out of his mouth like an out-of-control firehose.

"I'll tell you anything you want to know. Anything." he glanced at the array of instruments on the table. He whimpered and gasped. "Anything."

I didn't fight the grin the swept across my face at his cowardice. He had been so ready to hunt me. Promised to put me in a box. To kill the people dear to me. Now he was begging for his life. I didn't need to know anything else.

"Please," the Duke wept. "I can pay you. Handsomely. I can make you an extremely wealthy woman."

I took his face in my hands, jerking his head toward me to look him in the eye. The black latex squeaked with the motion. He flinched.

"I am a wealthy woman."

West had taken a step backward to give me space. Space to do my work. I beckoned him forward.

"Would you mind holding his head still? I have a feeling this mouth is going to be a nuisance."

"What? No!"

Those were the Duke's last words. At least, the last intelligible ones. West's hands bracketed the man's jaw, pinning his thumbs on the masseter muscle to force the man's mouth open. My fingers traced along his lips.

"You wanted to play games with me."

I snatched at his tongue and pulled. Hard.

"I win."

The Duke's screams were sweeter than any symphony. They made me dizzy with delight. I glanced at West who simply nodded as I adjusted my hold on Kaia's knife and brought it to the pink writhing flesh I gripped between my thumb and index finger. It cut through like butter. Garbled screams echoed off of the tiled walls as the Duke's tongue hit the floor with a wet slap.

Once I had been afraid of the snarling beast I had within me. Feared that I'd become my father. That man was cruel without cause. Without purpose. My father spent his life studying cruelty. He let it control him. Let it hurt everyone around him.

I mastered it. Mastered myself. He was a finger painter of malice and I was Michelangelo.

I also hadn't wanted West to see this side of me, but I wasn't worried about him anymore. This gift. It was a show of acceptance. He didn't ignore the monster inside of me. The wrathful beast who would always seek to balance the scales. He understood it. Understood me. And loved every ugly part of my soul.

"Let's begin."

EPILOGUE

Lilith

THREE MONTHS LATER

My hands were shaking. Actually shaking. Wrapping my fingers around the porcelain, I bent over and took a breath. I'd never been nervous before. Not like this. It singed every nerve as it rushed through me.

"Zia?"

Daniel's voice called through the bathroom door, full of concern.

"In a minute, buddy."

I pulled a paper towel from the dispenser and dried the slight sheen of sweat from my face as I repeated the same thing to myself over and over again.

You deserve this.

Shaking fingers smoothed my hair. My pinky dragged along my lips to make them perfect. With another deep breath, I turned and opened the door for my nephew. Looking smart in his suit, he looked me over from top to bottom. My eyebrows raised on their own, as if even they wanted to know what he thought.

"Pretty," he said with a smile.

"Really?" I asked as I ran my hands over the front of my dress, fingers snagging on the tiny silk-covered buttons.

He nodded. Yes. Good. A sigh of relief wooshed out of me. Without my sister here, I got ready on my own. Lanna offered, but I thought taking her away from West felt wrong. He needed her.

Daniel held out his small hand. A gentleman already. I took it, squeezing his little fingers as I came into the hallway.

"Oh wait." I stopped and released his hand, turning back to the powder room. I slipped the rings back on my fingers. Kaia's emerald-cut diamond glinted up at me from my right hand. I couldn't do this without her. Not today. "Alright. I'm ready."

Daniel and I went through the living room. Delicious scents came from the kitchen. Bootlegger's head chef was ours for the night. I eyed a Parker House roll as we passed and nodded to the chef.

"Hey."

Lanna was waiting for me on the patio. She smiled down at Daniel, who hugged her at the waist.

"She's ready," he said into her belly.

"She's almost ready," she said and released him, turning to the patio dining table. I felt the urge to reach out and touch her dress. The pale amethyst velvet looked light as it rustled in the warm evening breeze. She handed me a few gathered flowers, carefully tied with a black ribbon. I laughed at the blooms.

"Lilies?"

"It was that or wolfsbane," she grinned as her eyes dipped to the tattoo on my chest, peeking out from the ivory neckline. It felt wrong to hide the wolf now.

The sun was beginning to dip below the horizon. Soft orange rays peeked through the flowers and vines. My grandmother's wisteria blossomed beside fat lemons, scenting the air with their sweet perfume.

"Someone's waiting for you," Lanna said, a broad smile firmly in place now. "Let's get you to the garden."

Daniel and I walked together into the yard, holding hands tightly. The quiet look of happiness on his face reminded me of the way his mother looked when he was born. Despite everything. Our grandfather had died only minutes before. The man she loved was killed not long before that. Despite all of that pain, she had that same serene look on her face when she held her son. Her memory brought tears to my eyes. I gave Daniel's hand a little squeeze.

"I wish your mom was here," I whispered.

Daniel looked around the yard. Looked at the wisteria and lemons. At the splintered knife target I'd forgotten to put away. At the ring I wore on my hand that had belonged to her. The one I explained I'd save for him. He squeezed my hand back and smiled at me.

"She is."

Blades of grass cushioned my every step. Their cool caress on the soles of my feet. It felt right, somehow. To do this in bare feet. Most of our time had been spent together in the ring. On the mat. Skin to skin. Lupo had even proposed doing this at the gym.

"It's where you two met and you own it anyway, so why not?"

I'd just laughed at the idea.

I loosed a shaking breath as we approached the garden. Everyone was here. Everyone was waiting. Casey and Clayton waited, the first dressed in a breezy pale blue summer dress. Some soft pink crystal dangled from her neck. Clayton stood beside her. A respectful distance. But his eyes were locked on the red curls that danced in the breeze around her face.

Lupo wore a suit. Even when I'd told him it was a casual event. He waved me off. He'd clearly influenced his son's attire since I saw Nico standing nearby in an almost identical blue suit. They both looked at me and smiled. My stomach fluttered at the attention. And so many eyes on me.

There were only six people. Only six other than the two of us, and it still felt like too many. Too many people would know if I screwed this up. Too many could say they were here when I'd promised everything and failed. Failed to uphold another vow.

When you're used to violence and withholding, someone who gives you their love openly and without cost is unsettling. Terrifying, even. And this? It was the ultimate act of faith.

"Come on, Zia," Daniel said patiently. I hadn't realized I'd stopped walking.

It was only a few steps. A few steps that brought me into his view. Standing there under the arch that was covered in jasmine blooms, the few beams of remaining sunlight clinging to the long strands of his hair like even it knew he was something worth holding on to. The linen pants he'd put on fit perfectly. Sand colored. The white linen shirt he wore barely concealed the ink beneath. I could almost see the wolf tattoo on his ribs that matched the one over my heart. To mark the other vow he'd made to me.

Everyone there was smiling at me. West's smile was a thing of beauty. Filled with promise. With love. As soon as I saw that smile, it all went away. The fear. The uncertainty. All of it.

Lanna joined her brother under the arch as Lupo took his place beneath it. Every step I took felt too fast and not fast enough all at once until finally I was there, under that arch with them. Daniel gave my hand a small squeeze. Reassurance from a seven-year-old.

"Who presents this woman to be married?" Lupo started in a soft voice he reserved for only one person.

"I do," Daniel said proudly.

I leaned down and kissed him on the cheek, wiping away at any lipstick that remained. Lupo directed West to take my hands in his. I stood, stepped forward, and our hands found each other under the little blooming flowers of jasmine.

"Hi," West smiled, moving to tuck a loose strand of hair behind my ear.

"Hi," I laughed.

Part of me still couldn't believe it, as I stood there with his hands in mine. That someone so strong, so kind and good would want to bind their life to mine. But he did. He chose me just as I had chosen him. And as we said our vows to each other, I felt the raging beast inside of me curl up to rest.

HALE. MRS. WEST Hale.

The name made me smile. No, actually, it made me grin like an idiot. It would really be Lilith Rhamnusia Caccia Hale, but I liked it all the same.

After hours of sitting around the table in the backyard, eating and laughing with what I could now call my family, everyone had finally gone home. Daniel, now permanently living with his grandfather, had been the most reluctant to leave what had once been his home. It broke my heart a little, but gave me an idea. A way to make it right.

"Hello, wife," West grinned at me from the bathroom's open door, one muscled arm propped above his head. Wearing only the linen pants, my man was a sight to behold. Golden skin. Thick muscle. That stunning smile. I was lucky. So goddamn lucky.

"Hello, husband," I returned, dabbing my face dry after washing it clean of makeup and tears. I'd laughed so hard, I cried. I cried during our short ceremony. I cried, thinking of my sister, who should have been standing beside me. Tears had never tasted so sweet.

"Are you almost ready for bed?" He asked as he bracketed me in with his hand on either side of the counter. Burying his face in my neck, he inhaled and kissed the sensitive skin. I eyed the gold band glinting on his left hand, the inside engraved with a simple phrase next to tiny chips of our birthstones.

You and me.

"Just about."

West's head rested on my shoulder as his arms banded around my waist. The fabric of my tee shirt, his tee shirt, bunched around me with the movement. I'd started sleeping in it ages ago. Before this happened. Before we happened. After he had saved my life and taken me to his safe space. It was so soft. So comfortable. Sleeping in anything else was impossible. Like my skin had known that West was my safe space, a secret I'd been keeping from myself.

"How long will this take to heal?" West asked, turning my arm to take a closer look at the wound on my bicep from where my implant had been removed.

"I don't know," I said, my gaze following his. "It doesn't hurt anymore."

West nodded and stood up again, shucking the linen suit pants he'd been wearing off and throwing them toward the hamper. Missing it by a mile. I gave him a flat look.

"Not even married a full day and you're already getting on me about clothes on the floor," he laughed.

With a roll of my eyes, I chuckled and walked to the pants on the floor. They followed my damp washcloth into the hamper. As soon as I turned to face him again, he bent down and threw me over a shoulder.

"Hey!" I squeaked. West's chest rumbled with laughter beneath my stomach. A broad hand slapped my ass before tossing me down onto the mattress.

"We need to get started," he grinned down at me. His eyes flicked to my still flat stomach.

"It's been like four days. Nothing's going to happen that quickly."

I scooted backward, making room for him as he climbed onto the bed to kneel between my legs. His hands slid up and down my thighs, kneading the muscle and squeezing the softer bits until my oversized shirt was pushed up around my waist. West bent over to kiss the exposed skin, moving down to the sensitive flesh between my belly button and panty line.

"Well," he said between kisses. "Never say never, Trouble."

My head tipped back as his mouth moved lower, lavishing my sensitive bud with licks and sucks through sheer fabric until it was pushed aside. Fingers slid through me, testing the slick opening with teasing strokes until they slid inside. His tongue and hand worked at me relentlessly until I was brought to the shimmering void of release.

"West," I panted as I yanked my shirt off and threw it across the room.

He jumped up to remove his underwear as I shimmied off my own. Though he was only away a moment, I missed the feel of him. When his body was over mine, covering me completely, he looked down at me and smiled.

"Don't worry. You won't."

"I won't what?"

"Ever get tired of this. Of me. You never will."

His hips pushed forward, stealing my response as I gasped around the intrusion. My breaths were short and shallow as he began moving in me. As pleasure simmered in my blood again and I savored the feel of his bare skin on mine, I found the words before they could be washed away.

"Cocky bastard."

This happened every fucking time.

Every time I felt uncertain of anything, his touch drove my fears away. Years ago, I was a dangerously broken thing. I'm still broken. Maybe I always will be. But West sees the fragmented parts of me. Sees my cracks and shattered pieces. Over time, his love eroded the sharp edges. Turning me over in his tide. In his sand. Until the shards couldn't cut me anymore.

EPILOGUE

WEST

ONE YEAR LATER

Gone again.

I'd awoken in our bed without her beside me. Again. Waking up without her was unsettling, but hardly unusual. Especially lately.

The sun peaked through the trees, bringing its pale golden light to the forest surrounding around the cabin. Not much about this place had changed since we left it. I'd given my sister a license to escape to the mountain cabin that had once belonged to our father whenever she liked, and we benefited from her cleanliness.

Padding softly out of the bedroom, I looked into the bathroom. No Lilith. A few short steps told me the kitchen and living room were also absent of her. A glance out the window told me the Bronco was still in the driveway. Her boots were still by the front door, but my flannel had been missing from the chair beside our bed.

But there was coffee in the pot.

I snorted and stepped outside, pulling on my sweatpants, still in search of my wife. The word still felt like a wish. My wife. Mine. It had been a year since that day in her garden and it still felt surreal to me. That I'd met the woman of my dreams. That she'd said yes to me. That I get to wake up with her in my arms. Well, usually.

After the wedding, Lilith told me she'd decided to let Lupo move into the house with Daniel. The man seemed beside himself. His home quickly became Nico's and Daniel got to resume his residence in his old room. It was all very heart-warming, even if it left us homeless for a little while. Lupo invited us to stay while we looked for a home, but starting a family is private work. At least it was private most of the time.

Only about a month after leaving the Caccia estate, Lilith bought us a home. It was larger than anything I would have dreamed of for our first home together. It was old, but it still whispered of her family's breathtaking wealth. Our wealth, I guess, even if it was still hard to think of myself as someone with that kind of money. Though we moved in right away, the place required a lot of work. It was because of a particularly rigorous plumbing upgrade that I'd suggested we escape here.

The deck creaked beneath my bare feet as I approached her from behind. Lili had wrapped herself in one of my flannels. She turned at the sound of the wood, perfect pink lips smiling faintly at me, and then returned to her original position. The shirt was still far too large for such a small woman. But at least now the belly was getting there.

"Good morning," she said quietly, as though she was trying to respect the sleeping trees. A steaming cup of coffee sat on the wooden armrest beside her.

"That better not be what I think it is," I scolded, eyeing what was definitely a cup of coffee. I'd told her a dozen times she can't do that.

"Relax, Daddy. It's decaf."

She looked up at me as I placed my hands on her shoulders and bent down to kiss her forehead. The hand that had been stroking her stomach stalled its motion as she closed her eyes and hummed a tired groan.

"What are you doing out of bed?" I muttered the question into her hair. "You need to rest."

"This," she said as she patted her rounded belly, "is kicking up a storm. I couldn't sleep, so I came out here. I didn't want to wake you."

"My girl's a fighter already. Just like her mother."

Lili rolled her eyes and laughed. Her attention returned to the greenhouse I'd built for her. The one I gave her when I brought her here for her birthday last October. She gave me the real gift that night when she told me she was pregnant with our first child.

I'd never forget her shaking hands. The tears lining her eyes. She'd been afraid. Not to tell me. We'd wanted to start our family right away. But she was still afraid to become a mother. As I wiped away her tears, she told me she was afraid because she didn't know how to raise a child.

"My mom and dad weren't exactly model parents," she'd said between sniffles.

I didn't tell her I knew she would be a good mother. I didn't say that her fear was insane because I'd seen how she was with her nephew. The warm and soft side she reserved for him. How fiercely she protected those she loved. Instead, I'd just held her in my arms and let her cry, wondering if she could hear my heart thundering at the idea that I was going to be a father.

Eying her cup of steaming coffee again, I suspected she hadn't fixed herself anything to eat. The woman still could barely cook worth a damn, but I guess that wasn't a skill required of an all-powerful billionaire mafia boss.

"Are you hungry?"

"Always."

When I first met Lilith Caccia, I was a broken man. My world was empty without her in it. Those gorgeous eyes. The way she laughed. Knowing her made me want to work on myself. Not because I wanted to be better for her, but because she made me want more for myself. So I worked on myself and I became the kind of man who could stand by her side. Because that's what love does. Love doesn't fix you. It just creates space so you can fix yourself.

I knelt beside her and placed a hand on top of hers. Our fingers intertwined as she let her head rest against the back of the wooden chair. She was so incredibly beautiful like this. Sunlight gilded her shining black tresses. It was a spectacular thing, even when it was a damned mess. As I took in those gold irises that looked at me with exhaustion and undiluted love, I hoped our child would have their mother's eyes. I supposed I'd find out in a couple of months.

"I'd love some French toast."

"You know the rules, Trouble. You have to earn that."

Her answering smile was lupine. My dark and wild thing. Something I'd never be able to tame. Never wanted to. I was going to enjoy every unpredictable moment with this girl. My wife. For the rest of my life. Lili and me. She was everything to me. And as I felt our daughter kick, I knew she would be everything to me, too.

Lili and Kai, the little girl who was soon to come. I hadn't imagined this all those years ago as I locked eyes on her. My girl. I'd entered that gym a broken, lonely man. And now?

Now I'll never be alone again.

ACKNOWLEDGEMENTS

Lilith Caccia has lived more in a year and a half than I have my entire life. It took this long to tell her story, but it wouldn't have happened without a story of my own. It started with a move to Colorado from my lifelong home in Southern California. Though I had been a lifelong reader, it had been a long time since I picked up a book for fun. It's amazing how studying something can remove joy from it.

That's what happened to me. Like West, I loved books. Found friends in books. Escaped pain by immersing myself in a new adventure. Until I got my undergraduate degree in Literature and Writing and ruined everything.

That is... until I moved away from everything I knew and found myself longing for friendship. I sought connection in one book. Then another. And another until I couldn't put them down again and remembered that reading isn't just a pastime, it's a way to live one thousand lives in a single lifetime.

Then I picked up a pen and started writing again.

The first few words I wrote for Nemesis changed the trajectory of my life. Though I had always dreamed of an abstract future that involved being an author, it never seemed like something that would take shape. But, like with all things, you make space in your life for the things that matter to you.

ACKNOWLEDGEMENTS

This series was born in stolen hours before and after work, on long afternoons every weekend, and in the in-between spaces of my life. My notes app is still drowning in phrases I scribbled into it at all hours of the night.

It would be weird to thank myself, right? Screw it, I'm doing it anyway. Thank you, me, for doing the thing. Even when you were tired. Had writer's block. Whatever. You did the damn thing. I'm proud of us.

"Thank you" feels too small for the things people have done to help me get here, but until I find better words, they'll have to suffice. First, and most importantly, I'd like to thank my mother for being so supportive of me through this journey. Thank you for showing me that I can do hard things. For being my champion and my example. Also, your ability to look the other way while proofreading the spicy scenes for me deserves a freaking medal.

Second, I'd like to thank my husband. From handling things around the house so I could spend time writing to championing my works to everyone you meet, there isn't a thing you've done for the sake of these books that I don't appreciate. Thank you for encouraging me to pursue my dreams and for listening to me read scenes out loud to you, even when you didn't always feel like it. Also, sorry for all the times I shushed you while I was writing something down.

For my brother, Michael, my built-in best friend. Thank you for constantly reminding me that creative works are cultivated with heart. For Sara, the best beta-reader a girl could ask for. Your reactions never failed to make me laugh.

To the rest of my family and friends. Thank you for your kind words, your recommendations to friends, and your warm hugs. Every single supportive smile. Every single congratulatory text message. They all mean so much to me, as do all of you.

To Alison and Natalia, thank you for making these books beautiful.

And lastly, thank you to my readers. All of you. Thank you for loving a character who was deeply flawed and a little reckless. But most of all, thank you for reading three whole books about her. Thank you for welcoming Lili and West into your hearts.

Printed in the USA
CPSIA information can be obtained
at www.ICGtesting.com
LVHW030534131024
793557LV00009B/782